SPIDER'S WYRD

Adrienne Miles

Brick Cave Media
brickcavebooks.com

Spider's Wyrd

Copyright © 2024 Adrienne Bengtson

PAPERBACK ISBN: 978-1-938190-91-9

All rights reserved. No part of this book may be reproduced, distributed, or transmitted in any form or by any means, including but not limited to electronic or mechanical methods, for purposes including data extraction, machine learning, or training artificial intelligence technologies or systems, without the prior written permission of the author/publisher or in accordance with the provisional of the Copyright, Design and Patents Act 1988 or under the terms of any licensing permitting limited copying issued by the Copyright Licensing Agency.

Printed in the United States of America.

The characters and events in this book are fictitious. Any similarity to real persons, living or dead, is coincidental and not intended by the authors.

Cover Illustration Artist: Thitipon Decruen
www.xric7.com

Brick Cave Media
brickcavebooks.com
2025

Dedication:

In memory of
Elton R. Miles
Thanks, Dad.

SPIDER'S WYRD

Adrienne Miles

Brick Cave Media
brickcavebooks.com

PART 1

Starfighter Down

Chapter One
Starfighter

Ulla Thorsdaughter fired and the second Sparhawk attacker exploded. She tumbled her Goshawk starfighter out of the debris path and checked her screens—no more Sparhawks, thanks be. Bits of agile fighting machines glittered, reflecting the light from the star Bailey-Duran.

A River Pack smuggler ship emerged from behind the cloud of wreckage. It and its illicit cargo of high-end biomass jumped out-system from much too close to Bailey-Duran's third planet and disappeared.

Ulla checked on her wingman. "Goshawk Two Two, Goshawk Two One. Status?"

Silence.

Ulla scanned her displays. Was Two Two drifting? *Goddammit, Jeff! Say something!* She waited as many seconds as she dared before speaking. "*Valiant*, Goshawk Two One."

Control on the bridge of Ulla's battleship answered, "Goshawk Two One, *Valiant*."

Jeff's comm sent out an excruciating burst of static and went silent.

Shit. Ulla spoke into her comm. "Request emergency Gate recovery for Two Two."

"Goshawk Two One, *Valiant*. Initiating emergency Gate." Ulla's wingman vanished from her screens. He and his Goshawk were safe inside the cargo Gate on the battleship's flight deck.

Ulla remembered to breathe.

Her comm crackled again. "Two One, *Valiant*. Status."

"*Valiant*, Two One. Two bandits gone."

"Two One, *Valiant*. Copy two bandits gone. Count debris clouds."

Ulla rechecked her displays and spoke. "Two debris clouds."

"Two One, home."

"Homing." Ulla was still setting her course when her sensors lit up. The tiny image of the UW&NS *Valiant* burst into the brightest, fastest-growing debris cloud she had ever seen.

Training took over. Emotional reactions could get you killed.

The United Worlds and Nations' other in-system SpaceCom battleship, the *Resolute*, was outside range, making rescue in space unlikely. The smugglers had led the *Valiant* and her starfighters too far from the rest of the fleet. She would have to ditch on the ground. She set course for the ocean near Bailey-Duran Three's Port of Newcastle, well outside the shipping lanes but within easy reach of rescue forces at SpaceCom's new headquarters there.

She was well on her way when her Goshawk shuddered and a trouble indicator winked on—Sparhawks again.

What the hell? Local crime pack smuggler protection typically feinted and ran.

Ulla lined up her sights on the lead attacker. "Today, I am lucky. Are you?" Under the circumstances, that was an outright lie, but the rote phrase had helped settle her mind for fights since before she'd joined SpaceCom. She squeezed off a shot. The lead Sparhawk exploded, a chunk of its debris clipping her attitude control bank. As redundant systems strove to keep her Goshawk under control, the second bandit appeared in her sights. She got off another shot. It hit.

Alone again, Ulla fought to control her wallowing fighter as successive rocket banks burned up and forced others to compensate. The Goshawk's controls went useless. It tumbled erratically toward the planet until the last rocket bank, mercifully, pushed in the correct direction, burned up, and quit.

Ulla let her seat's landing restraints wrap and inflate around her arms, legs, and body. She clicked her helmet back into the head restraint and waited in gut-wrenching silence. Finally, the atmosphere grabbed the ruined Goshawk and peeled its outer body away to free the egress pod, which shuddered, steadied, and hurtled downward.

Damage had rendered Ulla's landing guidance useless; she'd land wherever the laws of physics put her. Ballistic reentry was steep, hot, and rough. The pod's first parachute slammed open, slowed its descent enough to ready it for the next chute, and broke free. Breathing turned into hard, deliberate work as the series of parachutes grabbed at her pod. When the main chute finally opened, she spent an eternity floating in plain sight down to the ground. At long last, the landing rockets fired. The pod landed hard, bounced, skidded down an incline, and was still.

The pod's emergency power kicked in, its screens winked back on, and the comm automatically screamed for help over SpaceCom's emergency channels. Ulla took a deep breath and disentangled herself from the seat restraints. As soon as the surface conditions test sequence told her she was on land and neither freezing, overheating, nor being attacked, she overrode it, unsealed her helmet vents, and set the pod's vent to outside air. Bailey-Duran Three's air was better than Earth's, and she needed some.

Her surface-position screen said she was deep in the backcountry of the continent called Hoffnung. SpaceCom's Bailey-Duran sector headquarters was in Newcastle City, on Hoffnung's west coast. Unfortunately, that was many hundreds of kilometers away. She couldn't Gate there; the nearest Gate was well on the other side of a big crosshatched swath in the middle of the map marked "Electronics Unreliable / No Energy Weapons." *Dammit.*

Ulla adjusted the settings to print a low-tech map she could carry with her. If Rescue couldn't reach her here, she might have to walk some distance to find a place where they could pick her up.

Once the map replicator spit out its tough, thin sheet, she looked more closely. Aside from a nearby hill marked "Restricted," this looked like agricultural land. Ulla folded the map and put it in one of the many pockets on her flight suit.

She made sure she had all her ground survival gear, including the old-tech projectile sidearm SpaceCom—which, in this case, actually did know best—had issued her. She snagged her water bottle from its nonregulation place behind the seat and stuffed it into its purpose-made pocket on her survival vest opposite the sidearm.

Rescue should have answered the pod's automatic distress call by now. Ulla checked her screens but found no ships or satellites in range. The map indicated she was in a valley; maybe she needed to be on higher ground for her comm to work. She ensured her handheld comm unit was fully powered up, opened the hatch, and climbed out.

The pod had landed near a creek in a narrow floodplain between two tall bluffs. No wonder her comm couldn't reach much of the sky. Ulla sniffed the air and smelled smoke. Frost covered the blackened tree branches and smashed underbrush at the top of the bluff where the pod's landing rockets had fired. A big, ugly gouge marked where the pod had skidded its way down.

Frost? The air wasn't nearly cold enough. Oh, well. At least the fire was out.

She took off her pressure gauntlets and laid them just inside the hatch, then removed and pocketed the soft gloves that lined the gauntlets. Next, she took off her helmet, tucked the gauntlets inside it, and placed them in the seat she'd just vacated. After a moment's consideration, she also took off her boots and many-pocketed flight suit, peeled off her thin but very tough one-piece emergency pressure undergarment, and chucked the sweaty mass of impermeable material back inside the pod. There was a reason starfighters shortened "pressure undergarment" to "PU." The PU liner—long underwear that went between the PU and her skin—was soggy with sweat. She put her flight suit back on over the damp liner, pulled on her boots, and rechecked her gear. Then she locked the egress pod and took another look at her surroundings.

A fresh pile of cow droppings lay on the ground less than two meters from the pod. Where there were cattle, there would be people.

Please, no trolls. Let the people be human.

Her rational self knew that the trolls, whose actual name she could not pronounce and for whom the polite term was "Elders," were half of a local alliance that belonged to the United Worlds and Nations. As a UW&N SpaceCom officer, Ulla had sworn to protect them. She'd been doing that in this world's sky less than an hour ago.

Still, being around them gave her the willies.

Human herders who called themselves On'oi had formed an alliance with the Elders to run this world's ongoing—and to the untutored eye completed—terraforming project. Ulla's impression was that the On'oi and Elders ran the planet outside the city-states where the ports, merchants, and SpaceCom's local headquarters were.

SpaceCom's official line was to contact the On'oi or the Elders if you found yourself dirtside in the backcountry. Locals in the downtown Newcastle bars called the On'oi herders and said they were arrogant and not to be trusted.

The *Valiant* exploding wasn't in the playbook at all.

Ulla's thoughts played back the firefight, and a chilling theory formed in the back of her mind. This part of space—the Edge—was claimed by its human and Elder residents and by a species called the Yotne, whose members were almost twice as tall as humans, and at least as ruthless.

The Yotne often employed disembodied spirits, that humans called Dwellers, to infiltrate places they were getting ready to attack. Had the starfighters she and Jeff fought just now been Dweller-possessed?

Please, no. But it would explain why the smuggler escorts had attacked instead of doing their usual divert and run.

With luck, Ulla would be out of here and up on the *Resolute* in a few hours. But if that didn't happen, she had to know what was going on before contacting anybody who wasn't SpaceCom.

* * *

The bluffs enclosing her landing site were many meters high and almost vertical, so Ulla decided to follow the creek upstream. As she walked, it grew narrower and deeper, and more boulders littered its banks. The climb became steeper, and before long, she reached a waterfall, which poured off the rock face at the head of the box canyon.

Ulla backtracked and found a tributary stream she could follow almost to the top of the bluff. She scrambled up and found herself on flat, rocky ground in a stand of mature forest. She pulled the comm out of her pocket and activated it. Its power indicator and status light glowed back at her, but the damned thing couldn't find a single ship or satellite.

She expanded the little comm's list of emergency frequencies, including local and commercial ones she hadn't expected to need—still nothing.

Being in the middle of nowhere would explain that, especially if the *Resolute* was below her horizon. She made some quick calculations; at the moment, she was on the other side of the planet from the main shipping lanes. That would put the commercial ships and Bailey-Duran Three's new space station below her horizon along with, more than likely, the *Resolute*.

She would keep trying. Something was bound to orbit overhead sooner or later, assuming anything friendly was left in the sky. Had the strike on the *Valiant* been part of a larger Yotne attack?

Ulla shut down that train of thought and scanned the map again. While her position was well outside the Electronics Unreliable zone, the waterfall at the top of the box canyon was part of the restricted area's boundary. Pity—the restricted area was the highest ground around here. Depending on why it was restricted, Ulla might go up there anyway. She could see the hill from here, and the roof of a large building—or possibly a group of buildings—was visible above the trees.

She tried her comm again. There, just above the horizon—a commercial ship! No sooner had Ulla locked the little comm unit onto the signal than all its lights flashed at once. It squawked and went dead. By the time Ulla got the comm working again, the ship had disappeared, and there was nothing else in range.

She was almost too spent to care.

Daylight was fading fast. She needed a place to rest, preferably where the comm unit could see the sky. She found a thick stand of stickerbushes and squirmed underneath until she came to a hollow in the middle. It didn't look like anything had slept there recently, so she settled in, ate an energy bar, and drank some water.

She tried the comm again. Still nothing above the horizon, but this piece of ground would rotate underneath the shipping lanes early tomorrow morning. She set the comm unit to passive identification mode and made sure it would wake her if it received any signal.

All the worries and fears she'd pushed back all day flooded her mind, setting aside any chance of sleep. The Yotne hadn't been near the Bailey-Duran system in living human memory, but if their Dwellers were possessing local people, the Yotne would not be far behind. The UW&N had sent SpaceCom here to catch smugglers and discourage piracy. There weren't enough forces in-system to stop a Yotne offensive. And who would help Jeff's widow raise their two little boys?

Ulla forced all thoughts of lost shipmates out of her mind as best she could. That would have to wait until she had the luxury of introspection. Instead, she lay under the stickerbushes, shivered, and tried to quiet her racing brain. Exhaustion finally won, and she slept.

* * *

At sunup, something bellowed. Fighting the urge to get up and run, Ulla lay face down in the chilly dawn and listened.

Less than ten meters away, Terran cattle grazed peacefully. She sat up and checked her comm; still full of static. She had a drink of water, ate another energy bar, and contemplated what to do next.

If she couldn't make contact with SpaceCom, she'd have to risk local contact. Hoffnung's backcountry was On'oi territory. Technically, at least, that was in her favor. But contact was unlikely to happen in the middle of a pasture. She got out her map and found a track leading from the restricted area to a town about ten kilometers away. She wadded up the energy bar wrapper and jammed it in her pocket with the map. She stuck her water bottle in its pocket, then wormed her way out of the stickerbushes.

She had not quite reached the gravel track when she heard the crunch of bipedal footsteps coming from the restricted area. There was more than one set—maybe three or four? Ulla moved to duck behind some bushes but brought herself up short. The cattle had looked well cared for. The people, who were still hidden among the thin woodland scrub, were more than likely the farmers whose place this was. With her comm still showing nothing but static, she ought to make contact with them.

Still, caution might be a good idea. Ulla stayed hidden and waited for the group to come closer. Two of the people who emerged onto the open part of the track were human men. The third was at least two-and-a-half meters tall.

Yotne? *Please no.*

But no, the eetee's skin was as gray as a Terran elephant's.

Not a Yotne. This eetee was a Bailey-Duran Three Elder, part of the Alliance that SpaceCom was here to protect. What the city people called a troll.

Very like the one in her most frequent nightmare.

Ulla knew she ought to make contact, but she just couldn't. The group left the track and headed for the canyon she had emerged from the previous evening.

Running after them would be counterproductive, she told herself as she headed for town. There would be time enough to rise above a lifetime of recurring nightmares.

Chapter Two
Guild Member

Olwyn Wittber, the UW&NS *Resolute*'s telepathic communications contractor, gathered her shopping bags and unfolded her tall frame out of a taxi in front of SpaceCom's Bailey-Duran sector headquarters. She savored Newcastle's daylight and salt air and adjusted the hat SpaceCom asked her to wear when in Newcastle. At least the city's dress code had kept her face and neck from being as sunburned as her arms after three hours dirtside.

As the taxi drove away, she pushed her brand-new spectacles up on her nose. Never mind that their presence on her face told anyone who cared to look that she had a physical disability her parents could easily have had cleared up before her conception. She could see, and her eyes no longer stung from wearing expired insertables. These clunky local eyeglasses were the best her employer, the United Telepathic and Paranormal Practitioners' Guild, would pay for now that they'd extended her six-month SpaceCom contract to a full standard year.

She headed for the installation's Gate. The day was half gone, and work would be piling up aboard the *Resolute*. Until midday yesterday, hers had been an easy job aboard a ship assigned to patrol the Bailey-Duran sector and whose main port of call was this pleasantly backward Earthlike world. Since the BD sector was part of the Edge between human and Yotne space, everyone got combat pay even though nothing ever happened here.

There'd been smugglers to chase, plus the occasional pirate, but not much else to write home about.

"Guild Member!" Lieutenant Commander Mary Nkosi, head of starfighter intelligence support on the *Resolute*, jogged up to meet her.

"Mary!" Olwyn stopped to wait for her. "What are you doing on the ground?"

Nkosi caught up with Olwyn. "Sat in on the debrief of the second starfighter from the *Valiant*." They walked together toward the Gate terminal.

Olwyn transferred her shopping bags to her left hand so she could open the door. "The one the itinerant mine workers' co-op rescued and towed to BD3 Station with their ship?"

Mary nodded. "Lieutenant Fergus McCauley. Medical kept him overnight at the station, and he arrived dirtside this morning." The two women got in line at the counter.

Olwyn pulled her security badge out of her pocket. "There's a third starfighter." Rescue had asked her for telepathic help in the search for the one on the ground where conventional comm didn't work. A fat lot of good that had done.

Mary fished out her SpaceCom ID on a chain around her neck. "Spider—um, Lieutenant Ulla, um, Ursula Thorsdaughter. Rescue hasn't heard a thing."

"Friend of yours?"

Mary nodded. "We were shipmates at Binder Station."

"Some On'oi sighted her alive and active on the ground yesterday." Which, though a godsend, was odd. Aside from one human Olwyn had found nearby who used an artificial psi blocker—who the spokesperson for the Hjralma-On'oi Alliance's research facility at Castle Chisos had identified as a visitor from Earth—she'd found nobody in the landing area who thought in Standard or Terran English.

Olwyn's purchases were getting heavy; she juggled her shopping bags and security badge as she transferred the bags to her right hand. "An Alliance telepath contacted me while I was downtown. A farmer saw her pod land several hundred kilometers east of here. By the time he reached the pod, which was pretty banged up and scorched, the starfighter had climbed out and walked away."

"How'd he know?"

"Tracks leading away from the locked pod matched

SpaceCom's standard flight boots in her size," Olwyn said. "This morning, he and two friends saw her from a distance. She was walking toward the nearest village."

Thanks be! Mary didn't say it out loud.

Did the woman have psi talent? Olwyn hadn't seen her name on the Guild rosters. "It's a damn good thing they spotted the starfighter because I couldn't find her," Olwyn said. *Thorsdaughter probably has a psi blocker. Why didn't Personnel TELL me?*

"I wouldn't think she has one," said Mary. "Starfighters don't, usually." *Oh! Those last few weeks at Binder she did. But it wasn't like Guild standard.*

Was Mary even aware she'd responded to an unspoken thought? And what did 'wasn't like Guild standard' mean? Olwyn would sort that later.

The person in front of them collected his token and went out a side door toward the tactical Gate SpaceCom was using while construction crews put the finishing touches on the permanent Gate. Olwyn stepped up to the counter and flashed her Guild medallion and security badge. "UW&NS *Resolute.*"

The attendant pushed a button, and a reusable token slid out. "Next group for the *Resolute* is in five minutes. You can make it if you hurry." Olwyn pocketed it and stood aside.

Mary showed her ID. "*Resolute.*" Her token slid across the counter with no human intervention, triggered instead by proximity to her SpaceCom ID. The two walked outside and waited.

When the lighted display over the Gate's portal flashed "UW&NS *Resolute,*" they entered and surrendered their tokens. The portal shut, and they waited with a handful of other spacers for it to open onto the *Resolute*'s quarterdeck. Onboard biometrics were working today, so there was no need for ID. Olwyn, a confirmed civilian, waved cheerily to the watch stander and ducked into a corridor.

Mary followed her. "I'm glad I ran into you," she said. "We need to talk. Do you have a few minutes?"

"Sure." Olwyn pressed a button on the bulkhead to summon the elevator, and they made their way to her Guild cabin on an upper deck. It was as far from the center of the ship as one could be and still breathe air.

* * *

Olwyn tossed her shopping bags onto the deck under her tiny desk. She took off her hat, fluffed up the short, sweaty brown curls it had squished, and activated her comm panel. Mary sat on the guest seat that doubled as a bed.

The comm panel blinked to life, and a long queue of messages popped onto its screen. Olwyn scanned subject headers and decided she had at least half an hour before any of them went critical. She turned to face Mary. "What's up?"

Lieutenant Commander Nkosi reached behind her in the cramped quarters and shut the door. "Dwellers."

Dear gods. That meant Yotne. But Yotne hadn't been seen in the Bailey-Duran system in living human memory. Most people who lived in BD3's coastal cities thought Dwellers were a myth. Olwyn hoped she had misheard.

Mary's face looked bleak. "You did not mishear."

You heard my thoughts. Olwyn spoke telepathically.

"Sorry; I didn't mean to eavesdrop." Mary said. "I need to talk to you about that."

"After the Dwellers."

The Intel officer nodded. "The official report will be in your message queue," she said. "I wanted to give you a heads-up that both of the starfighters we debriefed from the *Valiant* described engagement tactics that are much more Yotne than pack smuggler."

"Could their adversaries have been Yotne?"

Mary shook her head. "They flew Sparhawks, which are the older starfighters the local organized crime packs bought up to fly cover for their smugglers. They hire human mercenaries, usually ex-SpaceCom pilots, to fly them."

Olwyn didn't understand. Why couldn't a Yotne fly a Sparhawk? Sure, the Yotne were eetees, but they were bipedal, with two arms, opposable thumbs, and a head where humans would expect to see one. For a species that wanted to see humankind dead, they were depressingly intelligent.

Mary sighed. "The average Yotne is almost three meters tall," she said, "and Sparhawks are optimized for humans. Not enough room inside. But if Yotne Dwellers possessed human pilots, they'd likely use Yotne tactics."

Olwyn took off her spectacles, laid them on the desk, and rubbed the aching bridge of her nose. "Tell me about your psi talent."

Mary squirmed. "I've meant to come and see you ever since I got back from ground leave at MitSmith Corporation's beach resort in Landfall last month. I have some telepathic talent—but my range is so short that the recruiter's Guild rep wrote it down under Remarks and checked the 'no' box." Mary settled down. "My first year at the Academy, the Guild rep there taught me how to use and control what little I did have." She squared her shoulders. "But after spending a week on the ground here, my range improved, and my...other talent feels stronger than it was."

"Go on."

Mary didn't answer right away. "How much experience do you have with Dwellers?"

"None, thanks be." Olwyn stopped tapping at her comm panel. "I've studied them, of course. It's a requirement for most Guild contracts."

Dwellers were disembodied spirits that usually allied with the Yotne. They could and did possess whatever intelligent life-forms they found most useful. The Dwellers might once have been Yotne themselves, but nobody knew for sure. At least nobody in human-explored space knew. A ghastly series of mental impressions Guild trainees had to learn came to mind.

Mary trembled and shielded her thoughts tightly.

Olwyn thought she'd kept the images to herself. "You are a very strong telepath."

"Stronger lately. This was my old range." Mary stretched out her arms and tapped bulkheads on both sides of their cramped quarters to illustrate. "It's maybe ten times that now."

Olwyn put her spectacles back on and tapped at her comm panel. "May I open your record?"

"Sure. It'll be about three pages in."

The record was full of phrases like "outstanding team player," "rapport with others," "master instructor"...

You use your psi.

"I do," Mary said.

"How can you bear the ship's godawful psi shield that's

always in the background?" That was among the reasons the Guild cabin was so far from the center of the ship.

Mary shrugged. "It's just white noise. I can't hear it unless I'm right next to a source point."

"Well." Olwyn drummed her fingers on the desk. "You're not alone. Since we've been here, I've had half a dozen spacers come see me about psi talent they didn't have before. *If this keeps up, the Guild had better send somebody, not me, to train them all.* If a fight with the Yotne was brewing, there was no way SpaceCom would release anyone for off-site training. "Do you have any new psi talents?"

"No. Just the increased telepathy range—and strength, too." Mary blushed. "Sometimes when I hear a person's thoughts, I think they're speaking out loud."

Olwyn tried and failed to discern what classified matters Commander Nkosi carried in her mind. "Your privacy skills are good; the rep at the Academy taught you well. I think you'll get the hang of your stronger psi listening skills if you pay close attention. Come see me if you have any problems—but I think you'll be fine." She took off her spectacles and rubbed the bridge of her nose again. "Tell me about your other psi talent."

Mary shivered. "I can...kill Dwellers without harming their hosts."

Oh, sweet Mother of Light. Olwyn chose her audible words more carefully. "That's a skill the Guild doesn't list. Please tell me everything you can."

Mary took a deep breath. "I grew up in a little archipelago on Leviathan. Our island had a Dweller incursion when I was sixteen."

"Go on."

"It's as though people you know well have acquired a—second soul." Mary paused. "I'm pretty sure only telepaths can see that." She breathed—looking for gumption? "The second soul matches the profile you projected; it can only be described as evil."

Evil that usually chose to work on the side of the Yotne. Olwyn shivered. "Leviathan pushed the Yotne back, did you not?"

Mary grinned, but not happily. "We did." She seemed unsure of what to do with her hands. "That's when I, uh, killed the Dwellers."

And?

"The first was pure reflex, self-defense." Mary went even quieter. *The rest were...not. Their hosts survived, Dweller-free—except for horrific dreams and memories.*

Nothing Olwyn had found in the Guild archives had even hinted that any living being could survive Dweller possession. "That makes you a hero, you know."

Mary looked down. "I said nothing at the time. And I've only ever mentioned it once before."

Olwyn did not understand. "Why not?"

"Do you think I'd risk a witchcraft conviction?" Mary asked, astonished. "It was Leviathan!"

Olwyn scrolled through Mary's SpaceCom record and double-checked a date. "You were at Binder Station last year when the Yotne attacked." *What really happened?*

Mary went quiet for a long minute. She took a deep breath. "It was—complicated."

Olwyn waited.

"You're Guild." Mary spoke as though her statement was self-explanatory.

"Oh, that!" Olwyn sighed. "I promise you, the waste of biomass who was Binder's Guild rep at the time is a one-off." *The whistleblower who got him fired should have free drinks for life.*

Mary met Olwyn's gaze. "You're welcome."

???

Mary showed her the ghost of a smile. "No worries, I'm not much of a drinker." She stood up to look over Olwyn's shoulder. "Next screen." She placed her index finger on the Guild rep's comm panel. "That classified link there. It'll want my biometrics."

Olwyn leaned aside and let Mary open the link.

"Please read the whole thing first." Mary sat back down, visibly shaken. *Once you've finished, I think I'll be able to talk about it.*

Olwyn read. She'd already studied the Guild investigation that had come out a few months ago about Binder, which had tried and failed to make sense of the botched and incomplete original reports. The classified document Mary had just opened put things into perspective and included many more details.

The Yotne had attacked the Binder system and had sent Dwellers to possess key defense personnel and prepare the way. Nothing new there.

Alert cargo transfer workers at Binder Station had noticed some of their coworkers acting oddly, and soon after, the station's Guild rep had verified Dweller possession. Station security had evacuated as many non-possessed people as they could out of that section of the station. By keeping people away from the hundred-meter zone, they'd stopped Dwellers from jumping to other, safer hosts, and then were able to seal the bulkheads and empty the air from the affected section. With no other potential hosts in range, the Dwellers died with their existing hosts. Standard, if brutal, procedure.

The Yotne attack on the station had been part of their larger campaign. Humanity and its allies prevailed, due in part no doubt to timely eradication of Dwellers. That much was in all the Guild reports.

This report said more. There'd been more Dwellers, and several cases of probable Dwellers, passing through multiple hosts on Binder Station to get to key personnel in MitSmith's station control center, SpaceCom's command center, and the flight deck. One of the warehouse compartments had been evacuated unnecessarily, killing five completely non-involved people.

Several hours later, six people blacked out within minutes of one another and revived within an hour at most. All remembered being Dweller-possessed; all of them recounted to a Guild board the series of hosts "their" Dwellers had possessed before possessing them, and, as best as anyone could parse eetee memories, what those Dwellers were up to.

Two hosts were maintenance technicians on the flight deck. Another was a chief in the adjacent flight maintenance control center, and the fourth was a member of station management on safety duty in the station's main control center.

Half an hour later, two starfighters had blacked out in flight. Their safety systems had kicked in and Gated their Goshawks back to the station. They, too, suffered no ill effects.

Unless you counted a lifetime of Dweller nightmares.

Olwyn kept reading.

A seventh person blacked out, a starfighter whose Goshawk Gated automatically back to the station five minutes after the others, barely a minute after her wingman's Goshawk developed a stuck jet. In her case, there was no mention of Dwellers.

Olwyn finished reading the text and turned to Mary. "Somebody was doing at Binder Station what you did on Leviathan."

"It wasn't me." *Except for the Dweller on the MitSmith safety officer. He was maybe a meter away on the other side of the bulkhead.* "I had a debriefer on the flight deck, but I was in the Intel workspace in the SpaceCom command center, next door to the station's main control center in the middle of the station." Mary took a deep breath. "My, uh, Dweller-killing ability has the same range as the rest of my psi talent. No way could I reach out and touch the flight deck from there, let alone the starfighters in space." *The Guild rep at Binder called me a street witch.*

To your face? Olwyn was shocked. One did not mock those who had limited telepathy skills.

No, but he thought it, and I heard it. Mary's shoulders sagged.

"Any idea who killed the other Dwellers?"

"No. I debriefed the two starfighters when Medical and Psych were done with them. The Dwellers possessed them when they stepped into their Goshawks on the flight deck, but out in space, something destroyed those Dwellers." Mary took a deep breath. "Then a third starfighter blacked out. The fourth had a stuck jet."

"Stuck jet?"

Mary nodded. "Torch—Lieutenant Gav Psarakis. The opposing jets on the other side of his Goshawk compensated, so he had some control, but he was out of the action and couldn't recover on the flight deck. He'd have set the whole damn thing on fire."

That was a part of shipboard life Olwyn tried not to think about. She hoped Mary didn't see her squirm. "What happened next?"

"They tried everything, but the jet wouldn't shut off," Mary said, "until suddenly it did."

"How?"

"Nobody knows. But there were human handprints on his Goshawk's emergency shutoff panel that hadn't been there when he launched."

Seriously?

"It's documented on the security recordings from the flight deck."

Olwyn took a deep breath. "He shut the jet down, then."

Mary shook her head. "The panel's on the outside—designed for flight-deck use. And the prints didn't match any of the maintenance team who recovered the Goshawk."

Which meant somebody, or something, had touched the Goshawk with bare hands in space. Nope. Not possible.

Agreed. But it happened. Mary opened a link to a set of images. "See?"

Holy shit. Olwyn sat back. "Did they ever match up the prints?"

Mary nodded. "Torch's wingman, Spider. The last starfighter to black out. The timing's wrong. Video shows her flight-checking her own Goshawk before they launched; she didn't touch his. When his jet malfunctioned, she'd already blacked out. Her Goshawk's emergency system Gated it back to the flight deck. By the time Torch's jet shut off, out in space, the medics had Spider on a gurney headed for the elevator."

Maybe, just maybe..."Did anyone mention seeing a ghost?" Olwyn asked.

"You're joking."

"No, really."

"There was a rumor about a ghost three meters tall—big as a Yotne. It showed up in the elevator on the way to Medical." Mary sighed. "The MitSmith emergency med tech who was on call said he saw it drag Spider's ghost inside by the scruff of her neck and stuff her back into her body."

Could the starfighter called Spider have psi talent, and her "ghost" been an astral projection? Olwyn would have to check. She said only "That's—unique."

"Yeah."

"Binder's on the Edge too." *Weird stuff happens out here sometimes.*

"Mmm-hmm." Mary reached over to tap another link on Olwyn's comm panel. "The ghost thing didn't make it into the official report, but there was so much talk about it that the investigators included it in the notes."

Olwyn read. "Lieutenant Ursula M. Thorsdaughter." She looked up. "She's Spider?"

Mary nodded. "Spider is Ulla's call sign." *I so hope she makes it back safely.*

* * *

After Olwyn filed her report about the Alliance sighting of Lieutenant Thorsdaughter near Castle Chisos, she took off her spectacles, put her elbows on her desk, and sat, face in hands.

Dwellers. Much as she had studied them, she'd never been in contact with one—that she knew of. The way Mary Nkosi had described them, Olwyn ought to be able to recognize shipmates on the *Resolute* possessed with a "second soul." She telepathically scanned as best she could, but to do a proper job, she'd need to have the psi shield turned off. She made a private note in a paper notebook. On the bright side, the psi shield was said to be as much of a problem for Dwellers as it was for her.

What about BD3—an entire planet that was home to lots of people who had psi talent? This close to the Edge, surely a local adept could tell her more about Dwellers even if the City-States people were in denial. She'd ask the Alliance liaison at SpaceCom's dirtside headquarters in Newcastle.

She made another note on her readpad and flipped through the messages on her comm panel. There was a single urgent request among reams of administrative trivia. Predictably, the captain wanted her to scan for Yotne.

That task, unfortunately, was familiar.

Olwyn composed herself, got comfortable in her seat, and started scanning. She knew that taking half an hour to look for Yotne in a star system was a crapshoot, but half an hour was her own very human body's limit for peak performance while sitting still.

Most people had no clue how really, really big star systems were. Back in the day, astronomers Lowell and Tombaugh took over two standard decades to get from Lowell's concept of "Planet X" to Tombaugh digging in and finding Pluto at the end of a long, methodical search. Who was she to think she could find something the size of a fleet at a similar distance?

She scanned anyway. Lowell and Tombaugh hadn't had access to modern scanning techniques, and certainly not to psi.

Here on the Edge of human-explored space, the logical place to start was the side of the system facing Yotne space. She'd try the area where, last week, she'd noticed something off, but undefinable. Nothing there. She widened her search, taking care as she did so. If Yotne were present, they must not find her out.

Her back ached, she needed to pee, and she'd found nothing of interest. Maybe she ought to—there! Damn. She scanned again, very carefully.

Yotne presence, muted by Yotne military psi shields. *Damn, damn, damn.*

Chapter Three
Found in Water

Ulla stopped at a riverbank to get her bearings. The road turned upstream toward the town the map called Chisos. A cable ferry plied back and forth between the town's docks and a big encampment on the other side that was almost surrounded by the river's oxbow curve.

On the far side of the river, human shepherds and their dogs led freshly sheared sheep across a pasture behind a group of tents that other humans were erecting. On this side, half a dozen giant eetee draft animals that looked a little like humpless camels with big heads stood patiently, while long-necked, llama-sized creatures fidgeted, their pale fleece sparkling in the intermittent sunlight. The sparkly animals had to be capraglamas; they were as distinctive as Intel said they were. Assuming that was correct, their herders—uh, keepers—would be On'oi.

A man rode a big draft animal into the water; the other exotic stock followed and swam for the other side.

The wind picked up; a nasty-looking storm over the mountains to the northwest was heading their way. Growing up at MitSmith's mining station on Farwell had taught Ulla well about flash floods. Unless she missed her guess, that storm was about to send this river's water level way up.

A handful of fat raindrops splattered on the ground as the last shiny animal scrambled up the far bank. Ulla stuck the map in her pocket and headed for town.

She had gone maybe three steps when a relentless

half-meter wall of water, deadwood, and trash appeared from around a curve upriver. It piled into the ferryboat, which rocked as its cable parted. The boat wobbled, swung from its cable's newly single axis on the other side of the river, and slammed into a sandbar. People swam through the floating cargo and pulled themselves onto the opposite bank as the river rose even higher.

Then Ulla saw the child in the water. A little girl fighting the current and losing fast. Ulla was the only adult this far downstream. If she could swim powerfully enough, at just the right angle, she might—

No. Just no.

Her heart told her brain to shut the hell up.

All the trash in the water mapped out the currents, at least on the surface. It also made diving a terrible idea. Ulla slid down the bluff on her rear end, pushed off with as much force as she could, and swam for a place where the current might push her on course to intersect with the child's. In seconds, she found herself immediately downriver from the terrified little girl.

Ulla reached out. "Grab hold!" The child grabbed her, and they both went under. Ulla got a better grip on the kid and relaxed enough that they could float to the surface. She spat out water and murmured, "Relax, little one, so we can swim together. You understand?"

The kid gave her a blank look but relaxed just enough.

Ulla let the current carry them around the bend to a sandbar, where they were able to stand up. The child grinned and waved at three men running along the top of the bluff.

Holding hands as the water lapped higher around their ankles, Ulla and the little girl scrambled around tangled piles of wood and trash. When they reached the shallow water between the sandbar and the riverbank, Ulla picked up the child, braced herself against the current, and waded across.

The men, followed by a dripping-wet woman, half-climbed, half-slid down the bluff. The child jumped out of Ulla's arms, scrambled over debris, and ran to hug a big, red-headed man. He picked her up and handed her to the woman, who hugged her tight and helped her scramble up the bluff and away.

As Ulla's heart rate slowed toward something

resembling normal, she took a deep breath and gave thanks that she and the child hadn't both drowned.

One of the men shouted in Standard. "Lieutenant!"

Ulla needed to move, and fast. Where she'd been standing on sandy ground moments before, the water had now risen to her knees. She picked her way through piles of deadwood and trash. Whole trees had been uprooted and carried here. Loose branches floated free.

"Starfighter! On your right!" Standard again, in a different voice.

Ulla looked up. A huge branch bore down on her. She jumped to avoid it, tripped, fell facedown, and heard something crack. Gods, her ankle! Just then, the branch rolled sideways and floated harmlessly away downstream. How'd that happen?

When she tried to stand, her left foot buckled under her.

The men hauled her to the top of the bluff, where they all sat, breathing hard. Tents, people, and livestock were everywhere. The water below them was still rising.

The man who'd called out first turned to Ulla. "Ankle?"

She nodded. "Twisted it in the debris."

"Can you walk?" That was the other Standard speaker; he was a little taller and had a neatly trimmed dark beard.

"What do you think?" Ulla blurted. She was cold, wet, keyed up, and covered in mud. As the rain turned into sleet, she started shaking and couldn't stop.

The big redhead, who had been sitting quietly and staring into space, turned and spoke briefly in some other language with the clean-shaven man who spoke Standard.

The bearded man stood. "Starfighter, the chieftain has asked us to bring you to his tent."

She looked up at him from where she sat on the ground. "And?"

"It's warm and dry there. You can get your foot seen to."

Out here? Until this flood subsided, the town across the river might as well be on another continent.

"Of course," he said. "There's a healer with us; we're setting out on a months-long trek."

She hadn't asked out loud.

* * *

The chieftain's tent was round, warm, and surprisingly large. The redhead and the man with the beard carried Ulla inside, where a petite, brown-skinned woman with dark hair pulled back in a long braid waited.

The woman spoke and gestured to a pile of clothing at the foot of a sleeping pad.

The bearded man translated as he helped Ulla sit down on the pad. "This is Ingeborg Yensdaughter, the physician's apprentice," he said. "She's asking you to get out of your wet clothes and put these on." He picked up the clothes and held them out to her. "The physician will be here as soon as she has changed into dry clothes, too. The child you fished out of the water is her daughter."

That was one way to make contact.

Dry clothes would be a mercy. But everything Ulla owned on this planet was in the pockets of her wet, muddy flight suit and survival vest.

The men ducked outside through the larger of two tent flaps. The woman named Ingeborg looked at her and waited.

Equipment and money would be of no use if Ulla died of pneumonia, so she unloaded her pistol and replaced it in its holster. She put the unused ammunition in a purpose-made pocket next to the holster. Then she took off the vest and set it, mud, firearm, and all, on the ground cloth, pointed in what she hoped was a safe direction. She took her right boot off easily enough. The left one was a problem. The boot's padded liner, meant to protect the pressure undergarment she'd left behind in the egress pod, had felted itself to Ulla's sock. Together, Ulla and the woman gently eased the assembly off Ulla's swollen foot.

Ulla took off her remaining sock and her flight suit, piled them next to the vest, and peeled off her long underwear. Now that she was stripped down to her underpants, the unmistakable odor of ripe sweat in all that gear could no longer be ignored.

Ingeborg blinked, nostrils flaring slightly. She filled a basin with warm water, found a cloth and a bar of soap, and set them down where Ulla could reach them. Ulla took off her underwear and took as complete a bath as possible with the limited tools at hand. The warm water stilled the last of her cold shivers and, with the soap, helped get rid of the old sweat mixed with river mud. Ingeborg handed

Ulla a fresh basin of water when the first one got too filthy, so Ulla even had a go at washing her hair.

Being clean felt so good.

Ingeborg handed Ulla a towel. Being dry felt even better.

The tall woman from the encounter below the bluff ducked inside. She must be the physician, then. Ingeborg handed Ulla a warm blanket to wrap up in and spoke briefly with the newcomer. Then the physician sat down in front of Ulla and spent a few long minutes lightly probing her foot, knee, lower leg, and swollen ankle with her fingers. She said a string of words Ulla did not understand and wrapped the ankle tightly in a strip of cloth.

Ingeborg handed Ulla dry underwear that looked too big. Awkwardly, because she was sitting at ground level and her ankle really hurt, she changed into dry everything—underwear, an oversized shirt, a medium-length full skirt, and a thick, cuddly sweater.

Ingeborg piled Ulla's wet, filthy gear near the entrance, where the ground cloth was already muddy with footprints. At a muffled "heya" from outside, she opened the tent flap. The shorter of the two Standard-speakers, the one without a beard, ducked through the entrance, carrying a well-worn leather case. He conferred briefly with the physician, then sat down next to Ulla. "She says it's not broken."

"How does she know? She didn't do a scan." The woman hadn't manipulated Ulla's injured foot or even poked at it very hard.

He opened his case. "Did she spend several minutes touching the injury with her fingers?"

Ulla nodded.

"That was a scan. She used psi." He reached into the bag, brought out a handheld medical sensor, set it next to her foot, and activated it. Once the image in the little viewing chamber was clear, he held it up for Ulla and the healer to see. "See? Not broken—though in a few months, you may wish it had been. That's a nasty sprain." He enlarged the image and focused on a group of ligaments. "If you stay off your foot and let it heal, you can probably avoid surgery. None of the ligaments are—quite—torn through."

"You sound like you know what you're talking about."

"I'm a doctor."

"Then why—"

"Hanni Rubensdaughter is the senior physician here; she's perfectly competent." He powered down the sensor and put it away. "I do have a United Worlds and Nations license and a MitSmith contract number if you want to see them."

Ulla shook her head. She tried forming her next question and just couldn't.

Hanni spoke to the doctor, who laughed. "I'll bet your briefers mentioned that some people on this world use what SpaceCom calls paranormal skills and that you likely ignored everything but telepathy as superstition and nonsense."

Exactly so. Ulla felt her face grow warm. She changed the subject. "I can't send a message to anything in orbit, yet your sensor works. Why?"

"Dumb luck," he said. "We're already in a place where, half the time, it won't activate. Once we're well inside the Electronics Unreliable zone, it won't work at all."

None of this was getting her up and out of this tent. "What happens next?" Ulla asked.

"With your ankle?" he asked.

She nodded.

The doctor and the healer spoke with each other in that other language. Finally, the doctor spoke to Ulla in Standard. "Stay off your injured foot. Hanni will get you some ice and make a place for you in her tent where you can rest and keep it elevated, at least while we're in camp. When the swelling goes down, we'll see."

Well, shit. Ulla poked at her bandaged ankle. How would this affect her chances of flying?

Hanni said something else and the doctor translated. "You can eat with them and have a warm place to sleep. Her little girl can't wait to see you."

* * *

Ulla dozed under a warm blanket inside a creaking, flapping tent. Sleet blew in on cold drafts around the edges and melted in the warmth from a vented stove. Water ran off the thin, sturdy ground cloth and soaked into the entrenched ground around its edges.

Something, maybe stew, simmered on the stove. It

smelled delicious—onions, maybe? Possibly mutton, too, and spices she couldn't identify. A child sang in a language that might almost be Classical English, or the variant they spoke in this world's city-states, but wasn't.

A warm little hand grasped hers.

"Stelle, let the starfighter rest." Hanni turned from the pot she was stirring.

What just happened? The woman hadn't switched languages.

"But, Ma, I'm showing her how we talk."

Without a word, Hanni gave her young daughter "the look," instantly recognizable by human parents and children everywhere. Stelle's chin quivered. Her mother relented, knelt down to her level, and hugged her. Then she gently led the child aside, sat her down, and gave her a spoon and a bowl of stew. The little girl solemnly scooped up a spoonful and blew on it before putting it in her mouth.

Hanni picked up another bowl. "Are you hungry, Starfighter? You've been asleep for several hours."

Real food after a diet of energy bars! Ulla was starving. She sat up and pushed back the blanket. Somebody had given her injured foot its own pillow.

"Here." Hanni put a tray on the ground cloth next to Ulla. "There's stew and bannock, and—oh, I forgot. Just a minute." She ducked outside and brought back two lightweight camping mugs full of cold beer.

She set one down beside Ulla and fished a small bottle of commercial anti-inflammatory. out of her pocket. "Nathan left these. One tablet should do for half a day."

"Who's Nathan?" Ulla asked.

"He's the offworlder healer. You met him this afternoon." Hanni gave the bottle to Ulla before turning back to cover the stew pot and adjust the stove.

As Ulla ate and drank, Hanni moved around the tent, wiping, tidying, and stowing clutter. Ulla's freshly laundered clothing hung on a line strung near the stove. Where were the rest of her things?

Hanni reached into a jumble of saddles and tack and pulled out a cloth bag and handed it to Ulla.

Another unasked question answered.

"I hope you don't mind. I took the liberty of cleaning your pistol before it could rust." Hanni pointed toward the sidearm, recently cleaned and lubricated, sitting on an improvised shelf, out of the child's reach. "That's a nice Smith."

Ulla caught herself before she shrugged. The Smith projectile pistol was standard SpaceCom issue in places where energy weapons did not work. Instead, she said, "Thank you," and took the bag. She resisted opening it to check; that would likely be rude.

Finished with housekeeping, Hanni resumed knitting a half-finished wool sock on four tiny knitting needles. Little Stelle tootled away peacefully at a singing game.

Ulla finished eating and settled back with the last of her beer. Who were the On'oi, really? The SpaceCom briefers said they traveled with their livestock every summer and inspected most of the planet's surface in the process. It was part of the terraforming project the On'oi shared with the trolls. The briefers had also said that almost all On'oi had some kind of psi talent.

The only other reference Ulla could think of, other than a few holoshows, was the odd way some Newcastle locals said goodbye: "Don't let the herders get you."

The woman flinched. *Damned Newcastlers.* She stopped knitting, drew a couple of deep, quiet breaths, and resumed working on the sock. *We are On'oi. Guardians, not 'herders.'* She took another deep breath and let it out slowly. *And do not ever call the Hjralma 'trolls.'*

Ulla heard the woman as clearly as if she had spoken out loud, which she hadn't. "Sorry, just going on what I heard."

The healer put down her knitting and spoke out loud. "You have the Gift, then."

"What Gift?"

"Mind-talking."

"Do you mean—" Ulla had no idea how to say "telepath" in this language.

Hanni nodded. "Yes. That is the word in Standard."

Ulla shook her head. "SpaceCom tests for that. I've always tested negative."

"You might test again when you get back to SpaceCom." Hanni turned her attention back to her knitting.

Ulla finished her beer. "How is it that suddenly we can speak and understand each other?"

"I can't say." Hanni glanced at her little daughter.

"When I figure it out, I'll let you know."

Ulla was exhausted and, more or less, safe. For the first time since she'd landed on Bailey-Duran Three, she slept deeply enough to dream.

* * *

Flames crackled and roared as buildings caught fire. Ulla peered through thick smoke as soldiers half-ran, half-skidded down the slope toward the shuttle behind her, hustling the VIPs they'd rescued away from the fire. More soldiers sprinted out of the shadows with well-dressed civilians.

The wind shifted; sparks and embers flew closer. Patches of dry brush caught fire.

The pilot's voice crackled in the comm pickup. "We can't stay."

Velasco, Cheylik, and Jones were still out there with, one hoped, the rest of the evacuees.

A tall, gray eetee stepped gracefully from the shuttle. That would be the troll. A shower of sparks engulfed her—for some reason, Ulla knew the eetee was a her—and her lightweight robes caught fire. The flames faded quickly and died, leaving holes in the cloth. The troll brushed at the ash with her hands and picked her way across crushed grass and brush. "I can help."

A low, cold draft blew across the ground, pushing sleet that sizzled and evaporated.

Ulla rolled over, half-awake now, and pulled the blanket up around her shoulders to block the draft coming into the tent. The damn sprain woke her up completely.

Just as well. Whoever Velasco, Cheylik, and Jones were, she hated, hated, hated their firestorm dream. No need to close her eyes and finish it. She knew how it ended.

Chapter Four
Rescue Meeting

Power tools whined in the corridor outside the only finished conference room in SpaceCom's brand-new Bailey-Duran sector headquarters. Olwyn stretched her legs under the table and waited for the conversation between Admiral Rosen and the Rescue Service Lead to cool down. Idly, she wondered if they were painting her new office today. Even though she'd been approved for the Headquarters job, she couldn't move in until the Guild's new replacement for her *Resolute* billet arrived.

The Hjralma-On'oi Alliance liaison seated across the table from her, opened his mouth to speak, then thought better of it.

"Mr. Eselgroth, I understand about not sending a rotorcraft into the Electronics Unreliable zone." As the admiral got angrier, her speech grew quieter. "Can't you at least get a backcountry vehicle in there? An animal-mounted expedition will take weeks."

"No, ma'am." The Rescue Lead was adamant. "Even if we could rely on shielding to keep the electronics working—which we can't—the terrain is too rough even for an overland camion. And there aren't any roads where Lieutenant Thorsdaughter is."

A heavy flittercraft taking off from the nearby Port of Newcastle rumbled overhead. Conversation paused.

Roads, yes. Highways for your big honking military camions, no. The Alliance liaison caught Olwyn listening. He ventured a faint smile.

She returned his glance. *It's more about rough ground and mountains, isn't it?*

It is. Further thoughts shielded, the On'oi turned his attention back to Rosen and Eselgroth.

What was the liaison's name again? She consulted the meeting agenda on her readpad. Balanced Trade Enforcement Agent Skuli Branson. Maybe he could tell her who could provide a local perspective about Dwellers. There were enough people on BD3 with psi skills that somebody must know something.

"—so, I recommend you take the On'oi Council of Chieftains up on their offer to return Lieutenant Thorsdaughter." Olwyn had worked with Craig Eselgroth before; she spotted the body language that said he was frustrated. The way this meeting was going, pissed off was coming right up.

Admiral Rosen turned toward Mr. Branson. "Who will you assign to bring her home?"

"Thom Yensson, who was in contact yesterday with Guild Member Wittber. He's a land-use inspector for the Alliance's Planetary Restoration Project, assigned to a special project for the Council of Chieftains. He's escorting a Terran physician on a medical education exchange with the group that picked her up. He and the Terran have offered to escort the starfighter to Newcastle when the exchange is over."

"How long will it take?" asked Rosen.

"The trekking group is assembled now," Branson said, "near a place called Chisos, on the other side of the mountains east of here. Good news is, they're headed in our direction anyway; Flint Clan's summer pasture base camp is near Bald Mountain."

"How far will that put them from a working Gate?" Rosen asked.

"About a week overland, if the weather's good." The Alliance liaison glanced at his notes. "The educational exchange has three weeks more to go. They should be at Bald Mountain by then; they'll leave from there."

"Four weeks in all, weather permitting." Admiral Rosen was not pleased. "That's almost a standard month."

I've worked with the Terran doc before; he's solid. And if the Council of Chieftains picked the High King's son to ride herd on Flint Clan, he's solid too.

Startled, Olwyn realized those thoughts came from the Rescue Lead, not the Alliance liaison. Was Craig's psi security blocker wearing off? She'd have a private word with him after the meeting.

In the meantime, it looked like they'd be working with the son of the elected head of the Council of Chieftains. But, what did Craig mean by "ride herd on Flint Clan?"

Eselgroth sighed. "Ma'am, it's not my first choice either, but the starfighter's in good hands."

"Then we accept the Council's offer." Admiral Rosen snapped her readpad shut, signaling the end of the meeting. "Make it happen."

* * *

After Admiral Rosen left, Olwyn, Craig, and Skuli got to work.

Craig tapped his stylus on the table. "We need to contact Lieutenant Thorsdaughter. And we need to talk with Nathan and Thom."

Olwyn adjusted her new spectacles. "Can you tell me more about the Terran physician?"

"Dr. Nathan Steves, the Terran doing the educational exchange," Craig said.

Educational exchange, my ass. Skuli Branson's On'oi earrings caught the light as he glanced at Eselgroth. Why were there two in his right ear and none, not even an empty piercing, in his left?

Olwyn kept picking up stray thoughts from the On'oi liaison. *Out loud, please, Mr. Branson.* She continued out loud. "If we three are going to work together, we have to work from the same page." She rested her elbows on the table and leaned forward. "Why are Mr. Yensson and Dr. Steves really out there?"

Craig and Skuli looked at each other. A long moment passed.

Skuli finally spoke. "Thom Yensson is a land-use inspector with the Planetary Restoration Project. A group of farmers on Flint Clan land, right in the middle of the Electronics Unreliable zone, updated their irrigation systems. Tagging along with Flint's trek is a convenient way for him to travel for the final inspection. And since Thom facilitated Dr. Steves's exchange project with a highly regarded traditional healer in Flint Clan, they might as well travel together."

Really? Skuli Branson's neat explanation might convince a table full of headblind players in a game of chance, but Olwyn could tell there was more to all this. She stared at him. He stared back.

Skuli turned to Craig. "Guild rep's cleared, right?"

Craig nodded.

"Fine," Skuli said reluctantly. "Here's what's going on. The Alliance wants to restore the Ancients' major Rings to their historic positions. Thom Yensson does have actual land-use inspections to do for farmers on Flint Clan's land, but the main reason he's on trek with them is to represent the On'oi Council of Chieftains and make sure Flint moves the Ring from Bald Mountain back to Landfall where it belongs." *Not like last year.* "Nathan Steves has his back. The two of them are old friends."

Olwyn had read about the Rings. Didn't they have something to do with the locals' ongoing terraforming project?

Not exactly, Guild Member. Skuli made eye contact with Olwyn. *And we call it planetary restoration.*

"Let me get this straight," Olwyn said. "Mr. Yensson is in the backcountry on an iffy assignment, and his backup is a traveling doctor from Earth." She pushed her spectacles back up on her nose. "But who is Nathan Steves, really?"

"Dr. Steves travels a lot, meets people, learns things. He's a competent physician and we're happy to have him." Skuli looked across the table at Craig. "If SpaceCom debriefs him after every trip, that's none of our affair." *Can't hurt for you lot to get to know us better.*

Craig glared at him.

"How much does Admiral Rosen know?" Olwyn's question broke up the incipient staring contest.

"She's been in the briefings." Craig shrugged. "She knows the important parts; the rest falls under 'not worrying the commanding officer unnecessarily.'"

So, this fraught situation was their safest choice for getting the starfighter back. No wonder Admiral Rosen was unhappy.

"Why do they want to move the Ring?" Olwyn cut short the rest of her question as another loud flittercraft took off above them.

Skuli waited for the noise to subside. "Legend says that in the time of the Ancients, twenty major Rings protected this world. Then, when the Ancients moved a Ring from Landfall to Bald Mountain, that's when the Yotne got in."

"Yotne, on the surface?" There were Yotne artifacts scattered throughout the Bailey-Duran system, but this was the first Olwyn had heard of humankind's worst enemy reaching the surface of Bailey-Duran's third planet.

"Most Hjralma make a habit of blasting anything and everything Yotne back into its original chemical elements." Skuli made eye contact with Olwyn. "But that's another story."

Shit. Olwyn had more homework to do about this place.

Skuli leaned forward. "Quick history lesson. It seems all the Rings have to be in their original places for their protection to work. Once the Ancients died out, about thirteen hundred of your standard years ago, the Yotne arrived. It took them five hundred years to extract everything they could from this world. The Yotne left, the Hjralma arrived, and the first Terran settlers arrived a few years later. That would have been over eight hundred years ago." He sipped his coffee. "Some scientists at Newcastle University think that resonance between two incorrectly placed Rings is why electronics don't work in that part of west Hoffnung. There are a handful of places at sea with the same problem. Wasn't an issue with traditional navigation, but we're in the modern age now. They want to fix that."

"By getting the Ring off Bald Mountain?" Olwyn rubbed the sore spot where her spectacles dug into the top of her right ear.

Skuli nodded. "By putting all the Rings back where they think they belong. The Ring functionality researchers are working with some archaeologists to refurbish an empty Ring seat for Flint's Ring off Landfall Mainland, on a tidal island called Great Knob. Assuming they're correct, and that they can apply the right, um, magic, for lack of a better term, they aim to restore the Ancients' planetary defense system."

The right magic? Even to Olwyn, who had been born into the Guild, that sounded like a profound stretch. "Are you ready to contact Mr. Yensson?"

"Not quite. I need some more information from Admiral Rosen," Craig said. "I'll be right back."

After the door closed, Olwyn set her spectacles on the table. "I didn't mean to eavesdrop. I apologize."

"No need. I thought I'd kept myself to myself." Skuli smiled. "You're a powerful telepath."

"Thanks." Olwyn rubbed the bridge of her nose.

"New spectacles?"

She nodded. "Never worn them before." *Gods, they're painful.*

"Those are pretty thick. If they're your first, how did you see before you got 'em?"

She laughed. "I've used corrective inserts since I was a child. Now that our six-month deployment has stretched to who knows how long, my last pair expired."

"SpaceCom doesn't send you new ones?"

"From the Reynoso system, when the list says a suitable substitute is available locally?" *You're funny.*

"You're the first SpaceCom person I've seen who uses them."

"Oh, there's a handful of us who have similar dirty little secrets." *Pretty soon, you'll be seeing lots of new pairs of spectacles around here...* "At least as a Guild contractor I don't need a vision waiver to keep my job." *Before you ask, yes, my parents could afford genetic correction. In the Guild, it's not done, though, because it'd disrupt the Registry Plan.*

Registry Plan?

She put her spectacles back on; making conversation with a blurred head and torso was unsettling. "The holoshows and sensational news reporters call it the 'studbook.'"

Skuli tapped a pencil on his little notebook that lay open on the table next to his readpad. "That's a real thing?"

Olwyn nodded, hoping the Guild might one day recommend a partner she could stand to be in the same room with. *There has to be a better way.* She changed the subject. "Most On'oi have psi ability. How does that happen?"

"We avoid inbreeding and hope for the best. The Rings play a part, too."

"The Rings? SpaceCom's intel briefers say they're

archaeological curiosities, nothing more."

"What does your Guild say?"

Olwyn had delved deep into Guild literature before deploying here, and aside from a paper that attempted unsuccessfully to pinpoint the Rings' power source, had found very little. "Only that the ratio of people with psi abilities is greater here than most places." *But only a few scholars put that down to the Rings.*

"Offworlders with established Gifts often find they're stronger after they've been here a while. Offworlders whose Gifts are latent suddenly have the real thing." Skuli paused. "Depending on the Gift, that can be traumatic if it's unexpected."

That would explain Mary Nkosi's experience, and the spacers—seven now—who'd come back from surface leave with psi talent they hadn't had before. *So, it's 'normal.'* When might she find time to train them all?

There surely would be more. *Dammit.* Olwyn had to reassess needs, negotiate a new contract with SpaceCom, and request more Guild members.

Was her own talent getting stronger? "What's your range, Mr. Branson?"

"Average, maybe a little longer."

"Which is?"

Enough to hail somebody in the next valley over. Way more than I need to cover a capraglama herd. "About twenty kilometers, give or take. And I can work with longer-distance mind-talkers easily if they hail me."

"Did you hear any thoughts from Craig Eselgroth?" *Or, the gods forbid, from Admiral Rosen?*

He shook his head. "No. Should I have?"

"No. I thought I heard his psi security block leaking, is all." *So it's just me, then.*

Chapter Five

Beginnings and Endings

"You can walk on this. But not too much, and when your ankle hurts, get off it." Nathan Steves made the last fitting adjustments on a modern orthopedic boot while Ulla sat on a big rock in front of Hanni's tent. The smell of roasting meat had joined the ever-present scent of campfire smoke; there was supposed to be a feast tonight.

He held out the boot. "Let's see your foot."

With his help, she eased her swollen foot into the boot. He adjusted something and fastened the buckles. "Try it."

Ulla took a few experimental steps across the low-growing local forage. This was so much better than sitting on her butt—and she wouldn't have to lean on Hanni every time she needed to go outside to pee.

"Once you can get your own boot back on, we'll talk about graduating to this." Nathan held up a purpose-made canvas wrap that had way too many straps.

"Where did this come from?" She sat back down and examined the sturdy composite boot. "Please don't tell me the On'oi packed it just in case."

"No." He laughed. "If this had happened in the backcountry, they'd improvise with whatever they had. Town's right over there, so Stelle used telekinesis to fly it across the river."

"You're kidding me."

"Well, yes. Yes, I am." He paused, watching her face. "Her father helped; she's little."

Behind her, a man laughed.

Was Nathan serious? *Do they really expect me to believe impossible things?*

"Not at all, Starfighter." The laughing man turned out to be the other Standard speaker from yesterday. "Stelle wanted to do something for you, so her da let her help him mind-move your new boot."

"You too?"

He sat down next to her. "Me too, what?"

Ulla sighed. "Reading my mind. Hanni's been doing it all morning."

"Sorry. I thought you were using your Gift."

"Gift?" Hanni had called it that too.

Nathan rolled up the used cloth bandage. "What the High King's son is trying to say is that most On'oi are telepaths. A lot of them have other psi talents too."

"Like Stelle's da, yesterday, when he used telekinesis to nudge that floating branch away." The man with the beard used the Standard term.

So that had really happened. Ulla shivered.

The High King's son held out his hand to her. "It was rude of me to eavesdrop on your thoughts. I won't do it again."

Ulla reached out to shake his hand. "Have we been introduced?"

"Um, apparently not, sorry." Sunlight caught his eyes and they sparkled. "I'm Thom Yensson, and you are?"

I'm pretty sure you know. "Ulla Thorsdaughter." They stayed, hands touching, longer than they needed to. Dear gods, those eyes were blue.

She broke contact and made a mental note to avoid further physical interaction with Prince Blue Eyes here. *Back to this universe, Spider. Now.*

Spider?

Starfighter call sign, a semi-official nickname. Shit. She was doing it, too. Mind-talking.

Just so you know, High King is an elected office. Myself, I'm a humble civil servant.

So he'd heard her snark. That was awkward.

He broke the silence first. "How well can you walk in that thing?"

"No," Nathan said, clicking his medical kit shut. "She is not making the trek on foot."

"I didn't say she was." He turned to Ulla. "Will you

come to the pasture with me? We'll find a camdeer you can ride."

"Can't you bring one over here?" Nathan asked.

"We need a camdeer who gets along with her. It'd be better for the starfighter to go to the paddock and find a volunteer."

"Gets along with?" Ulla asked. *A volunteer?*

Nathan grinned. "On'oi. Get used to them, Starfighter."

Ulla followed Thom through the camp. She would not admit how badly her ankle hurt and hoped she could make it all the way to the paddock.

He turned to face her. "May I?"

"May you what?" Ulla asked.

"Carry you," he said. "You're hurting."

Was this a normal local thing? "Um, sure." He seemed like a decent guy.

Her answer was barely out of her mouth when he picked her up in his arms and kept on walking. So much for avoiding physical contact.

* * *

"Look at the river!" Thom turned so she could see it too.

A spectacular curve of water lay between them and the village. Most of the debris had floated away, and the water was a deep, muddy brown. The spring thaw must be well underway in the mountains.

The ferryboat lay on the near bank, its severed cable partly submerged in the water. Several people were clearing away branches and trash from around the dock's pilings while Piet, Hanni's husband, stared at a spot in the sky over the river.

Ulla followed his gaze as he mind-moved a stick through the air toward the workers at the dock. When the stick reached them, a worker pulled hand over hand on the long, thin cord tied to it.

"They're replacing the cable," Thom said. "Piet just landed the guide cord. See the crew on the other side? They're attaching a bigger cord now."

Sure enough, the string in the river was now big enough to see from where they stood.

A cloud blew over the sun, but only for a moment.

The water under the bluff gleamed with broken patches of reflected light.

Thom turned and walked on. "It'll take them a while to work up to the actual cable and install it. But the ferry should be good to go by the time the water level drops back to normal."

"Does this camp ever flood?" Ulla asked.

"Not usually." He set her down so he could open a gate at the edge of the camp. "But it's just as well we're leaving tomorrow."

* * *

Once they were through the gate, several camdeer wandered over to investigate. Ulla sat on a rock while Thom wandered among them. He made a low whistling sound, and one of the towering, four-legged creatures craned its long neck down toward his hand. When Thom gave it a treat and scratched its broad, shaggy forehead, it followed him.

"Here." Thom handed Ulla a piece of carrot.

The camdeer bent down, delicately accepted the carrot from Ulla, and nuzzled at her pockets, looking for more. Thom had told her its name, which she could not even begin to pronounce.

She reached for another carrot from Thom and held it out to the camdeer. "May I call you Snowball instead, big fellow?" Again, gentle lips took the carrot for huge teeth to grind up.

If Snowball were smaller, had a hump, and pads instead of hooves, he could pass as a camel. As it was, he was the size of a Maybelle draft horse. With that big head, the effect was impressive.

How did one mount such a giant? Obligingly, Snowball knelt one end at a time. Should she climb on?

"Have you ever ridden bareback?"

"No." Ulla and her brother had ridden horses when she was about Stelle's age, but Grandad or one of the vaqueros on his ranch had always saddled the horses for them.

"Don't start now." Thom reached out, and Snowball offered a spot between his ears for Thom to scratch. "This guy's gentle, and he likes you. We'll saddle him for you tomorrow." He patted the camdeer on its big flank. Snowball got to his feet and lumbered away to graze.

"Let's stay here a while." Thom sat on the ground facing her. "I talked with the *Resolute*'s Guild representative this morning."

"You did what?" Oh. Telepathy. "What did the Guild rep have to say?"

"She relayed a conversation for me and the team that've been tasked to bring you back. They work for the Director of Operations at SpaceCom's sector headquarters in Newcastle. Do you know Admiral Imelda Rosen?"

Ulla nodded. So, Rosie had got promoted again and was in-system!

"Short version is the On'oi Council of Chieftains has contracted with SpaceCom to get you back to Newcastle. Nathan and I are going there in a few weeks; you're welcome to join us."

That sounded extraordinarily convenient. "How do I know you're telling the truth?"

He sighed. "A Mr. Eselgroth from your Rescue Service is coordinating your return from SpaceCom's end. He told me to tell you that the word of the day, when you got into your Goshawk last week, was 'imperious.'"

So it had been, but this man had ways of finding that out that had nothing to do with SpaceCom.

You're right, but why would we?

He was doing the psi thing again; had he meant to? "No idea," she said. "Can you do better?"

Thom's eyes widened the tiniest bit. "Sorry. I must not have shielded my thoughts sufficiently." He pulled the conversation back on track. "Eselgroth said you would ask." He paused and cleared his throat. "He says Admiral Rosen told him that on your first deployment, you kept a tattered toy rabbit wrapped up in a bag with a bottle of aquavit that you stashed behind the ventilation grille nearest your pillow."

Then-Lieutenant Commander Rosen had been Ulla's flight commander—and she knew about Pink Wabbit? Ulla felt her entire body blush.

"He said Admiral Rosen described it as more gray than pink. Its embroidered face had been redone at least twice." The man had the grace not to laugh.

"A childhood toy. Only thing I had left from my dad."

Rosie must have found the contraband during a routine inspection.

"She didn't have the heart to write you up for it, so she put it back."

"All right, I believe you." Ulla could absolutely imagine Rosie doing that. "Thank you, I'm in."

"It'll take weeks, but we'll get you back." Thom reached into his pocket for a small, well-worn notebook and dove into administrative details. "I'll be your point-of-contact; Nathan will be alternate. If you want to contact SpaceCom, talk to Hanni. She can send a message to their Guild rep. If she's busy, Flint has a couple other long-range mind-talkers here on trek. Hanni can introduce you. Nathan and I will be gone for a couple of days next week. I'm sure Hanni and Piet will take good care of you."

"What do you mean, take good care of?" Ulla was an adult, or had been the last time she checked.

"Trek'll be a new experience for you," he said. "And there's your injured foot."

There was, indeed. Ulla wiggled the toes on said foot and immediately wished she hadn't.

"Any questions?"

She shook her head. "I'll come find you when I think of some."

Thom turned a page. "The admiral dictated this herself. She said you'd want to know." He handed the open notebook to Ulla.

The page was full of the round, connected squiggles the locals called writing. Ulla shook her head. "I can't read it."

"Sorry." He took the book back. "That's the mind-talker's transcription."

"The mind-talker?" Ulla didn't understand. "You're a telepath."

"My range is soulslayer-short. Flint Clan's primary interstellar-grade mind-talker—you'll meet her before long—received the Guild rep's meeting request and handled the administrative stuff. When that was done, the Guild rep maintained the meeting link with me. I relayed for Nathan, and the Guild rep relayed for the head of your rescue team—Mr. Eselgroth's headblind."

Headblind? Did that mean "normal"? And what was a soulslayer?

Figures of speech. Tell you later.

Was he listening in on her thoughts again?

Before Ulla could call him on it, Thom switched to audible speech. "Sorry; I didn't mean to eavesdrop. Your Gift is really strong."

"It isn't a 'Gift,'" Ulla retorted.

After an awkward pause, he turned to the next page and held the book out to her. "Here's the list in Standard letters. These pages are yours. I'll slice 'em out for you if you want."

It was a list of shipmates who had survived the *Valiant* explosion. She scanned the names. *Bejarano, Yong D.* Ulla smiled. The young ops clerk with the bad tooth must finally have gone dirtside to get it seen to. He'd picked a good day for it.

De la Cruz, José M. Oh, good. What about Fergie? He'd flown with José that day. *McCauley, Fergus B.* Ulla remembered to breathe. Fergie made it!

Thom studied her face. "Is Fergie somebody special?"

No. Ulla was beyond caring about telepathic politeness. *No more than any shipmate.* Not for—had it been five standard years?

She read on. *Papas, Margaret E.; Papas, Nikolas R.* Nik and Mags had been on well-deserved ground leave at the beach resort in Landfall. *Thorsdaughter, Ursula M.* For Starfighter Operations, that was it. She scanned the rest of the names and recognized many, but not all.

Nearly six hundred souls had been aboard the *Valiant*. Two pieces of paper, written on front and back, listed those who remained. Pages the size of her hand.

Mutely, Ulla handed him the notebook. Using a small folding knife, he removed the two sheets for her. She folded them, put them in her pocket, and sat there staring at nothing.

"Are you all right?"

She started to nod and caught herself. "No. I'm not." Tears brimmed. "So many people."

He stood up. "Would you like some privacy?"

Ulla shook her head. She couldn't speak. *The whole damn ship.* Shoulders trembling, she sobbed. Tears flowed. Snot ran down her upper lip. She wiped at it with her hand.

You look like you could use a hug.

She nodded. *Yes, please.*

As he took her in his arms, she laid her head on his shoulder, snot, tears and all, and wept.

When she had no more tears, she sat up. "Please, forgive me."

"What for?"

"I'm not in the habit of losing my shit in front of strangers." She dried her face with the back of her hand.

Thom gave her a handkerchief. "I'd be more concerned if you hadn't. That's a hell of a loss."

"Thanks."

Any time.

"Out of all those people," she said out loud, "I'm still here." *Why?*

Not something I can answer, Starfighter.

Chapter Six

Heroes, Danger and Drink

Late that afternoon, Hanni fastened the last button on little Stelle's dress. "Remember your manners tonight, sweetie."

Ulla folded her flight suit and put it on top of her other things in a bulging cloth bag. Her survival vest, with her water bottle and sidearm, fit nicely over her borrowed sweater.

Given, not lent. Hanni rummaged through a bag. *The sweater is yours now.*

Ulla was beginning to lose track of Flint Clan's piecemeal donations. In most cases, she had no idea whom to thank for what.

Hanni offered Ulla a hairbrush. "No worries." She grinned. "I need this back when you're finished with it."

Ulla's hair, neither curly nor straight and seven standard months out from a buzz cut, couldn't be styled properly, but at least she could coax out the tangles. Maybe it was finally long enough to tie back with the ribbon somebody had given her.

Hanni looked in the mirror. "You can say a general thank-you to everyone tonight when it's your turn to speak."

Ulla almost dropped the hairbrush. "When it's my turn to WHAT?" Somebody might have mentioned that tonight's festivities included public speaking!

Piet ducked in through the door. "It isn't a formal event, Starfighter. Standing up to toast your ancestors and heroes is nothing compared to fighting Yotne in space." *You'll do fine.*

Ulla took a deep breath and gave Hanni her brush back. *You have no idea.*

Let's set that topic aside for a minute. "Here." Piet handed Ulla a brand-new saddlebag. "This is for you. We brought it across the river from town with the last of the pastries."

Across the river with the last of the pastries?

"Oh, Ulla." Hanni burst out laughing. "We have to have pastries for dessert tonight. It's tradition. Since the river's up, the mind-movers flew the bakery boxes across from town." *So glad the beer came over three days ago with the advance group.*

Still not making sense. Ulla was beginning to lose track of what was said out loud, what wasn't, and whether it even mattered. She set down her new saddlebag and unbuckled its cover.

Sorry. "Tonight's the night before we leave for trek," Hanni said. "If the river weren't up, there'd be lots of people here from town for a big farewell party." *Come here, Stelle. Let me braid your hair.* "It's an excuse to feast on things we won't get on the trail."

Like beer and pastries. "What about fresh fruit?" Ulla asked. In Newcastle, fresh fruit was a treat.

"Too early for fresh fruit." Hanni parted Stelle's hair and started braiding one pigtail. "We'll have blackberries at Summer Pasture before long."

Ulla supposed Summer Pasture must be the trek's destination.

Piet nodded. "Summer Pasture gives the stock—and us—good food and a solid base camp."

Ulla didn't bother telling him she hadn't asked.

I thought you had; sorry. "Please look through your new things," Piet said. "Hanni's ma told me to make sure everything fits."

Hanni tied off Stelle's first pigtail with a red ribbon and started braiding the next. "My ma lives in Chisos. Council sent her shopping for you; she told me to tell you she had a grand time doing it."

Ulla sat down on her sleeping pad and opened the bag. It was fully stocked with a travel toiletries kit, a small pile of underwear, fresh socks, and a cup like all the adults in

Flint Clan had clipped to their belts. It also held a towel small enough for camping and big enough to dry a person off.

"What's this?" Ulla held up a pocket-sized notebook like Thom's, two pencils, and a tiny folding knife.

Piet grinned. "You may have noticed nobody has a readpad out here. A notebook serves pretty much the same purpose."

Ulla hadn't seen a graphite pencil since her earliest days in the isolated Big Bend country in Earth's Republic of Texas. They hadn't had comm there, either. At least, Granddad had taught her how to sharpen her pencils with a knife.

Ulla opened a resilient waterproof container, which was full of what the Newcastle apothecaries stocked on shelves euphemistically marked "ladies' supplies." Not her usual brand, but it'd do. She had two new shirts and a pair of new trousers identical to the gently used pants she had on.

Tucked beneath those, she found a pair of hiking boots and a holster for her Smith. No wonder Piet wanted to make sure everything fit. Clothing could be altered, but the holster and boots would have to be exchanged if they didn't suit. A belt was already threaded through the loops on the holster.

Assuming Ulla's injured foot would one day revert to its usual size, everything fit. And she would absolutely have to get up in front of the entire Flint Clan and thank them.

Not the whole clan. Hanni tied off Stelle's second braid and grabbed jackets for herself and her daughter. *Just those of us on trek.* "You'll get a chance to watch and see how it's done. Your turn will be somewhere in the middle." *And Thom and Nathan will be right there with you.*

You think that makes it easier? Ulla gave up sorting psi from spoken word. She took off her survival vest, put on her new belt, and holstered her pistol. That done, she clipped her new cup to her belt and followed her hosts outside.

* * *

"Do people get, um, verbose?" Ulla asked Thom as she

sat down between him and Nathan at a long folding table.

"Only if they've had too much to drink." Thom filled their mugs from a pitcher, then placed it next to a flickering lantern.

Ulla traced a roughly stenciled logo on the table that matched the logo on a row of sheds at the edge of the lighted area—Chisos Municipal Park, maybe?

Shh! Dev's talking!

The chieftain lifted his cup. "To the world!"

There was a thunder of, "To the world!" and "Hear! Hear!" Ulla watched and imitated the others as they lifted their cups, drank, and deliberately splashed a few drops on the ground.

They started in on the heroes and ancestors while Flint Clan's teenagers bustled around the tables serving food. People spoke; cups emptied.

"These toasts will go on forever." A woman across the table pointed to a pitcher of water. "The world gives us water, too, Starfighter. If you'd rather not get grogged, the heroes and ancestors will understand completely."

Thom smiled, nodded, and topped up Ulla's mug with beer.

People took turns according to where they were seated. Most recited from memory, though a few spoke extemporaneously with varying success. Nathan gave a rousing, well-crafted speech in a Terran language Ulla couldn't place.

Finally, it was Ulla's turn to speak. She stood up and steadied herself on the table's edge to keep weight off her injured foot. Bonus: her hands couldn't shake if they were busy holding her up. She swallowed. "First," she said, doing her best to hide the quaver in her voice, "thank you all very much for your hospitality and your generosity. I look forward to getting to know you better."

Piet beamed at her from his seat with his wife and daughter three tables over. *See, Starfighter? I knew you could do it!*

There were still the heroes and ancestors to get through. Ulla swallowed again, silently extending her heartfelt thanks to the teacher she'd hated for making all his students memorize poetry.

"Words are not my strong point," she said. "A Classical English poet wrote this on Earth long ago. It still applies:

"These, in the day when heaven was falling,
The hour when earth's foundations fled,
Followed their mercenary calling
And took their wages and are dead.

Their shoulders held the sky suspended;
They stood, and earth's foundations stay;
What God abandoned, these defended,
And saved the sum of things for pay."

Ulla raised her cup. "To Thor Bjornson and his Berserkers, defenders of Binder Station!" She drank and sat down.

Nathan grinned. "Housman."

"'Epitaph on an Army of Mercenaries.' It's pretty obscure," Ulla said, surprised. "How did you come across it?"

"Undergrad at Oxford; they still teach Classical English there." Nathan nodded toward Thom. "That's where I met this guy."

The Oxford in England, on Earth?

Thom shook out a napkin and placed it on his lap. "Thor Bjornson is your da?"

Ulla nodded, unwrapping a roll of flatware from the pile in the middle of the table. "'Epitaph' is his favorite poem."

"Bjornson isn't dead, though—is he?"

"Not that I'm aware of." She speared a chunk of potato with her fork. "The Berserkers were between contracts, last I heard." She tucked into her dinner.

Thom stood and raised his cup. Everyone got quiet and turned to their table. "To another defender of Binder Station—a starfighter who slew eight Yotne in a single day." He turned to face Ulla. "I raise my glass to Ulla Thorsdaughter!"

Ulla's cup would not budge. From her place between her parents, little Stelle stared at Ulla, giggled, and raised her cup of water.

Bless her, the child was making sure the offworlder knew how to accept a toast. Ulla remained seated and hoped her facial expression was appropriate. *For goodness' sake, Hanni, tell your daughter to let go of my cup.*

The toasts kept coming. A warm feeling, only partly due

to the alcohol, started somewhere around Ulla's middle and filled her up. People called out their ancestors' names, including First Settlers, long dead, and others from places like Belfast and Mumbai and Copenhagen and Papeete, dead even longer.

When dinner was mostly gone, trays loaded with pastries appeared. If there was coffee, Ulla never saw it. Eh, they were camping. She bit into a delectable chocolate éclair and washed it down with beer.

The chieftain raised his cup again. "To this summer's trek!"

Once everyone had drunk to that, people cleaned off their tables and rearranged them around an impromptu dance floor. A few musicians gathered where the head table had been and started playing a dance tune.

* * *

"What do you think so far?" Nathan asked in Standard. He sat beside Ulla on her bench and topped both their cups with more beer. With the table and lantern gone, their little seating area was dark.

Ulla answered him in Standard. "So, so many things to wrap my head around. But they contracted to take me to Newcastle. That's something."

He stared out at the dancers. "They treating you okay?"

Ulla nodded. "Little Stelle thinks I'm the best thing ever. I'm surprised she let me out of her sight."

Nathan smiled. "I think she's done for the night." They watched Piet and Hanni leave quietly for their tent, Stelle asleep in her father's arms.

They sat until Ulla had to fill the silence. "So, you went to university with Thom Yensson."

"His father wanted him to get a good Terran education and go into galactic politics. Help put the Bailey-Duran system on the map. Thom was happy to oblige. But when he saw what a hot mess we Terrans have made of Earth, he knew this world could easily go down the same path."

Ulla sipped her beer. "He changed his course of study?"

"Oh, no. He got his degree in galactic affairs, and he'd be good at politics if he put his mind to it. But almost all his elective classes were in what Terrans call the Earth Sciences—enough that he needed less than a year of study in Terrandessay to go to work with the Planetary Restoration Project when he got home."

"Terrandessay." Ulla set down her cup. "That's the forbidden continent, right?" She didn't want to think about the bureaucratic hoops the locals would have made her jump through had she crash-landed there.

"Yep." He nodded. "Their terraforming testing ground—it's where the Elders and the First Settlers made some initial traction on restoring breathable air. They still use it for species introduction and testing adjustments to the system." Nathan thought for a minute. "If you'd landed in, say, the Great Prairie or the Southern Rainforest, Balanced Trade Enforcement would have made you stay in your egress pod, packed you off to SpaceCom within half a day, and only sent your pod back after they killed its microbial load."

"Really?" Ulla sighed. There was no use wishing herself back with SpaceCom; she was here now.

Nathan spread his arms wide, indicating everything around them. "This world—Bailey-Duran Three to us—is Thom Yensson's first love."

Ulla wiggled to find a more comfortable position on the bench. Her foot ached. "Not to the exclusion of people, I hope."

"You mean romantic love?"

"I suppose." While Ulla had only been making conversation, she wouldn't mind knowing the answer.

Nathan sipped his beer. "He had a pretty serious relationship at university. It didn't work out, though."

"So, he's not…with anybody…at the moment?"

"I don't think so," Nathan said, laughing. "I think he's glad to be out on trek; in Chisos, he was fresh meat."

"Because he's the High King's son?"

"Not so much that—he's a new prospect who's not off limits."

"What do you mean?"

Nathan looked out at the people dancing. "The On'oi have a clan system," he said. "A few generations after the First Settlers landed—and by the way, they weren't the first; the Hjralma were already here, and the Ancients predate them—the human families who developed psi power had serious trouble with inbreeding."

"They tried too hard to give their kids psi talent?" Ulla

asked.

"Yep." He nodded. "What they got instead were birth defects, stillbirths, and miscarriages."

Ulla cradled her cup in her hands. "Like why the Guild have their studbook."

"Exactly. The human settlers looked into the library their great-greats had brought over on the ship from Earth, studied the matter, and devised a clan system that's a composite of systems from several different Terran cultures."

"Which means?"

"It boils down to not mixing genetic material with anyone who has a grandparent who belongs to the same clan as any of your four grandparents. They gave each family with psi talent a clan name, set the rules, and went from there." He sipped his beer. "Not sure they thought through the cultural and political implications at the time, but it serves the original purpose well."

That made sense. "So if everybody here is Flint Clan, they're all off-limits to each other." Ulla sipped her beer. "What about the married couples?"

"On this trek?" Nathan drank the last of his beer and filled his cup with water. "Husbands are Flint Clan; their wives are from somewhere else."

Ulla finished her beer and set her cup on the bench next to the pitcher. "Wouldn't Thom be fresh meat here, too? Or did the unattached women stay home?"

"Good question." Nathan sighed. "In a normal year, you'd be correct. But this year, there are only three unmarried women on trek—one of whom is his sister—and they are all in established relationships."

"His sister?" Ulla was confused.

"Half-sister." Nathan filled Ulla's cup with beer before she could stop him and ask for water. "Thom's mother died when he was little. She was Raven Clan; that makes him Raven Clan too. Ingeborg's mother is Flint Clan."

Just stop! My brain is full. Ulla forgot Nathan couldn't hear psi. She was glad she wasn't staying on Bailey-Duran Three.

"Talking about my sister, are you?" Thom appeared out of the darkness with a pair of folded canvas armchairs and a fresh pitcher of beer. "As long as you remember she's betrothed, why don't you go ask her to dance?"

Nathan took the hint and left.

Thom set the pitcher down and opened up a chair. "For you."

Ulla gratefully accepted the new seat.

"Lift your foot." He gently slid the bench under Ulla's boot and sat across from her. She relaxed against the back of her chair. Oh, that felt so much better!

Thom disappeared into the darkness and came back with a lantern, and they sat in companionable silence for a while.

Ulla sipped her beer. It was cold and delicious. And she felt the alcohol working its magic.

It wouldn't do to "get grogged" out here, though, at least not until she knew these people a lot better. Might as well start with the one in front of her; was there a particular form of address for the High King's son?

"Thom works." He glanced at her half-empty cup. "More beer?"

Ulla held it out for him to fill. "Granny always said never try to outdrink a local."

He tut-tutted and poured. "You're not drunk."

"In another pint, I will be." Sooner than that actually, and they both knew it. Ulla leaned back in her chair.

A laughing couple dashed past them.

Ulla sighed and drank some more. "Thank you for the shout-out. How'd you find out about Binder?"

"I asked the *Resolute*'s Guild rep if you had any decorations I could brag about to Flint Clan. She read me the citation for your Gallantry Star."

"Why?" Ulla sipped unsuccessfully. She'd run out of beer.

He poured her another pint. "Some people here would just as soon see you dead. That's why I brought up your status as a hero."

Oh, gods. "Who?" She set her mug down on the ground. "Why?"

He inclined his head toward a dancing couple. "Emil Rikson and Salli Marvinsdaughter, mainly." Even from here, Ulla could see the woman was just going through the motions.

"Do they hate offworlders on general principle, or do they have a special grudge?"

"Salli's brother and his wife died in last year's

basement explosion in east Newcastle-Outside-the-Wall. It's said they were making bombs for River Pack."

The *Valiant*'s briefers had mentioned the explosion in a briefing about organized crime in the local city-states. Ulla remembered an overhead image of a yawning, blackened basement in an otherwise neat row of townhouses. "Do they belong to River Pack?"

Thom shook his head. "Just Salli's late brothers-in-law. Her brother was good with explosives, but in his personal life he tended to think with…not his brain." He sighed. "Salli took the loss very hard, and Emil is at his wit's end about it."

"I was on a ship between Binder and Reynoso when that happened."

"Your presence here represents to Salli why her brother and sister-in-law are dead."

Ulla was grateful that looking over her shoulder was already a deeply ingrained habit.

"You're safe enough with us while you're injured, but you surely noticed we all go armed. When your ankle heals enough for a fair fight, it won't take much for Emil or Salli to call you out."

"Anyone else?"

He shook his head. "Most everybody is just here to live their own lives. Your presence is a novelty, nothing more. I'm hoping your status as a badass hero will keep it that way."

"Thank you." They sat and watched the dancers. Binder Station came to mind. Had that really been just over a year ago? Ulla drank some more. Maybe alcohol would help her brain process what had happened there, what had really happened to the *Valiant*, why the Yotne existed, and why this man was being kind to her.

"How did you kill eight Yotne fighters in one day?"

"What?" Ulla jumped. "Sorry, I was thinking about something else."

"I noticed." He glanced at her empty cup. "More beer?"

"Yes, please." She held it out for him to fill. She'd lost the ability to defend herself effectively at least a pint ago; at this point, she might as well drink up. "You asked about Binder Station."

He nodded.

"Three different sorties. Binder was strapped for

starfighters. Our last sortie was a bitch." They'd escorted a shuttle full of children to safety. Her wingman had died, and she very nearly had, too. Odd things had happened. She did not elaborate.

"I thought two or three kills were a big deal for a starfighter."

"One kill is a big deal." She sat quietly for a moment. "It was, um, a target-rich environment."

Thom lifted his cup. "To starfighters!" They drank.

Ulla drained her cup and set it down firmly, marring the effect when she missed the chair arm. "Killing sucks."

Chapter Seven
Untidy Psi

The next morning, Ulla and all her body parts swayed in the promised saddle as Snowball lumbered along with the rest of Flint Clan. Her headache outdid her throbbing ankle, and her stomach needed to mind its own business.

They had only been on the move since a cold breakfast she hadn't eaten, but it seemed like forever. At daybreak, Flint Clan had pulled down their tents and packed clothing, cooking gear, and household items with the speed and precision of long practice. Capraglamas, camdeer, sheep, and people formed a column that gathered momentum and settled at an easy walking pace.

The column turned slightly and Snowball turned with it. Ulla looked up. *Oh, gods. Light.* She shut her eyes and concentrated on not throwing up. Thanks be the camdeer knew where to go; it wore no bridle and she had no idea how to guide it.

She might have heard somebody laugh.

Snowball plodded and swayed as Flint Clan pressed on. Ulla felt blisters forming on her behind. Nobody else rode a camdeer—this rawboned gait had to be why.

"Good morning, Starfighter!" The Terran doctor's voice was much too loud.

Ulla risked opening her eyes. "Good morning, yourself!" She slipped and grabbed hold of saddle leather just in time.

Nathan pulled a medical injector from his shirt pocket. "According to every telepath in Flint Clan, you need this."

"Huh?"

"They say you're projecting your feelings. Look: almost everybody is limping." He pulled the cap off the injector. "Did you take an anti-inflammatory this morning?"

"Of course, I did, but I doubt it stayed down."

"I thought as much." He held up the injector. "Stop for a minute."

The camdeer, unbidden by anything Ulla did, moved out of the flow of traffic and stopped.

"Stick out your leg." The doctor found a vent in the orthopedic boot and injected a painkiller right through her sock.

Relief was swift. "Thank you. That feels much better."

"I'm sure our friends agree." He held out a large flask. "I can't cure a hangover, but this will help."

Please. No medicine. "What is it?"

"Water. Drink it."

She swallowed hard. "I couldn't."

"If I were you, I'd dismount first." His voice was far, far too chipper.

The camdeer sat down ponderously, one end at a time. Ulla compromised by swinging a leg over the front of the saddle, sitting sideways on the animal as she sipped very carefully. The water stayed down. She drank some more, then stopped, not wanting to overdo it.

Nathan reached into his pocket again and brought out a hunk of bread. "Eat this."

"Are you serious?" No way could she keep food down.

"Just eat a little at a time once you're moving again."

Ulla had her doubts, but she accepted the bread. "Here's your flask back."

He eyed the bottle on Ulla's survival vest. "Is yours full?"

"Yes."

"Drink all of it. We're stopping by water at midday and you can refill it then."

She tucked the bread into her pocket and swung her leg over the camdeer's back.

Nathan reached up and adjusted the cargo tied in front of her saddle. "Try hooking your left leg around here; it'll help elevate your foot. This guy should be fine as long as you don't whack him too hard with your boot."

Ulla propped her leg on the repositioned cargo bundles.

Her back was going to hurt like hell in the morning, but her foot already felt better. Snowball stood up.

Nathan broke into an easy jog. "Hang on! We have to run to catch up!"

You son of a bitch. Ulla squeezed her eyes shut as the camdeer lumbered after him.

* * *

Late that morning, they paused to rest by a small stream. Ulla slid off the camdeer's back as soon as it had stopped and knelt.

"Rough ride?" Thom had been walking beside her for the last kilometer or so.

"Very." Ulla stretched. "Now I understand why you people walk."

Thom said nothing, but the corners of his mouth twitched.

"With electronics not working, I understand about not using modern vehicles, but what about horses? They'd handle this little dirt track just fine. You have pigs and cattle and dogs and goddamn pine trees from Earth! Why don't you have horses?"

"Your language!"

"My butt hurts."

"Not nearly as bad as the rest of you." He held out a bag containing dense bread, cheese, and dried fruit. "Eat. Then we'll talk."

Ulla could not contemplate eating a meal, but she pulled the bread Nathan had given her from her pocket and nibbled on it experimentally.

"Give me your water bottle and your cup." Thom held out his hand. "I'll fill them for you."

"Thanks." Ulla watched Thom walk down to the spring. Tall and well-built, he had long, wavy black hair tied back with a cord. In his right ear he wore two compact, mismatched earrings and none in his left. He waited his turn with the others at the spring, chatting and carrying on, then rolled up his sleeves, showing brown, well-muscled arms as he rinsed cups and bottles, then filled them. *If that man isn't already spoken for, there'll be a queue.*

Some of the people by the spring laughed and looked

toward her. Damn! Was she projecting again?

Thom returned with their water and handed her the cup he had filled. "Yes, you're projecting again. Want some dried fruit?"

Ulla blushed.

Much to her surprise, she was hungry. She had finished Nathan's bread and eagerly reached for fruit. She munched on the small, sweet pieces. They tasted almost like raisins only better.

Thom handed her a piece of bread. "How's the hangover?"

She swallowed. "Why do you ask? Reach out with your Gift and find out."

He cut off a hunk of cheese and gave it to her. "Gentlemen don't pry."

Ulla laughed. "I'm still hungover, but it's getting better." She drank the last of the water from her cup. "Ladies don't project, do they?"

"No. Expedient as it might be to monitor your every thought, Starfighter, we're getting very tired of the contents of your head."

"Thank you, I think."

Thom refilled her cup. "Did you really have no idea you had a Gift?"

Ulla shook her head; her mouth was full. She swallowed. "How do I turn it off?"

"You don't." He wrapped a piece of bread around some cheese and ate it. "I'd like to show you how to control it, at least enough so you can keep yourself to yourself."

Ulla was skeptical. "Is there time? We'll be moving soon."

"I think you'll catch on quickly." He paused. "This isn't something I can tell you how to do; I'll have to show you."

"How?"

He polished off the last of his lunch. "May I establish a mind-talking link with you?"

"Do I have a choice?"

Thom laughed. "Not really. Flint Clan will have my head if they have to share one more minute of your aches, pains, and personal problems."

"Oh, gods." Did people know about her visceral reaction to the Hjralma?

He nodded. "But most of us have heard your recurring

nightmare, so people are trying to cut you some slack."

Ulla groaned. Sorry didn't begin to cover sharing a dream that involved soldiers, an eetee, and fire. "What do you want me to do?"

Thom shifted his position." Get comfortable, and sit still."

Ulla did. She waited. Nothing happened.

"Pay attention."

"To what?" A twig snapped in the tree above them, and she glanced up to see what might be up there.

"This." Thom said quietly. Ulla's mind filled with memories and disconnected thoughts that were not her own, and she saw through more than one set of eyes.

"Is that what I've been doing to you?" she asked, amazed.

"I'm exaggerating to make sure you see, but yes, you have been. Watch!"

Ulla's thoughts were her own again. "How did you do that?"

"I told you it had to be shown—now!" The contents of his mind flowed into hers once more, then shut off abruptly.

This time, Ulla thought she understood what he'd done to control his flow of thoughts. She tried it herself.

It must have worked. Thom smiled. A crease he'd been carrying between his eyes smoothed and disappeared. She almost reached out to touch the spot.

"Headache gone?" she asked.

"Yes, thank you."

"You'd have felt better soon." Ulla fished the bottle of anti-inflammatory tablets out of her pocket. "I think I can keep one of these down now."

Thom laughed. "Don't give yourself airs, Starfighter; you just learned what small children learn the minute their Gifts show up." He said an eetee word, or maybe he was only clearing his throat. "Are you sure you didn't know?"

Ulla flushed. "Where I'm from, you wouldn't want to have psi. Not on Farwell, and certainly not on Earth."

Thom put his arm around her. "I've lived on Earth. I know."

"Yeah." Ulla shivered in the warm sunlight.

"I hear the Guild pays well," Thom said. "Why didn't

you ever test?"

"I did test. SpaceCom requires it." Aware of their closeness, Ulla sat up straight. Thom removed his arm from around her shoulder. "I'm a starfighter, not an adept. My psi scores have always been low."

Ulla enjoyed the sunshine on her face. She changed the subject. "I thought you were from around here."

"Close enough," he said. "My da's house is about four hundred klicks north of here, on Worldtree ground."

Now that she knew how to look, she saw well-kept towns in his mind's eye nestled among snow-capped mountains. "When we were linked, I got the impression you grew up in Newcastle," she said.

"I did." He stretched. "My ma died when I was little. I lived with my aunt and uncle in Newcastle until Da remarried."

Ulla tried to look into his mind again, but he'd stopped sharing thoughts. *Sorry. I didn't mean to pry.* Oddly, all three of the adults whose images she'd picked up from Thom's long-ago memories looked familiar.

No harm done. "You've probably seen Auntie and Uncle; they're featured in one of SpaceCom's local orientation holoshows—Renata Connersdaughter and Padraic Willemson. He's the Alliance's Minister of Trade. And Da's in the news all the time." He looked off into space, thinking. *Do you need another lesson on keeping thoughts to yourself?*

Oops. Sorry. Ulla tried the thing he'd shown her.

It must have worked because she had to ask her next question out loud. "What's a soulslayer?"

Thom jumped. "Hmm?" He must have been deep in thought.

"You said the word yesterday. It came up again in your thoughts."

"It's a Deadly Gift." He undid the top two buttons of his shirt.

Ulla raised an eyebrow.

"No worries, Starfighter." He pulled his shirt collar aside. "You need to know this." He showed her a faded blue triangle tattooed below his left collarbone. "If you need to render first aid to a stranger who's unconscious, look for the soulslayer mark first."

Ulla remembered that from SpaceCom's newcomer

orientation. The briefers had said the locals expected it, but— "Why?"

"A bad startle reaction from a soulslayer could get you both killed. Don't risk it."

* * *

"Who's Mr. Sanders?" Thom topped up both their cups with water.

"Who?" Ulla had been daydreaming.

He bagged up what was left of their lunch. "A mentor? A teacher?" *He's been at the back of your mind all day.*

"Oh!" She smiled. "Mr. Sanders was a family friend on Farwell. Finished his indenture to MitSmith Corporation before we got there, but he couldn't afford to leave. Nice old guy; he ran a karate dojo, tutored people in Terran English, Standard, and math, carved turquoise, kept a garden, whatever it took to make a living."

Ulla hooked a finger into a thin chain at her neck and pulled out two pendants. "He gave me this," she said, pushing aside her SpaceCom ID. She held up a small, stylized image of a bear done in turquoise. *Mama used to call me Little Bear.*

"Where did he get the turquoise?"

"Some of the copper miners' families must have paid for lessons with lunchbox turquoise."

"What's that?"

"Turquoise sometimes occurs in copper ore. But even with indentured and convict labor, mining the turquoise is too labor-intensive for MitSmith to make a profit on it. So it goes out with the waste. The company looks the other way, mostly, when miners help themselves to small amounts."

"What was your Mr. Sanders doing on Farwell?"

"He never said." Ulla could not imagine the gentle, discerning teacher choosing a miner's life on the Edge. "Knowing him, he most likely spoke truth to power one time too many."

"He told you that you have a Gift, didn't he?"

So he had, though Ulla's younger self had put it out of her mind over a standard decade ago when she got accepted at SpaceCom's officer academy and put Farwell behind her.

* * *

"I know one doesn't normally inquire how a person came to be on a penal world like Farwell, but what was your family doing in the Republic of Texas?" Thom asked as he walked beside Ulla and Snowball the next morning.

"Mama was an RT citizen. Her people are ranchers, not far from the Marfa Natural Gate. She took us kids to Texas when she left Dad."

"You lived with your grandparents?"

"Only for a little while. By the time I was ready to start school Mama had a job with MitSmith's mining division. We lived in Grand Saline."

"The big salt mine in east Texas?"

Ulla nodded. "She was in management—worked in the head office."

Now I've met a real, live Texan.

She smiled. "I was born a military brat, had triple citizenship till I came of age. When I had to pick among the Commonwealth of Virginia, where I was born; McKay Settlement, where Dad's from; and the Republic of Texas, of course, I chose Texas."

He looked up at her. "Riding a camdeer isn't like the Texans riding in the holoshows."

"I only ever rode horses on visits with Granny and Grandad—till Mama took a promotion at MitSmith's copper mine on Farwell Three. We moved there a couple of years after I started school."

He ambled along beside her and Snowball. *Farwell? By choice? Unbelievable!*

Ulla couldn't help overhearing. She weighed what to say, and decided on blunt truth. "You can't get any farther than that from Bailey-Duran and still be in human-explored space. Mama was piss-terrified of trolls."

"Oh." He looked straight ahead and kept walking. *You do know the Hjralma don't like to be called trolls.*

Yes, but I need to learn how to pronounce the word first.

You can call them Elders. They're all right with that.

Something else had been bugging her. "Why did you drunk me up?" she asked.

He looked up at her, all innocence. "Did I?"

Ulla laughed. "I take full responsibility for drinking

what was in front of me, but a certain On'oi—and his buddy—kept my cup full. Was that on purpose?"

Busted. "Fastest way to prove you are who you say you are."

What?

He walked along, staring at the trail in front of them. "We knew you were there, ever since you landed, but couldn't pick up your thoughts. Fripp told us to let you be, that you had to decide on your own to join us."

Really? They'd known she was in the backcountry since she landed? "Who's Fripp?"

"Senior spinner."

"What's a spinner?"

He switched from Dialekt to Standard. "It's a rare psi talent. They say spinners of wyrd can modify the space-time continuum."

"Modify how?"

Thom shrugged. "They just can."

"Oh! 'wyrd' with a y." Ulla felt her headache coming back.

"Yes, that one." He nodded.

"Like the Fates, then, or the Norns." Ulla rode along, processing that. "Those are old myths from Earth."

"Myths, yes—but where did the idea come from?" They followed the column up a short, rocky slope. "At Fifth River, you were in just the right spot to rescue the younger spinner."

Did he mean Stelle?

Thom nodded. "Twice now in your dreams, you've told an adversary you were lucky—and you won." He looked up at her. "I'd bet money that's what you did at Binder Station."

He uncapped his water bottle and took a drink. "You use luck to your advantage, and all of a sudden, your mind-talk went from unreadable to off-the-scale loud. And clumsy. Does that mean you don't know you're an adept? Or does it mean you're trying to fool us into thinking so?"

"If I were an adept, I'd be Guild by now." Ulla shuddered; she would never have seen the inside of a Goshawk. Instead, she'd be working inside her head, in a climate-controlled room in some dreary, undisclosed location.

He smiled. "Never fear. We're all painfully aware now

that you are who you say you are."

That was something. Maybe the hangover was worth it.

"But, Lieutenant, you do have formidable psi talent, and you dream regularly about the senior spinner."

The Elder in her nightmares was real, then? *Shit.* "I'm a starfighter. I only want to get back where I belong."

He trudged along. "Working on it. But Spinner Fripp asked me to tell you that when you're ready, she'd be delighted to meet you."

Chapter Eight
Soulslayers

By the time Olwyn emerged from the new permanent Gate inside SpaceCom's Gate terminal, the star Bailey-Duran rested on the horizon. The shipping crate-sized tactical Gate she'd expected to walk out of sat unused at the edge of the transfer plaza's expanse of freshly cured concrete. Scavenger birds cried overhead as she looked for Skuli Branson, the Alliance liaison.

"Heya!" *Guild Member!* Skuli waved from where he stood next to a sporty little open cabrio.

Olwyn's heart sank. How would she fold her long legs into that tiny thing? She steeled herself as she crossed the plaza to meet him. "Thanks for arranging a meeting."

"Glad to do it." He opened the passenger door and slid the seat back for her, revealing ample forward legroom where she'd expected the cabrio's inner workings to be. Gratefully, Olwyn got in. Skuli made some adjustments on the control panel and they made their way out the perimeter gate onto the Newcastle trunk road. Low as the windscreen was, Olwyn felt no wind in her face. She raised a hand above her head and felt air flowing over them past an invisible barrier. "Force field extension?" she asked.

Skuli grinned. "It's adjustable—designed for humans and Elders both." He steered them through a crowded roundabout onto a cobblestone street Olwyn knew led to the city center. As traffic noise picked up, he switched to telepathy. *Have you eaten yet?*

No, I haven't. She'd been working flat out all afternoon.

Trade Ministry dining room's closed for the evening, but they'll have left something for us in the kitchen, he said. *We're using their secure conference room to meet with the Matthias Carroll Memorial Society's Dweller workgroup.*

The Matthias Carroll Memorial Society—isn't that the soulslayers' watchdog organization? What did they have to do with the Dweller defenses she'd asked about?

Dwellers are souls. Skuli whipped the cabrio expertly through another roundabout. *The soulslayers have been doing some thinking about how to use their Dark Gift for good.*

Dark Gift?

Another name for soulslaying. Sounds pretty dark to me. Their street ended at Landfall Square and he turned right. "By the way, soulslayers prefer to think of the MCMS as a mentoring society that also enforces boundaries." *Not a watchdog.*

Skuli drove halfway around the square to the Hjralma-On'oi Alliance Trade Ministry's service gate. He parked in back, over a charging tile in a multi-stall garage that must once have been a stable. The other half of the building still was. Two enormous local draft animals and a pair of imported horses looked up with mild interest.

Before getting out of the cabrio, Skuli asked, "How would you like me to introduce you?" *I've never heard you use more than two of your four names that SpaceCom puts on meeting agendas.*

How thoughtful! "You mean Olwyn Dara Wittber Argeles?" Olwyn asked.

Skuli nodded.

"Olwyn Wittber is plenty," she assured him. "The forename my friends use, plus my father's surname." *The rest are Guild tradition.*

* * *

Olwyn and Skuli went in the back way; the front door was kept locked after business hours. They crossed an open cobbled area and stepped into a large professional kitchen, dark except for an electric light over the big commercial stove.

A man wearing upscale business attire and four On'oi earrings moved a pot of stew from the stove to the cart.

"Heya, Victor." Skuli turned on the rest of the lights while Olwyn breathed in the aroma of cooking meat, onions, and spices.

"Thanks." Victor wiped his hands on a towel. "Here's the cart the kitchen staff made up for us, but there isn't any butter for the bread. Do you know where they keep it?"

"I think so." Skuli disappeared into the walk-in cooler.

A bowl of pesto sat next to the bread on the cart, but Olwyn kept her mouth shut. She was pleased she could understand the gist of their mostly City English conversation.

"Victor Jamesson." The businessman extended a hand to her. "You must be the Guild rep."

As they shook hands Olwyn lined up appropriate City English words in her head before speaking. "Olwyn Wittber. Glad to meet you."

Skuli emerged from the cooler with butter and a fruit bowl he'd found. "Victor is president of the Matthias Carroll Memorial Society."

The businessman grinned and switched to Standard. "We're the strong, short-range mind-talkers your Guild tries not to anger." He switched back to City English. "Matti's upstairs; we just got done with the emergency MCMS board meeting."

"Matti's the one who found the double-souls in the warehouse district?" Skuli set the butter and fruit onto the food cart.

"He can tell you all about it." Victor pushed the cart toward the elevator. "Neal's staying, too."

"Great," Skuli said. "Neal knows more about magic than the rest of us put together."

* * *

In the conference room, Olwyn glanced at Skuli as she filled a bowl with stew. *All I needed was a sounding board and some local perspective.*

We need a sounding board, too, Guild Member, and a broader perspective. It works out.

A flat, ring-shaped object the size of a dinner plate sat on a thick mat in the middle of the table. Nobody else paid the slightest attention as Skuli sang nonsense syllables and it glowed with swirling figures.

"There!" He served himself a bowl of stew and reached for a roll. "We can speak freely."

What did you just do? She hoped only Skuli could hear her question.

Skuli glanced up at her. *Utility Ring. I sang it up to keep the conversation in this room private.*

Olwyn had read about On'oi utility Rings but had never seen one in action before. *It's beautiful! What do the markings say?*

You can see those?

Of course. Couldn't everybody?

Then we must find someone to teach you properly.

What did he mean by that? Olwyn would have to wait to find out. The meeting was starting.

As they ate, introductions flowed naturally, in a pidgin mix of City English and Standard. On top of being president of the Matthias Carroll Memorial Society, Victor was also a manager for a prominent local seagoing shipping line. Matti Brown, seated next to Victor, was a detective with the Newcastle City Guard, and Neal Erikson was a professor at Newcastle University. Likely in physics or anthropology. Olwyn couldn't picture stodgy Newcastle Uni offering coursework in magic.

Soulslayers, it turned out, were exactly what their name implied. Victor, Matti, and Neal had been born with a very unpopular psi talent.

The Society was an educational and self-policing group, not unlike the Guild, except it was composed only of soulslayers. While the Guild was also a clearinghouse for paranormal employment, the Society existed purely to keep its members out of trouble. "Let me get this straight." Olwyn pointed with her spoon at Victor. "You have a psi talent that kills."

"Yes and no," said Victor. "The Dark Gift extinguishes souls. A body with no soul, no spark of life is, of course, dead."

Or, depending on one's philosophy, more than dead. "So, the soul is gone." Olwyn put her spoon down; she wasn't hungry anymore.

"That's why we police ourselves," Victor explained. "The Dark Gift cannot, must not, be used to murder."

"People do that?" Olwyn was appalled.

"Sadly, yes." Victor set down his fork. "Not often, but it happens."

"What do you do when it does?"

"Once guilt is proven in court, the murderer is executed by a Society member, using the Dark Gift." Matti placed his empty bowl on the cart. "It happened in Esperanza a couple of years ago. One of their younger adepts drew the odd lot and executed the murderer."

A psi talent like that was nobody's Gift. Olwyn changed the subject. "I thought we were here to talk about Yotne and Dwellers?"

"We are." Neal stacked his empty bowl on top of Matti's. "We think we can use the Dark Gift to kill Dwellers without harming the hosts."

Like Mary Nkosi had. Olwyn took a deep breath. "How do you use the…Dark Gift against Dwellers?"

"We're still working that out." Neal poured himself more water and looked around the table for other glasses to top up. "Unlike the ghosts we hear about in stories around the fire, Dwellers present as two people in one body. If the Dweller has been in place long enough, it will have stuffed down most of the victim's personality, keeping just enough of the host's distinctive traits, language, and habits to keep others from suspecting."

Mary had called them "second souls." Olwyn took a drink of water to cover her unease. "Can you illustrate?"

Neal inclined his head toward Matti, who said, "Before we knew what they were, I found two 'double-souls' right here in Newcastle, in the warehouse district. May we link minds so I can show you?"

Olwyn set down her glass and concentrated on the memory he shared. "Dwellers." *Oh, dear gods.* "Where are they now?"

"I don't know." The detective sighed. "When we went back, they weren't there."

Didn't you LOOK? Olwyn used private telepathy; she didn't want to call him out in front of everybody.

He shook his head. *Guild Member, I'm the only officer in the Newcastle City Guard who admits to having a Gift. And my Gift barely reaches the street outside this building.* "It's probably just as well," he continued. "If the Dweller-ridden had been there, the Dwellers could easily have migrated onto us."

"What kind of psi range does the average soulslayer have?" Olwyn asked. Guild protocol was to keep at least a hundred meter distance from known Dwellers, the longest distance they'd been known to migrate.

"Short," said Victor. "Very short."

"Two or three meters is not uncommon." Neal had already loosened his collar. He removed his cravat, rolled it up, and put it in his jacket pocket. "Often less."

So, they could kill Dwellers, but only from well inside Dweller range. On the other hand, they couldn't project their own psi farther than they could use it.

Skuli poured himself more water. "What you're proposing sounds right up there with bow-hunting for wild pigs. How do you plan on identifying your targets before you become theirs?"

"Spotters." The professor and the detective spoke in unison.

"A soulslayer can link with an adept who has range enough to find the Dweller," Matti said. "The two work as a team."

Bow-hunting for wild pigs, indeed. "Has anyone done it?" asked Olwyn. "Or are you talking theory?"

"Legend says it's been done," said Neal, "including improving range by sending the soulslaying impulse through a linked spotter. Theoretically, it's possible."

Olwyn did not need psi to detect skepticism at the table.

Victor, now in full businessman mode, said, "There haven't been any Yotne or Dwellers here in recorded history."

"Dwellers are real." Skuli pushed away his bowl. "How do you apply a legend in combat?"

Victor sighed. "This sort of thing is completely outside my experience." *I'm a businessman, not a soldier.* "That's why I want your opinions, and"—he nodded to Olwyn—"to involve the Guild."

Olwyn's brain went to an old recipe—*first, catch your rabbit.* "You'll need to experiment and practice. For that, you need Dwellers."

Victor folded his napkin. "Guild Member, will you help us?"

Olwyn pointed to the utility Ring. "Make a hole in your shield, and I'll see what I can do."

* * *

Once Olwyn was able to send her consciousness out from the conference room, it was easy to distinguish soul from soul. There were no Dwellers in Newcastle and none in the countryside nearby. She went further afield; what was that in the mountains about two hundred klicks east? She scanned the place again and found no Dwellers. False alarm? Nevertheless, she made a note with a pencil on paper. This excursion would have no digital record.

She kept searching across the surface of the planet. She ranged farther east and found nothing in continental Hoffnung except the uncertain blip in the mountains. She turned her attention to the west—shouldn't neglect the water surface—past the big MitSmith resort on Landfall Mainland.

She'd had no idea so many people lived on those scores of tiny islands, far beyond the big island they called the "mainland."

Shit. An island in the middle of nowhere teemed with Dwellers; "double-souls" far outnumbered the non-possessed.

"I've found your test subjects." Olwyn took a drink of water to cover her unease. "How do we locate them on a map?"

"If I link, can you share what you see?" Neal asked. "I've spent some time in those islands."

"Remote viewing isn't one of my talents," she replied. "I'll have to look through someone's eyes there—is it emergency enough for that?"

"Do it," said Victor. "I'll deal with any repercussions."

Olwyn linked with Neal. She was startled at the strength of his Gift, short-range as it was. She found an islander who was not—or at least not yet—Dweller-ridden, and looked through his eyes. Shell pavement on an empty small-town street. Nothing to see but nondescript walls. Then, when the man rounded a corner, the view of a compact harbor. Olwyn couldn't identify the ships; she hoped Neal could. The stranger walked past a row of shops. There was a grocer, then maybe a hardware store, then a menu on the wall outside a bar.

Neal opened his eyes. "Got it," he said. "That's Sheltertown, on New Vatersay. The island in the distance is Kettlerest."

Olwyn cut the link and got out of the stranger's head as fast as she could.

* * *

Victor broke the silence. "What about next steps?"

Neal took a sip of water. "I have an idea."

The man was a university professor. Olwyn wondered what practical knowledge he could possibly have about Dwellers, about the Yotne.

Not much, Guild Member, but I'm On'oi. We Guardians grow up hunting. "One of my grad students—Sean Patel— is from Kirkhilo. It's a town near the MitSmith resort on Landfall Mainland. Sean'd be a good spotter. He's also a very capable Ring singer, though, I doubt we'll need that."

There was new information, Olwyn decided, and then there was overload. Ring singers. Dwellers. Soulslayers. Weird somethings in the mountains east of here. Legends that might be true after all. And just when she thought almost all the adepts on this world were On'oi, here was a roomful of adepts in urban business attire, talking about grad students and "next steps." She narrowly avoided putting her face in her hands.

Skuli's voice brought her back when he asked Neal, "Just you and Sean?"

"Maybe." Neal paused. "His sister works for MitSmith at their Landfall headquarters in Kirkhilo; she's married to a soulslayer. Sean and I can go for a visit. It would be natural enough for the four of us to pack up a boat and go camping for a few days on Kettlerest."

"That'd give you some redundancy." Skuli settled back in his chair.

"It helps me too," said Neal. "Sean and I need to stop by Great Knob while we're in Landfall and check in with Miles and Thad Rogers. They're working on Ring seat prep." *Should be ready by the time Thom Yensson is back with the Landfall Ring.*

Matti said nothing. Olwyn detected skepticism from the city-bred detective—who obviously had been around the On'oi long enough to keep his mouth shut.

"Miles is in Landfall now?" Skuli asked. "Is Aubrey with him?"

Miles Rogers. The name rang a bell, possibly from Olwyn's reading about the Bailey-Duran system. Wasn't he married to the famous archaeologist Aubrey Rogers?

Neal nodded. "Hey! She's planning a new dig on Kettlerest. If the Rogerses go with us, we'll have a reason to be there. We'd likely camp on Kettlerest anyway."

"They're offworlders," Skuli said, "headblind and no longer young. Is that wise?"

Neal thought for a moment. "Actually, yes. I've been in tight spots with them before; they'll be fine. And a couple of headblind people might be useful." *Think about Odysseus and the sirens.*

Matti nodded. "You'll need continuous monitoring."

As much as Olwyn wanted to volunteer, she could not leave the job she had.

"Trade Ministry can provide long-distance communicators, in shifts, around the clock," Skuli said.

Of course they could. But SpaceCom had another resource to offer. "I just interviewed a SpaceCom officer whose psi talent appears to be, um, similar to yours," Olwyn said. "She's completely untrained, but she killed a Dweller last year when the Yotne attacked Binder Station. And when she was in her teens, she killed four Dwellers on Leviathan when the Yotne tried to take over that system. I can ask her commanding officer to send her with you."

"Leviathan? That world's mostly water, isn't it?" Neal said.

"Commander Nkosi grew up with small boats if that's what you're asking."

Neal grinned. "Yes, please. We'll find her a spotter."

Olwyn wiped up the circle of condensation her glass had left on the table. "I'll have a word with the captain."

Chapter Nine
Journey

A few mornings later, Ulla swayed more or less comfortably as Snowball lumbered along through the cool, sunny morning. After the first excruciating minutes, when every tight muscle she had was asked to stretch, contract, or do both to match his gait, her body relaxed to the inevitable. Now, if she could keep her weight off the hot spots she'd developed yesterday...

"Heya, Starfighter." Piet had jogged up behind her. He slowed to match Snowball's pace. "Have you seen Hanni and Stelle?"

"No, not since we broke camp." From her vantage point astride the camdeer, Ulla looked along the stream of people and animals.

There they were, up ahead. Stelle waved. *May I ride behind the Starfighter? Please?*

Ulla glanced at Piet. He was preoccupied; were he and his wife having a telepathic parental discussion? Hanni and Stelle stepped aside from the trail to let others pass.

Piet looked up at Ulla. "Do you mind if Stelle rides with you?"

"Not at all—if you think I'm steady enough in the saddle."

He laughed as they drew even with Hanni and Stelle. "You'll be fine; our Little Star was riding before she could walk."

Snowball stepped off the trail and knelt. Piet picked up his daughter and settled her on the bedroll behind the starfighter. Ulla felt trusting little arms wrap around her middle as Snowball lurched to his feet and ambled back onto the trail.

They had been going along for a few minutes when Hanni reached into her pocket and pulled out three small, soft balls of felted sheepswool, green, blue, and yellow. "Stelle, why don't you show the starfighter some mind-moving?" The balls flew up and danced about a meter above Snowball's head. They tumbled in the air, then raced off in a line, up and away, returning to chase one another around Ulla and Stelle.

Stelle laughed. Snowball plodded on, not distracted in the least.

"'Ulla," Hanni said, "you're next. Observe what Stelle's doing."

Observe? How?

Hanni, walking beside them, watched the balls tumble playfully. *Listen with your mind.*

Ulla tried but had no idea what to listen for. They rode along with colorful bits of felt flying around them. The green ball faltered; was Stelle getting tired? Suddenly, the ball dropped free, headed straight for the ticklish spot between Snowball's ears.

Would that make him bolt? *Shit!*

Just shy of its target, the ball zoomed straight up.

"Good job, Starfighter!" Piet raised his arm. The green ball turned and cruised into his hand.

Ulla looked on, amazed. "Did I do that?"

Hanni and Piet nodded. Stelle giggled.

The other two balls still danced in the air. Suddenly, they shot up high and descended in free fall. "Da! Think fast!"

Kids. He reached out again, and the blue and yellow balls changed course so he could grab them. He handed the felted balls back to Hanni. "Little Star, how would you like to walk with Auntie Maribet?"

"Oh, yes!" Snowball left the trail and knelt again; Stelle held out her arms and let her da swing her down to the ground.

Once Snowball resumed his place on the trail, Ulla glanced back at father and daughter. "She's a beautiful child. You must be very proud."

Hanni smiled. "We are." *That said, we all have our*

moments.

Don't we, though. They traveled together in silence.

"I still haven't figured out how she taught you to speak Dialekt."

"She held my hand. Then I understood what you were saying."

Hanni stared straight ahead as she walked. *My daughter, spinner of wyrd. If she's this powerful now, what will adolescence look like?*

She's a sweet, loving soul. It's bound to be fine. Ulla refreshed her standing mental note never to have children.

Hanni blinked. "You heard that? I thought I'd kept that thought private."

"Sorry." This psi stuff was so damn awkward!

"Where did your Gifts come from?"

"I have no idea." Ulla sighed and remembered to relax into Snowball's gait.

"Well, you have Gifts now." Hanni took off her sweater; the day was warming up.

Ulla grinned. "The felt balls were fun."

"Expect more of that sort of thing." Hanni tied her sweater around her waist as she walked.

Ulla reached forward and scratched Snowball's neck. "That was a teachable moment, then."

"Of course it was. That's how children learn." Hanni walked a few more paces, considering. "If you're going to travel with us, you have to control your Gifts."

Ulla shifted her weight off a hot spot on her rear end. "How?"

"As a beginning, I'd like you to spend mornings with Stelle and me."

"Like we just did?"

Hanni smiled broadly. "That was a preview. Some days we'll do more, and some days we'll do nothing at all—at least nothing children recognize as 'school.' Oh, and don't be surprised if one or two Hjralma pop in from time to time."

Ulla couldn't say it; the word still put her in mind of a cat expelling a hairball.

Hanni coughed. The corners of her mouth twitched. "You may call them Elders if that is easier," she said. "They help us out when a student gets into territory none of us do well." *Stelle does that more and more lately.* "I imagine you've seen the word written down; it transliterates into Dialekt as h-j-r-a-l-m-a, and the same in City English and Standard."

The eetee in her nightmares. The briefers couldn't pronounce it, either; they'd called them trolls like the Newcastlers did. Ulla's heart sank.

Oh, you poor dear. Hanni mightn't have spoken aloud, but Ulla felt her compassion. "Are the Elders in your dreams always so terrible?"

Dreams?

Hanni looked up at her. "The one you had last night was...very disturbing."

"Sorry, I don't remember dreaming last night."

"People don't always remember dreams." Hanni didn't break stride as she rolled up her shirtsleeves.

"Was I projecting? Sorry." Had Gav suffocated again in his Goshawk at Binder, or was it the new dream where pieces of the *Valiant* engulfed them all?

"You've gotten better at keeping yourself to yourself. I was awake and noticed you seemed restless; your nightmare spilled out. What do you know about spinners?"

It had to be the firestorm dream, then. "Nothing," Ulla replied.

Only what Thom had mentioned on the first day of trek when he'd taught her to shield her thoughts. The eetee in the firestorm dream always offered to make her firstborn daughter a spinner in exchange for opening a path through the flames for three of her troops. They were always the same three: Velasco, Cheylik, and Jones. In the dream, the bargain was completely worth it. Awake, she had no idea who those people were.

Hanni reached up and smoothed Snowball's saddle blanket. *Oh, Starfighter, you have so much to learn.*

Piet overtook them with an easy jog. "Thom and Nathan are on their way back from Thom's irrigation inspection. They'll likely be at tonight's camp before we are."

They made good time. Ulla watched a flock of birds take off from a nearby stand of bushes.

"Tonight, you'll move into the single women's tent," he said. "Hanni can introduce you this afternoon."

Hanni added, "You'll be with Ingeborg Yensdaughter, who is a very accomplished adept. You've met her; she's my apprentice."

"Thom's half-sister, right?" Ulla asked. There were so many people to keep track of.

"That's her," Hanni said. "There's also Kamna, my junior apprentice, and Maribet, who is as strong a mind-talker as any Guild rep. She's tutoring Kamna in the finer points of mind-talk; I want you to join their lessons. I think the four of you will get along well." *I wouldn't fault you for wanting to be with them instead of with us old, married folks.*

The old, married folks might want their privacy back. Ulla smiled, hoping Piet and Hanni hadn't heard that thought. "Thank you."

"Don't thank me yet," Hanni retorted. "You're in for some hard work."

Chapter Ten
With the Ladies

Flint Clan didn't stop for lunch that day. Instead, Hanni and Ulla kept moving and munched on bread, cheese, and dried fruit. Then Hanni dropped back to walk with Piet and Stelle. Early in the afternoon, the column slowed. Ulla saw people up ahead dismounting, sorting gear, setting up camp. Snowball left the path and picked his way among people, tents, bags, and tack until he stopped in front of a tent two women were adjusting on its conical frame of poles.

Starfighter! Stelle, jumping up and down, emerged from the sagging main flap. "Here's your new tent!"

Snowball knelt. Ulla dismounted and stretched.

There! Somebody lifted and fastened the fabric from inside and the tent lay smooth. Hanni emerged as a tall, slender woman wearing a large sun hat finished securing the bottom edge of the fabric.

"Heya, Starfighter!" The woman with the hat stood and held out her hand. The fair, freckled skin on her forearms was red and peeling above a line where gloves must have been. "Welcome. I'm Maribet."

"Thanks." Ulla shook her hand. "Name's Ulla." She turned to unfasten her bedroll and saddlebag.

Maribet adjusted the main tent flap. "For now, unload, drop your gear in the tent, and get out your dirty laundry."

Stelle looked up at Hanni. "Ma, can we go to the hot springs now? Please?"

"Hot springs?" Ulla paused at the tent entrance. "Is

that why we didn't stop for lunch?"

Hanni nodded. "Yes. We'll stay through tomorrow night. It makes a good break between the first few days' shakedown and the rest of trek."

Ulla put her saddlebag and bedroll on an empty spot inside the tent. When she came back out, Snowball, still seated in his comfortable spot in the sun, looked at her with big, dark eyes. What was she missing?

Oh. Piet and Hanni had taken care of the livestock at the end of each day's travels. It was surely Ulla's turn to do that now, and she had no idea how to proceed. As a child, she'd rubbed down horses once or twice, under supervision. Snowball was most certainly not a horse, and horse saddles only slightly resembled the contraption he had on. She scratched him between his ears.

From somewhere beyond her line of vision, Piet laughed. *Send him along with Hanni, Starfighter. Time enough to learn wrangling when you're steady on your feet.*

* * *

Ulla followed Maribet into the tent, where the other woman rummaged through a pair of well-worn saddlebags and built a pile of laundry. Ulla took off her smelly clothes and put on her clean-enough flight suit.

Maribet put her hat back on and picked up her laundry bundle. "Do you mind if we take a detour? I need to stop by the garden patch and see if the aloe made it through the winter."

Garden patch? "Fine by me." Ulla tossed her toiletries kit onto her laundry, wrapped the bundle in her biggest dirty shirt, and ducked outside.

They walked through the camp toward a stand of large boulders near the water. As Ulla followed Maribet through the grass toward the sunny side of the rocks, burrs attached firmly to the exposed bits of her sock. Maribet pushed through a stand of low-growing bushes with tiny blue flowers toward a dry, chest-high stalk of faded yellow. "This rosemary wants to take over the world."

While Ulla picked burrs out of her sock, Maribet used a folding knife to trim small, fragrant branches to make space for a knee-high bunch of puffy, spiky leaves at the base of the stalk. Setting the rosemary stems aside, she cut off a big, spiky leaf and added it to the pile. "For sunburn. Looks like you can use some too."

Ulla could. While her initial spacer's sunburn had turned mostly to tan, the skin on her face and neck still itched. Her mother had kept a spiky patch of the same aloe species just outside the kitchen door on Farwell. As had her granny in Texas.

Aloe was such a humble remedy for the multitude of ways this universe could burn you. People kept planting it because it worked.

While Maribet sliced open a fat aloe leaf so they could smear its juice on their sunburns, Ulla took in their surroundings. Aside from a few patches of the spongy, low-growing forage the camdeer and capraglamas liked so much, most of what grew here belonged in a holoshow set on Old Earth.

Maribet grinned. *Holoshow production is big business on the Esperanza coast for that very reason.*

"How did so many Earth species take hold here?" Ulla asked, preferring words to thoughts. Telepathic conversation was still unsettling.

"Sorry. I thought you meant to use mind-talk." Maribet gathered the rosemary and the rest of the aloe leaf into a bundle. "The First Settlers brought them. Legend has it that, long ago, the Yotne conquered the Ancients, took this world, used everything up, and left. Then they conquered the Hjralma, blew up their home world, and dumped them here, sink or swim."

That didn't sound quite right. "The Yotne don't take prisoners." *Unless they have a reason.*

"True." Maribet shrugged. "It's a legend. Who knows what really happened?" They recrossed the grassy patch and headed for the river. "The Hjralma are good at planetary restoration, but they had very little to work with. Enter the First Settlers with a ship full of cryo-stored samples from pretty much every biome on Earth. The two groups got together for pure survival, and their scientists went to work in Terrandessay, which was almost bare at the time, and started propagating what they had."

Terrendessay? The forbidden continent? "I've seen it from overhead," Ulla said as they reached the brushy area near the river. "It's not bare now—it's beautiful!"

"So I've heard." Maribet stopped and held a springy

branch aside for Ulla to follow her on the faint trail. "Terrandessay's still the world's biggest climate control and air purifier. Legend says they started by planting grasslands and prairie, then got to work on the forests."

So the Hjralma and the First Settlers had brought back the planet Bailey-Duran Three from the brink of death. Which might explain why the Yotne had allowed the Hjralma to live. But Maribet's legend felt like it was missing something.

"If it helps any, the Hjralma are no friends of the Yotne." Maribet kept walking.

Ulla followed, unconvinced, as they emerged from the brush onto the riverbank.

"The Hjralma are all about three things: restoring this world to its former glory, restoring the Ancients' Rings, and keeping the Yotne the hell out." Maribet took off her boots and socks. "Those things inform everything they—and we—do. I think that's what keeps them alive."

Where was this woman getting her information? SpaceCom's briefers had only mentioned terraforming in passing. They'd told people to stay away from the forbidden continent so as not to be eaten by wolves or arrested by Balanced Trade Enforcement, but that was it.

"That's the city-states for you." Maribet shrugged. "I grew up in Newcastle with the best private education a young lady's parents can buy." She took off her clothes and added them to her laundry bundle. "I only learned how this world really works after I joined the On'oi and studied at Castle Chisos."

Ulla wondered how much of SpaceCom's local knowledge, informed by the city-state where its headquarters lay, was just plain wrong.

Maribet waded into the water with her laundry and started scrubbing. Ulla hesitated; should she wear her orthopedic boot into the steamy water?

Heya, Starfighter! Ingeborg waved from the bank of the swimming hole, at least twenty meters away. *Boot'll be fine. Take off your sock first, so it doesn't get squishy. And get rid of the stickers.*

Ah, the joys of telepathic communication. Ulla did as she was told, then undressed. She stuck the little toiletries kit into her right boot, folded her flight suit, and balanced it on top of the stack. What should she do with her Smith?

Oh! Just over half a row of spikes driven into a big rock above shoulder height were draped with firearms. Hanging her pistol in its belted holster on an empty spike, Ulla gathered up her laundry and joined Maribet in the water.

Up and down the bank, women and girls who weren't washing laundry were bathing, swimming, and splashing each other. Clothing was optional, and nobody cared.

Hanni swam up behind them. "Do you have some laundry soap?"

"Sure." Ingeborg tossed her a bar. "Here."

Hanni caught the soap and stood on the gravel river bottom beside them. She took off her shirt and ran the bar of soap around the collar and under the sleeves. "Have you seen Stelle?"

"Over there." Ingeborg pointed to a spot where the water had carved a hollow in the rocky bank. Stelle squealed with laughter as an older woman poured water over her soapy little head.

They washed their laundry and wrung it out. Ingeborg scrambled up the bank with it and spread it all out to dry on bushes in the sun. She paused to survey her handiwork. Then she raced back into the water. Ulla grabbed her toiletries kit and followed the other women. Where the hot springs bubbled up, someone had gone to some trouble to place big rocks in the water for people to sit on. At least Ulla assumed so; the place was much too conveniently laid out for nature to have been the sole designer. They had driven spikes into the rock face above them, which at the moment were hung with towels and a few more pieces of lethal hardware.

Ulla got out her soap and stashed her toiletries bag in a convenient niche in the rock. She dropped to her knees in the water and immersed herself up to her neck. A fine, hot current flowed from up ahead, near the rock face. Several people gathered there, including Hanni, Stelle, and a young woman Ulla had seen but hadn't met yet.

Ulla sank below the water level to get her hair good and wet, then came up for air and swam toward them. Hanni paused bouncing her daughter up and down in the water to scoot over and make space on the hewn rock bench.

"Thanks," Ulla said, "but I'd like to soap up and get

clean first." She stood up in the hip-deep water and started washing.

Wow! The starfighter is just a regular human! "Heya, Starfighter," the young woman said out loud. "I'm Kamna. Hanni says you're in our tent now."

"Heya, Kamna." Ulla soaped up her hair. *Yup, I'm a regular human.*

Sorry. The adolescent blushed. *My big mouth.*

You never know; I could be an exotic green-eyed eetee, hey? Ulla smiled, hopefully reassuringly, and sank back into the water to rinse off.

Thom says you were born on Earth, so you can't be an extra-terrestrial! Kamna smiled. *But you do have green eyes.*

Young Kamna had a sense of humor, then. *Shouldn't we be talking out loud?* Ulla asked her.

Yep, we should. Was that an eye roll? *But first, I want to know why you wear your hair that way.*

Oh. Ulla swiped at her brown mop of wavy not-a-haircut, which was currently wet and plastered to her head. *Tradition.*

???

It's a starfighter thing. Ulla sat down next to Hanni and Stelle. *We shave our heads right before a deployment and don't get another haircut until we get home.* The practice, grounded in the needs of historic shipboard life before artificial gravity was the norm, was a mild irritant for the higher-ups, which made it all the more attractive among the starfighters.

Ulla sighed. The *Valiant*'s current deployment had been extended so many times that her starfighters had set up a betting pool about who would be the last to cave and get a haircut.

Chapter Eleven
Telepathy for Beginners

After dark that evening, Ulla sat at the fire with Kamna and Maribet. Ingeborg had already gone to bed.

Sparks flew when Maribet put the last of their big logs on the fire. In time, it would catch fire and keep them warm for the rest of the evening.

Maribet sat on the ground across from Ulla and Kamna. "Tonight, we're going to work on monitoring—looking for and listening to whatever thoughts you can find."

"Just humans?" Kamna turned up the collar on her jacket; the fire hadn't yet caught up with the night breeze.

"Not necessarily, though if you find any intelligent life that's not human, Hjralma, or capraglama, I want to know about it."

"Capraglama?" Ulla was mystified.

"Capraglamas can mind-talk." Maribet poked at the fire with a stick. "The Hjralma bred them to support mind-work and Ring magic; Hanni and Piet can show you how that works."

"You've never heard them?" Kamna asked. *Especially Marigold; she's mouthy.*

Ulla shook her head. *There's a capraglama named Marigold?*

"Don't worry about it." Maribet settled, ready to begin. "I joined the On'oi as an adult, and I didn't hear capraglamas talk until I'd been training for almost a year."

Oh.

Back on task, Starfighter. "I hope I don't need to tell

you that you should not do this outside a training setting unless you have a very good reason. Monitoring may be a good way to stretch your skills, but it is still eavesdropping. What you see here stays here. Ulla, how much do you know about Gifts and personal privacy?"

"I had a lesson the first day we traveled."

"So you did." Maribet chuckled. "Your stomach has settled a bit since then, I hope."

Ulla swallowed. It would take time to live that down. "What do you want us to do?"

"Sit quietly." The fire caught a knot in the wood, sending sparks upward. "You two link with each other... all right...now with me...now go outward."

Nothing happened for quite a while. Then Kamna laughed. "Look! A baby!"

Ulla got the distinct impression of sitting in a friendly giant's lap, clapping her hands, and blowing bubbles. She laughed. The link faded.

"You have the idea; let's go farther out." Maribet looked at her two students across the fire. "Link—now!"

They followed Maribet's lead through the night to—a village? In her mind's eye—or maybe it was her mind's ear—Ulla heard muffled background noise as people cleaned up after dinner, settled down for the night, and got ready for bed. Sometimes they spoke a variant of Classical English, but mostly she heard raw streams-of-consciousness.

Maribet's mind traveled farther. Ulla and Kamna followed until Ulla heard the sea, scavenger birds, and cargo-loaders hollering in City English. It was still daylight there; how far away was that?

Maribet's voice intruded. *Did you say daylight?*

Of course, she had. If she took care, she could pick one person's eyes and see through them. And couldn't everyone smell the ocean and hear the loud scavenger birds?

Oh, sweet Mother of All. Maribet broke the link and spoke out loud. "Starfighter, did you see the light of day and hear scavenger birds just now?"

Ulla nodded. "I was monitoring like you said to. Aren't all the senses part of the package?"

Maribet shook her head. "Not usually, no." She took a deep breath. "Let's go back to Newcastle. This time, I'm going to link with a mind-talker. Pay attention to what I do, and then you try."

"Maribet, may I link with you and watch?" asked Kamna. *Newcastle's way outside my range.*

Certainly. Maribet sat up straight, relaxed, and closed her eyes. *Watch and learn.*

Ulla and Kamna linked with Maribet, who sent her consciousness to Newcastle City and said, via psi, *Alliance Trade Ministry, Maribet, Alliance Flint Clan.*

Skuli Branson here. Heya, Maribet.

Maribet. Heya, Skuli.

Skuli. Good to hear your voice. Teaching this evening?

Maribet. Yes. Glad you're on duty tonight.

Skuli. Thanks. Are you going to introduce us?

Maribet. You know Kamna Trentsdaughter. New student is Ulla Thorsdaughter.

Skuli. Glad to meet you, Lieutenant.

He knew who she was?

Skuli. I'm on the team with your Guild rep and Craig Eselgroth to get you home.

Ulla took a deep breath. *Uh, Ulla. Glad to meet you, Skuli.*

Maribet. Skuli, we're doing range-finding for the starfighter. I'll unlink now; she will attempt to hail you on her own in a minute.

Skuli. I'll be here. Ulla could tell from his tone of—voice?—that he was bored and happy to have something to do.

Maribet. Be nice, Skuli. Tonight's her first formal lesson.

Skuli. When was I ever not? The link faded.

At the campfire, Maribet stretched, then settled. "Try it, Starfighter."

Because she knew whom to find and where he was, renewing the link was almost as easy as linking with a person right next to her. *Skuli Branson, Ulla Thorsdaughter.*

Skuli. Heya, Lieutenant. Gods! Are you sitting by a campfire?

Ulla. Yes. What of it?

Skuli. Link us with Maribet; I don't have the range to hail her.

Ulla looked across their campfire, made eye contact with Maribet, and linked.

Skuli. Your new student's transmitting vision, sound,

and smell as well as words. You know that, right?

Maribet, eyes large, dropped all pretense of comm protocol. *I know it now.*

For a long minute, nobody said anything.

Finally, the man in Newcastle spoke. *Do you plan to hail the Resolute today? Guild Member Wittber is on duty for another hour or so.*

Yes, Skuli, we ought to. Maribet sighed. *Thanks.*

Any time. He paused. *Hey, Maribet—how's my baby cousin doing?*

Thom Yensson? He's fine. Maribet opened her eyes. *As you would know if you'd read his report that I transmitted this afternoon.*

That went to Planetary Restoration, Mind-Talker.

Ulla listened to the psi stream, fascinated that she could sense the man's tone of voice.

Thom's all about ecosystems; I'm Balanced Trade Enforcement. The man in Newcastle wasn't being arrogant; he was trash-talking with an old friend.

Oh, Skuli! Maribet countered. *I'm so relieved you're on the job protecting the galaxy from illicit Bailey-Duran strawberries, chocolate, and turnips.*

Balanced Trade Enforcement's job was to keep BD3's biomass on BD3 and keep invasive species out. But—turnips? Ulla stretched her cramped leg and wondered if she needed to drop out of the conversation.

No worries, Lieutenant, Skuli said. *We're almost done.* Then, and Ulla got the impression his next words were directed at Maribet, she heard, *You Flint guys treat him right, you hear?*

After they signed off, Ulla asked Maribet, "What was that about?"

Maribet sighed. "Skuli and Thom Yensson have been friends since they were kids. Even though they're only distant cousins, Skuli sees himself as the older brother Thom never had."

* * *

After some more practice, Maribet ducked inside the tent and returned with a lantern. "Let's hail the Guild rep before it gets any later. Starfighter, I'd like you to translate."

Ulla was surprised. "You speak Standard."

"Not well enough." *Yet.* "Ulla, get your notebook and a pencil."

Ulla pulled her notebook out of her pocket and dug into another pocket for her pencil. "What do you want me to write?"

"The date, time, who we link with, and any notes you think are important." Maribet lit the lantern, sat down, and turned to a fresh page in her notebook. "Kamna, you're welcome to observe if you want."

Maribet linked the three of them and ranged outward past the planet's surface. Ulla knew the *Resolute* lay roughly in the path they were searching, so how did Maribet know where to look? Presently, they heard a babble of voices, mostly in Standard, muted by buzzing energy that blurred individual words and thoughts.

"It's a scrambling device for psi energy," Maribet explained. "A bigger version of the blocker Nathan uses."

Kamna's eyes grew wide. "How do they do that without Rings?"

"No idea," said Maribet. "Most SpaceCom ships have them. The bigger MitSmith facilities usually have a room with one, and so does the SpaceCom headquarters in Newcastle." *And the cities' crime packs have a few.*

Maribet drew their attention to a solitary, disciplined presence just outside the *Resolute*'s psi shield. *There she is, Starfighter. Hail the ship.* Maribet opened her notebook and held her pencil, ready to write. *Go on.*

Ulla thought back to the comm protocol Maribet had used to hail the Trade Ministry. SpaceCom's standard protocol ought to work well enough. She cleared her throat unnecessarily. *Resolute, Valiant Goshawk Two One.*

That certainly got the Guild rep's attention. *Valiant Goshawk Two One, Resolute. Stay linked.* They waited a moment, then the presence spoke again. *What are YOU doing on this channel?*

I'm the translator, said Ulla, in Standard, *and very new at this.*

Go ahead. The voice sounded bemused. Ulla relayed the instruction to Maribet in Dialekt.

Maribet responded in Dialekt. *Maribet, Hjralma-On'oi Alliance, Flint Clan: Olwyn Dara Wittber-Argeles, United Telepathic and Paranormal Practitioners' Guild. Here is a new avenue of communication for you with Lieutenant*

Thorsdaughter.

Ulla relayed Maribet's words in Standard. After a few long seconds, the telepath spoke. *Wittber. The duty officer sends compliments. He thanks you for your consideration.*

Ulla translated for Maribet. "Anything else?" she whispered.

Maribet changed position on the cold ground. *Maribet. Flint Clan sends compliments. Thank you.*

Ulla translated and heard herself repeated politely.

Wittber. Stand by. Ulla heard muffled speech she wasn't sure was meant to be heard. *Informal relay for Admiral Imelda Rosen.*

The voice relaxed. *Spider! How are you!*

Rosie! This was like comm, only clearer and faster. *I'm fine, other than not flying.* Shit. She'd just called an admiral "Rosie." Ulla swallowed. *Congratulations on your promotion.*

Thank you. I hear you're injured.

Sprained ankle. It's on the mend.

Heal it up and get back here. The words were pure Imelda Rosen; the voice was not. *We need you in the sky.*

Yes, ma'am.

Take care, Spider. Rosen out.

Ulla stared into the fire and tried to process what they'd just done.

Valiant Goshawk Two One, Wittber.

Ulla jumped when the Guild rep spoke. She'd forgotten they were still linked. *Goshawk Two One.*

Wittber. Request we terminate this SpaceCom communication and relink immediately for Guild business.

Maribet wrote one last paragraph in her notebook, signed and dated her work, and turned to a fresh page. Ulla scribbled a few notes in hers and wondered if she'd be able to read them tomorrow. The link dissolved.

Maribet, Ulla, and Kamna waited by the dying fire.

Maribet Elliot, Hjralma-On'oi Alliance, Flint Clan; Olwyn Dara Wittber-Argeles, United Telepathic and Paranormal Practitioners' Guild.

Heya, Olwyn.

So they knew each other? Ulla supposed they would; professional telepaths of that caliber were more than likely a very small community.

Lieutenant Thorsdaughter?

Who? Oh! *Spider here.* She wasn't used to hearing her patronym on voice comm.

Welcome, Spider. This conversation is informal; would you prefer we use your call sign?

Aye. Not that Ulla cared which of her names they used. "Aye" slipped out because dropping military voice comm conventions did not come naturally.

Maribet used perfectly good, if heavily accented, Standard. *Olwyn, we're checking out the starfighter's range. Will you stand by to receive?*

Certainly. Ulla detected skepticism on the other end.

At Maribet's nod, Ulla dropped out of the link. She took a deep breath, searched for the adept they had only just been talking with, and found nothing but space. Oh! Relative to the spot on the ground where she sat, the *Resolute* was moving fast. She searched again, tried the most likely angle, and widened her focus.

Guild Member, uh, Wittber, Spider here.

There was a long silence on the other end. *Welcome back, Lieutenant! Maribet, sorry I doubted you. She's very strong.*

Maribet scribbled some more. *Thought so.*

Is she getting formal training?

Tonight's her first night.

Spider, how much do you know about psi communications security—privacy, setting boundaries?

Not much. Ulla didn't suppose twenty minutes spent learning to keep a hangover private qualified as SpaceCom security training. She thought she heard *That was you?* followed by stifled laughter.

The Guild member spoke. *Maribet, let's talk later.*

I'll be happy to. Maribet poked at what was left of the coals. *Tomorrow? It's getting late, where we are.*

It's night there, isn't it? And my routine hailing hours are almost over. Tomorrow, then.

Just before Ulla dropped out of the link, she overheard Maribet. *You must not have heard; I don't use the name Elliot anymore.*

Chapter Twelve
Debrief

The next morning, Ulla and Thom crossed the earthen dam by the swimming hole and hiked up the gentle slope of the meadow on the other side.

"How was your trip?" Ulla asked.

"Eh, work is work," Thom said. "The farmers out here know all about irrigation systems; all I did was certify their new build for the Planetary Restoration Project." He laughed. "Nathan had a field day—taking in the sights and practicing his Dialekt with anybody who'd stand still."

Ulla laughed, lost concentration, and tripped on a rock.

Thom reached out to steady her. "How's your ankle?"

"Fine, so far." The swelling had gone down. She'd considered trying her new hiking boots today, with the canvas brace, until Thom had invited her to walk out for a picnic. She opted to wear the big boot for one more day. The extra physical protection had better be worth the grass burrs in her sock.

Thom stopped, surveyed the ground for rocky spots and insect colonies, and, once satisfied, spread out a ground cloth from his rucksack. "This spot should do nicely."

They were not quite half a kilometer from camp, with a clear view on all sides. They'd gained enough elevation to see the camp and the herds spread out below them. Ulla watched an Elder pop into view outside Hanni's and Piet's tent. How had he done that? No matter; Hanni and Stelle greeted him and the three of them sat down together. While Hanni had told her Elders would visit to help with psi training, this was the first Elder Ulla had seen in camp. She was glad she wasn't there.

Up here, clear, warm sunlight competed with a cool breeze. This morning was just right—as long as you hung on to anything that might blow away.

Thom set his rucksack on the ground cloth. "Business first; the Guild rep's waiting."

"Works for me. I brought the map. Do you want to see it?"

"Not now, thanks. You may want it for reference."

"Why the elaborate cover?"

"This picnic? I thought it might be a nice change of pace. Besides, Flint Clan needn't know everything."

Ulla studied him. "What needn't they know?"

He reached into the rucksack and pulled out their picnic bundle. Then he dug out a hefty round leather case. "SpaceCom wants a debrief from you, soonest."

Of course, they did. "What's in the case?"

"Utility Ring. Borrowed it from the chieftain." He set the case shallow side down in the middle of the ground cloth and unbuckled the deep cover, revealing a thick Ring about as big around as a dinner plate.

Ulla opened her water bottle and took a drink. "Why are we out here?"

"Communications security." He undid the picnic bundle and set out bannock, cheese, and dried fruit. "Since you have the Gift, the *Resolute*'s Guild rep would normally relay for you and their debriefer."

That had to be why Guild Member Wittber had asked about communications security last night. "Did she tell you I'm leaky?"

He laughed. "She didn't need to."

"Touché." Ulla reached for a piece of dried fruit. "Flint Clan's bound to know what you and I are up to."

"Probably. If anyone asks, tell the truth." He sliced off a piece of cheese. "But they don't need to hear the debrief itself." *Who'll pry when a man and a woman go off on a fine, sunny day for some privacy?*

Had he meant her to hear that? Ulla rolled her eyes. "We're in full view of the camp."

"They'll think it's sweet. It's our first date."

First date, my ass.
Not going there, Starfighter. Not going there.
Ulla's face went hot.
Thom laughed. His eyes were very, very blue this morning.
She looked down at the Ring. *Spider, don't even think about it.* "What's the plan for the debrief?"
"The Guild rep links with me. I voice-relay for you; she relays for the debriefer on the *Resolute*. You're to stick to spoken word only." His eyes twinkled. *Spider, you did think about it.*
Stop it! We're working. Ulla took a deep breath. "All right, then." She settled more comfortably on the ground cloth. "Let's do it. Hail the *Resolute*."
"In a few minutes, Ms. Wittber-Argeles will hail me." *I can't even hail our own camp.*
Oh. He'd mentioned that on the night of the party. She hadn't meant to strike a nerve.
"No offense taken, Starfighter. But you do need to stop using what you call 'psi,' at least during the debrief." Thom paused, listening. "It's time to activate the Ring."
"What?"
"Another layer of communications security; it's to keep other telepaths out of your mind." Thom placed his hand on the Ring and sang a brief string of syllables in no musical scheme Ulla had heard before. The Ring's dull surface turned shiny, reflecting sky and puffy clouds. Something swirled around inside it under the glare. Runes maybe?
"It took almost a week to get SpaceCom to sign off on using a Ring for this," he said. "Don't screw it up. No mind-talking."

* * *

Thom spoke out loud. "*Valiant Goshawk Two One, Resolute.*"
Ulla did her best to keep her thoughts to herself. "*Resolute, Valiant Goshawk Two One.*"
Thom ran through the greetings. "Olwyn Dara Wittber-Argeles, United Telepathic and Paranormal Practitioners' Guild, relaying for Lieutenant Junior Grade Hector Ortega, Operations Intelligence, Starfighter Support, UW&NS

Resolute. Lieutenant Commander Mary Nkosi, Director of Operations Intelligence, UW&NS *Resolute*, is also present."

Ulla had worked with Mary Nkosi at Binder Station; they'd both been reassigned in the aftermath of the Guild's foul-up there. So, Mary got her promotion after all!

"Ortega. Proud to meet you, Lieutenant. Please authenticate and verify call sign and mission information."

Ulla did, and the familiar routine began.

Ulla explained how Goshawks 21 and 22 had scrambled in response to yet another smuggler. Its Sparhawk escorts had turned and flown away, just like they always did once they'd got the SpaceCom fighters flying in the wrong direction.

"Thorsdaughter. They were just testing us, like always. Suddenly, they turned and fired on us; we engaged. Goshawk Two Two was hit." Ulla paused, thinking about Jeff Xu's widow and two little boys.

She took a deep breath and went on. "I destroyed both attackers. UW&NS *Valiant* Starfighter Ops Gated Jeff, uh, Goshawk Two Two, back to the ship approximately one standard minute before the ship exploded."

Thom's eyes widened even as he maintained the uninterrupted link with the Guild member.

Ulla swallowed. "Having no options for recovery within range of my remaining air," she said, "I set an atmospheric reentry plan for a point near Newcastle Harbor on BD3's surface. Shortly thereafter, two Sparhawks attacked me. I destroyed them, but my Goshawk sustained damage that must have neutralized its surface-recovery guidance. I then executed a ballistic reentry and landed in the backcountry in west Hoffnung."

Ulla shivered. One did not "execute" a ballistic reentry from space in a damaged starfighter; one hung on and hoped to survive. But SpaceCom's preferred dry narrative style helped her and her listeners keep going.

"Ortega. Usual pack mercenary tactics?"

"Thorsdaughter. Negative." Ulla poked at the idea she'd hoped to disprove. "Their tactics were more like what the Yotne used at Binder Station. And the ones who attacked felt different."

"Nkosi. Felt different how?"

"Thorsdaughter." Oh, shit. She'd have to own up. "When I fight, I do a psi thing to make the adversary, uh, less lucky." There. She'd said it.

Thom's eyes widened again. "Ortega. Lieutenant Thorsdaughter, are you still there?"

Ulla cleared her throat. "Aye."

"Nkosi. Lieutenant Thorsdaughter, what was your impression of the adversaries at the time?"

"Thorsdaughter." How could she best put it? "The adversaries flew like Yotne. And they felt like Yotne. But they were flying Sparhawks." The average adult Yotne was as big as an Elder; a Yotne would not fit inside a Sparhawk.

"Nkosi. In your experience, Lieutenant Thorsdaughter, what might that impression indicate?"

Ulla didn't want to go there. "Dweller possession of human pilots, consistent with Yotne Dweller actions at the Battle of Binder Station." The theory she'd hoped to ignore was the only one that fit.

The rest of the debrief involved her activities on the ground. Ulla kept the narrative simple and did not mention psi again. The Guild rep already knew, and Ulla had no desire to remind Ops about anything that could keep her from flying.

Thom spoke again. "Ortega. Thank you, Lieutenant. Do you have anything to add? Any questions?"

"Thorsdaughter. Nothing more. Thank you."

"Nkosi and Ortega. Thank you, Lieutenant Thorsdaughter. Out."

Glad that's over. Ulla stretched and pretended to relax. "Why don't we get on with our picnic?"

"Let's." Thom powered down the Ring and put it away in his rucksack.

Ulla sliced more cheese and bannock for them. "Trail food." She gestured to the valley around them. "All this for a setting," she teased, "and you bring trail food."

"It's what was available." Thom smiled.

"Actually, it's perfect." She picked up a handful of dried fruit. "Thank you."

"You're welcome." He brushed crumbs from his fingers. "Let me see your map."

She pulled it out of her pocket and handed it to him.

He sighed. "They were supposed to fix that."

"Fix what?"

He pointed to the map. "Here's where you landed." He moved his finger slightly, pointing to the hill in the middle of the restricted area. "Did you see a large structure on top of this hill?"

Ulla nodded.

"That's Castle Chisos, where the Elder leadership live, and where the best of us study how to use our Gifts."

Maribet had mentioned Castle Chisos. Ulla ate and listened.

"Castle Chisos would have been, by far, the safest place for you to go. As it is, they're the ones who coordinated your return with Flint Clan. But if you'd gone straight to Castle Chisos, they'd have taken you in and gotten you back to SpaceCom."

Ulla's heart sank. "Do they have a Gate?"

Thom shook his head. "They're too close to the Electronics Unreliable zone. But they'd have arranged a fast escort to take you overland to Newcastle."

Well, shit. "What about the restricted area?"

"That's for flittercraft," he answered. "Approaching Castle Chisos on the ground would have been fine."

Ulla would still have had to wait for the river to subside. But if she'd gone to Castle Chisos instead of striking out toward the town with the same name, would anyone have been in a position to rescue little Stelle when the ferry crashed?

Thom tore a bannock in half and offered a portion to Ulla. They ate in silence.

When they'd finished, Ulla sat, thinking. *Dwellers. For sure. Damn.* Dwellers in-system meant the Yotne weren't far behind; they used Dwellers to prepare the battlespace for their invasions. *Not again.* She lost interest in eating.

"In the debrief it sounded like you've been around Dwellers before," Thom said. "Farwell?"

Ulla shook her head. "I was in Goshawk school when that happened. My mother and brother were in the thick of it. They died."

She did not want to think about her brother Andrew's last few messages, there at the end. "The Dwellers at Binder Station were my first."

"In the station itself?"

"They got into an outlying warehouse wing."

"What'd Binder do?"

"Sealed the wing off, kept everybody the hell away, so the Dwellers didn't have anybody in range to migrate to.

Station Control flushed the air out." Thanks be the hosts' alert shipmates had noticed something was off and that a Guild rep was on-site to confirm.

"What happened to the people the Dwellers possessed?"

"They died when Central evacuated the space." They were dead anyway. Nobody survived Dweller possession.

"Can you show me what Dwellers look like?"

What a silly question! "They're souls without bodies; they don't look like anything at all."

"No, no. With your Gifts, you must have sensed them."

"I didn't have 'Gifts' back then."

Thom's eyes narrowed. "What about the 'lucky' thing?"

Ulla paused. "Well, yes. That, and I've always been able to spot Dwellers. It's weird."

"Can you show me?"

"Are you sure?" Ulla so did not want to revisit those memories.

He nodded. "Please."

She linked her mind with his and thought back to a few choice incidents, including her most recent contacts in the sky above Bailey-Duran Three.

Thom's face paled. He blinked, as if to clear the image.

"You did ask." Ulla picked a fragment of dried fruit off the ground cloth and rolled it in her hand. "Shall we head back?"

They stood up, shook the ground cloth, and folded it up so Thom could lash it to the outside of his rucksack. He offered her his hand. "Walk you to camp?"

She smiled. "Why yes, thank you." She let him help her up.

Shivers. The good kind. Dammit!

Thom hitched at his belt and shifted his stance awkwardly.

I felt that. How blunt ought she to be?

I can handle blunt.

She had to say it. "As attractive as I find you, Thom Yensson, there are two rules I do not break."

"What rules are those?"

"Don't fuck in your workgroup, and don't fuck in your chain of command." *I can see us heading straight for Rule Number One.*

Me too.

They stared at each other, frustrated.

"Shall we revisit this once you're back in Newcastle?" he asked.

"Oh, yes!" *I'd like that very much.*

Chapter Thirteen
Fire and Ice

Five days and many kilometers later, Ulla shivered, pushed the tent flap aside, and peered out into the early-morning fog. Flint Clan had been stuck in place for two days, waiting for wet weather to lift. The rain had stopped last night, but everything left uncovered was sopping wet.

Well, fire duty was fire duty. While the other women slept, Ulla pulled on her clothes, stumbled out, and poked a stick into what remained of their fire. The coals and ashes were wet and cold all the way down to the bottom layer. She used a small shovel to scrape off a place to start a new fire and hobbled to the woodpile Kamna had stacked and covered last night. She selected a few dry sticks, carried them to the spot she'd prepared in the fire ring, and stacked them. She added some dry, fluffy seed pods she'd collected from this camp's wild garden before the rain had started. They would make good tinder when she lit them with one of Flint Clan's chemical matches.

Wishing briefly for an energy beam weapon that would just light the pile on fire, she struck a match on a dry-enough rock. Thanks be, a tiny flame burst from the match's tip. Carefully shielding it from drafts, she held it under the dry, fluffy bits. The match burned until the flame reached her fingers and ignited nothing. Swearing, she dropped the match, which promptly went out. The fluff didn't look that wet.

What to do? A career in starfighters hadn't prepared Ulla for this kind of ground-operations job. She chuckled;

if she were a groundie, she'd have that energy beam, and this chemical-match exercise would be academic. Except, energy beam weapons did not work here. She needed coffee to think that through again.

Lacking an industrial heat blower or even warm sunshine, could she mind-move the water out of the wood? She picked up a small stick and applied herself. Slowly, as she concentrated on what the stick was made of, everything that wasn't "wooden stick" slid out and off. Water dripped. Bugs crawled out. Ulla held the stick at arm's length to finish drying it out. This stuff worked!

Having successfully dried her test subject, Ulla turned her attention to the fire-to-be she had just laid. Touching the materials was no more necessary for this job than it had been for juggling Stelle's felted practice balls. As the water dripped and puddled underneath the little stick structure, she mind-moved it into big globules she could shove into a low spot outside the fire ring. There, she had used psi for something productive!

Encouraged, she took another chemical match from its waterproof pouch, struck it on the rock, and shepherded the tiny flame to its special spot amid the tinder. The tinder caught and flared tentatively.

A puff of wind blew it all out, leaving most of the match intact in her hand.

Dammit, they were going to have a fire if she had to beat it into submission!

Frustrated, she stared at the spent match. She'd removed water from wet wood in a series of very tiny, precise mind-moving actions. Fire was no more than oxidation; how tiny could she go with this? *Let's find out.* Still kneeling by the fire pit, she studied the match in minute detail.

FWUMP!

Ulla jumped back as the small fire she'd laid damn near exploded. Something smelled; that would be her clothes burning. She dropped, rolled, and came up muddy. Thanks be that her outer layers were all wool. She looked around the camp. What else, among all these tents, might have caught fire?

Do not worry, Child. It is contained.

Who said that?

Ulla spun toward the source of the mind-talk. An

Elder, appearing out of nothing, stood across the fire ring from her.

Contained, my ass. Ulla could hear flames crackling. Her hand hurt where she'd held the match and there was a fire to put out. She turned her head wildly; where was the flame? And why didn't the eetee DO anything?

"If you insist on teaching yourself fire-starting, this is a good day for it." If the Elder hadn't been two-and-a-half meters tall and gray-skinned as an elephant, her smile would have looked downright human. She—Ulla wasn't sure how she knew the Elder was a she—set down a garden trowel, which promptly disappeared. She bent and wiped her big muddy hands on neatly trimmed Terran grass, which appeared and disappeared as she touched it. It sure as hell wasn't growing here by the fire ring.

A thin tendril of smoke rose from the woodpile.

The Elder turned to follow Ulla's worried gaze. *Just as well.*

A tentative flame licked up from the center of the loosely stacked woodpile. What did "just as well" mean? Was the Elder going to stand there and let it burn?

No, Child. The Elder motioned for Ulla to stand next to her. *If you are going to start fires that way, you must learn to put them out that way. Observe.* A little over half of the fire's base stopped burning, just like that. *Your turn.*

Whose 'child' were you thinking of? Addressing that would have to wait. Ulla had to concentrate on the burning twigs. This time, thinking tiny was easier. The idea seemed to be to slow the fuel down, so to speak. A new flame went out almost as soon as it ignited.

You are on the right track. Do more. Now.

You think? The fire was almost as large as it had been before the Elder had put out the first bits. Was she just going to let it grow?

No, Child. Focus. You started it, you put it out.

I'll show you 'child.' Ulla concentrated on the fire again, followed it down to its base, embraced the base with her mind. While the analytical part of her brain wasn't clear about the process, she could feel cooling, a slowing down of the oxygen and flammable matter involved. Combustion decreased, stopped.

Keep at it. Bring it back to the temperature it should be.

Ulla kept at it, whatever *it* was. Frost formed on burnt

wood.

The Elder relaxed. *That is more than enough. You did well.*

Ulla looked at the extinguished woodpile, then at the Elder. Now that the emergency had passed, she studied the visitor's craggy, gray face again.

No doubt about it. This was the eetee in her nightmares. Ulla stepped aside, hobbled away, and ran into a force field.

With one hand on the force field to steady her, Ulla bent over and threw up. When the heaving stopped, she wiped her mouth with her bare wrist, trying and failing to keep vomit off her sleeve. She stood and returned her attention to the fire pit and the tall, gray figure beyond it. *You're not really here, are you?*

Only in projection. I was working in my garden when you started the fire.

I'm making this up, then. Given her delusional state, Ulla hoped she could still tag along with Thom and Nathan to Newcastle. Even a psych discharge from SpaceCom would be better than this waking conversation with her own personal monster from under the bed.

Ulla decided her imagination must be working overtime. The Elder in her nightmares wore a formal gown, not muddy trousers and a sheepswool pullover.

What nightmares?

Why was it still here? *"Give me your firstborn daughter, and I'll clear a path through the fire for your soldiers."* The inside of Ulla's mouth tasted terrible. *Velasco, Cheylik, and Jones.* Ulla hobbled back to the fire pit and picked up her water bottle with shaking hands. She swished, spat, and took a long, cold drink.

Does this dream trouble your sleep?

All my life. She had other recurring nightmares, mostly about Binder Station and some new ones involving the *Valiant*, but that was beside the point.

"Oh, Child." The Elder sat down heavily. There must have been a seat where she was; from this end, she looked like an Elder sitting on a piece of nothing. "Those are the dreams of another."

"You could have fooled me." Ulla poured water on her sleeve and scrubbed off vomit. Her right thumb and a couple of fingertips were blistered, and the right side of her face hurt.

"I am so sorry." The Elder turned and focused her eyes on something Ulla could not see. "That borrowed dream will not visit you again. You have my word."

Ingeborg opened the tent flap, stretched, and stepped outside. "Morning, Starfighter. Coffee ready yet?" She was mid-yawn when she noticed the Elder. "Heya, Spinner Fripp! What brings you here?"

Still yawning, Ingeborg smacked into the force field. "Sorry. Private conversation?"

"Not anymore," Fripp said. The force field dropped and smoke dispersed.

Ulla, done with words, plopped down on a rock and stared into space.

Ingeborg sniffed, took in the small, struggling fire in the ring, the frost melting on the woodpile, and Ulla's muddy, disheveled appearance. Her eyes grew wide. "Starfighter, did you—"

Fripp nodded.

Ingeborg took charge. *Ladies, we have company. Kamna, please take over fire duty and make us a pot of coffee. Maribet, help Kamna make breakfast.* Taking a closer look at Ulla, she spoke out loud. "You've burned yourself. I'll get some aloe."

Fripp stood up. "I cannot stay, but we must talk." She brushed the last of the dried mud from her fingers. "Are you staying here, today?"

Ingeborg nodded. *Road's soupy.*

"Then I will see you and your tent mates back here in two hours. Please invite the chieftain and Hanni Rubensdaughter." Fripp's projection glanced at something in her world. "And I will need capraglamas for support. Please, arrange that."

"I'll ask, but I'm sure it'll be fine. Please, excuse me. I need to gather those aloe leaves."

"Of course." As Ingeborg walked away, Fripp studied Ulla's face. "The burn on your cheek is not as severe as it feels; Terran aloe will be sufficient. Let me see your hand."

Too overwhelmed to protest, Ulla held out her hand for inspection. Ugly blisters swelled where the matchstick had exploded against her thumb, fingers, and palm.

The skin between Fripp's big eyes furrowed exactly as a worried human's might. *The burn is in an awkward spot.*

On trek, it will almost certainly become infected.

Kamna mended the cooking fire, set the kettle to heat, and rummaged in the grub box while Maribet mixed and patted out dough for bannock. She tested the griddle and laid the bannocks down to cook.

Fripp beckoned. "Kamna, you have the Healing Gift, do you not?"

"Hanni says so," Kamna said as she opened a packet of ground coffee. "But I've only just started training."

Fripp smiled. "All I need is for you to link with me and touch Ulla's hand. I will do the rest."

Kamna washed her hands, sat down next to Ulla, and gently grasped the starfighter's injured hand. "Like this?"

"Place your thumb as close to the burn as you can without causing more damage. Watch carefully; I need to look through your eyes."

As Kamna focused on the injured spots, fluid seeped and blisters shrank. Slowly, discolored skin turned bright pink, smoothed, and paled almost to its original color beneath the swiftly drying layer of loose skin that had covered the blisters.

"Exactly so," Fripp said. "Thank you."

Kamna let go.

Ulla stared at her hand, then at the Elder. "How did you do that?"

"I hope to teach you," Fripp said, her projection fading. "Wear clean gloves for a few days. Let the dead skin slough off as it will; your hand will be tender." Then the Elder disappeared.

Ulla sagged on the rock, spent. Which improbable thing ought she process first? Maribet handed her a cup of coffee and a plate full of food, so she ate breakfast instead.

* * *

Two hours later, the fog had lifted and the ground was drying. Kamna, exhausted from expending the energy required to heal Ulla's hand, was asleep inside their tent.

Ulla, holding the moist side of a sliced aloe leaf against the burn on her face, sat on a ground cloth in the pale sunshine with Maribet and Ingeborg, facing Hanni, Fripp, and Chieftain Dev Aronson.

That fatigue is why we use mindborne healing sparingly.

Fripp was eavesdropping again.

We are not eavesdropping, Child. Hanni and I are still testing you.

It didn't look like anyone was doing anything. Hanni had her notebook and pencil out; occasionally, she added to an ever-growing list.

Hanni turned toward the chieftain. "We should include Granny Kate."

"Katrin Ostapsdaughter? In her capacity as the trek's senior member of the Matthias Carroll Memorial Society?" Dev sounded surprised. "The starfighter's mind-talking range doesn't fit the soulslayer profile."

A soulslayer? *Would you PLEASE stop talking as though I'm not here?*

"Nevertheless"—Fripp's projection ignored Ulla and glanced down at something the rest of them could not see—"the starfighter has the Dark Gift. I can train her, though we ought to let the Society know, as a courtesy."

Dev stood up to bring his face level with Fripp's. "I will not have a soulslayer in this community who has not sworn the Society's oath."

"What oath?" Ulla asked.

Ingeborg brushed an insect off her shoulder. "It begins and ends with 'Never in anger.' I'm not sure about the rest, but Thom can fill you in."

"I'm a military professional." *Gratuitous mayhem isn't my thing.* "Would the oath I've already taken suffice?"

Dev looked thoughtful, then shook his head. *I trust you, Starfighter, but not everyone does.* "You have to remain on this world until the Matthias Carroll Memorial Society deems you fully trained." He addressed Fripp. "There will be no uncontrolled deadly Gifts in Flint Clan while I am chieftain. Granny Kate or Thom Yensson can swear the starfighter into the Society today and begin training."

Wait a minute! Ulla looked up at Fripp, who'd just said she would train her. Better to have the nightmare eetee for a mentor than be stuck dirtside.

Fripp smiled ever so slightly. *Be at peace, Child. The Society's oath is for safety. They will insist you remain in-system until you are proficient and safe, but they cannot restrict you to the surface if you demonstrate safe and conscientious practice.*

Ulla swallowed. "Fair enough." She could deal with

that.

Hanni reviewed the list she'd made. "She has every single Gift we can test for." *Merciful gods, the woman is a spinner of wyrd.* "Starfighter, where were you born?"

"The Commonwealth of Virginia," Ulla answered.

"Is that on Earth?" Hanni asked.

"It is." Ulla wondered what that had to do with anything.

The On'oi looked at each other. Ingeborg spoke first. "She's 'found in water' right enough."

Dev shook his head. "Even if 'confirmed in fire' just happened, what about the rest of the prophecy?"

"It hasn't happened, yet?" Hanni sighed. "Ulla, I know you've already consented to training during the brief time you're with us, and the Society can get you up to speed with the Dark Gift—but your Spinner's Gift changes everything."

A Spinner's Gift? As in, Ulla was one of the Fates? *Not bloody likely.*

Child, you use your Spinner's Gift when you fight. I have seen you do it twice. That was Fripp, again. *You invoke it when you tell your adversary that you are lucky.*

The fight that had landed Goshawk 21—Ulla—here. Where else had Fripp seen her?

The Binder System. You defended MitSmith's station there. Fripp rested her big eyes on Ulla. *How did you think you were able to do the work of a dozen starfighters?*

Dev looked from Elder to starfighter. "Out loud, please."

Fripp and Ulla both faced the chieftain.

He straightened to his full height. "Ulla Thorsdaughter, you are our guest—an offworlder, not a clan member. By law, we cannot train an outsider not covered by the Society in the deadly Gifts."

"What deadly Gifts?" Ulla knew she shouldn't interrupt, but this was her life they were discussing.

"Other than the Dark Gift?" Dev looked tired. "Fire and Ice—and the Spinner's Gift. I cannot allow an unsworn possessor of those Gifts among us. Nor can I send you away; not only did Flint Clan contract with SpaceCom to give you food, shelter, and clothing for your journey to Newcastle, you share the bond of lives saved with Stelle Pietersdaughter and her parents."

* * *

An hour later, nobody had moved, but Ulla's psi testing was finally over. She hadn't asked for psi talent. Neither was it likely to go away.

Decision time. Could she travel for a few weeks with these people, unsworn? She did need psi training, which in that case would come from the Guild when she got back to SpaceCom. That meant joining the United Telepathic and Paranormal Practitioners' Guild, whose only flying members were communicators like Olwyn. It seemed to Ulla that most of the Guild worked inside their heads in windowless rooms. She would not willingly trade flying a Goshawk for that.

She could strike out on her own—but her ankle wasn't up for that yet. And she would still have to deal with the Guild.

Ulla could take Fripp up on her offer to take her in and train her. But if working with Fripp meant deserting from SpaceCom, that was a hard "no" as far as Ulla was concerned—which was just as well because in no way would she trust the rest of her life to the much-too-recent monster from under the bed.

Wait. There was another choice. "Are you inviting me to join Flint Clan?"—*so I won't be an outsider?*

"Yes." Dev sat, facing her. "Yes, I am." *The starfighter's quick!*

Fripp nodded approvingly.

"I understand I need to learn to control my psi talents." Ulla would not call them Gifts. "I'm willing to do that. But I have to fulfill my obligation to SpaceCom. I won't be an oath breaker."

"You needn't leave SpaceCom," said the chieftain. "The Alliance belongs to the UW&N too. SpaceCom doesn't care what member nation you're from."

SpaceCom might or might not allow her to keep on flying. Still, her chances had to be better outside the Guild.

"A 'yes' means Alliance citizenship, right?"

Dev nodded.

Ulla's Republic of Texas citizenship was linked only to childhood memories. At age Standard eighteen, she'd picked Texas over McKay Settlement—Dad's home—and the Commonwealth of Virginia where she'd been born because of the link to the only kin Mama spoke to.

After a flurry of condolences when Mama and Andrew died, none of those people had written to Ulla again. Granny and Grandad were dead. A stranger had bought the ranch.

If Ulla had a home, it would be in Aurora City on Reynoso Tres, where her things sat in a storage locker because maintaining an empty flat while deployed made no sense.

Dev shut his notebook and put it and his pencil in his pocket. "If you need time, know that Council needs to meet and agree first." *They will; it's the only viable choice.*

Ulla breathed in the fresh air—growing plants, charred wood, sheep droppings and all. She surveyed the people, the tents, the livestock, wild birds chattering in the trees, the sunshine, the clouds, and the shadows they made on the mountains. One could do worse.

She sat up straight and squared her shoulders. "Yes, if Council will have me. Thank you."

Chapter Fourteen
New Guardian

Less than an hour after Ulla said "yes" to Chieftain Dev, she was officially a soulslayer, having sworn the Matthias Carroll Memorial Society's "Never in Anger" oath in front of soulslayers Kate Ostapsdaughter, Thom, and Kate's teenage grandson, Wat Henrikson. Then, in the tent Kate shared with her daughter-in-law and grandchildren, she gave Ulla the characteristic triangular soulslayer's tattoo. She used a little mallet and a tiny row of sharps that looked like a miniature rake but felt like an instrument of torture, while Thom stretched the skin between Ulla's left breast and her collarbone and held it still so Kate could work.

Once Kate embellished Ulla's triangle with what looked like a skinny letter *T*, Thom relaxed his hold on Ulla's skin. Kate handed her a mirror, so she needn't crane her neck to see her new ink.

"What's the *T* stand for?" she asked.

"It's not a T; it's a spindle," said Thom. "Because you're a spinner of wyrd."

Kate's brow furrowed. *Can't have people misinterpreting that.* She took the mirror from Ulla. "I need to draw some more. Hold still." She tap-tapped what Ulla later assumed was a stylized little puff that came together in a thread that made an *S*-curve and then wrapped around the spindle.

Ulla could have done without the extra flourish. She kept her mouth shut till Kate had packed her tools safely away.

No sooner had Ulla buttoned up her shirt than she heard Hanni's telepathic voice.
Starfighter?
Yes?
I have an hour free between now and supper. Please meet me in our tent so I can get you started learning Ring song.

* * *

Ulla opened the flap on the tent Hanni shared with Piet and Stelle and ducked inside. This afternoon, Hanni was alone.

"Welcome!" Hanni reached for the ever-present pot of coffee warming on the stove.

Ulla unclipped her cup and held it out for Hanni to fill. "I thought the chieftain said I need to be a Flint Clan member before you could train me."

Hanni shook her head. "That's for deadly Gifts." She topped up her own coffee and gestured to a soft seat on the ground cloth facing the utility Ring Thom had used for Ulla's debrief with SpaceCom. "Thom says you can see the Ring's markings; that means you have at least some capacity for Ring work." She sat down opposite Ulla, with the Ring between them. "For safety's sake, you need to know at least the basics before you leave us for SpaceCom."

Ulla set her cup down. What could possibly be dangerous about a communications scrambler?

As soon as Ulla settled in, Hanni touched the Ring and sang a dozen or so notes. The space went absolutely dark. The only sound was their breathing. Ulla couldn't even sense the faint undercurrent of psi activity she'd become accustomed to.

"You wanted to know how a small artifact like a utility Ring could be dangerous," Hanni said out loud with just a touch of humor.

Ulla's neck grew moist with sweat. The air wasn't moving. Shit! Were they...

"The Ring is letting nothing in nor out," Hanni said, "including air."

Ulla reached out and touched both sides of the bubble-shaped force field Hanni had just made. Her spacer's mind calculated how long their existing air would last; she fought down panic and forced herself to breathe slowly.

Hanni waited an excruciating minute before she sang nine syllables in a more-or-less musical sequence. Light returned, and the temperature dropped to match the rest of the air inside the tent.

Ulla took a deep breath of precious air and let it out slowly. *What did you do that for?*

To get your attention. "Utility Rings are most commonly used for privacy, but they have other uses." Hanni took a sip of coffee. "You just saw one of the lethal uses—privacy carried to the extreme. Before we leave this tent, you're going to be able to sing a Ring down."

"You mean deactivate it?" Ulla asked.

"Yes. Even if you do nothing more with Rings, you at least need to be able to do that." *Let's get started.*

* * *

There was so much to process, Ulla reflected as she lumbered along on Snowball's back. It was hard to believe that just over a week had passed since she'd placed one hand on Flint's utility Ring, sworn an oath, and joined Flint Clan. In those few days, Fripp, Kate, and Hanni had given her just enough emergency psi training to keep her out of life-threatening trouble.

They'd settled into a routine. Ulla continued to sit in on Stelle's lessons in the mornings. She'd spent three evenings with Hanni, learning more about Rings. Other evenings, she kept working on mind-talk with Maribet and Kamna. Mind-talk practice was much more interesting now that Maribet trusted the starfighter to share her thoughts only with the intended recipients.

Sometimes, especially on days when they camped in one spot for more than one night, Piet took Ulla aside to work with the capraglamas. Ulla found she had a knack for gathering the mindstreams of multiple capraglamas to combine their uncomplicated power with her own Gifts for whatever paranormal task fell to hand.

On travel days, Granny Kate rode pillion behind Ulla in the afternoon and taught her about the Dark Gift.

Kate, thanks be, turned out to be a delightful person to spend time with. Even—no, especially on the afternoon when Ulla, overwhelmed with her new position among the

On'oi as an adept with so, so many new skills, broke down in tears. Kate hadn't said a thing. She'd just hugged Ulla, held her steady, and kept Snowball galumphing along with everybody else.

Kate didn't drink alcohol. "If I start," she'd said, "I find it hard to stop. So, I don't." Her subtext was that the Matthias Carroll Memorial Society would see her dead if she couldn't control her Dark Gift.

Ulla, who had not repeated her early epic drunk, was not similarly restricted.

As for who Matthias Carroll was, he'd been the first poor soul to startle a badly injured soulslayer. Things had not ended well for either party.

Granny Kate was Ulla's official Society mentor, for now. "Thom Yensson would be the logical choice because he's going to Newcastle with you, and I'm not," Kate had said. "But if you don't honor your oath, I don't think he could bring himself to kill you." *You must have noticed he has a crush on you*—this from the senior Society member on trek.

Shit. On so many levels.

Still, Ulla couldn't help but like Kate Ostapsdaughter. The long-married, long-widowed grandmother understood people so very, very well and loved them anyway.

The first step in slaying souls—after understanding that one never, ever did it without a very clear and valid reason—involved understanding what healthy souls were made of. Granny Kate had studied souls for at least twice as long as Ulla had been alive. Kate's psi range might be short, but when she did connect, she saw everything, including your illusions and what they hid.

Ulla thought back to the first time she'd linked minds with Thom. He had that same mind-penetrating ability; was it a soulslayer thing? She rode along, daydreaming.

Kate let go of Ulla's waist and had a drink from her water bottle. *Thom's a good man. You could do a lot worse.*

Maybe—if they lived on the same planet. But a woman could dream.

Why don't you act on it?

Granny Kate had caught her in mid-shiver. *It'd be—unprofessional.*

Maybe, maybe not. Sooner or later, you'll want to take up with someone.

Not a chance. Ulla sighed. *Oh, Kate. I am so not from here.*

* * *

Another week passed. One sunny day, just as Hanni and Stelle dropped back in the column to join Piet for lunch, Kate showed up next to Snowball. "How are you doing, Ulla?"

Fine. Ulla set a mind-link with Kate, whose range was too short to hail Ulla on the camdeer's back from where she stood on the ground. *Want a ride?*

Thanks, no. We're stopping soon.

They had reached a wide meadow where people were spreading out to rest and eat. Kate picked a spot with two handy rocks to sit on; Snowball followed her and knelt to let Ulla climb down.

Ulla rummaged in her saddlebag for bannock, cheese, and dried fruit, then grabbed her water bottle and joined Kate, who was already eating.

Once Ulla had settled in next to her, Kate said, "You have questions."

That was direct. Ulla's mouth was full, so she used psi. *What brought that on?*

I've been listening to your inner skeptic every afternoon for two weeks. Kate waved her arms to indicate everything around them. "All this. Being one of us."

I'm astonished that people are so accepting. Ulla swallowed so she could speak out loud. "I'm still an offworlder."

Kate shrugged. "The cynics are keeping their mouths shut." She cut herself another slice of cheese. "Opening yourself up so people could share what you felt when you grabbed the Ring and took your oath went a long way." She popped the cheese into her mouth. *Some were quite surprised that you could touch a Ring.*

"Why couldn't I?" Ulla asked. Surely her lessons with Hanni must be common knowledge.

Kate shook her head. *Your lessons are no secret, but most people aren't paying such close attention.* "Only about a third of humans can touch Rings at all."

Ulla bit off a mouthful of bannock and cheese. *Seriously?*

Kate reached for some dried fruit. "Piet Erikson, for example. He's very Gifted with capraglamas and other stock, with mind-moving, and with mind-talk. But if he touches a Ring, it'll burn him." *Even though his brother Neal is one of the world's foremost authorities on Ring work.*

"Is it a psi thing?"

"No." Kate shook her head. "It's quite random. And nobody knows why."

Ulla thought back to Thom singing up the utility Ring for her debrief, even though his mind-talk range was, in his words, "soulslayer-short."

"Thom can, I can, you can. Piet and a whole bunch of other people can't." Kate packed up the remains of her lunch. "And then there's a family of headblind offworlders in Newcastle who can. They are really good at Ring song—but they need spotters to give them feedback because they can't see the runes."

It was time to get moving again. Snowball knelt, and Ulla stashed their eating utensils in her saddlebag and got on. Kate settled in behind her. As they rode in silence, Ulla poked at the small, polished flint stud in her left ear and mused about the oath she'd taken on Flint Clan's Ring to uphold honor, courage, kindness, prudence, justice, temperance, and fidelity.

At least the list of virtues was familiar.

* * *

They crested a hill and entered yet another valley, where a river meandered along the valley floor. Just before they reached the floodplain, they passed a working archaeological site; a vast, modern roof soared on posts above a rambling collection of hewn-stone structures.

"What's that?" Ulla asked.

"The Ancients' Villa," said Kate.

Ulla stared as they passed what must once have been a substantial property. Fascinated, she was glad that it took a while at walking speed. "I'd love to spend some time poking around there."

"If there's time, you can. We're almost to Summer Pasture." Kate pointed. "Bald Mountain."

The top of the mountain in front of them had been visible for days. Now they were at its foot, and within about half an hour's ride from three low buildings and an elevated water tank.

As they drew closer to the semi-permanent camp, Ulla saw tents going up along one edge of a grassy square anchored on two other sides by the river and the buildings. The fourth side remained open to acres of pasture where the capraglamas, sheep, and camdeer were settling down.

Ulla smelled food roasting and heard what had to be the whine of a working machine shop from the building nearest the river. There was a waterwheel, probably the power source. Next to the shop was a long, low building with people coming and going. The third building was smaller, with a peaked roof and a wide, raised porch on two sides.

The mood was festive. A handful of people jogged out to meet the column of travelers. A big, well-built man snuck up behind Ingeborg and scared the living daylights out of her; they ran ahead, laughing. Kamna walked hand in hand with a young man Ulla had not seen before.

Kate released her hold on Ulla's waist and waved at the young couple. *Kamna's friend is Jon Craigson. His grandmothers are Mountain and Thistle; grandfathers are Gandras and Elg.*

Ulla was mystified. Why was Kate going on about grandparents?

His clans, dear. Kamna's grandmothers are Flint and Worldtree; her grandfathers are Hammer and Waterbasket. She and Jon are perfect for one another.

Ulla thought back to what Nathan had told her about the On'oi clan system as insurance against inbreeding.

Exactly. Kate settled back into her seat behind Ulla.

Ulla opened her water bottle, drank, and capped the bottle. *How do people keep track?* Was the system functional, a tradition, or both?

Tradition that serves its function quite well.

Nathan had said as much, the night of the farewell party. Ulla put away her water bottle and concentrated on the road ahead.

"Turn around," Kate said. *No, not you, Snowball.* "Ulla, you turn around in the saddle; I want to show you something."

As soon as Snowball was safely on course, Ulla looked back at Kate, who pointed to her ears. "You want to know how we keep track of people's clan affiliations."

Ulla sighed. She still had trouble with control. As loud as her thoughts must have been, she might as well have asked.

Kate switched to mind-talk. *In which ear is your Flint earring?*

Left. Ulla resisted the urge to fiddle with it.

Kate nodded. *A woman's clan jewelry is worn on the left. Your Flint earring has a blue stripe around the bezel; that's because you weren't born Flint but joined as an adult.*

True. Both Hanni and Maribet had offered their spare blue-striped earrings when the need arose. Mind-seeing told Ulla that hers had once belonged to Maribet.

You and I are Flint Clan. Kate pointed to the polished flint stud in her left earlobe. *You by oath, me by birth. The upper earring on my left is for my father's mother's clan, Raven.*

Kate's upper left earring matched the lower one on Thom's right ear.

That'd be his mother's clan—Thom's Raven. Kate chuckled. *I thought you said you hadn't looked that closely.*

Ulla blushed. *What's in your other ear?*

Kate pointed to her right ear. *These were my Wat's clans. His ma was Worldtree; his da was Thistle.*

Ulla was confused. Wasn't Kate's grandson named Wat?

Kate nodded. *Young Wat is named for his grandda.*

Who, Ulla surmised, would have been Kate's late husband.

Her mentor nodded and sat back. Ulla faced forward again; Snowball seemed relieved that they'd finished squirming.

So, a Guardian with one bare ear isn't married. Ulla mulled the social implications.

Usually, said Kate. *People who are widowed usually keep their partners' earrings. If they remarry, they add their new partner's shiny wares to the lineup. And divorced people who have children often keep their ex-partner's set.*

Why?

Kate sat up and waved to someone in the distance. *It's a daily reminder for their kids about who they are and where they're from.*

If, Ulla decided, she'd had to stumble into a new

culture, this one that so valued family and connections was not a bad one. But thinking about all the permutations of family affiliation, as mapped out by people's jewelry, just to figure out who was dating material—never mind dictating with whom one stood in times of trouble— made her brain hurt.

I'm glad both sides of that occurred to you, Starfighter. Kate rested a gentle hand on Ulla's shoulder. *As for dating, don't fuss about it. The blue stripe on your earring means that, for you, the field is wide open.*

Snowball picked his way among tents, people, and baggage. He stopped and knelt by a conical framework of tent poles.

"Granny!" Two young girls raced to greet Kate, who slid expertly off Snowball and retrieved her small bag from the saddle.

They hugged. "Have you been good for your ma and da?"

"Yes, ma'am." They jumped up and down, then raced back to unfold the tent.

"Kids." Kate smiled. "Heya, Claudia." She hugged her daughter-in-law. "Did Henrik get the sauna up and running?"

"There are people using it already." Her daughter-in-law laughed. "Young Wat grabbed his da out of the workshop the minute we got here, and they went to get wood for our cook fire."—*and talk soulslayer stuff.*

Young Wat's Dark Gift had surfaced during the first week of this trek to go with his newly defined muscles and wispy facial hair. Ulla figured he couldn't wait to compare notes with his soulslayer father, who had arrived early to help prepare the semi-permanent camp for the rest of them.

"Enjoy your son while you can." Kate helped Claudia lift the tent onto its conical framework of poles. "Next summer, he'll trek with your brothers in Mountain."

* * *

Snowball carried Ulla to the single ladies' campsite, where the others had erected the poles and waited impatiently for the tent. The camdeer knelt, and Ulla slid off.

Ouch! Ulla landed wrong on her bad foot, which until this moment had been feeling and working well enough. She kept her mouth shut and loosened the straps on the rolled-up tent.

Kamna's friend Jon picked up the tent, unasked. "Starfighter, sit down. You're hurt."

"Thanks." Ulla tightened the shield on her thoughts; she hadn't meant for anyone to know.

She sat while Jon and Ingeborg's red-bearded giant spread the tent out on its poles and tied it down. Kamna unrolled the ground cloth inside while the men unloaded gear from Snowball, removed his saddle, and sent him off for a rubdown and a rest with the other camdeer.

That done, Ingeborg and Kamna tossed their things inside and disappeared into the forest with their men.

Maribet took the heater inside and put it together. She poked at the flue hole with a stick; Ulla mind-moved the canvas aside and adjusted it to suit the light breeze. They unrolled their bedding and were home.

"How's your ankle?"

"I think I tweaked it a little, getting down off Snowball," Ulla admitted.

Maribet raised an eyebrow but said nothing. She dug dirty clothes out of her bag and made a bundle of them. "Let's do laundry."

Ulla could not face getting down in a cold stream and pounding rocks on shirts.

Maribet laughed. *Me either.* "If we hurry, we can snag space in the automatic washers."

"What?" Ulla had already stretched out on her sleeping pad.

"Modern washing machines. In the bathhouse." Maribet spread her roomiest long-tailed shirt on the ground and piled laundry on it.

Ulla closed her eyes. "You go. I'm exhausted."

Maribet laughed. "There's a sauna. You know you want it."

Kate had told her about the sauna. "Can't, at least not today." *Not good for new ink.*

Oh. Sorry. Maribet pushed aside the tent flap with her bundle, then turned to Ulla. "Kate'll let you have a shower, right?"

"A shower? Out here?"

Maribet nodded. "Indoor plumbing. And the tank behind the sauna makes plenty of hot water."

There were no hot showers on SpaceCom vessels. Ulla hadn't had one in months, not since taking ten glorious days of leave at MitSmith's beach resort on Landfall.

She rolled to her feet and grabbed her bag. "I'm in."

* * *

The laundry took up one end of the long, low bathhouse near the river. Inside, half the commercial washing machines were full and sloshing. There was no electrical wiring, but the floor vibrated. Ulla peeked outside. The laundry had its own little millrace and waterwheel. There had to be a power takeoff for each machine.

Maribet scooped commercial detergent from a common bin and tossed it and her clothes into a washer. She stripped off what she was wearing, threw that in, and set the machine running.

"Dressing room's there." Maribet pointed to a door. "There are shelves where you can put your things. Showers are on the right; the sauna is straight through the door at the end of the room." Then Maribet was gone.

Ulla pulled her dirty clothes out of her bag, loaded them and some detergent into a machine, and puzzled out how to make the damned thing work. Then, she stripped down and tossed in what she was wearing. She fished out clean clothes, her toiletries kit, and her towel and set the bag by "her" washer. Then she headed for the showers.

She turned on the water just long enough to get wet and shut it off while she soaped up. Wait! This was dirtside! Her only limit was the capacity of the tanks. Well, that and social pressure not to hog all the hot water. She oughtn't fog the place up completely; that'd be bad for the tattoo. Ulla turned the water on, rinsed, and let hot, liquid goodness flow down her back. Gratuitous, decadent water circled the drain. The sauna would be nice, but this shower was the stuff of a spacer's dreams.

Chapter Fifteen
Who We Want

Ulla couldn't sleep.

The cooking fires had burned down, though a few people lingered outside and talked by lantern light. They weren't noisy, not anymore. But her brain could not stop turning over all the new things she'd learned and all the things she still needed to learn. How many things did she not even know she needed to know?

She might be headed back to SpaceCom but, like it or not, the community she'd just joined was going to be part of her forever.

She rolled onto her side and pretended to sleep, not wanting to disturb Maribet, who had turned in early, too.

Ulla must have drifted off. When she woke, the camp was dark and quiet. Ingeborg and Kamna were still out. Worried, she put out a discreet telepathic search.

Oh. Ingeborg and Dannel had taken a blanket to a private spot. Kamna and Jon were similarly engaged inside the little traveler's tent Dannel must have agreed to vacate for the night.

Ulla backed out hastily and left them alone.

Sleep eluded her, but she wadded up her pillow and tried anyway.

What about Thom? Maribet was wide awake too.

Why did everyone think Ulla and Thom Yensson ought to be an item? She closed her eyes and lay still. Half-sleep eventually came.

Starfighter!

Nestled alone under her blankets, Ulla felt Thom's body beside hers, under different blankets. He rolled over and flung an arm across her. She grabbed his hand and they embraced.

This was the best dream ever! Ulla relaxed and settled down to sleep. The embrace felt real. She turned her face to his, and they kissed.

Oh, how she needed this!

He brushed her hair back with his hand, and she wrapped her legs around his waist—more kissing. Neither of them, apparently, slept wearing pants. She undid the buttons on her shirt—so much better! Together, they rolled over.

Ouch! Ulla rolled over onto her bad ankle and woke up.

"Are you all right?" Maribet spoke out loud. Thom, or his shade or whatever it was, was gone.

Ulla sat up and buttoned her shirt. "All good."

"You two shared a dream."

Some dream. Ulla shivered, embarrassed. "How much did you, uh, hear?"

Pretty much all of it.

Oh, shit. Ulla felt around in the dark until she found her wadded-up blanket. *Did I project again?*

No. I looked in because you were thrashing around. I thought you were having one of your nightmares.

At least the whole damned camp hadn't been in on it.

Ulla stared into the dark. She envied Ingeborg and Dannel. But... "What about Kamna and Jon?"

"What about them?" Maribet asked.

"They're so young."

"Not that young." Maribet settled back into bed. *Not here.*

What if they make a baby?

"Unlikely." *They've both been taught how not to.*

Disease?

"Almost nonexistent in the backcountry," Maribet said, "and there are remedies." *Let it be. They're FINE.*

Maribet was right. If Kamna was old enough to go on trek as an adult, she was old enough to bed down with Jon. Ulla pulled her blanket up under her chin. She liked Kamna. *What about broken hearts?*

She heard a sob from Maribet's side of the tent.

"Sorry." Ulla hadn't meant to strike a nerve.

Maribet wept.

They lay in the dark, wide awake. Eventually, the sobs diminished, and Maribet took a deep breath. Ulla pretended to sleep.

As the night wore on, a pencil beam of moonlight made its way through the flue hole and crossed the tent floor. Eventually, the beam landed on Maribet, who still lay curled in misery. Ulla got up and crossed the short distance between them.

When she put her hand on Maribet's shoulder, the energy that came back was sexual. Ulla left her hand where it was.

Very slowly, Maribet let down her shields. Ulla picked up a jumble of thoughts. When Maribet spilled a long-ago memory of her father beating her, Ulla drew back.

Maribet cried harder. "I knew that's what you'd think."

"About what? That your father beat you? That's appalling!"

"No. The other."

"What other?"

Maribet hung her head. *Women.*

What about women?

I...like women.

What did that have to do with anything? Ulla quashed the impulse to burst into laughter. Maribet was deadly serious and beyond anxious. Ulla chose her words carefully. "Why would that even be an issue?"

"Among the On'oi, it isn't." Maribet sighed. *In Newcastle, it's against the law.*

Having no idea what to say, Ulla lit the lantern. Tears ran down her friend's face. Who had broken Maribet's heart?

Susana. But it's not her fault. "My lover in Newcastle married Old Man Schiller."

Wait a minute. "What do you mean, 'married'?" And who was Old Man Schiller?

Maribet nodded. "You must not know much about Newcastle. Schiller is rich. So is Susana's family. It was a lucrative match—especially considering how much older he is than her." *That's how families like the one I grew up in hang on to their fortunes.*

Rich families maybe, but Ulla had seen plenty of

women in Newcastle who made a perfectly good living in the trades or as shopkeepers.

Maribet shook her head. *I'm glad for them. But the family I left thinks they're too good for common work.*

The family you left?

Not by choice. "My father disowned me after Susana and I got caught the second time." Maribet wasn't crying anymore. "Her husband came home early from a business trip." She smiled a little. "I had to climb out an upstairs window; she threw my clothes down after me."

That was an unexpected image of quiet Maribet with the upper-crust City accent. *Is it funny in hindsight, then?*

A little. "By then, I was a mind-talker, completely self-taught. Thom's aunt and uncle took me under their wing and sent me to study at Castle Chisos. Flint Clan needed a long-range mind-talker, so they took me in."

Why hadn't Maribet moved on? She must have had offers.

"Oh, yes. But I love Susana."

Married or not?

Maribet wiped away tears and smiled. "Widowed. I got word today that her husband died."

"Is there any reason for you to stay away from Newcastle?"

"Legally? No." *Old Man Schiller was too embarrassed to prosecute.* "The only other time we got caught, we were both underage. That record's been erased."

Well?

I'll think about it.

Chapter Sixteen
Breakfast, Interrupted

Early the next morning, Ulla met Thom leaving the bathhouse as she was going in.

"Heya, Starfighter."

"Good morning."

They stood, blocking the doorway until a mother and two children shouldered their way past them. Thom and Ulla moved to one side.

He did not look happy. "You might have told me you changed your mind about your unbreakable rules."

I haven't. "Maribet says it was a shared dream."

"It was private until you showed up," Thom said. *Oh, gods. Maribet heard?*

I'd hoped you'd forget when you woke up.

A dream like that? Um, no.

I was asleep, and then we were in bed together. It was a DREAM!

"It started out as a dream," he said. "Once you arrived, it was real."

"Oh, no, it wasn't!"

"In a physical sense, no. But in mind-work it certainly was." *Do you have any idea how strong your Gifts are?*

He thought she'd done that on purpose? What nerve! "It won't happen again."

Thom's thoughts went shuttered. "Um, Starfighter? Different topic."

"What?" Ulla shifted from one foot to the other; there were flush toilets inside the bathhouse, and her need was urgent.

Sorry. "Just one thing."

Would he get to the point?

"Nathan and I are going up Bald Mountain today with the group who're bringing back the Ring. If all goes well, we should be back here in a day or two."

It's that close?

He nodded. "A stiff half-day walk. They'll need time to sing up the Ring, power it down, pack it up. Climb's steep, Ring's heavy—but there's a good road most of the way." *Wish I knew how the Ancients built it.*

Uh, "Safe travels."

Thanks. "The morning after we get back, you, Nathan, and I leave for Newcastle with the Ring. Be ready."

Oh! "I'll be ready." Ulla ducked past him.

* * *

As Ulla emerged from the bathhouse, a rooster crowed. *Chickens? Here?* That opened up intriguing possibilities.

Maribet looked up from stirring a pot of oatmeal and dried fruit. *Advance team brought 'em from Hovey.* She nodded in the general direction of the town on the other side of the ridge. *No eggs yet.*

Ulla shooed Maribet away from the pot and took over stirring duty. Once the oatmeal was ready, she moved the pot to a flat rock at the edge of the fire ring and ladled herself a bowl. Then she filled her mug with coffee and sat down to eat while Maribet ran off to the bathhouse.

Awkwardness with Thom aside, the day was shaping up brilliantly. Small, puffy clouds sailed across an endless blue sky. The sun had already dried most of last night's dew. Spoon and mug still in hand, Ulla stretched out her arms and turned her face to the sun. A light breeze ruffled her hair. Idly, she watched Ingeborg and Kamna share breakfast with Dannel and Jon in front of the men's little tent.

Ulla breathed deeply, taking in as much fresh air as she could. Mornings like this did not happen shipboard. Well, there'd still be oatmeal and coffee. And dried fruit.

Starfighter! Maribet waved energetically at her from the Council House steps.

Ulla ate another spoonful of oatmeal. *What?*

Relaying for Kate Ostapsdaughter. Emergency meeting for soulslayers, right now, in Council House.

Ulla wolfed down the rest of her meal, wiped her empty bowl and spoon, and set them down by the fire ring. She topped up her coffee mug, pocketed her notebook and a pencil, and headed for Council House.

* * *

Ulla stepped inside the Council House door and waited for her eyes to adjust.

"Welcome." Granny Kate greeted her from where she sat at the head of the table. Her son, Henrik Watson, sat on her left, Thom on her right. Everyone else had brought coffee, too. The utility Ring, activated to block sound and psi, sat in the middle of the table.

Were Kate and her family the only soulslayers in Flint Clan?

Kate shook her head, picking up on Ulla's thoughts. *There are two other families. They...stayed home this year.* She turned toward Henrik. "Where is young Wat? He ought to be here by now."

Discreetly, Ulla scanned the immediate area as she took a seat next to Henrik and found Wat racing toward Council House.

Henrik opened his little notebook and fished a pencil out of his pocket. "He went out early with Ryan. They're working with the sheep in the far pasture."

Thom smiled. "He still wants to be an animal healer, does he?"

Henrik nodded. "Kid's good with livestock." *Too bad he doesn't have the Healing Gift.*

Sympathy manifested on everyone's face.

Ulla realized she was the only soulslayer in the room who had additional Gifts. She had, by far, the longest telepathic range. By the standard of any place else in known space, soulslayers had remarkable psi talent. Compared to their own community; however, they were practically headblind. What did that do to young soulslayers' career choices?

It isn't pretty, Starfighter. The look Thom gave her was indecipherable.

The door burst open. Young Wat, breathing hard,

almost forgot to shut it before sitting down next to Thom.

Kate had just opened her mouth to welcome him when her facial expression shifted. *Katrin Ostapsdaughter here, go ahead.*

Ansel Flett, Lesser Knob, Landfall, linking for Matthias Carroll Memorial Society members Neal Erikson and Mary Nkosi, and for José Redland, trusted guest. Miles Rogers, trusted guest, is also present for relay. Then the communicator faded into the background. Ulla tried to figure out how he did it.

It'll come, Lieutenant. Watch and learn. Nobody else at the table reacted as Mr. Flett juggled his private comment with the conference itself.

Neal. Never in anger.

Everyone around the table replied, *Never in anger.*

Neal. Sorry about the short notice. Just found out that you plan to dismount the Bald Mountain Ring tomorrow. We have new information you need to know.

What did the Ring have to do with soulslayers? Ulla looked around the table; apparently, she was not alone in her curiosity. And when had Mary Nkosi become Society Member Mary Nkosi?

There are approximately sixty Yotne-affiliated Dwellers on and near the island of New Vatersay, western Landfall Archipelago. We just got back from an exploratory trip, testing what we can do with the Dark Gift against them... Neal Erikson's voice trailed off.

If I may—Mary. Sorry, we go on not much sleep. Main points: Yotne want a major Ring, they know you are to power a Ring down and move it from Bald Mountain to Landfall, and we found Dwellers on New Vatersay that Yotne, uh . . . Lieutenant Commander Nkosi's organized brief foundered in her hunt for Dialekt words.

Neal. The Yotne have assigned a group of Dwellers to take the Ring while it's in transit.

Thom. Mary, please continue in Standard. I'll translate.

Thom for Mary. Thank you.

Katrin. Any idea if the Dwellers are still confined to Landfall?

There was a pause, then, *Thom for Mary. Probably. But their hosts can Gate anywhere but the area you're in, where electronics don't work.*

At least the annoying problem with magic, or whatever

it was, had a silver lining. But Ulla could hear Thom's brain turning over a zillion contingencies for the upcoming trip to Newcastle even as he translated for Mary, who was still speaking.

The other big takeaway is that the Ancients' legends are true. Soulslayers can kill Dwellers without harming their hosts further. We've been...doing that.

Thom, Kate, Henrik, and Wat picked up their pencils.

Ulla, wishing for a readpad, did the same. Young Wat, wide-eyed, locked eyes with her. She understood exactly how he felt.

Mary was still talking. *We'll send a formal report as soon as possible, but here is what we found that you may find useful in the near term.*

So, a SpaceCom intelligence officer believed they were about to find Dweller-killing tactics useful. The familiar excitement kicked in as Ulla put pencil to paper.

Neal. First, thanks very much to Lieutenant Thorsdaughter and Lieutenant Commander Nkosi for your vivid descriptions. That got us up to speed quickly on identifying Dwellers.

Mary Nkosi had prior combat experience with Dwellers? Ulla could hardly wait to see her in person and find out more.

Those of you who have been in the Society for a few years have witnessed at least one execution. The process for killing a Dweller is the same—except that, because the individual target has two souls, you must take care to banish the Dweller and leave the host untouched.

Thom, for Mary. Fortunately, it is almost always obvious which one is the Dweller.

Almost? Who the hell had they run into?

Neal. We found several different methods that work for identifying and neutralizing Dwellers. Ulla could hear the extreme fatigue in his voice. And "neutralizing?" Either this man spent too much time with SpaceCom Headquarters types, or he had been reading too many thrillers.

Thom, for Mary. As soulslayers, you need to know that as long as you are conscious, you can kill Dwellers, even if they try to occupy your mind. You need only isolate the Dweller and do the deed, whether the Dweller is attached to a host or in midtransfer to a new one. And if you are unconscious, the Dweller has no immediate reason to possess you.

Perhaps, short range was not as big a problem as it seemed.

Mary continued. *A soulslayer's greatest personal danger from Dwellers is plain old kinetic deadly force. Once the Dwellers recognize you as a soulslayer, they know not to try to possess you. Their own best defense is to kill you. Becoming overwhelmed is also a danger. Each Dweller engagement takes energy, and your human body can only do so much.*

Neal Erikson issued an out-of-order, nonverbal affirmative. Had he nodded off?

José. Two things a spotter can do for the soulslayer, besides finding Dwellers to slay, are monitor the soulslayer's energy level and create shields around both of you when necessary. Dwellers can't pass a strong shield, but neither can the Dark Gift, so it's a value judgment.

Katrin. What about amplifying the soulslaying Gift to extend its range, like in the legends?

Neal. Yes and no. A spotter can extend range, but the process is dangerous and poorly understood. Until we know more, I do not recommend it.

Silence around the table.

Katrin. Do I understand correctly that you set out with a party of eight—three soulslayers, three spotters, and the Rogerses?

Neal. Yes.

Katrin. Where is the rest of your party?

There might have been a sigh at the other end of the link.

Neal. Sean Patel, who served as my spotter, is at the hospital in Kirkhilo. Emma Lemaire, spotter for her husband, soulslayer Magnus Lemaire, is Mr. Patel's sister. She and Magnus are with Sean. Aubrey Rogers conveyed them there; none of us soulslayers or spotters is fit to drive until we get some sleep.

Granny Kate waited.

Thom, for Mary. Mrs. Lemaire is beyond angry with her brother and Dr. Erikson. Dr. Rogers—Aubrey, not Miles—stands ready to make them behave.

Katrin. What happened?

Neal. Minutes after Sean and I successfully tested range extension, he passed out. We cut our experiment short and came here. *Don't know why he passed out, but it may be related to the fact that soulslayer power is stronger than the power of most adepts.*

Thom. How is he now?

Neal. He's awake and still has his Gifts. We'll know more when the healer's finished with him.

The rest of the meeting was pure business. Mary and José covered the various methods for isolating a Dweller while putting oneself and one's spotter in the least possible danger. Then Mary gave a quick recap of what had to have been two hair-raising days between two small islands.

Ulla got a kick out of how the celebrated archaeologist Aubrey Rogers, with the Lemaires riding shotgun, had shuttled each catch of rescued Dweller hosts to the hospital on Landfall Mainland, looking for all the world like an older lady making a beer-and-grocery run.

They'd had to make sure that, as far as the Dweller community on New Vatersay was concerned, the Dwellers and their hosts disappeared without a trace. The "camping party" hadn't been equipped for a pitched battle.

Thom for Mary. Are there any further questions?

Ulla was pretty sure her brain was full.

Katrin. None for now, thank you. Once we process what you have told us, I'm sure we will.

Neal. Just ask. But please hold nonemergency questions for a few hours. We need sleep.

Outside the window, Bailey-Duran hung maybe an hour and a half above the horizon. It wouldn't be daylight in Landfall for another three hours.

Those people hadn't risen early; they were still up.

Katrin. Thank you. Get some sleep.

The link dissolved. For a long moment, nobody inside Council House said a word.

Kate broke the silence. "The Society's been alerted; Neal spoke with Victor Jamesson before he hailed us. Victor and the High King will have spoken by now about the Dwellers."

Ulla glanced at Thom. *Who's Victor Jamesson?*

Thom set down his pencil. *President of the Matthias Carrol Memorial Society.*

Oh. Thanks. Kate must have mentioned him. Ulla felt herself blushing.

"The Society recommends that any target of value to

the Yotne, and anyone traveling overland, especially with valuable cargo, be guarded by a soulslayer and spotter," Kate said.

"Just as well, then, that the starfighter and I will travel with the Ring." Thom pocketed his notebook.

Kate nodded, sang down the utility Ring, and shut her notebook.

Henrik opened the door to find Flint Clan Council gathered on the porch, waiting to get in.

"Emergency Council meeting?" Kate asked.

Chieftain Dev nodded. "You and Thom Yensson stay. We need your input."

* * *

When Ulla stepped outside, Ingeborg waved from the end of Council House's wide porch where she stood with Dannel and Jon. The two men were deep in conversation with a clerk at a portable desk. Jon signed a paper and gave it to the clerk, who gave him a different piece of paper. He folded the document and put it in his pocket.

Jon smiled as Ulla approached. "Heya, Starfighter."

Dannel hugged Ingeborg. "Jon has his sheep back. We're off."

"I'll miss you," Ingeborg said. "Come back soon."

Jon and Dannel jumped off the porch and headed for the pasture, where Kamna was minding half a dozen sheep. Kamna and Jon hugged, and then the two men, the sheep, a camdeer, and an ever-circling dog headed for Mountain Clan's summer pasture in the adjacent valley. Kamna trudged up the path toward the ladies' tent.

Ulla was puzzled. "Kamna's not joining us?"

Ingeborg laughed. "She's going out to gather willow shoots. Hanni asked me to review with you what you've learned about Rings."

Because I'm leaving? And what would Kamna do with willow shoots?

Ingeborg nodded, then grinned. *It's spring. Kamna's jumping on the willow project while you're still here to help.*

Ulla shrugged. She had no illusions about how little she knew about her new community. If Ring song were a new language, she was at the stage where she could find the toilets, bargain poorly in the market, and order a meal as long as she didn't mind culinary surprises. "How much Ring song do I really need to know?"

"More than you've had time to cover with us." Ingeborg opened her pocket notebook to a list of talking points.

"I can't read the squiggles."

"That'll come, Ulla," Ingeborg said. "Your Gift is very strong; you absolutely must be able to use it safely—but at this late date all we can do is review what you've learned so far."

"You know I'll be back in the sky in a few weeks, right?" Ulla fished her notebook out of her pocket anyway.

"Even with no Ring, there's plenty we can do while Council finishes their meeting," Ingeborg said. 'Let's use that picnic table over there." She hopped down from the porch; Ulla remembered in time to step down sedately with her good foot.

They sat at the table. "I know you've been working on the basics with Hanni," Ingeborg said, "but before you leave you at least need to be familiar with dual-voiced Ring song." She looked up and got a crease between her eyebrows. *Shit. There's Dmytro. I should have told him to wait.*

"Dmytro?"

Ingeborg closed her eyes for a moment, probably mind-talking. "Dmytro Robson." She opened her eyes. "He was going to sing the other voice."

Ulla was vaguely aware that some Ring songs required more than one voice and a spread of at least three octaves.

"Extra layer of security," said Ingeborg. "For instance, it is impossible for one person working alone to power down a major Ring. That requires verification from a second person, singing in a different octave."

Ulla stared across the plaza toward Bald Mountain. "That's what they plan to do up there, isn't it?"

Ingeborg nodded. "That Ring hasn't been powered down during any of our lifetimes. That's why Gib and Hanni are going." *They're the two best Ring singers in Flint Clan.*

That made sense. "Anybody else going, other than Nathan Steves and your brother?"

"Dean Gregson and Rilla Marcsdaughter," Ingeborg said, "as backup. Also, a major Ring is heavy and awkward to carry." *It'll likely take at least four people to get it down from the top of the mountain to the road. The camdeer can carry it from there.*

So, Thom's going as soulslayer. What's Nathan's job? Could he even touch a Ring? Did he even know?

Ingeborg shivered. "Thom's original job was—and still is—to verify to Da that Flint actually moved the Ring this time. And for all Nathan's a headblind offworlder, he can handle Rings just fine." *He has Thom's back.*

This time? That meant there had been a last time. And Nathan had Thom's back—had things gotten ugly?

Ingeborg's answer was roundabout. *We had a different chieftain last year. He did not move the Ring.* She did not elaborate.

"What does the major Ring do?" Ulla asked.

"Rings," Ingeborg said. "Plural."

Oh.

Ingeborg shifted into teaching mode. "There are twenty major Rings, big ones like the one up there. We think the Ancients made them; we use them to gather and focus energy for big...projects."

"Big projects like terraforming?"

Ingeborg nodded. "Yes—among other things." *On this world, we call it planetary restoration."*

That's what the Alliance is for?

Partly. "Back to Ring work: it's a partnership. The Hjralma have powerful Gifts, but their voices don't work with Rings. We humans have to do the singing."

Ulla stared into the middle distance between them and Bald Mountain. "Why does Flint Clan need to move the Ring?"

Ingeborg sighed. "Some researchers at Castle Chisos think it was built for the Great Knob Ring Seat in Landfall."

"So, how did it get here?" Ulla asked. Flint Clan clearly considered it "their" Ring.

"No idea." Ingeborg tucked a stray lock of hair behind her ear. "We thought it had always been here—until the researchers found out differently, through inscriptions the Ancients left behind. Our Bald Mountain Ring Seat contains fewer Ancient runes than any of the other Seats. Current theory is that the Ancients moved the Ring there from Great Knob, and there aren't many runes because the Yotne invaded shortly after. They don't know for sure because there's a gap in the record. The Elders' recorded history starts a few hundred years later."

Ulla thought back to what Maribet had told her. "Didn't the Yotne conquer the Ancients, lay this world bare, and dump the Elders here later?"

Ingeborg swatted at a lace flier. "That's the campfire story, with the First Settlers showing up just in time with a ship full of life-forms from Earth. What really happened is likely somewhere in the middle."

The Council House door flew open. Kate jogged toward the tent she shared with her son's family. Hanni and Piet emerged, looking displeased. Piet hugged his wife and went back inside. The other two Ring singers stepped outside with Gib Rikson, and they all joined Hanni.

From their picnic table, Ulla and Ingeborg watched a pair of camdeer with lightly packed saddles amble up to Council House. One knelt as Granny Kate fixed a small bag to its packsaddle. It lumbered to its feet, and the group hiked away beside the camdeer toward Bald Mountain.

Where were Thom and Nathan?

Chapter Seventeen
The Yotne Gate

Olwyn had just unpacked the last box in her new office in the command wing of SpaceCom's Newcastle Headquarters when the comm panel beeped. She sighed. At least it wasn't her replacement on the *Resolute*, asking, again, about something he could figure out for himself. He would have used psi.

She left a stack of family holograms unopened on the shelf over her desk, bent down, and tapped to answer.

Craig Eselgroth's face filled the screen. "I'm in Intel, with the ground forces analyst," he said. "Come down here. There's something you need to see."

Her holos could wait. Olwyn went down the corridor, past the soulslayer and the guard, and through the command post's vault door. She tiptoed behind spacers working at their consoles and slipped through another door into Intel's big windowless cave of an office suite. The silent presence of the facility's active psi shield made her skin crawl. She'd so hoped to have left that behind on the *Resolute*.

"Oh good, you're here." Craig peered over an ensign's shoulder at an overhead image of a craggy mountaintop surrounded by thin forest. The ensign's finger rested over a tiny, squarish shadow nestled between cliff and trees.

Olwyn adjusted her spectacles and leaned closer. "What's that?"

Craig stepped back.

The ensign stood up from his workstation. "Guild

Member." He reached down to adjust the image on the screen. "You'll want some context." Their field of view widened. The mountaintop remained in the center of the screen, but now the view included a river and a—town? No, all but three of its "buildings" were tents.

"That's Flint Clan's summer pasture camp, where Lieutenant Thorsdaughter is." The ensign sat down again for better access to the image panel controls. "She's waiting for them to unmount an artifact—they call it a major Ring—from this installation up here." He pointed to a spot on the rocky mountaintop. A faint path wound down to the camp from the spot.

It dawned on Olwyn that this man was not an ordinary ensign. She couldn't read the thoughts underneath his artificial psi blocker, but she could read the devices on his uniform and the crow's feet around his eyes. He'd been a Marine for at least ten standard years and had done some seriously hairy ops. Which explained why this newly minted officer was allowed to function as an adult in this place.

He glanced at her, comprehending. Did he have psi talent? No, she decided. He was simply an excellent reader of people. He probably got reactions like hers all the time.

"What's the concern?" she asked.

He enlarged the display and brought the focus to the mountain's rocky cap. "There's the Ring that Flint Clan is set to power down, pack up, and move. There's the top of the trail they'll have to take to get there."

An indistinct, doughnut-shaped object sat at the top of some steps that were cut into the rock. "Are the steps scaled for humans or for Elders?"

"Scaled for humans," he said. "Which confirms that the artifact is just under a meter across."

Olwyn waited for him to say more.

"Did you see Commander Nkosi's dispatch from Lesser Knob this morning?" Eselgroth asked.

"The Landfall Dweller experiment on New Vatersay?" She knew they'd had to cut it short. "They're safe, then, at Lesser Knob?"

The ensign reduced the size of the image to half his screen and brought up a written document.

Olwyn pushed her spectacles up on her nose and bent down to read. It did not take long. *No. Just no.* She stood up straight. "Do the On'oi know the Yotne intend to have their Dwellers steal a Ring?"

Both men nodded.

"Matthias Carrol Society knows, too," Craig said. "They're already working with the Council of Chieftains. And they're asking for volunteers."

Well. Olwyn stared with renewed interest at the image the ensign enlarged to fill his entire screen. She followed his finger as he pointed to the rectangle he and Eselgroth had been studying when she came in.

"That's a Yotne lightweight tactical Gate. Somebody had to have packed it in, in pieces, on foot. See how the Gate is out of sight of anyone on the trail or at the Ring's location, but close enough for easy access?" He pointed to a rocky shelf that looked perilous to Olwyn, though she had to admit it was plenty wide enough for two people walking abreast.

But why? "I thought Gates didn't work there," Olwyn said.

"They don't." The ensign expanded their view on the screen. "But somebody who uses Yotne equipment obviously thinks that's about to change."

"Flint Clan needs to know," Eselgroth said. "Now."

"To communicate, I need to get outside the psi shield," Olwyn said. "Is there an unshielded place close by where we can bring up this same image and speak freely?"

He thought for a minute, then crossed the big room and disappeared into the command post. Almost immediately, Olwyn felt the psi shield power down.

The Intel ensign returned. "Everyone here has a personal psi blocker. We don't need the facility psi shield, for now."

Why had it been in use at all, then? Olwyn sighed and rubbed the tight spot at the back of her neck.

She reached out to Maribet first, who was busy communicating for someone else. Who was their other dedicated long-distance communicator? She thought for a minute. Oh, yes! The trad medic, who only spoke Dialekt.

Olwyn tried her best to think in the rudimentary Dialekt she was learning. *Hanni Rubensdaughter, Alliance Flint Clan: Olwyn Dara Wittber-Argeles, United Telepathic and Paranormal Practitioners' Guild, relaying for SpaceCom Bailey-Duran Headquarter personnel Mr. Eselgroth and*

Ensign—she peeked at the ensign's name tag—*Strom, SpaceCom.*

Silence, for most of an excruciating minute. Then, *Olwyn, Hanni. If you are trying to contact Flint Clan at our summer pasture, I can't help you. Sorry.*

???

I'm not there. There was another stretch of silence, then, *Guild Member, I must sign off. We are on a very steep mountain trail. Try Maribet.*

In the time it took for Olwyn to figure out how to say *Maribet is occupied; who should I contact instead?* in Dialekt, the link had dissolved. She tried hailing Thom Yensson but couldn't raise him.

Well, shit. In theory, Olwyn could link with any adept in Flint Clan's camp, but with whom? Not Lieutenant Thorsdaughter, who was still learning how to keep her thoughts to herself. With everything that was going on near Bald Mountain, contacting some random person was a no-go.

There was a reason SpaceCom had an Alliance liaison. And he needed to be in on this. *Skuli Branson, Olwyn Dara Witt—*

Heya, Olwyn.

Thanks be! Quickly, she brought Skuli up-to-date. *Craig Eselgroth and Ensign Strom need a relay to Thom Yensson and to Flint Clan—preferably their chieftain—on trek near Bald Mountain. Neither of Flint's on-site interstellar-grade communicators is available. Whom do I contact?*

I'll ask. After a brief wait, Skuli was back. *Dmytro Robson. He's a trained communicator—continental-range, not interstellar.*

That'll do, thanks. Olwyn released the breath she didn't know she'd been holding.

Shall I have the Trade Ministry's communicator hail him for you?

Yes, please! Oh, and Skuli?

What?

Stay in the link. Olwyn sat back and waited.

Chapter Eighteen
A Fight Brewing

"Heya." A man joined Ingeborg and Ulla at the picnic table. "Any idea when Council will be finished with the utility Ring?"

Ingeborg looked up at him. "Heya, Dmytro." *Nope, sorry.*

No worries. He nodded toward Council House and its closed door. "What's going on?"

Ingeborg shook her head. "No idea." *Doesn't look good.*

Dmytro shrugged. "If you can get hold of the utility Ring later today, find me and we'll try again."

Ingeborg stood and stretched. "You and I might as well go help Kamna gather willows."

Ulla cut her reply short as Dmytro suddenly stared into space.

Eyes wide, he excused himself, turned, and ran to Council House, where he pounded on the door until they let him in.

Ulla stared at the closed door. "What was that about?"

"No idea," Ingeborg said. *The willows are waiting.* "How's your ankle?"

Ulla wiggled her foot and decided to ignore the twinge that had bothered her since her clumsy dismount. She tightened the canvas brace. "We'll be outside, right?"

Ingeborg nodded.

"It's fine. Let's go." With her return to SpaceCom more defined, Ulla was all for getting as much fresh air and sunlight as possible.

* * *

They hadn't yet been cutting willow shoots for an hour when Ingeborg's eyes went wide. Maribet's telepathic voice rang out. *Ingeborg, Ulla—Council House, NOW!*

Ingeborg sheathed her knife and called out to Kamna. "Did you hear that?"

Kamna tossed a stick onto the growing pile. "Go. I'll take these back to the tent and get started."

Ingeborg and Ulla hurried to Council House.

"Shut the door." Chieftain Dev pushed a large sheet of paper into the middle of the big, central table. It was a map of Bald Mountain. All the chairs were full, so Nathan got up and offered Ulla his. She sat gratefully. Her ankle hurt from the sprint she ought not to have done.

Thom's little notebook, open to a surprisingly detailed two-page sketch of a Yotne tactical Gate, lay next to the map. The utility Ring privacy shield was active.

Starfighter. Dev turned the notebook so Ulla could see the sketch clearly. *You know what that is, right?*

Of course. She overheard Thom explaining to Ingeborg; the rest of those assembled would have covered this ground already.

"Two days ago," Dev said, "SpaceCom asked their newly arrived ship, the *Dauntless*, to take images of this area as she passed over us." He pointed to Thom's sketch of the Gate. "They found this." He moved his finger to a spot on the map, high on Bald Mountain's shoulder. "It's right here. Gib's party tried to take it out, but they can't get to it because part of the trail has collapsed." He turned a page of the notebook to show a drawing of a surprisingly wide rock shelf: one side snug beneath a cliff, the other side open to a very long drop-off. A gully yawned between the viewer and the tiniest corner of the Yotne Gate, just around a bend behind the cliff.

Shit. But why? There was no way that Gate could work out here, any more than any other electronic device.

"Current theory is that the issues we have in this area with modern technology will resolve as soon as we power down the Bald Mountain Ring." The chieftain flipped the page back to Thom's sketch of the Gate. "We're told the Yotne want a Ring; there's the means for them to take it."

Ulla kept her mouth shut as the familiar adrenaline

rush kicked in. But . . . weren't Thom and Nathan supposed to be on the mountain?

Thom's blue eyes met hers for a brief moment. *Leadership squabble.* He did not look pleased.

If the Gate worked, the fact that Landfall was a quarter of a world away from here was no barrier at all. As for the broken trail, tactical bridging materials could easily be the Gate's first cargo.

Thinking of the broken trail, Ulla wondered how the men would reach the Gate.

There are other trails, Starfighter. Dmytro's voice. *I've been stomping around on Bald Mountain all my life.*

Dev shut the notebook. "Ingeborg."

"Sir?"

"Dr. Steves is leaving shortly with Dmytro and Thom to destroy the Gate. You will be the only healer left in camp." Dev paused. "In the best of worlds, all will go well, and that will not matter. But if things go badly . . ."

Ulla heard everyone in the room complete that sentence in their heads.

* * *

Nathan and Ingeborg stepped outside with Maribet, doubtless to plan and arrange reinforcements.

"Starfighter."

"Sir?" Ulla sat up straight under the chieftain's gaze.

"You have three jobs," he said. "The first is to stay in this camp—at least in body." He smiled slightly. *I'm well aware of your Gifts' range.* "Your primary objective remains to return to SpaceCom on time and in one piece."

Ulla managed not to roll her eyes at his emphasis on those last three words.

"The second job," he continued, "requires your Gifts."

Thanks be! He would not make her sit on her hands.

"You are the only one among us who has real-world experience with Dwellers. Be alert for them. Once the Ring is powered down tomorrow morning, I want you to keep watch over this entire area." *I trust you are the least likely of us to freeze up if and when Dwellers—or Yotne—appear.*

Adrenaline rush, indeed. "Yes, sir."

Piet Erikson spoke. "If you are not busy with Dwellers, I could use help with the capraglamas. If things get hectic,

I'd like you to help channel mind-work support for Gib and Hanni." *Or for anybody else who needs it. Gods, this operation has too many moving parts.*

"Of course," Ulla said. "Same as what we practiced last week?"

"Same kind of link." Piet took a drink of water. "Different job is all."

"Piet." The crease between Dev's eyes deepened. "About the capraglama pen—you removed the fallen tree. Did you replace the keeper's seat that was in it?"

"No, sir."

The two of them engaged in a staring contest—no doubt deep in private conversation.

Finally, Piet spoke. "With all due respect, sir, the keeper's seat is an empty tradition. Flint Clan's capraglamas are family; we work best on the ground together."

More staring. Finally, Dev closed his notebook and turned to Ulla. "Starfighter, your Hjralma mentor asked me to relay a directive from her."

Which was?

"Under no circumstances," he said, "will you use your Spinner's Gift to influence any outcome whatsoever. Fripp specified, and I quote, you will not use the phrase, 'Today, I am lucky.'"

Ulla swallowed. She was pretty sure her outward demeanor remained professional.

Do not fret, Child. I will show you other, less perilous ways to achieve the same objectives.

Ulla looked around. *Fripp?*

The Elder's low-pitched laughter, for Ulla's mind only, rose and then faded away.

* * *

After that, things happened fast. Two camdeer showed up in front of Council House, their packsaddles loaded for travel, heavy work, and possibly a hunting expedition, if the collection of wrecking bars, rifles, and ammunition meant what Ulla thought it did. There likely were explosives in the saddlebags. She sincerely hoped that Thom and Nathan knew how to use them.

Thom grinned. *I've been clearing fallen boulders off trails since I was a kid. It's fun.*

You think we have enough? she asked. *Could what they had even touch the Gate's fortified inner works?*

We don't have anything fancy. One of the camdeer knelt; Thom double-checked the contents of its bags. *Don't worry, Starfighter; Nathan's an expert.*

With explosives?

Thom nodded.

Who is he, really?

Old friend from university, Starfighter. Thom closed the last saddlebag and scratched the camdeer's ears. Once they had checked the other camdeer, the three men began their hike up the trail to Bald Mountain.

Since Piet wanted her help, Ulla followed him to the pasture where capraglamas and camdeer placidly munched Terran grass. A gate at one end stood open. Last week, Piet had shown her how to herd a few select capraglamas into a pen and help them settle down and make a mind-link. They'd used extra power from the capraglamas to mind-move a fallen tree off a fence rail, then repaired the fence. They'd chopped the tree up and stacked the wood. There'd been a few rotten boards nailed to the branches. Piet had pulled out the nails to be straightened and reused, and he'd tossed the boards onto the pile with the rest of the wood.

"Why's there a pen?" she'd asked as they worked.

"Working capraglamas pay no attention to their surroundings," Piet had said. "The pen keeps them from wandering off."

She wondered now if the boards had been the keeper's seat, whatever that was, that Dev was so concerned about.

Piet lifted the gate latch so roughly it almost came off. *Don't ask.*

All righty, then. She wouldn't.

Piet settled himself, walked out into the pasture among the capraglamas, and called them with mind-talk. He gave them treats when they nuzzled his pockets.

"I think we'll work with these guys right here," he said finally, as he scratched random capraglama heads and shooed the animals who pestered him the most. "Morning comes early. Might as well be ready." He wandered deliberately toward the pen, bonding and coaxing.

Once they were in, Ulla swung the pen's gate closed and latched it.

"Thanks." Piet stood in the center of a multi-animal nuzzle-fest.

"Need anything else?" Ulla asked.

"Not right now, thanks," Piet said. "Maybe later. I'll call if I need you." *With your range, you can work from wherever you are.*

Maybe, but she preferred being able to see what she was doing. Ulla headed back to camp.

* * *

"Heya, Starfighter." Kamna set aside the willow shoot she'd just stripped the bark from. She patted a spot on the ground between her and Ingeborg by a pile of unprocessed willow in front of their tent. "Have a seat. The more, the merrier."

Ulla sat, having no idea what they expected of her.

"Strip the inner bark like this." Ingeborg made a few swift motions with her knife. Supple bark peeled off her branch like parchment from gummy candy and then split into two layers. Ingeborg tossed the outer layer into the fire and dropped the pliable inner layer into a basket.

Ulla tried it and had to resort to prying bark off her small branch with her fingernails.

"Here, Starfighter." Kamna leaned over to help. "Cut through both layers of bark; the wood won't let you cut too deeply."

Unless I slice my thumb off. Ulla tried doing what Kamna showed her. Sure enough, the bark peeled back nicely and split into layers as advertised. "What's this for, anyway?"

"Salicylates." Ingeborg's knife moved as fast as ever. "Anti-inflammatory, same as what's in that bottle of offworlder pills Nathan gave you for your ankle."

Really? Ulla's skill improved with each branch, but she saw no pharmaceutical-manufacturing speed trials in her future.

The three worked silently, companionably. The pile of unpeeled branches diminished, and the pile of strips in the basket grew. Kamna short-stopped the smallest, smoothest bare shoots, for weaving into a basket. The bigger ones went next to the woodpile to dry out.

Miraculously, at least to Ulla, they finished the job

before dark. Ingeborg, having offered to cook as a thank-you to Ulla and Kamna, sautéed mutton and wild onions for a stew, put it on the fire to simmer, and disappeared with the willow bark. Kamna started weaving her basket while Ulla lay back on the ground and stared at the sky. Maribet was nowhere to be seen. Smart woman.

Or...a quick check with psi told Ulla that Maribet and all of Council were still at work.

Ulla sat up and checked on the stew. "Where'd Ingeborg go?"

"She's spreading out the bark to dry." Kamna reached for another bare willow shoot. "There's a rack in the attic over the laundry."

They sat like that, Ulla keeping an eye on the stewpot and Kamna, fingers flying, weaving at high speed while they still had daylight.

After a while, Ulla served herself a bowl of stew and watched the sunset. Here in the mountains, you didn't actually get to see Bailey-Duran set, but the pink, red, and gold light it threw on the clouds, the peaks, and the taller trees was spectacular. Ulla leaned back to enjoy the show—one more thing she wouldn't see from the *Resolute*.

I'm told there are plenty of spectacular sights in space.

Ulla almost aspirated her supper. *Ingeborg?*

Savoring the moment, Starfighter. Ingeborg stood right behind her, laughing. *You're hard to startle.*

Ulla coughed hard, regained equilibrium, and swallowed a piece of stew meat down the correct pipe. *I was—preoccupied.*

Ingeborg lifted the tent flap and stowed her empty basket inside. *Me too.*

Ulla scraped the last bits of stew from her bowl and licked the spoon. "Have you heard from Thom?"

"No." Ingeborg sat next to Ulla.

"Finished!" Kamna said, tucking the last loose twig into the edge of her new basket and holding it up to the firelight.

"Nice!" Ulla knew, in theory, where baskets came from, but she had never seen one progress from growing plant to finished product in a single day.

Kamna stood, shook out her hands, and took her new basket into the tent while Ulla and Ingeborg sat, exhausted, in the gathering darkness.

Ingeborg unhooked her mug from her belt and filled it with water. *In so many ways, today was so normal.*

Ulla nodded. *War is like that. It's a mix of normal and... not.*

War. Do you think it will come to that?

Hope not. But having the Yotne interested in you is never good.

Halfway up Bald Mountain, something flared. They watched a trail of sparks skitter downhill and go out. Then the mountain went dark again.

What was that? Ingeborg radiated anxiety.

Um, sparks? Ulla tried, unsuccessfully, to project calm.

"Starfighter," Ingeborg said in a carefully unbothered voice, "please link me with Thom. He, Nathan, and Dmytro are out past my range." *That had better damn well be why I can't hear them.*

Ulla scanned the mountain. Nathan's buzzing psi blocker was still intact. Thom and Dmytro were linked with Chieftain Dev, among others. Ulla withdrew; there was no need to disturb them.

"They're fine," she told Ingeborg. "Thom and Dmytro are mind-talking with Council."

"Thanks." Ingeborg sat down. "What the hell happened?"

Maribet appeared out of the darkness and sank onto the ground next to the fire. "They pushed the Gate off the ledge. Those sparks you saw were ferrous metal Gate parts scraping flint outcroppings on the way down." She grabbed the stewpot. "Mind if I polish this off?"

Was there any left?

Just crunchy scum. I don't care. Maribet scraped the bottom of the pan and ate. Once she was finished, she said, "I'm going to bed. Gotta be back at Council House when they unmount the Ring in the morning."

Ingeborg put the pan to soak and followed Maribet into the tent. Ulla scanned the area one last time for Dwellers and other hostiles, found none, and banked the fire for the night.

Chapter Nineteen

Bad Day at Bald Mountain

"Goshawk Two One, BDSYS Rescue. Respond!" The voice, with a tinny little klaxon in the background, came from inside her saddlebag.

Oh, gods. Not another dream. Ulla pulled the covers over her head and burrowed into her pillow. Early-morning light seeped in anyway.

Light? *Shit!* Fully awake now, she rolled out of bed. They were going to deactivate the Ring at sunup. Gate or no Gate, she'd promised to watch for Dwellers, and she still needed to be available to help Piet.

Hastily, Ulla pulled on her clothes and boots, begrudging the extra time it took to strap up the ankle brace. Maribet was gone, her sleeping pad rolled up neatly, but Kamna and Ingeborg were still in bed.

"Goshawk Two One!" her saddlebag squawked again. Something inside it vibrated at a slight delay behind the klaxon.

Why the hell was SpaceCom's Bailey-Duran System Rescue calling her?

Oh, crap. Her emergency comm unit had called them! Ulla ripped the bag open, dug through socks, shirts, and underwear, removed the offending device, and stepped outside. She flipped a red toggle switch that had been useless until this moment. The klaxon stopped. "Rescue, Goshawk Two One. Sorry about the hot beeper. I'm safe on the ground, enroute home as planned."

"Goshawk Two One, Rescue. Stand by."

"Aye, aye." She waited. Then the comm unit's power indicator flickered and winked out.

What to do? She could use psi, but with whom? The rescue dispatcher for the Bailey-Duran system would be at SpaceCom's Headquarters in Newcastle, where the hour was wicked early. Olwyn Wittber worked there now, but the Guild member kept banker's hours. Was there an Alliance adept on watch in the command post? How did one identify such a person among all the other telepaths in Newcastle?

That was there. She was here. Piet?

Morning, Starfighter. She heard barely restrained laughter. Well, she'd earned it. *No worries, we're fine. I'll call if I need you.*

Ulla scanned the area for Dwellers and found none. She coaxed the fire to life, started a pot of coffee to brew, and scanned Newcastle for an adept who could close the loop for that poor dispatcher about her emergency beeper.

Starfighter!

Maribet?

Mind-talker in SpaceCom Headquarters looking for you. Talk to him; I need to keep a link open for the Ring party.

* * *

Well! That had been awkward. At least SpaceCom knew that electronics were working out here. She hoped they would start using some. West of here, Thom said, the roads got better. A modern vehicle, even a farm camion, would shorten the trip to Newcastle. She dreamed bigger and wished for a rotorcraft. That could put her—and Thom, Nathan, and the Ring—there tonight.

Daydreaming, Ulla scrubbed out the stewpot and refilled it with rolled oatmeal, water, and dried fruit. Once the oatmeal thickened, she served herself a bowl and added some of the goat's milk young Wat had brought by last night. Breakfast in hand, she watched another glorious, sunny morning unfold.

As she sipped coffee, Ulla sent her consciousness up the mountain. The Ring party was coaxing and belaying a heavy, round package, encased in leather and secured with ropes, down a precarious slope. No way could they carry that thing on the narrow, zigzag trail. Two camdeer waited at the top of the Ancients' graded road.

She didn't find Nathan, Dmytro, and Thom on her first pass. That was worrying. Oh! There they were, headed for the box canyon where the Gate had fallen.

Ulla did not have a groundie's understanding of such things, but weren't the ultralight tactical Gates extremely difficult to destroy? The munitions she'd used as a starfighter to blow up Yotne Gates in space were seriously kick-ass. She'd heard stories of Yotne popping out of nothing, drawn only by the heavily armored, resilient Gate engine.

Somebody on Bald Mountain shared her skepticism. That was reassuring.

Heya, Starfighter.

Oops. She hadn't meant to be so obvious. *Heya, Thom.*

No worries. I've been hoping you'd scan in our direction.

Had he, then? *You were at the meeting, Guardian. That's my job.*

Still, good to see you.

Ulla set down her coffee mug. *May I look through your eyes?*

Go ahead. Thom walked behind Dmytro. Through Thom's ears, Ulla heard Nathan's footsteps and the familiar sounds of camdeer and creaking saddle leather bringing up the rear. *Ulla, how are you at mind-seeing?*

You mean finding? Pretty good. It was a Gift she'd always had, improved exponentially when Hanni taught her how to do it right. *Witched water when I was a kid, why?*

Thom stopped walking and turned his—their—gaze toward a ridge far below. *We think the Gate landed on the other side of those rocks. Can you tell us where it is?*

Maybe—Ulla unlinked from Thom's mind. For a minute, she sat by the fire in camp, drank her coffee, and considered how to proceed. It would help if she knew more about Bald Mountain's topography.

Maribet?

Starfighter! What's up?

Thanks be, there was a lull in activity inside Council House! *May I come get a look at the map of Bald Mountain?*

Dev answered right away. *Of course. Don't knock; just come in.*

Thanks.

She paused to wash her face and comb her hair—no need to show up to Council looking like she'd just rolled out of bed.

* * *

Ulla slipped quietly inside Council House and went straight to the map on the table. "May I?" she asked. Dev nodded. She carried the map to the window facing Bald Mountain and compared the ink-and-paper likeness to the real thing.

"Thanks." She returned the map to the table, went outside, and sat cross-legged on the porch with Bald Mountain in full view. Ulla focused on the ridge between her and Thom's box canyon. Then she closed her eyes and concentrated.

There definitely was a large, recent artifact in there. Something moved. It felt mechanical, not animal. She didn't like that, not at all.

Finding was all well and good, but she needed to see what was going on. She relayed what she'd found to Thom and Dmytro, and to Maribet.

Anything else? That was Thom, linked through Dmytro.

I wish. Suddenly, Ulla had a clear bird's-eye view of the canyon, charred brush, broken Gate parts and all. Four robots scurried among the wreckage, intermittently popping up into the air to spread a framework of lightweight metal beams around the Gate's blackened engine. A new Gate engine sat off to one side, ready for installation.

Let's nip that in the bud. The beams were only half-connected. She reached out with mind-moving to knock them down.

Yow! Her effort met a powerful psi shield.

You all right? Thom stood on the ridge opposite her.

Yeah. Startled. She flew her consciousness across the valley and settled next to him.

Three men stared at her, wide-eyed.

What?

"Ulla, how did you get here?" Nathan asked.

Nathan could see her? Just in case, Ulla spoke out loud. "I'm on the Council House porch, doing the mind-seeing Thom asked for."

Thom blinked. "Starfighter, you're doing that projecting

thing the Hjralma do." *Don't move but be aware you look like you're sitting in midair.*

"You're talking out loud," she said, amazed, "and I can hear you."

"And we can hear you." Nathan was getting over his initial astonishment. "What did you see?"

Oh. The view Ulla had shared with Thom and Dmytro was no use to Nathan. "The Gate you pushed over the edge is smashed, but it must have had enough engine left for them to send robots and repair parts through," she said. "They're almost finished re—"

They watched, speechless, as four robots, rotors whirring, lifted the repaired Gate over their heads and flew toward the spot where it had originally been.

Nate, Thom, and Dmytro fired. At least two of their bullets glanced off the Gate's protective force field. Both camdeer knelt as Thom and Dmytro dumped all nonessential gear from their saddles onto the ground, remounted, and rode hell-bent up the mountain. Nathan opened a dropped saddlebag, grabbed a small package, and scrambled up the ridge behind them, rifle in hand.

Ulla changed position again, dodging a tree while she went for more altitude. She could see the Gate from where she hovered.

Stay in the treetops. The Yotne cannot harm you if you keep your projection thin enough to let branches pass through.

Fripp? Ulla waved her arm through a branch; it passed through like the arm of a ghost.

You have the correct idea, Child. Be no more present on the mountain than you already are.

Ulla would have appreciated hearing some finer points of this business.

Stay grounded where your body is.

Where was Fripp?

Landfall. I cannot coach you now; we have much to do here.

Of course. Somebody had to keep a lid on the Dwellers in New Vatersay.

* * *

Olwyn Dara Wittber-Argeles! Dmytro Robson, Alliance

Flint Clan, linking for Thom Yensson at Bald Mountain.

Snug in her room at the Pordenone Hotel, Olwyn rolled over in bed.

Guild Member! Wake up! The man's telepathic voice had an odd cadence to it.

She opened her eyes. It was still dark outside, or at least as dark as it ever got on Newcastle's posh and brightly lit Landfall Square.

Olwyn here. She stumbled out of bed, put on her spectacles, turned on the lights, and grabbed a notebook and pencil. She wasn't about to use her readpad and expose this conversation on the hotel's primitive comm network.

Thom. Yotne robots have repaired their tactical Gate on Bald Mountain and moved it to its original position. We expect Dwellers soon.

Olwyn. Electronics are working there?

Thom. Yes, though this may be intermittent. Flint's reactivating the Ring.

She overheard him, or maybe Dmytro, direct a camdeer at a fork in the path. They were riding, then, and fast. That explained their thoughts' rhythm.

Well, shit. *Olwyn. What is Lieutenant Thorsdaughter's status?*

Thom. She is well and is under orders to remain in camp.

That was one worry taken care of. *Olwyn. Does SpaceCom Headquarters know?*

Thom. Yes. The Ring party and Flint Clan Council are linked with Levi Dirkson at your HQ through Maribet. Recommend you go to Headquarters immediately.

Olwyn. Will do. Thank you.

The comm panel on her wall beeped for attention. Headquarters. She crossed the room, turned off the panel's video pickup, and pressed Answer. "Guild Member Wittber-Argeles here. Working, please stand by."

What else did she need to know from the men on Bald Mountain? *Olwyn. Have you notified Mr. Craig Eselgroth, SpaceCom Rescue Service?*

Thom. Yes.

Olwyn. Thank you. On my way. The link dissolved.

Olwyn addressed the comm panel. "Guild Member here."

By the time the spacer on the other end finished reciting the recall order, Olwyn was dressed.

Heya, Olwyn. Skuli here.

Olwyn headed for the bathroom. *You heard, then.*

Yes. Through his ears, she picked up the sound of an unfamiliar ground vehicle starting. *Want a ride to HQ?*

Yes, please.

I'll be in front of the hotel in five minutes.

She grabbed a jacket and her readpad, locked her door, and tiptoed downstairs to the hotel's entrance hall. At the buffet outside the closed dining room, she got in line behind a handful of yawning SpaceCom officers. She boxed up fruit, boiled eggs, and pastry to go. Skuli drove up in a Trade Ministry staff car as she fastened the lid on a cup of coffee.

* * *

Ulla sat her projection among the branches of a tall tree, near the place on Bald Mountain where the trail to the Yotne Gate met the Ancients' road, and watched the Yotne robots make final adjustments. Mind-moving was no use—the Yotne psi shield held firm.

Granny Kate and Dean Gregson pelted down the road and ducked into the underbrush beneath Ulla's perch.

Ulla waved down to them. *Heya.*

Holy shit! You really are a spinner! Exclamations notwithstanding, Dean lay still, quiet, and flat behind a stickerbush, watching and listening.

Heya, Starfighter. Kate eased into position about a meter away from Dean.

They waited.

Dean rolled sideways and got behind a boulder. *Kate, can you mind-talk at this distance?*

Yes, thanks.

Ulla cruised her projection through the treetop for a better view and found a perch where she could see into the Gate's yawning entrance. She was dimly aware that somebody, back in camp, had shoved a bannock with molasses-nut spread into her right hand and a mug of coffee into her left. She set the mug down on the Council House porch and spread her hand on its smooth wood flooring. Fripp had said to stay grounded. Ulla stretched, then hopped down and sat on the ground. She ate and drank. Firmly established, she returned her projection to the treetop across from the Yotne Gate.

Lights winked on inside the Gate. A stack of beams appeared; it took almost no time for the robots to use them to bridge the chasm. Ulla poked at them with mind-moving, but they, and the bridge, lay maddeningly inside the Gate's psi shield. She longed to put a bullet or six through every last one of those robots.

Wheet-sproiiing! A rifle round glanced off the Yotne force field. Ulla's projection—and all four robots—turned to find the source; Nathan disappeared among boulders on the opposite ridge.

They needn't waste their energy on the bridge. Eventually, anybody who came out of that Gate would have to leave its shielded bubble.

Waiting sucked.

* * *

Despite the heightened alert status at Headquarters, Skuli had no trouble getting the Trade Ministry's shiny sedan past the guards at the front gate. He pulled into a reserved parking space with a charging tile.

Olwyn got out, brushed crumbs from her shirt, and retrieved her coffee. *This is the Alliance Trade Minister's parking space.*

Skuli grinned. *This is his alternate staff car.*

They jogged inside through the biometrics station and up the stairs toward the command post, where a guard stopped them at the door. A man whose collar lay open to display a distinctive triangular blue tattoo sat in a chair on the guard's left.

The man's eyes twinkled just a bit. *Heya, Guild Member, Skuli.* He gestured thumbs-up and the guard stepped aside.

Skuli nodded to the soulslayer. *Morning, Aden. Caught any Dwellers?*

Not inside. We got one at the front gate about an hour ago. Host was River Pack; he woke up right away.

Skuli reached for the door handle. *Does Matti know?*

The soulslayer nodded. *The host had an outstanding arrest warrant. Matti's interrogating him now. Then he* turned his attention to a group of spacers waiting behind Skuli and Olwyn.

Skuli opened the door. "After you, Guild Member."

She stepped inside. *River Pack. Are they a Newcastle crime family or from farther down the coast?*

Newcastle. Skuli followed her into the command post. *Matti Brown—he's the detective you met at the soulslayer meeting a couple of weeks ago—spends his working life chasing after them.*

Well. That was interesting. But it would have to wait. The Alliance's mind-talker at the comm desk was barely keeping up with a slew of links.

Morning, Levi. Olwyn set her things down on the console next to his and skimmed through the stack of paper notes and sketches he'd made. "I can take some links."

He looked up from his notetaking. "Thanks, Guild Member. Get briefed first. If General Zhou doesn't need you, I could use help on the Bald Mountain piece." *All hell is busting loose in west Landfall.*

* * *

Inside the Yotne Gate on Bald Mountain, lights flickered. The robots stopped abruptly, paused, and resumed their work, lugging at half-speed.

Maribet's voice sounded clear in Ulla's head. *Gib and Hanni unpacked the Ring; they're singing it up now.*

Ulla sent her projection on a quick jaunt up the hill. Around the first bend in the road, the Flint Clan adepts had the Ring out on the ground. If it had stopped electronics from working before, it likely would again.

Dweller! Dean's voice jerked Ulla's attention back to her treetop.

Three men emerged from the Gate.

Wait. Wait...

The men crossed the bridge. A beam of light shot from Granny Kate's empty, outstretched hand, hit one, and laid him flat. *Dweller gone. Host is stunned.* Kate rolled sideways and hid behind a different bush as a bullet ripped through the one she'd been hiding behind. Ulla was impressed. Where had the peaceable woman learned that?

Kate dropped another intruder with another

improbable-looking light beam. *My grandparents were in the Squatters' War. They taught us well.*

Ulla did what Kate did. Curiously, no light betrayed her projection's position. She zapped another Dweller and watched a beam of light spring from the base of the ridge where Nathan had been—the ridge between this location and her physical body, in front of Council House. Killing Dwellers felt oddly familiar; Ulla put that down to Kate's teaching skills.

Even as the Gate flickered, Dweller-ridden intruders kept coming. Ulla lost count; she and Kate may have missed a few. Each time she killed a Dweller, she lost a little more energy. In that way, the Dark Gift was like any other—the human body had its limits.

The light inside the Gate steadied and brightened, illuminating Dweller-ridden fighter after Dweller-ridden fighter.

Kate nailed another Dweller. She must have lost concentration as she rolled sideways because instead of taking cover, she came to rest in the open. Her body jerked as a Dweller's bullet hit her in the head.

Ulla concentrated on killing the Dwellers pouring out of the Gate. Where the fuck was Thom?

A Dweller shot Dean.

Ulla put everything she had into killing Dwellers, until sudden pain bloomed in her chest and she found herself sprawled on the ground in front of Council House.

The Council House door flew open. Two Council members emerged.

One, a woman, jumped off the porch and put an arm around Ulla. "Are you all right?"

Ulla was still taking inventory. "I think so." Eyes, ears, hands, feet, brains—no bleeding. She took a deep breath and almost passed out from pain in the right side of her chest. She managed to point and say, "Hurts here," before closing her eyes and surrendering to extreme fatigue.

People gathered around them. Ulla was dimly aware of Ingeborg and others helping her up off the cold ground onto a folded blanket on the porch. Pain tore through her chest when they lifted her.

"Starfighter, what happened?" Ingeborg probed the spot with gentle fingers, and with her mind.

"No idea. Dweller shot at my projection." Was that

what Fripp had tried to warn her about? Ulla started to tremble. Then she blacked out.

She woke when Kamna sat her up and propped a cushion behind her back. Ulla started shaking again. "Oh, gods. Kate and Dean—"

Kamna tucked a warm blanket around her. "Be still."

Ulla tried to relax. "Where's Ingeborg?"

"Busy."

Oh, no. "Did they...attack the camp too?"

"Not so far." Kamna held up a cup of water for Ulla to drink. "Ingeborg is getting ready."

Chapter Twenty
The View from Headquarters

Inside the command post, Olwyn and Skuli watched the briefer change the scale on his map display. "Yotne Dwellers confirmed in three places. Island called New Vatersay, western Landfall Archipelago." He changed the scale again to show the wreckage. "SpaceCom Atmospheric Forces took out two Gates there. The locals and some trol—uh, Elders—have them bottled up on the island."

"Flint Clan briefed us while we were driving," said Olwyn. "Where are the Bald Mountain Dwellers coming from?"

The briefer shifted the display to an overhead image of Newcastle. He zoomed in on the warehouse district near the river. "There's a Gate inside this warehouse. Alliance Balanced Trade Enforcement agents—most of them adepts—are working with soulslayers and the Newcastle City Guard. They expect to mount an attack any minute."

"Is that the warehouse the Newcastle City Guard identified?" Skuli opened his pocket notebook.

The briefer nodded. "The Guard don't advertise the fact, but their lead organized crime investigator is a soulslayer. A few weeks ago, he noticed something was off but found nothing unusual there until this morning."

So, it was the warehouse Matti Brown had mentioned in Skuli's ad hoc meeting with the soulslayers about Dwellers. They'd found nothing? Really?

Skuli paused his note-taking. *I was there, Guild Member. The day after you found Dwellers on New Vatersay,* the Newcastle City Guard asked BTE to do a 'routine inspection' at that warehouse. Didn't find a damned thing.

Olwyn settled at the comm station next to Levi. *Olwyn Dara Wittber-Argeles ready.*

The mind-talker spared her a glance. *Request you connect with Maribet. She's with Flint Clan Council. Link with Dmytro Robson too. He's on Bald Mountain with Thom Yensson and Nathan Steves.*

Olwyn found Dmytro, who did not acknowledge as he was occupied. She reached out to Maribet next.

Levi shoved pencils and a paper logbook from his console to Olwyn's. "Be alert for other On'oi messaging from Hoffnung," he said quietly. "Balanced Trade Enforcement and Council of Chieftains are active."

Maribet. Request you monitor Flint Clan Ring party on Bald Mountain. Chieftain has another conversation; I'll be back shortly.

Olwyn. Will do. She sent her consciousness up the mountain from Maribet's location. Thom and Dmytro were linked with each other; she found Nathan's buzzing psi blocker nearby. Dmytro was spotting Dwellers for Thom to kill. No wonder he'd been unavailable. She ranged outward and cringed at Dweller-presence. She had a brief impression of a slew of unconscious humans and a few who had recently awakened, but she wasn't about to hijack anybody's eyes just to see more clearly.

Only a little way uphill, she found Hanni Rubensdaughter singing challenge-and-response syllables with a man Olwyn didn't know. A third person stood guard.

Olwyn Wittber, Bailey-Duran Coalition Headquarters. Maribet asked me to monitor; request your permission. She detected relief on the other end.

Uh, Rilla Marcsdaughter. Yes, please.

Will I disturb the singers if I monitor them?

Unlikely. The guard sounded so very young. *Just don't...say anything while they're working.*

Olwyn looked in on Hanni, who was linked with someone, or something, else. Capraglamas, maybe? A couple of Guild papers mentioned them, but Olwyn had never seen capraglamas in action before. Fascinating. She listened quietly as the two Guardians sang and activated the Ring.

An audible curse word snapped Olwyn's attention

back to the command post. Across the table from her, a man stared at a blank screen. The other screens were working.

"West Hoffnung?" Olwyn asked out loud.

He nodded.

"They just activated the Bald Mountain Ring."

Olwyn turned her attention back to Bald Mountain, to Hanni. Except that a Dweller had latched on to Hanni's mind, intent on singing the Ring back down. Olwyn checked the male Ring singer; he was Dweller-ridden too.

Olwyn watched, powerless, as Hanni's mind fought the Dweller, which apparently found its new host too difficult. The Dweller marched Hanni's body right off the cliff and migrated to the young woman who'd been on guard duty. Dweller-ridden, she and the man sang.

Olwyn didn't sense capraglamas anymore. She did sense, through what she could still read in the Ring singers' minds, the Ring's power fading.

Dmytro Robson! Olwyn Wittber! Respond!

Dmytro. We know! On our way!

She checked; he and Thom Yensson were at least half a kilometer away—far, far outside soulslayer range.

Olwyn. Permission to monitor.

Dmytro. Sure. Just be the fuck quiet!

Through Dmytro's eyes, she watched the two camdeer cover distance. Fast as they were, they weren't fast enough.

Dmytro and Thom rounded a switchback, slowed, jumped off into the bushes, and sent their camdeer running away downhill just in time to watch Dweller-ridden Gib and Rilla, with a man wearing City clothing, carry the Ring across the bridge and into the Gate.

Thom threw a beam of light through the Gate entrance, then another and another until there were no more Dwellers.

Rilla and Gib reappeared at the Gate entrance, dragging the Ring between them. Gib looked up and saw Thom and Dmytro.

"Take cover! Gate's deploying!"

Olwyn dared not ask.

Thom and Dmytro jumped, rolled, and slid backward into a gully. Olwyn watched brush pass by Dmytro's face; dirt flew.

Then a loud boom and a lot more flying dirt. Olwyn felt

Dmytro hug the ground. A few small rocks bounced past. Then it was quiet.

Dmytro Robson, Olwyn Wittber. Status?
Dmytro. Thom and I are alive. Ring's gone.

Chapter Twenty-One
Aftermath

Gradually, Ulla stopped trembling. She did not black out again. Her chest and shoulder burned like fire, and she was exhausted from so much psi activity. Breathing was harder than usual, but, hey, she was still alive!

Then she coughed and found herself curled up on the porch floorboards in a ball of pain.

"Starfighter." Kamna steadied her, helped quiet her coughing fit, and pulled her back to a sitting position on the blanket. The young woman's gentle voice was every bit as authoritative as Hanni's or Ingeborg's.

Or Fripp's.

Ulla leaned back against the cushion. "You'll go far, kid."

Kamna, preoccupied with—mind-talking?—did not answer.

Ulla didn't have the energy to pry.

Kamna looked up. "Starfighter, can you walk?"

"Sure." Ulla got halfway up, stifled a cough, and plopped down unceremoniously.

"I'll take that as a no." Kamna's face got that "mind-talking" look again. Soon after, Ingeborg and a man moved Ulla across the square to the bathhouse, onto a sleeping pad in the laundry room, with pillows arranged against the wall at her back.

Ulla looked up at the row of washing machines. "Why here?"

Ingeborg turned her attention from the big metal

cylinder bolted to the wall. "It's out of the weather, clean, and has running water." *I hope it's—*

Ulla couldn't make out the rest of Ingeborg's mind-talk. Putting two thoughts together was hard.

"I was afraid of that." Ingeborg adjusted a gauge on top of the cylinder and connected a hose. She crossed to the main doorway and shouted to somebody outside. "We've got to use it! NO fire, anywhere near here!" She turned around. The distant look crossed her face again. Concentrating hard, Ingeborg readjusted gauges on top of the cylinder, fastened a small mask on the free end of the hose, and popped it over Ulla's nose and mouth.

Coherent thought came back, just like that. *Oxygen?*

Ingeborg nodded. "Tank's from the welding setup in the machine shop," she said. "Took me forever to find the connectors in Hanni's gear."

You did beautifully, dear.

Who was that?

Heya, Starfighter. I'm Emli Clarksdaughter.

"Flint Clan's senior healer," said Ingeborg. "Chieftain's wife. She talked me through the oxygen setup."

Ulla knew for a fact that Dev, Thom, and Nathan shared a bachelor tent. Where was Emli?

Chisos. The town Flint Clan had set off from, weeks ago. *We can't all be on trek.*

Ingeborg looked out the window. *Emli, will you monitor the starfighter? I have to go.* She met young Wat Henrikson at the door and pointed to a sleeping pad Kamna had rolled out next to Ulla's. "Sit there. Kamna, stay with Wat and Ulla." She stepped outside.

Wat limped across the floor. He held his side and tried not to wince as he sat down.

"Heya, Wat." Talking didn't work well with the mask so Ulla switched to mind-talk. *Cracked rib?*

"Ryan says so. Told me to come see Ingeborg."

Ulla heard footsteps and voices outside but couldn't make out words. Even though everyone's thoughts were shielded, Ingeborg's stress leaked through.

Two sets of heavy, coordinated footsteps went away. A lighter set—Ingeborg's maybe—crunched across the gravel to the bathhouse door. Then retching, a flush, more footsteps, water running in the washbasin.

Footsteps crunched on gravel again, and Ingeborg

came back in the laundry room door. She knelt on the floor next to Wat. "Piet's dead."

He nodded.

Ingeborg reached for Wat's hand. He allowed her to take it. "Ryan said to tell you he saw the whole thing. He told me you did very well."

"But Piet's dead."

"He was linked with Hanni and the capraglamas. When the Dweller got Hanni, the capraglamas bolted." Ingeborg looked Wat in the eye. "Once they knocked Piet down, there was nothing anyone could have done." She paused. "Ryan says you saved a lot of lives—and the pen—when you opened the gate to let the capraglamas run."

"Gate faces away from camp; they just ran and ran." Young Wat tried to hide a sniffle. "You should have seen the camdeer rounding the capraglamas up—like giant sheepdogs. One camdeer stood and guarded Piet, and another stood over me till Ryan could get help. Wouldn't let any other stock near us."

"Really?" Ingeborg's hand tightened on Wat's.

He almost smiled. "I always knew camdeer were underrated."

Ingeborg took a deep breath. "Let me have a look at those ribs of yours. Where does it hurt?"

* * *

Ulla must have drifted off. She woke to the sound of a rotorcraft landing very close by.

Ingeborg met someone at the door. A man in a SpaceCom Atmospheric Forces flight suit came inside. They spoke quietly.

A Guardian wearing City clothing and On'oi clan earrings came in and set down something big on the other side of the bank of washing machines. A flight-suited woman followed with more gear.

The Guardian sauntered over to Ulla. *Heya, Starfighter. We finally meet in person.*

Was this Thom's friend who worked at the Trade Ministry? Ulla wondered if he used mind-talk so she would recognize his telepathic voice. *Are you Skuli Branson?*

"Yep," he said. "But I'm Balanced Trade Enforcement's liaison with SpaceCom; I help out at the Trade Ministry when I can." He grinned. "I've been keeping Thom out of trouble since he was six years old."

Ulla doubted that last statement. But Skuli seemed like a good guy.

Somebody in a flight suit bent over Ulla. The woman's insignia meant "Rescue Force" and "Medic." "Hold out your arm, please, and make a fist." She cleaned the crook of Ulla's elbow and stuck in a big needle with a contraption on it.

Ulla winced. *What's the needle for?*

The medic taped the needle in place and attached an IV tube to the contraption. She dug into a bag, found a diagnostic bracelet, and fastened it around Ulla's wrist.

You're in pain, Ingeborg said. *Now that technology works, your mind needn't be clear.*

???

No further need to use your cognitive ability as an index of your O2 level.

The medic glanced at the readout on Ulla's cuff. "When did you eat last?"

"Breakfast. And a snack, later." Ulla pulled off the mask and said it again.

"Hypoglycemic too." The medic stuck the mask back on Ulla's face. "Mr. Eselgroth, grab me a—"

Ulla lost the thread of conversation among a confusion of letters and acronyms. Having finished with Ulla, the medic turned her attention to young Wat.

"That's a welding tank." The man named Eselgroth studied the assembly Ingeborg had put together. He glanced at the readout on Ulla's diagnostic cuff and nodded approvingly. "Purpose-made adapter. Nice."

Ulla's mind fuzzed up. She could tell the man used a psi blocker, but she couldn't punch through it. "You're him."

"What?"

"Eselgroth." Ulla couldn't talk in the damn mask. She pulled it off. "Pink Wabbit."

"Wait a minute." He stuck the mask back on her face. "Let me help you." Mr. Eselgroth went around behind the washing machines and returned with a largeish kit. He fished out one end of a slender hose from the kit's main compartment, rummaged in an outside pocket until he found a loop of similar hose material with a pair of little protruding tubes, and connected things. Then he pulled the mask off her face and stuck the tubes up her nose, securing them with a loop of hose behind each of her ears. He shut off the valve on the big tank. "Might as well save Flint Clan's oxygen. We have plenty."

The little tubes were better than the mask. But he might have asked first.

"You're welcome." Eselgroth studied gauges on the kit. He checked the diagnostic cuff again, nodded, and sat on the floor beside her. "Now, where were we? Pink Wabbit?"

"Authentication, weeks ago. The stuffed toy Admiral Rosen told you about, that I stashed behind the HVAC grille when I was an ensign?" Another coughing fit threatened. She managed just in time to say, "Don't you ever tell another soul."

"No worries, Lieutenant." He put an arm around her shoulders while she coughed and helped her settle back on the pillow when she was ready. "Your secret's safe with me."

* * *

"Up you come, Lieutenant." The medic's voice woke Ulla.

She blinked. When had she gone to sleep? Or maybe this was part of the fuzziness that had taken hold of her mind.

Maribet held the oxygen kit and IV bag while the medic and Mr. Eselgroth helped Ulla onto a litter. Young Wat was arguing with Skuli and Ingeborg that he could walk just fine, thank you. Skuli and Ingeborg won.

They carried Ulla outside behind Wat; she shut her eyes against bright sunlight. Swaying. Footsteps on gravel. Voices. She hadn't meant to leave Flint Clan this way.

They set the litter down. She opened her eyes and saw a SpaceCom tactical Gate. Had they brought it on the rotorcraft?

A shadow passed between her and the sun—a man's face, backlit and unrecognizable. He put a hand on her good shoulder. "Starfighter."

Though her Gifts had deserted her, she recognized Thom's hand. "You're all right, then," she said.

He nodded. "Nathan and Dmytro are all right too."

"That's good." Ulla blinked and waited for the world to stop spinning. "What about…"

"Stelle?" he asked. There was a long pause. "Sorry. I forgot your Gift is shot. It's the poppy juice." He moved slightly, and the sun was back in Ulla's eyes. "Stelle's in good hands."

Poppy juice was supposed to make her not care. It wasn't working. "Did she…"

"See, with her Gifts?" Thom reached for Ulla's hand. "No. Claudia was watching her; she distracted her two girls and Stelle through the whole thing."

Just as well, Ulla decided, for Claudia. "Good." She tried to form a question, and her brain just couldn't.

"Stelle is with Claudia, Henrik, and their girls. Piet's parents are on their way here from Mountain's summer pasture."

One set of Stelle's grandparents, at least, was close by. Ulla's heart ached for them.

Two men emerged from the Gate and joined them. Maribet handed Ulla's medical paraphernalia to the one wearing a SpaceCom utility uniform and stepped aside with the other, who wore civilian clothes.

Ulla had just enough brains left to wonder what Maribet was doing.

"She's briefing her temporary replacement," Thom said. "She told me you convinced her to go back to Newcastle and take a chance with her lover."

"That's good." Ulla was so proud of Maribet. She grinned. "Are you coming to Newcastle too?"

Thom shook his head, gestured at the activity around them. A swarm of City men, Flint Clan members, and On'oi she had never seen before were erecting a tent, setting up equipment, and, wonder of wonders, talking over conventional comm. Climbing gear, bulging packs, and all sorts of equipment sat in the open, waiting to be organized and used.

"Who are all those people?"

"Tell you later." He squeezed her hand. "For now, Da and the Council of Chieftains want me to ride herd on them."

"Gate's ready!" A man in a SpaceCom Ground Forces uniform tapped at an operations console. The medic and Mr. Eselgroth picked up Ulla's litter.

Thom gave Maribet a quick hug. He looked down at Ulla, hesitated for the merest second, and planted a chaste kiss on her forehead. "See you in Newcastle, Starfighter."

PART 2

The Hidden Spinner

Chapter Twenty-Two
Newcastle

The solid doors of the Gate terminal slid open on a paved area next to Newcastle Hospital's emergency room. Hospital personnel met them with two rolling gurneys.

"Do what Cousin Skuli says!" Ingeborg's voice? Oh. She was talking to young Wat, not Ulla.

Cousin Skuli? Ulla's drugged mind decided that On'oi had genealogy databases where their brains ought to be. Ingeborg stepped back inside the Gate with Mr. Eselgroth and the SpaceCom medic. All three disappeared.

A man with a clipboard met Ulla and Maribet at the emergency room entrance. "Name?" He spoke City English.

Ulla hesitated. He repeated the question in Standard. The word was almost identical.

"Ursula Marie Thorsdaughter."

Maribet looked sideways at her.

The clerk checked off a square on a piece of paper. "Chaperone?" he asked, in Standard.

"What?" Ulla, feeling no pain, sat up and coughed. The clerk stepped back.

Maribet stepped up. "Maribet, uh, Elliot."

The clerk blinked, stood up a little straighter, and checked off another square.

What the hell? And why did Ulla need a chaperone?

Maribet whispered in her ear. "Newcastle law, Starfighter. When a minor or a female of any age requests medical help, a chaperone's required."

Ulla whispered back. "That's batshit!"

"Don't say that out loud, not here." Maribet squared her shoulders and smiled pleasantly at the clerk. When he left, she bent down and whispered to Ulla again. "Ursula Marie? Really?"

"My legal name," Ulla whispered back. "I thought you didn't use your birth surname."

"I don't—not normally." Maribet sighed. "It has its uses."

Later, Ulla would have vague memories of a SpaceCom flight surgeon and an exam, getting a room with a bed, a young Newcastle woman—a soulslayer, maybe—taking Maribet's place as chaperone, Maribet saying goodbye.

All Ulla wanted to do was sleep.

* * *

The next time she woke, it was nighttime.

A young Newcastle woman looked up from her knitting. "You're awake. Good." She spoke Standard with a faint City accent.

Who was she?

The woman set down the little sweater she was working on. "I'm Yasmin Tully. Thom's aunt asked me to chaperone."

Thom's aunt? The On'oi extended family network must have kicked into high gear.

"I'm a soulslayer. Young Wat Henrikson's in the room next door; his chaperone is my spotter." Yasmin stood up. "The spotter's Ed Jeppeson, from Trade Ministry Security. He says hello."

Who was Ed Jeppeson? Ulla tried to reach out with mind-talk and couldn't.

"No worries; your Gifts will come back when the poppy juice wears off." Yasmin smiled. "He says the two of you met last week during your mind-talk lesson."

Ulla closed her eyes and thought as hard as the drugs would let her. Maribet had had her link several times with different people at the Trade Ministry—Ed must be one of the Balanced Trade Enforcement agents who worked there.

Yasmin unbuttoned her blouse and pulled the collar aside to show Ulla her blue triangle. "Never in anger."

"Uh, never in anger." Was Ulla supposed to show off

her own tattoo? She tugged ineffectively at the neckline of her hospital gown, which was tied in the back.

"No need to show me your mark." Yasmin picked up a clipboard from a purpose-made rack at the foot of the bed. A blue triangle overlaid with the words *Matthias Carroll Memorial Society* in City English lettering was printed in the upper-right corner of the top sheet of paper.

Ulla sat up. "I'll bet that frightens the staff."

"Hospital staff are hard to scare." Yasmin grinned and put the clipboard back. "Besides, they know the Fourniers and the Tullys. We're stubborn patients, but none of us has ever slain a single soul."

"Huh?" Glittering conversation was not Ulla's forte at the moment.

"I was born in this building," Yasmin said, "as were my children."

"You're Newcastlers then."

"Yes—though we Fourniers are Second Wave. The Tullys have always been Newcastlers." Yasmin stood, picked up a covered plate from a warming tray, and found flatware and a napkin. "Want supper?"

"Thanks."

Yasmin removed the cover to reveal roast chicken, puréed vegetable soup, and boiled potatoes. She set the plate within Ulla's reach.

Ulla wasn't actually hungry. She ate anyway. "Second Wave?" she asked, between bites.

"My father's parents immigrated from Quebec." Yasmin returned to her chair and picked up her knitting. "My uncle Aden was Thom Yensson's first soulslayer mentor. When Thom lived in town with his aunt and uncle, we kids hung out together."

In Newcastle, then, which made this woman part of Thom's extended City family.

Yasmin paused to count stitches. "Thom's ma died when he was a baby. His da—"

"Yens Peacemaker?"

Yasmin nodded. "Yens Govinderson, yes. He took it hard. Padraic and Renata took Thom in while his da threw himself into politics. When the Peacemaker remarried, Thom went back to live with his da and stepma. But even then, Thom was back most summers for several weeks between the end of trek and the start of the school year."

"Back up a minute." Thom had told Ulla most of these things, but the remnants of poppy juice in her system made the conversation hard to follow. "Padraic and Renata are Thom's aunt and uncle, right?"

Yasmin nodded again. "Yes. Padraic's the Alliance Trade Minister; they live in private quarters in the big Trade Ministry building on Landfall Square."

That made sense. "Thom's stepma—she's Ingeborg's mother, right?"

Yasmin grinned. "She's exactly who that family needed; I think you'll like her."

Ulla finished her soup and stacked the bowl and spoon on her empty plate. She and Thom weren't that close. Why did everyone assume otherwise?

Chapter Twenty-Three
The End of the Day

On Newcastle's Landfall Square, Olwyn emerged wearily from the headquarters shuttle onto the foot of the grand steps at the Pordenone Hotel. By the time she'd relinquished her post, a slew of Alliance Balanced Trade Enforcement agents, the Newcastle City Guard, and who knew how many other sorts of cop had all arrived at Bald Mountain. SpaceCom and the BTE folks were easy enough to work with, but she was done relaying for local City men whose first experience this was with telepathic communication.

The Council of Chieftains had arranged with Flint Clan to put Thom Yensson in charge of coordinating all of them on-site. She did not envy him the job.

Olwyn checked at the hotel's front desk to see if anyone had left her a delightfully anachronistic pen-and-paper message. Nobody had.

The Pordenone's bar was still open. Newcastle City women did not drink in public, but Newcastle City barkeepers didn't seem to mind taking money from offworlder women who did. She sat down at a table in a dark corner, ordered a whiskey, and stared into space.

"May I join you?" Skuli Branson stood by her table.

"Sure." She waved toward the other chair. "Please, sit."

He took off his jacket and sat. "Thank you."

He ordered a beer. Neither of them spoke.

The time came for a second round. He bought.

She finally broke the silence. "What brings you here?"

"I thought you might want company." *You were up close and personal with Dwellers today.*

"Thank you." *I was monitoring Hanni Rubensdaughter when...when...* She couldn't say it.

A Dweller possessed her and marched her off a cliff.

There had been no time to regroup afterward. Olwyn had managed comm between Headquarters and Thom, Nathan, and Dmytro, who'd had to subdue the Dweller survivors—mostly River Pack enforcers from Newcastle whose own personae were arguably no better than the Dwellers that had possessed them.

She'd handled the initial comm to dispatch a medical evacuation rotorcraft to Flint Clan's summer pasture for Ulla Thorsdaughter and another member of Flint Clan. She'd helped coordinate the team of climbers who had recovered Hanni's body. There'd been at least two forensics teams at the Bald Mountain Gate site, and each agency had its own logistics organization and its own agenda. She'd served as the comm link so everybody could negotiate with Flint Clan, from whose summer encampment the investigators would have to come and go.

Local conventional comm had gone to hell when the partially activated Ring materialized inside a warehouse the City Guard had surrounded. The Ring had missed the warehouse Gate by at least three meters and materialized inside a wall of concrete and rebar.

That had to have been ugly.

An hour or so into that, a research group from Newcastle University had managed to put a shield around the malfunctioning Ring and stopped it from hogging the electromagnetic spectrum. Thanks be. If they hadn't, Olwyn would still be at work.

At the end of her shift, she'd transmitted General Zhou's summary to the regional SpaceCom Headquarters on Reynoso Tres—in which she'd revisited her entire day, with added carnage in western Landfall.

Her hand trembled as she set down her empty glass. *Mustn't shake, not in public. Unprofessional.*

Nonsense. You are a human being. Skuli covered her hand with his. *For all that your Guild treats its members like racehorses.*

Olwyn was pretty sure he hadn't meant for her to hear his last sentence. When the server came back, Olwyn covered her glass and asked for water.

Skuli and Olwyn sat in silence. Finally, he asked, "Have you had dinner?"

Olwyn shook her head.

Skuli reached for a menu. "Eat. I'm buying."

"Thank you." After today's marathon telepathy session, she was starving.

Chapter Twenty-Four
Hospital

Ulla woke at daybreak the next morning. The stuff the paramedic had given her yesterday had worn off. Her chest and shoulder hurt, but her mind was clear. She tried scanning with psi and found Skuli Branson in the room next door.

Heya, Starfighter.
Heya. Dweller-spotting?
Yep. Giving Ed a break.

Clear mind was good. She didn't want any more poppy juice. Ulla spotted her boots next to a sack in a corner. Her clothes, maybe? Where was her sidearm?

No worries, Starfighter. Skuli again. *Thom took your pistol for safekeeping before they Gated you here.*

Ulla leaned back against the pillows. The oxygen thing was still in her nose, but they'd untethered her other body parts and traded the paramedics' tactical diagnostic cuff on her left forearm for the hospital's sturdier one.

On a fold-out bed under the windows, Yasmin Tully stirred. What had her night been like, away from her family? Ulla could barely imagine the chores piling up in the young mother's absence. Yasmin had said her husband and her mother had things under control, but still . . .

The door opened. "Oh, you're awake!" A young man brought in two breakfast trays, stacked one on another.

"Shh!" Ulla gestured toward Yasmin. "She's still asleep!"

The warming unit from last night was still there.

He powered it up, set Yasmin's breakfast tray on it, and placed Ulla's tray on a rolling table that he pulled across the bed in front of her.

As soon as he left, Ulla pushed the table away. Thanks be, the oxygen kit was on wheels and portable. She got out of bed and found the toilet. She washed her face and hands, sighed at the face she saw in the mirror, and wheeled the tank back to her bed. She pulled the rolling table close, ate her mediocre breakfast, then slept.

* * *

She woke again when somebody knocked. Yasmin, who was now up, bathed, and wearing fresh clothing, answered the door.

"Good morning!" A SpaceCom flight surgeon strode in, followed by a tall woman who greeted Yasmin as if they were already acquainted.

"Morning." Ulla sat up carefully to avoid tweaking the painful spot inside her chest. She didn't cough. That was good. Now that the poppy juice had worn off, coughing really hurt.

The woman held out her hand. "I'm Olwyn." *Glad to meet you in person.* They shook hands. "Ingeborg Yensdaughter insisted I come with the flight doc on today's visit." The Guild rep grinned. *As though they could have kept me away.*

The flight surgeon held out his hand. "You may not remember me from last night. I'm Dr. Lym."

"Vaguely." Ulla shook his hand. "Things were, uh, fuzzy."

Olwyn got out of the doctor's way and sat down with Yasmin, who finished eating breakfast while Ulla dropped the hospital gown off her shoulders. The flight doc poked, prodded, and stuck a cold audio pickup on Ulla's bare back and chest. Then he fished a readpad out of his pocket and tapped at it. Ulla pulled the gown up and retied the laces as best she could.

He picked up the clipboard from the foot of her bed, flipped up a couple of pages, and wrote something with a pen. Once he'd read through all the notes, he shook his head. "Have you ever been shot with a projectile weapon?"

"Um, no." Had her projection been too substantial

for safety, as Fripp had warned her on Bald Mountain? "Someone did try, kind of." Ulla squirmed, tucking the drafty hospital gown more securely around her. How to explain? That her body had been safely in front of Council House when the Dweller shot at her projection on Bald Mountain? That she had no idea what really happened?

"Your extremely robust Hjralma-style astral projection got shot," Olwyn said, bailing her out. "The On'oi traditional healers say that because your body was several kilometers away at the time, you have pulmonary contusions and a wad of stuck magic, instead of—much worse." *Ingeborg's exact words included "sucking chest wound" and "half a liver."*

Ulla blinked. "Stuck magic?"

The Guild rep sighed. "I can't pronounce the local word for it."

Dr. Lym held up his readpad and pointed to a cloudy streak. "Pulmonary contusion is a fancy name for a bruise inside your lung. More than likely, it will resolve on its own." He moved his finger over a bright spot on the image. "There's a part of your lung, at one end of the contusion, that shows up as a blank spot on every image we've taken."

Olwyn nodded. *That's why he invited me.* "Emli Clarksdaughter and Ingeborg both wanted to send you to Castle Chisos."

Ulla shifted pillows so she could sit more comfortably. *As if SpaceCom'd let that fly.*

Exactly. "The On'oi say an injury like yours is rare but not unheard of," Olwyn said. "I recommend you take the Alliance up on their offer."

Ulla pulled the blanket up; she was chilly in the skimpy gown. "What offer?"

"In a day or so, an Elder who is a traditional healer will be in Newcastle," Dr. Lym said. "The Alliance Trade Ministry has offered to put both of you up in their guest quarters."

Ulla chose her words carefully. "You're letting me out of the hospital?"

He shook his head. "I want you here till you can breathe on your own. If you're like most healthy spacers, that won't take long."

Encouraging, but—the only Elder Ulla knew was Fripp. She had reached out, in projection, to Ulla during that last week with Flint Clan, obviously hoping for at least a tentative understanding. Ulla was aware, at least intellectually, that there was more to Fripp than her own recurring nightmare.

But still.

Olwyn confirmed her suspicions. "Elder's name is Fripp. *She and her colleagues are sleeping off what went down in Landfall.*

* * *

The Guild rep had just excused herself and stepped into the hall when a man with Piet's voice poked his head in the door. "Wat?"

He saw Ulla and Dr. Lym. "Oh, sorry, wrong room."

The man wasn't Piet, of course, but he looked a little like him: similar face, same broad shoulders, but thicker in the middle. He had a thinner, graying version of Piet's red hair.

Yasmin stopped counting stitches. "Wat's next door."

"Thanks."

"Wait!" Ulla knew this man—but from where?

Heya, Starfighter.

That voice...she recognized it. *Neal Erikson?* The exhausted soulslayer from the New Vatersay expedition—had that been only the day before yesterday? But there was something else.

"Are you Piet's brother?" Ulla asked. *Hanni didn't tell me you were a soulslayer.*

The ache she picked up from his tired soul spoke for him.

"I'm so sorry for your family's loss." Inadequate words, but she said them anyway.

"Thank you."

Had the man even had a chance to rest up from his adventures in west Landfall?

He stifled a yawn. *Kind of.*

She hadn't meant to project that last thought. His psi was probably strong like Thom's, just very short-range.

That, it is. The ghost of a smile crinkled his face. *No worries, Starfighter; it takes a while to recalibrate after being on poppy juice.*

Ulla's gown tried to strangle her; she tugged at the

corner she'd sat on. *How's your spotter?*

Sean? He's fine. Slept for a full day and a night and woke up claiming he'd figured out how to extend range safely.

That sounded delusional to Ulla.

For Sean? No, for him, that's normal. He's an incurable optimist. "I look forward to getting acquainted, Starfighter," Neal said, "but right now, I need to spring Wat out of here."

"How is he?" Ulla asked.

"Two broken ribs," said Dr. Lym. "Bumps and bruises. Kid's tough." He looked at Neal. "Are you taking him back to his family, at the camp by Bald Mountain?"

"Not right away." Neal shook his head. "He's coming home with me. Ingeborg Yensdaughter wants him to stay in town at least through tomorrow."

Ingeborg would.

That's not the half of it. Aubrey's in full doting aunt mode; she can't wait.

The archaeologist who did your "beer runs" in Landfall?

Yep. Aubrey and Miles Rogers live across the street from me. "Sorry to bother you," Neal said, and left.

* * *

The flight doc had just left when, through the open door, Ulla heard people talking in the hallway. One of them had a psi blocker like Nathan's.

Admiral Rosen, of all people, knocked on the doorframe.

Ulla tried to sit up and look presentable, but something inside her chest chose that moment to make a bid for freedom. Instead of greeting Admiral Rosen with a chipper "Good morning, ma'am," she took a full minute to cough up a wad of goo while attempting to hide how much it hurt.

When the coughing passed, the admiral handed Ulla a glass of water and a hankie.

"Thank you, ma'am." With shaking hands, Ulla wiped her eyes, nose, and mouth. She pretended the basin she'd just spat in did not exist.

Rosen stood next to the bed and waited while Ulla cleaned up. Then, she reached out and gave Ulla a big hug. "So glad you're back!"

"Glad to be back." Ulla inclined her head toward the

open bathroom door. Might the woman want to clean residual cough-slime off her black uniform?

"It's all right, Spider. Guild rep says I can't catch what you have." Rosen smiled. "Please, if you need to rest, rest."

Exhausted, Ulla lay back against the pillows. There was a reason why Rosie's other nickname, never used in her earshot, was "Mother Hen."

"You get well. We need you in the sky. And Starfighter?"

"Yes, ma'am?" Ulla tried to sit up again.

Rosen motioned for her to stay where she was. "Get a haircut."

* * *

Ulla had just dozed off after lunch when someone knocked at the door.

Heya, Starfighter!

Thom! I thought you were at Bald Mountain!

Gated back for a couple of hours. Auntie Renata and I brought goodies.

Yasmin got up and opened the door. "Auntie!"

"Yasmin! You're looking well." An attractive, middle-aged woman set down a large vacuum flask and hugged Yasmin. "Want a break? I'm already signed in as alternate chaperone."

"Thanks so much. Did you bring a soulslayer?"

"Thom's right behind me." Renata set the flask on the counter next to the plate warmer and opened it. "Want coffee before you go?"

"No, thanks. I'll get some at home." Yasmin picked up her jacket. "When do I need to be back?"

"Thom and I can stay for an hour."

Yasmin was out the door and gone.

Thom carried a basket in one hand and a familiar-looking saddlebag in the other. He set the basket down on the rolling table and placed Ulla's saddlebag next to her boots.

He bent down and hugged her. She hugged back. Oh, it was good to see him!

"Good to see you too." *Talk out loud. Auntie's headblind.*

Ulla gave Thom one last squeeze. *Where I'm from, that's called normal.*

"Auntie, this is Ulla Thorsdaughter."

Ulla held out her hand.

"Renata Connersdaughter." They shook hands. "So glad to meet you; Thom's said so many good things about you." The woman's thoughts were protected with an artificial psi blocker.

"Glad to meet you."

Thom got out cups; Renata poured coffee. Ulla rummaged in the basket and found napkins and a bag of pastries. She almost missed the small plates nested in the bottom of the basket. She got those out too.

Renata put pastries on plates. They each took a napkin and dug in.

Ulla pulled the bed covers up around her and rolled the long table under her chin. No need to drop crumbs between the sheets. "This is delicious! Thank you." She licked sweet glaze off her fingers. "How did you know to bring coffee?"

Thom and Renata both laughed.

"In the City-States, they don't think coffee is good for sick people. It's a real problem." Thom drained his cup. "Skuli's on spotter duty outside your door. He and I need to catch up." He disappeared into the hallway.

Renata pulled out a hard cheese, a packet of flatbread, and a tin of dried fruit from the basket. She set them on the little table between the two guest chairs before gathering up dirty plates and napkins to stuff back into the basket. She left the cups out; there was still plenty of coffee in the flask.

Ulla shook crumbs off her coverlet. "What's in the saddlebag?"

Renata smiled. "Clothes and some toiletries. And pajamas."

"Thank you!" Ulla was eager to get rid of the awkward hospital gown, but the clothes she'd arrived in were dirty.

"Do you feel up to taking a shower?"

Ulla swung her legs over the side of the bed. "Do you mind?"

"Not at all." Renata sat down in a guest chair. "If you need help, ask."

Ulla stood up. She would manage.

* * *

Six days later, Ulla smiled politely at the man who delivered her lunch. As soon as he left, she got up and moved her tray to the small table between the guest chairs so she and Yasmin could eat together. The oxygen tank sat unused beside her bed.

Soup again. Ulla liked soup, as a rule, but this hospital stuff was an unabashed purée of last night's steamed vegetables. She had a sandwich with mystery meat, a tired-looking apple, and all the water she could drink.

Yasmin looked up from the lunch she'd packed. *That looks vile.*

Ulla took another bite. The sandwich tasted pretty good. She ate the whole thing and was still hungry, so she applied herself to the dreadful excuse for soup.

She'd finished the soup and moved on to the apple when Dr. Lym showed up.

At least she had on her own clothes today.

"Well! You're looking much better!" The flight doc powered up his readpad.

"Thanks." She sat up straight, smiled, and tried to look extra-healthy.

"How do you feel?"

Like a better grade of shit than I did when I got here. Mental editor running at full speed, she said, "Much better, thank you." Bonus points for a chipper reply, lost points for coughing.

At least coughing didn't hurt as much now. Ulla perched on the side of the bed for yet another examination while Dr. Lym poked, prodded, and listened to her chest as she breathed in and out.

"You are much better." He picked up his readpad and entered data. "Good job on getting out of bed, by the way."

Ulla so wanted out of this place.

He tapped some more on his readpad. "You're not ready for duty yet."

True. "How much longer do I have to stay here?"

"You don't." He snapped his readpad shut. "The Alliance has a room ready for you at the Trade Ministry. You can get started on phase two with your Elder tomorrow." He unhooked the clipboard from the foot of Ulla's bed. "Mrs. Tully, would you and the guard in the hall give Lieutenant Thorsdaughter a ride to the Trade Ministry once the hospital's finished their clerical work?"

"Of course." Yasmin wrapped the unfinished sweater around her knitting needles and stuffed it and the yarn into a bag.

"Pleasure getting to know you, Lieutenant," Dr. Lym said. "Come see me when the Elder says you're ready."

Chapter Twenty-Five
Healing

Ulla peered around her new rooms in the Trade Ministry. "This place is enormous!" Much as she wanted to sit, she was too spent to climb into the nearest Hjralma-sized chair. A sofa scaled for humans faced two such chairs on a platform designed to put everyone on the same level. She wasn't climbing up there, either.

"High ceilings make it look big, is all." Ed set Ulla's saddlebag on the carpet inside the door. "Need anything else?"

Ulla picked up the bag. "Thanks, I'm good."

When the door clicked shut behind Ed, Ulla set the bag down. She didn't remember it being so heavy.

Yasmin carried it into the bedroom for her. Ulla followed. At least the furniture in there was built for humans. To the right, the bathroom door stood open. Thankfully, its fixtures were also human-scaled.

Her new rooms had enough cubic space to put up an entire flight of starfighters.

"The High King's apartment was the only place open on such short notice," Yasmin said. "He and Marta said you're more than welcome to use it for now."

Thom's parents said that? Exhaustion took over before Ulla could feel overwhelmed. She took off her boots and lay down, fully clothed, on the bed. She freed a pillow from its spot under the coverlet.

No sooner had Yasmin thrown a spread over her than Ulla was asleep.

* * *

At sunup the next morning, the room looked much less intimidating with light streaming through the tall windows. Having had a decent night's sleep helped.

In the front room, Ulla found a tall, round table with two enormous chairs and three human-scaled bar stools. A high kitchen counter stood across from the Hjralma-scaled seating area she'd seen last night. Someone had placed a low platform in front of the counter to render it usable by adult humans. There was a stovetop, a warming oven, and a tiny sink. Half a liter of milk sat unopened in a small MitSmith refrigerator. That and a bowl of fruit on the counter were the only food in the place. Meals would have to come from somewhere else.

She opened a cabinet and found a canister each of tea and ground coffee, a teapot, an automatic kettle, and a contraption that was probably the coffee maker along with an assortment of cups, saucers, glasses, little plates, and bowls. Flatware was in a drawer.

Ulla's sleepy brain wasn't ready to figure out how the coffee maker worked, so she set up the teapot. She filled the kettle and powered it up to boil while she went off to explore the bathroom and get dressed.

* * *

Good morning, Child.

Ulla had just slid onto on a bar stool with a cup of milky tea. *Fripp?*

Yes. Will you accompany me to breakfast?

The time had come, then. Hunger got the better of Ulla's hesitation. *Yes, please. Where?*

There was a knock at the door. *I will show you.*

* * *

Breakfast, it turned out, was served buffet-style in the Trade Ministry's commercial-sized kitchen. Humans and Hjralma lined the long, high tables with the same seating arrangements as the table in Ulla's room. She loaded her plate with eggs, beans, and grilled tomatoes. Fripp led the way to a table and found a spot where someone had already placed a tall stool across from a Hjralma-scaled chair.

Reassured that the table at least stood between them, Ulla set down her plate and climbed onto the stool. She grabbed a set of flatware rolled in a napkin from the pile in the center of the table. Fripp ate toast and drank coffee. This was no projection; her new mentor was right here.

Ulla wasn't sure how she felt about that.

Fripp set down her butter knife and reached a long arm across the table to Ulla. "We meet in the here and now. I am glad."

Ulla took the proffered hand; warmth and recognition flowed. She risked a smile.

Did a smile even mean anything to the eetee?

Of course, your smile has meaning. I have known humans for a long time. Fripp smiled back.

A sandy-haired man, wearing local business attire and an ornate chain of office, entered the kitchen. He moved like Thom did, and when he got closer, Ulla recognized his face from SpaceCom's orientation holoshow that had welcomed her group of newly arrived starfighters to this world. Thom's uncle.

"Welcome, Lieutenant. I'm Padraic Willemson."

Ulla turned in her tall seat and shook his hand. "Pleased to meet you, sir."

"I'm so glad you're here," he said. "Your quarters are all right, I trust?"

"They're more than all right, thanks."

"If you need anything, Fripp can tell you how to get hold of Renata's staff." Outwardly, the man was the picture of relaxed hospitality, but Ulla inadvertently heard his mind reviewing a wicked-heavy morning schedule. "Renata sends her regards. She's on a conference call that started half an hour ago."

They exchanged a few more pleasantries, and then he left. Ulla, bemused, cut up a grilled tomato and ate it. Did the Alliance Trade Minister squeeze time out of his schedule like that for all his guests?

No, Child, he does not. Fripp cradled her Elder-sized coffee mug in her hands. *You are special.*

Had he made the effort, Ulla pondered, because her new psi talents set her apart? Or because she was a friend of Thom's?

Yes, Child. The Elder sipped her coffee. *Both statements are true.*

* * *

After breakfast, Ulla followed Fripp down a back hallway to the freight elevator they'd taken earlier.
Ulla was tired of being treated like an invalid. "Where are the stairs?"
"They are there." Fripp gestured toward a door next to the elevator. "Are you sure you do not want to use the lift?"
Ulla opened the stairwell door.
The stairs were the standard U-shaped switchback type common in large human-constructed buildings, but there the similarity stopped. The center flight, sized for humans, was separated by a railing from a parallel flight that hugged the outer wall. That one had massive treads and risers covering the same distance at the same angle, with fewer steps.
Hastily, Ulla switched to the steps that fit. Fripp took the big steps and waited for her on the landing. By the time Ulla made it to the first landing, she could hardly breathe. Fripp waited for her to catch her breath, then they turned and took the next flight up.
Again, Fripp waited for her on the landing. Another flight rose between them and the floor they needed to be on. Ulla stopped, rested, pressed upward. When they reached Ulla's floor, Fripp opened the door to the hallway and guided Ulla to an upholstered bench opposite the elevator doors.
Ulla gasped for air. *This is only one floor above ground level. What the hell?*
Fripp put an arm around Ulla's shoulders. *Child, you have not yet fully recovered.*
Damn. Ulla's chest felt like it had a steel band around it.
With Fripp's help, Ulla made it to her room. She sank onto the platform by the sofa and concentrated on breathing.
Finally, she managed to speak. "Sorry," squeaked out; her voice wasn't ready yet. *This is worse than what I had at Binder Station.*
Fripp squatted down next to her. *This is a different*

ailment than we fought at Binder. It is not worse.
We?
You, your father's partner, and I.
Berit, the nurse at Binder Station who'd taken up with Dad toward the end of those long days when he'd camped out beside Ulla's bed after the battle.
Berit Gee, yes. Her Healing Gift is very strong.
Berit had psi talent? That was news to Ulla.
Mind-talk is not everything. She is an empath and, also, she has the Healing Gift.
From what Ulla knew of the remarkable woman who might as well be her stepmother, that made complete sense.
Fripp cleared her throat. "We digress. Can you stand?"
Ulla nodded. Fripp helped her onto one of the big easy chairs and piled pillows behind her. "I am sorry; this will not be as comfortable for you as the couch made for humans, but if we are to work magic together, we must touch one another." *If I sit on your couch, it will break.*
Ulla's voice was coming back. "What really happened that day Flint moved the Ring?"
Fripp settled into her chair. "You allowed yourself to be more present in your projection on Bald Mountain than was wise. Your physical body became involved in the actions of your projection."
Ulla had suspected as much, but could she have avoided getting hurt and still killed Dwellers?
"Your projection allowed you to see, hear, and interact on Bald Mountain, Child, but your physical body, in Flint Clan's summer pasture, did the work." Fripp extracted a pillow from behind her back and tossed it onto the couch. "Your projection need not have been as robust as you made it." *But that is hindsight. Let us heal your wound.*
Wound?
Indeed, Child. The Dweller host who shot you was a pack enforcer who almost certainly used expanding bullets. One such traveled partway through your projection.
Only partway?
Fortunately for you, the shot went a little high and to the shooter's left.
Missing Ulla's heart and guts.
"The bullet would have tumbled. You used magic to catch it, hold it, and form a barrier so it would cause no

further harm."

I did what?

Fripp's voice was human-stern. "That is the problem, Child. Your powers are strong. Until you learn how to control them, I must insist that you refrain from using any Gift a qualified instructor has not approved."

That made sense—but how the hell was Ulla supposed to refrain from instinctively doing things she didn't know existed?

Fripp brought a throw from the bedroom and tucked it around Ulla. "The barrier is still there, inside you. Pay attention while I take it apart."

What?

Watch, only, and learn. Fripp wrapped Ulla's hand in hers. *Do not use your own Gift; your body needs all its strength to recover.*

Something dissolved from around the sore spot, and Ulla could once again breathe deeply. For the first time since that day on Bald Mountain, both lungs filled, really filled, with air. She felt better already.

The next thing she knew, she was coughing up gunk.

Fripp handed her a handkerchief. "I thought this might happen."

When the coughing subsided, Fripp's big handkerchief was filthy, slimy, and a little pink.

"That was caught inside the barrier." Fripp found a washcloth, dampened it, and gave it to Ulla. She dumped the contents of the fruit bowl on the counter and set the empty bowl in Ulla's lap. "The best thing you can do is cough it up." *As the area clears, I will see what I can do to repair the damaged tissue.*

Fripp settled back into her chair and took Ulla's hand again.

Ulla watched with her mind's eye as, bit by bit, Fripp adjusted delicate lung tissue. Little by little, the Elder's Healing Gift set things right. Each time Ulla coughed, she felt stronger. Pain that had become constant melted away. At some point, Ulla moved into Fripp's lap.

What toll did mindborne healing take on an Elder? Ulla didn't know, but she was grateful. She fell asleep in Fripp's arms.

When the mid-afternoon sun woke Ulla, she was still in Fripp's lap. The Elder was fast asleep.

Chapter Twenty-Six
Life, Reconstructing

A week later, Ulla sat curled up in the same chair, reading. Pillows, blankets, printed books, and food and drink on a small table within easy reach, made the Elder-sized chair better than any childhood blanket fort.

Since her first healing session with Fripp, she'd had two more. The practical Elder had also sent to SpaceCom Medical for expectorant tablets and a course of antibiotics. Why waste magic where technology would suffice?

Now that she could climb stairs, Ulla had explored the residential part of the sprawling Trade Ministry building far enough to find a library that doubled as a common room, a balcony that overlooked the stables and garage in the rear service yard, and the tiny dispensary where, day after tomorrow, the traditional healer who was also a UW&N certified medic would inject the final dose of antibiotic into Ulla's rear end.

Today had a bright spot: company was coming.

The kettle beeped. Ulla slid down from her nest, padded in stocking feet to the counter, poured boiling water over coffee grounds, and lifted the lid of a cardboard box to peek at a dozen pastries the kitchen staff had packed for her. She'd carried the box up the stairs herself and hadn't needed the railing once. Dammit, she was almost well!

She put on her boots and laced them up.

Starfighter, your guests are here.

Thanks, Ed. I'll be right down.

* * *

Two men in flight suits and a woman wearing the maternity version of SpaceCom's black and white summer uniform stood gawping at sculpture, maps, and tapestries in the Trade Ministry's entry hall. Fergus McCauley, José de la Cruz, and—Mags Pappas was expecting?

José saw her first. "Spider!" The three of them came running and almost smothered her.

"Hey, guys!" Oh, it was good to see them! Ulla disengaged from the scrum. "Come on upstairs."

"Spider, you look way better than Admiral Rosen said." Mags backtracked to the front desk and retrieved a big duffel from behind the guard's chair. Fergus immediately took it from her.

"Mags?" Where was Nik? Had something happened to him? "You're, uh, pregnant."

"This little guy was a surprise." Mags patted her abdomen. "Nik says hello. He wasn't on today's flight schedule, but Commander Arsehole put him in at the last minute."

Thanks be! Kind of. "I heard Arnie was on the *Resolute*."

"Yeah. I'm told he prefers being called 'Commander Charbonneau.'" Mags made an uncomplimentary hand gesture. "They put Nik in D Flight, under him, because I was originally in B with Fergus and José."

Ulla led the way down the back hall to the elevator. She would not give herself a coughing fit in front of the *Valiant*'s other surviving starfighters.

* * *

Chattering, they filed into Ulla's front room. Fergie and José had come straight from their debrief; they'd flown today and had a couple of hours liberty before they had to Gate back to the *Resolute*, get dinner and some sleep, and fly again. Mags had been reassigned to ground duty at the new SpaceCom headquarters, down by the Port of Newcastle. She lived at the Pordenone Hotel, just across Landfall Square from here.

Ulla poured coffee while Mags moved the pastry box to the table in the seating area. José and Mags sat on the couch; Ulla took off her boots and sat cross-legged in her blanket fort.

Fergus opened the duffel and pulled out a bottle. He loosened the wires around the cork. They heard a pop.

"Bottle got shaken pretty good on the way over here," he said, holding the bottle over the sink until the foam subsided. "Got a towel?" *Mustn't piss off Spider's herder friends by spraying bubbly all over.*

That was no headblind thought leakage. When had Fergie developed psi? Also, when had he lost weight, and why did he have dark circles under his eyes?

Thanks, Fergie. "Towels are in the drawer under the warmer, to the left of the sink."

What? Mind-talk, definitely.

Thanks for not spraying champagne inside. "Champagne! What's the occasion?" she asked.

The psi's real, then. Shit. Fergus raised the bottle. "Four kills, Spider! Congratulations!" He handed the bottle to her; she drank and passed it to José. Fergus grabbed a bar stool and sat next to Ulla. José drank and gave the bottle to Mags.

Mags hesitated. Ulla could not hear her thoughts, just the quiet static of an artificial psi blocker. Was that a requirement for Mags's new desk job? "I'm not supposed to drink alcohol..." Mags's voice trailed off, then she lifted the bottle and took a sip. "Baby's got to learn who his mama is. Congratulations, Spider!"

She passed the bottle to Fergus, who downed his quarter of the bottle at one go. They passed it again. When his turn came, Fergus finished it off, got up, and set the empty bottle in the sink.

"Enough about me," Ulla said. "You guys had kills, too, right?"

José nodded. "Two apiece, confirmed. Fergie may have gotten a third."

Fergus shook his head. "Nope. If I did, it was effing magic."

"He did. We got some new information last week." Mags reached for a pastry. "Fergie, come see me in Ops; Captain Nault has me going through the new stuff." Mags clammed up abruptly.

"It's effing magic we're alive at all. It was a target-rich environment." Being out of champagne, Ulla raised her coffee cup. "To us!"

When they'd got past that, she asked, "How did you guys get back?"

José swallowed a bite of pastry. "I splashed down in the ocean just outside Newcastle Harbor. Only textbook thing I've ever done." He inclined his head toward Fergus. "His story is better."

"An itinerant mine workers' co-op picked me up, shared power and air, and towed me to BD3 Station." Fergus put down his coffee cup. "They'd have brought me inside, but their ship was full to capacity." He grabbed a pastry and broke it in two. "One of the *Valiant*'s outside maintenance crews got torn off with a piece of hull they were working on. They were safety-cabled to it; a surprising lot of them survived. The co-op picked them up."

Ulla resolved never to complain about the labor co-op ships' casual approach to space traffic management ever again.

Fergus broke the silence. "Where's the loo?"

"Through the bedroom door, on your right."

Ulla locked her thoughts down tight and waited until she heard the bathroom door shut. "Is he all right?"

José shook his head. "No."

"Ever since that week we spent on the ground, waiting to be reassigned after—*Valiant*, Fergie's been hiding inside a bottle." Mags put down her coffee cup. "He still flies sober, but he stopped to…fortify himself on the way here."

"Any idea why?"

"Big John had something he wanted to do aboard ship that last day. So he and Fergus traded flights. Fergie's been beating himself up about it ever since."

"But if John asked to trade—"

"Fergie doesn't care." José brushed crumbs into his hand with a napkin. "Says he had a premonition."

Fergie got scary-accurate premonitions sometimes. As had, he said, his granny back on Earth, who had taught him never, ever, to act on them.

"Yeah." Mags dug another pastry out of the box. "He swears he knew somehow that he needed to get the hell off the *Valiant*. He blames himself for John's death."

They heard the toilet flush. By the time Fergus joined them, they were making small talk.

Ulla got up to brew more coffee. "What's in the duffel?"

"New uniforms, mostly." Mags licked glaze off her

fingers. "Some administrative stuff. Crappy little issue readpad. You'll want to get caught up before you come back on duty. A few odds and ends."

José pulled out his readpad and glanced at it. "There's a line at the Gate," he said. "Fergie and I need to get going."

Ulla dumped used coffee grounds into the trash. "Want the guard to call a taxi for you?"

Fergus drank the last of his coffee. "Thanks; we'll get one from the queue in front of Hotel Row." *We'll walk Mags home first.*

Ulla walked downstairs with them and waved goodbye from the front door. *Starfighters. Aren't we the swashbuckling ones?* She made damn sure Fergus couldn't hear that.

* * *

Back upstairs, Ulla lugged the duffel into the bedroom and unzipped it. She pulled out a flat package and set it aside. Underneath, there were three brand-new gray flight suits already embroidered with her name, rank insignia, and a stylized device that was meant to be a spherical starfighter covered with jets but looked like a hedgehog. She had underwear, socks, a new pair of boots, and a garrison cap that went with any uniform she'd be likely to wear here. At the bottom of the duffel, she found two new sets of loose-fitting knit pants and shirts for physical training.

Ulla put her new clothes away, except for the flight suits. She couldn't wear those at Headquarters, not wrinkled like that. There had to be a laundry nearby; she would ask.

She opened the flat package. The first item was a piece of paper, a hand receipt painstakingly listed and signed by an ensign named Mikko Strom. The other sheets of paper were purchase vouchers: one for footwear, one for black and white service dress uniforms, and another to pay for new civilian clothes and personal effects. There was a printed list of approved vendors; shoemaker Aden Fournier was listed at the top. Small world. Ulla looked forward to doing business with Yasmin's uncle.

She found the readpad and set it on the nightstand for later. A jingling cloth bag held metal insignia to go on the black and white uniforms she didn't have yet. She shook the contents out on the bed; her ribbon rack was already assembled. Correctly.

Ulla needed to find Ensign Strom and thank him.

The folding hologram cases were next. When she unfolded the top one, a group image of her Goshawk squadron from the *Valiant* popped up. There they all were, looking dashing with freshly shaved heads in front of a cargo Gate. That would have been on Reynoso Tres when they'd deployed to Bailey-Duran. She set the hologram case on the bed and opened the next one. It was a double. On one side was a portrait of Mama, frozen in time at age forty-seven standard. On the other was a holo of Ulla's brother Andrew, similarly frozen at twenty-one.

The next two cases matched—a professional hologram of Dad, smiling, and another of Berit Gee. Background and lighting were the same in both. They must have gone together to have their holos taken. Ulla was glad the two of them were still together; at least life was treating somebody well.

She found space for the holos on a shelf on the wall over the seating area. That done, she settled into her big chair with the readpad. She might as well connect it and make a dent in her message queue.

She turned on the readpad and glanced through its file list. "Downloaded documents" were almost all SpaceCom administrative rules and regulations. She found a copy of her orders for D Flight on the *Resolute*; she was to report immediately upon medical release for flying duty. D Flight—that would be with Nik, under Lieutenant Commander Arnold Charbonneau, call sign "Arnie." Her brain translated the man's call sign automatically to "Arsehole."

Dammit. Well, at least she already knew one decent person in the flight.

She also found copies of the printed vouchers she already had, and that was it. The readpad had to be connected to a SpaceCom node before it could be of any further use.

Ulla opened the readpad settings. The Trade Ministry would have a good signal; they'd need it for their own business. Surely, they'd have a pass-through to UW&N, maybe even to SpaceCom.

No signal at all. Which was weird because she knew the Pordenone Hotel, right across the square from the Trade Ministry, had signal.

This was BD3; maybe the Alliance preferred hardwired ports and cables. Lacking a desk in her quarters, the next most likely spot for a port would be behind the table. Sure enough, she found a standard comm port. She rummaged through drawers and found a cable.

Ulla connected her new readpad to the port. A long list of "content unavailable" markers populated her message list. Chasing a connection was pointless when there had to be an obvious solution. She'd ask at dinner.

She powered down the readpad, climbed into her reading nest, and picked up a book by Miles Rogers that she'd found in the library. It had a chapter about spinners of wyrd.

* * *

Bailey-Duran Three: A World Remade seemed to be the respected folklorist's attempt to distill a career's worth of academic research into an accessible book for armchair travelers. The first pedantic chapter said nothing Ulla didn't already know, so she skipped to "About the Author" in the back of the book.

Dr. Rogers, it seemed, first came to BD3 to research Hjralma and On'oi concepts of fate. He and the On'oi had hit it off from the start and, a few years later, he and his equally respected xenoarchaeologist wife Aubrey Rogers returned to make their careers and raise a family. The "Acknowledgments" section that followed his bio mentioned Renata, Padraic, Marta, Yens, and the On'oi Council of Chieftains. There was a special thank-you to Dev and Emli of Flint Clan for helping Miles, Aubrey, and their young children settle in at Flint Clan's summer pasture. Aubrey had run the dig at the ruined villa nearby while Miles wrote the book Ulla now held.

How had he done that, Ulla wondered, with no electronic devices? She flipped to the chapter about spinners.

The first paragraph was a dizzying array of human religious and cultural takes on fate, wyrd, karma, and a lot of concepts Ulla had never heard of. The narrative, if you could call it that, bounced from Earth to Bailey-Duran and droned on about Bailey-Duran Ancients, Hjralma spinners of wyrd, and the recurring idea of the Fates personified, often in threes. The Greek Moirai and the Roman Parcae were just a start.

Here was a quote from the *Poetic Edda* where the dragon Fafnir described Norns. Norns, the dragon said, could come from anywhere; they needn't even be the same species.

Fafnir? Wasn't he the fellow who got turned into a dragon in a kick-ass story involving greed, gold, magic, a very special ring, and a crap-ton of folks killing each other? Maybe the narrative would pick up soon.

A few pages later, Dr. Rogers introduced Elder lore, including a translation of BD3's own "Prophecy of the Hidden Spinner":

Bred in fire,
Born in earth.
Tested in fire;
Found in water.
Confirmed in fire,
Protector in air;
Returned to fire.

Ulla thought back to the odd conversation among Ingeborg, Dev, Fripp, and Hanni, the day she'd first made Fire and Ice. They'd used similar phrases in Dialekt as though everybody knew them. Then they'd asked where she was born and gotten quiet when she'd told them.

She broke down the riddle.

"Bred in fire": Nope.

"Born in earth": Yes, if that meant "on" Earth. Translations could be tricky.

"Tested in fire": Binder Station, possibly.

"Found in Water": Um, yes.

"Confirmed in fire": Ulla looked at the scar on her right hand and touched the scar on her face. Yup.

That left "Protector in air," which sounded dashing. "Returned to fire" did not bear thinking about.

Well, her life didn't match the first line either. That was something.

Ulla slammed the book shut. This was right up there

with looking up a trivial medical issue and finding out that your stuffy nose could be a symptom of any one of seven fatal diseases.

It was time to go exploring again.

Chapter Twenty-Seven
Thom's Garret

The attic was the only floor Ulla hadn't investigated. She took the elevator; there might be more stairs to climb at the top of this massive pile of brick.

The elevator opened on a wide hallway flanked with Elder-scaled doors and lit by daylight from a big window at the other end. Aside from a peaked ceiling and zero effort expended on interior decoration, the hallway looked just like the ones on the lower floors. Daylight showed under every door, most likely from the dormer windows she remembered seeing, ages ago, from Landfall Square. The next-to-last door on the right stood open.

Instead of rattling doorknobs, she used her Finding Gift to peek inside the rooms. Her mind's eye found shelves and shelves of archival boxes stuffed with paper records. There were rooms piled high with unused furniture, an auxiliary pantry filled to bursting, and an armory lined with projectile firearms, a few larger weapons, ammunition, and maintenance supplies.

Really? She'd thought the Trade Ministry's main enforcement functions were housed in the warehouse district near the sea and sky ports.

A mechanical room on the other side of the hall most likely controlled the utilities for the whole building, including a secondary plumbing system with a cistern that appeared to be independent of Newcastle's city water system.

Heya, Starfighter.

Thom? Ulla had thought he was at Bald Mountain.
Just Gated back. Would've said hello but you had company.
That was fair. Ulla passed a room with a big electric generator, idle but recently serviced. *This place is a fortress.*
Thom's laughter rolled out of the open door. *Of course it is. The original owners built it when the City-States were still at war with each other.*
That explains it.
Yup. Thom's attention drifted back to a sketch he was working on.

Ulla reached the open door and peeked inside to see Thom working at a professional-looking drawing table. His pocket notebook lay open next to a large sketch of the Yotne tactical Gate on Bald Mountain exploding with the Ring inside it. He added a few more details to the big drawing, set down his pencil, and stretched. "Come in!"

Ulla sat on the only unoccupied seating, a battered but solid couch with worn upholstery. Why hadn't she heard him earlier?

This is my old childhood quiet place. "You had no reason to look and, from here, street level and the Trade Ministry's offices and lodging are outside my mind-talk range," he explained. "Uncle cleared this room out for me, back in the day, because he knew I couldn't hear Old Man Schiller's mind from this end of the building."

"Susana Schiller's late husband?" *The man Maribet climbed out an upstairs window to avoid?*

"The house next door." Thom jutted his chin in the direction Ulla had just come from. "He was a real piece of work."

"Sounds like good riddance, then."

"Not something I'd normally say about anybody," Thom said, "but in his case, you're right."

So, the window Maribet had climbed out of, naked, opened onto the Trade Ministry's rear service yard. "Let me guess," said Ulla. "Your aunt and uncle took Maribet in, used diplomatic immunity, political pull, or whatever to keep Schiller away from her, and set her on the road to a career as a professional mind-talker." Ulla didn't know Padraic well, but that was exactly what she would expect of Renata.

"They did that, and more."

Ulla smiled. The more she learned about Thom's aunt and uncle, the better she liked them.

Thom picked up a yellow pencil and went back to work.

"Why the drawing?"

"Documentation." He drew a series of beams radiating from the dark spot the Ring had become.

"What are the yellow rays?"

"That's what I saw."

Ulla picked up a similar drawing that had no such rays. "What's this?"

"That's what Nathan saw." Thom continued adding detail "Adepts often see more. Not always, and not usually the same. I have a meeting tomorrow with Maribet so she can validate my drawing of her description."

"What about Olwyn?"

"She came late to the party but, yes, she's a witness." He showed her another drawing, signed and dated. "As soon as you feel up to it, I need a statement from you too."

"Sure."

"How are you feeling?"

"Better. Bored out of my mind."

He smiled. "That's good."

Ulla groaned. "I am sick and tired of being an invalid!"

"Probably means you're not one anymore." Thom got up and sat next to her on the couch. He held out his arms to give her a hug. *May I?*

Ulla nodded and hugged back. A tingle went up her spine. All systems were, apparently, working. She cuddled up against him. They sat together for a while.

Um, Starfighter?

What?

We have unfinished business.

How could he talk about business when the electricity between them was so obvious?

A few weeks ago, a SpaceCom officer told me we needed to defer—this—until we were back in Newcastle. He whispered into her ear. "I'm not in your workgroup anymore."

So he wasn't. Ulla raised her face to his. They kissed.

Ever made love with another adept?

No. I didn't used to be an adept, remember?

Link minds, then.

Um, all right. Ulla linked her mind with his as she put her arms around him and pulled him to the couch. *Oh! Oh, indeed.*
I've never felt one of those from the man's viewpoint before.

* * *

Later, they watched the sunbeam from the dormer window creep up the wall. Ulla sat up, the coughing fit she'd successfully delayed hitting full force. At least coughing didn't hurt anymore.
Sorry. I thought you were better.
Ulla, still coughing, picked up her trousers from the floor. *I am better, don't worry.* She rummaged in the pockets and found a handkerchief. "Doc says heavy breathing exercise is beneficial." She grinned, started to sit back down, reconsidered, and bent down to pick up her underpants.
???
Not staining your upholstery, Guardian. "Is there indoor plumbing up here?"
"Just the emergency cistern tap in the hall." He pulled her onto his lap. *You can sit here.*
Ulla laughed and put her arms around him. "It'll be suppertime in half an hour." She nibbled on his ear. *Shall we have another go?*
He frowned. *Much as I'd like to, no.* He hugged her, then slid out from under her and got dressed. He picked up her shirt and tossed it to her.
She put on her clothes and sat back down, content for the first time in a great while. *That was delightful, Thom Yensson.*
It was. He smiled, plopped down on the couch, and put his arm around her shoulders. "I'd planned a more civilized version of this moment." *Hope the impulsive approach doesn't cause you any, uh, problems.*
What? Oh. "Not at all. I had my contraceptive refreshed just before mid-tour leave, about four local months ago." *And all my immunizations are up-to-date.* He must be aware that starfighters were not known for chastity.
Oh. Thom's single-word answer hung between them.
"I'd never knowingly pass along some awful disease,"

she said, "and I daren't risk getting pregnant." *In a combat zone, pregnancy's an automatic dishonorable discharge.*

"That makes sense." *Draconian as hell, but it makes sense.* Thom's shields closed up a little. "What about your friend? Looks like SpaceCom's keeping her."

"Mags, who was here today?"

"That's the one."

How could she even begin to describe the documentation nightmare Mags and Nik must have gone through when Mags turned up pregnant? "She and her husband must have proven to SpaceCom that they used approved contraception and it didn't work. Also, she's lucky there was ground duty available."

"You have to document everything?"

Ulla cringed. "I have to document this when I get back where my readpad is."

"That's barbaric!"

"I agree, but how is it different from the drawings you're working on?"

"You're right." Thom's shields relaxed, at least for her. *Conception and death are two sides of the same card.* He gave her good shoulder a quick squeeze. "So, Great Starfighter of the Edge, you have an image to maintain, do you?"

Thanks be, he wasn't put off entirely! "Yes, Guardian, I do." *Just so you know, I take full advantage of a great starfighter's ability to pick and choose.*

Glad I meet your standards, then. Thom pulled up a low table in front of her. "Put your feet up while I finish this drawing."

She rested her bare feet on the old, scratched-up table. Somebody had tried unsuccessfully to buff out a large scorch mark. Mind-seeing kicked in immediately. *Your attic retreat has a history.*

Was he blushing? "The table's the first piece of furniture I dragged in here when I was a kid." *Should have known.*

Ulla closed her eyes and relaxed into mind-seeing. Rainy days and books. Improbable kid plots involving treasure maps and pretend smugglers and pirates. Adolescent railing at the world. Young Thom learning to draw. She opened her eyes. "You grew up here, didn't you?"

"From before I can remember, till I was about six, yes." Thom put his pencil in a tray with the others and tidied up his drawing board. "Auntie and Uncle took me in after Ma died. Most summers, I went on trek with Da, with Worldtree Clan, till I grew into going on trek on my own, with Raven. Went to school near Da's place on Worldtree ground—but even after Da married Marta, I spent a lot of holidays here." He sat down next to her. *This pile of brick is home.*

"You didn't live in the attic." Ulla settled against his shoulder.

Thom laughed. "No. I lived downstairs with Auntie Renata and Uncle Padraic, in the Trade Minister's quarters." He put his arm around her. "I'm staying there now." *Renata updated the decor when I moved out and they gained a private guest room.*

I'll bet she did. Ulla snuggled in closer. He started to say something, then thought better of it.

They sat and enjoyed each other's company.

Feet still up, Ulla relaxed back into mind-seeing what the old table had to tell her. A utility Ring had sat on the scorched spot at some point—was that what so embarrassed him? She opened her eyes. *What goes on in your attic retreat stays in your attic retreat.*

Glad you understand. "About the utility Ring, Starfighter—Geoff Tully and I were barely in our teens when I mucked that up." *Cousin Neal saved both our asses.*

She laughed. "You can tell me about it when you're ready."

* * *

In her own room, after supper, Ulla cabled up her readpad and sat down at the tall table to catch up with several weeks' worth of messages.

The solution to her earlier connection problems had been simple: her room was directly above a secure conference room. When she'd first tried to connect, a utility Ring had been in use less than three meters away.

Her list of unread messages from the *Valiant* was short. A flight meeting that would never happen. A rude joke. A directive about what uniform to wear for ground duty. Thanks be she'd caught up before what turned out to be her last flight.

The next message header was an exuberant "HE'S HERE!!!" Ulla opened it and read that John Alexander Casey, Junior, had been born at ten in the morning on the 6th of January. So it had been January on—where was Big John from, anyway? The proud father had attached an image.

So John Casey had wanted to stay aboard that day to catch the daily message batch as soon as it arrived, which was why he, not Fergus McCauley, was dead now. Tears rolled down Ulla's face. No wonder Fergus drank.

Ulla could do with a drink herself.

Mercifully, the rest of her messages were from the living. Ulla deleted the outdated ones but kept the list of *Valiant* survivors.

She had a nice, long message from Berit Gee, Dad's partner, saying they were coming to BD3! The Berserkers had signed a contract with MitSmith to protect the company's assets in Landfall.

Ulla's heart sank when she saw the date; Berit had written a day or so after Olwyn Wittber had discovered Yotne in-system. Before Bald Mountain. She wondered if Dad and Berit were already on-planet. If not, she hoped they'd stay somewhere safe, and far away.

No, Thor Bjornson had signed a contract. He and his Berserkers would be there. The Alliance would just have to unstick the Ring and put it in place. There was still time. Wasn't there?

Her father had also sent a short note. She wondered if Berit had prodded him to write.

Ulla went back to deleting expired administrative trivia. She kept her Home of Record change, her orders for D Flight on the *Resolute*, and the flight doc's "sick in quarters" order.

She had an order to report for biometric security recalibration. Personnel had got hold of the images in her medical record of her spinner tattoo and the new burn scars on her face and hand. Next came a uniform waiver request form for an "item of overriding cultural significance." Of course. Admiral Rosen, a.k.a. Mother Hen, had to be the instigator. She would have noticed Ulla's earring at the hospital. The form was already filled out. She replaced "tribal earring (unspecified)" with "On'oi (Bailey-Duran

System) clan earring(s)," signed the form, and returned it. *What a difference an ess makes.*
Ulla looked up from her readpad. *Thom?*
He knocked at her door. *May I come in?*
She used mind-moving to spin the lock.
Thom opened the door and stepped inside. "Heya, Starfighter."
She slid down off her tall chair and hugged him. "Heya yourself, Guardian."
The spark was there, but he wasn't sharing thoughts. Ulla led the way to the couch. "What's up?"
Thom pulled a pair of small notebooks out of his pocket and took a seat. "It's about the documentation I was working on this afternoon."
"What about it?" Ulla settled in next to him.
"Council's moved up their schedule. Their courier arrived an hour ago, and he's leaving as soon as Maribet finishes her statement tomorrow."
"You said you needed a statement from me too." *Do you need it right now?*
There's time, first thing in the morning. "Can you meet me after breakfast?"
"Sure. Where?"
"We can use a conference room downstairs. I'll know which one tomorrow." He tapped the pair of notebooks against the armrest.
Thom shielded his thoughts—not a good sign. Ulla waited.
"These two notebooks have to go with the evidence package."
"And?" They looked like the notebooks Thom had carried on trek. She recognized the coffee stain on the one he'd drawn her portrait in, one glorious afternoon.
"I screwed up," he said. "Right after—Bald Mountain, I recorded my first impressions in my personal notebook. They should have gone in here." He held up the clean one. "These are my field notes for work."
"Why are you telling me this?"
"Because now both notebooks have to go into the evidence package." He handed her the stained notebook. "Council is building a case to persuade the United Worlds and Nations to escalate operations in this system."
"We're already at combat status."

"You were deployed here to catch smugglers and discourage pirates. Sending Dwellers to steal the Landfall Ring at Bald Mountain was a Yotne act of war."

"The UW&N won't need much persuading. It's not as though we ever stopped fighting." Ulla held up the notebook. "Council might not have to use this as evidence."

Thom nodded. "The whole lot may wind up in a box in the attic. I hope it does. But it could easily wind up on the floor of the UW&N assembly on Reynoso Tres." *And in the news.*

What was the big deal? Ulla opened the notebook. It was full of Thom's sketches, notes, lists.

"Please look through it," he said. "I don't want you to be surprised if anything here shows up in public."

She turned back to the first page and started reading. Here was a list of gear for the trek with Flint Clan, a note of Chieftain Dev Aronson's favorite whiskey, and weather reports. Thom had made and checked off two appointments: one for a physical exam and another to meet Nathan Steves at the Port of Newcastle passenger Gate. Text tapered off in favor of rough sketches. He'd drawn woods, deer, a river, a close-up view of the group of buildings on the hill near where she'd landed.

She turned a page and saw a spherical Goshawk egress pod. "You were there."

He nodded. "Turn the page."

She did and saw a detailed drawing of the console around the Goshawk's flight recorder. A schematic was in the corner of the page.

"You got in." *How?*

"An adept at Castle Chisos hailed Guild Member Wittber. She relayed for a maintenance tech on the *Resolute*, who talked me through the emergency access panel. Nathan got the recorder out." Thom shrugged. "If you can't find a mechanic, hire a surgeon."

"Where is it now?"

"Your flight recorder?"

Ulla nodded.

I expect your colleagues are combing through it. I brought it back in my saddlebag. "Craig Eselgroth took it to SpaceCom Headquarters."

Ulla stared at him. "Why didn't you tell me?"—*and why isn't this in your work notebook?*

"Until very recently, you'd have been unable to keep it secret." *Officially, Nathan and I were never there.*

Ulla turned a page. Here was a sketch of Piet and two other wranglers on camdeer, swimming stock across Fifth River. Thom had caught the action perfectly. *This is a great picture.*

Thanks. He relaxed just a little.

Ulla read Thom's notes about an unidentified Goshawk pilot, to whom he subsequently referred to as "LT T" in the pages following a handwritten copy of Ulla's Gallantry Star citation. He had scribbled down SpaceCom Rescue contact information, more notes, and a paragraph about a certain dilapidated stuffed toy the starfighter had packed with care on every deployment of her career. Two pages, front and back, of names in Maribet's careful, rounded handwriting, of survivors from the *Valiant*, followed by the stubs of the two leaves Thom had sliced out for Ulla.

Sketches of vegetation followed, and of animals, and children playing. There was a full-page portrait of Ulla with untidy hair and a pained expression on her face. Was this after they'd linked minds the first time?

His eyes twinkled. *What do you think?*

She kept going. While he'd never stopped recording other elements of Flint's trek, her image appeared more and more frequently. *Granny Kate said you had a crush on me.*

She was right. Was he blushing? "I would never bring this up, Starfighter, if this notebook could stay private." *I'm well aware of who and what you are.*

Ulla turned a page. There she was, on Snowball with Stelle seated behind her, felted balls zinging through the air. But the child was not red-headed, sunburned little Stelle. Her skin was darker, like Ingeborg's and Thom's. She had eyes like Ulla's, and her nose and cheeks were dusted with freckles not unlike the ones on Thom's shoulders. The little girl's short hair was tousled just like Ulla's.

"Oh, Thom." *She's beautiful.* Impossible, but beautiful. If the man had it this badly, how could Ulla avoid hurting him?

You might begin by not using the word avoid. "I won't apologize for indulging in pleasant fantasy." There was a catch in his voice.

Ulla didn't want to turn any more pages. "Is there anything else in here you'd like me to see before it goes to Council?"

"There are a few more, but you've got the idea."

"Any nudes?" She was thinking of their shared dream.

He took the book from her and flipped through it to a playful sketch, on two facing pages, of laundry day at the hot springs. "Here's the only nude: You're one of about forty people."

She laughed. "The UW&N and I can handle that."

He put his arm around her. She put her hand on his knee and leaned her head on his shoulder. *I never imagined I'd want kids.* Family and career were a mix she'd always shied away from.

There you go again, avoiding things.

The nerve! "*Life is about choices.* She stiffened but didn't move.

He kept his arm where it was. "Given a choice, I wouldn't fall in love with a starfighter who'll be back in the sky in a few weeks."

Ulla tried to lighten the conversation. "Maybe it's just a roaring case of lust."

"You know better."

Do I? Why was she about to cry? "I'm not good at long-term relationships." *They always end in shouting matches.*

"So," he said, "you've left a long line of exes behind you."

"Not exes as such; only two lasted more than a week or so."

"You haven't enough data, then."

Yes, I do. The spark she and Fergus McCauley had shared in Goshawk school had blown straight through flame to ashes, scant weeks after they'd registered as domestic partners so they could be assigned to the same ship. That was a deployment she did not want to repeat. Ulla had got a transfer to Reynoso Tres, where she met Evan Morgan and shared his flat in Aurora City near the SpaceCom base. Less than a year in, she and Evan had had the shouting match; both had been relieved when Ulla got orders for Binder Station. Her half of the furniture was still in storage. *I'm bad at partnering.*

"Still not enough data," he said.

"You've been eavesdropping all evening! Stop it!"

He took his arm off her shoulders and faced her. "Shall we have our shouting match right now?" he asked. "Get it over with?"

"NO!" Tears leaked out of her eyes.

He held out both hands to her. "You're exhausted."

She took his hands and held them. "I'm not as well as I'd like to be." At least she didn't need to cough. "I ought to go to bed."

They stood up, and she walked him to the door. "See you at breakfast tomorrow?"

"Of course." He gave her a hug. "Get some sleep."

She put on the soft pajamas Renata had given her, turned out the lights, and went to bed. Sleep took its own sweet time catching up with her.

Chapter Twenty-Eight
Who Ulla Is

Ulla woke, shivering and covered in sweat. She pulled the covers up around her neck and stared into the near darkness of the high-ceilinged bedroom. She willed herself to relax.

Fripp had promised her she'd have no more nightmares about Elders. Yet Fripp herself featured prominently in the dream Ulla had just had.

The most unsettling part was how big everything had been. Ulla, wearing stretchy pajamas with feet, had climbed up onto the chest-high seat of the sofa to cuddle between Mama and Dad. Her parents had been taller than Elders. Fripp, taller still and unable to stand up straight in their living room, had sat on the floor.

Well, shit. It was only a dream. Ulla turned on the bedside lamp. She took a deep breath and let it out slowly, willing the tide of emotion she'd caught from the adults in the dream to subside and fade back to where dreams lived.

She got up, padded into the bathroom, had a drink of water, and went back to bed.

She lay there, staring at the high ceiling. Fripp had said the "dreams of another" would not trouble her again, and Ulla hadn't dreamed about the groundies or their firestorm since.

Fine, Fripp had not actually promised she wouldn't have bad dreams about Elders.

Ulla turned off the light, fluffed her pillow, and

burrowed into bed. *It. Was. Only. A. Dream.*
Granted. But it was not the "dream of another."
Ulla's mind swirled. Her only memory of Dad, from the time before he saw her name on an after-action roster at Binder Station and shouldered his way to her hospital bed, was of him handing her Pink Wabbit through the open window of a taxi. She remembered waking up, much later, to blinding sunlight and bare, rocky hills on Granny and Grandad's Big Bend ranch. She had a few memories of the ranch—riding behind Grandad or one of the vaqueros, climbing with her brother Andrew among boulders, playing hide-and-go-seek in a vegetable garden with a pleasant, dark-haired woman. By the time Mama had gotten a middle-management job with MitSmith in Grand Saline, and Grandad had taken Ulla and Andrew to join her, Ulla had been big enough to remember most things.

The living room in the dream, if it was real, had to have been in Virginia, not Texas. Why had her parents separated? Mama had never spoken about that. When Ulla and her dad reunited, he only said he and Mama could not agree. When Ulla had asked what they could not agree about, he'd clammed up.

Here in the middle of Newcastle's dimly lit night, Ulla's brain crunched through what little data it had. Dad rushing downstairs with Pink Wabbit was family lore. Mama might have put that part of her life behind her, but Andrew had told Ulla that story every time she cried for her father. So, maybe Ulla didn't actually remember that bit in the taxi at all.

Why wasn't Andrew in her dream? Even though the grownups spoke quietly, how could her brother not have been awakened by the bewildering stew of emotions pouring off Mama and Dad?

Then Ulla knew. She did remember the taxi incident, but almost leaving Pink Wabbit behind, precious as he was, had been a side issue. The stricken look on Dad's face as he stood on the street outside their taxi window hadn't matched the void where Ulla should have felt how he felt. Mama, Andrew, and the driver had been in the taxi with Ulla, but she hadn't heard a single thought. Then she'd dropped her pacifier. When she couldn't make it fly back up to her mouth, she'd howled until her big brother ducked to the floorboard to retrieve it for her.

All through school, and after that at SpaceCom's Academy, she'd had the Guild's usual tests for psi. All had been negative. She'd always been good at finding things people had lost; she'd helped a friend of Grandad's witch water, had found well sites in the Big Bend desert.

There was the "Today, I am lucky" thing she'd used to win fights since she was a teenager on Farwell. For every victory that phrase had given her, she'd had a corresponding setback. This time, instead of giving her a head cold after vanquishing a school bully, had using those words got her shot down? What about the *Valiant*? Had she overdone things and...

No, she decided. No one person was that special. But the string of consequences linked to saying "Today, I am lucky" was too consistent to be superstition.

Then Ulla had met Flint Clan. Innocent little Stelle, the other spinner, had held the starfighter's hand to "show her how we talk."

Ulla and Fripp needed to talk.

Yes, Child, we do.

A wave of calm enveloped Ulla, almost like a mental hug from Fripp, even though she could tell the Elder Spinner was as upset as she was.

In the morning.

In the morning, then. Ulla fluffed her pillow and pretended to sleep.

* * *

It was just as well that neither Fripp nor Thom were at breakfast the next morning. Ulla put last night out of her mind as best she could and concentrated instead on Bald Mountain. She needed to provide a clear and accurate statement for Thom's report. Sitting in a chair opposite Thom in a spartan conference room, she related her tale into a readpad. Some corner of her mind managed to stay professional.

After last night's outbursts, a cool distance remained between Ulla and Thom. She kept it that way, the better to make it through her account of what had happened on Bald Mountain. Thom didn't seem to mind.

When she finished, Thom switched off the recording

function. "You okay?"

"Yeah."

He stared her down.

You win. "New dream last night."

Thom removed the paper copy of Ulla's statement from the printer and handed it to her. "Want to talk about it?"

Ulla focused on proofreading the transcript, making a few changes with a pencil. "No. Thanks for asking."

Thom spent several minutes tapping at his readpad. The printer hummed and dropped another copy. Ulla reviewed that one and signed it. Thom signed it, too, and tossed the draft copy into the shredder.

Ulla breathed out; tension lessened ever so slightly. "Glad that's over."

Thom folded her statement and added it to the bulging pouch. "Starfighter, it's just beginning."

She dug a finger into her tight neck muscles. "I know."

* * *

Fripp was waiting for her in a seating area at the end of the hall. Ulla dropped onto a chair next to Fripp's floor cushion. She had never seen a living being sit so still. Had the Elder Spinner not been wearing clothes, she might easily have been mistaken for a humanoid-shaped pile of rocks.

Your father thought that too. Fripp opened her eyes. "Why do you think Terrans call us trolls?"

If you are more comfortable conversing in public, we can speak here.

Ulla said nothing. It was easier to stare at the portrait on the wall in front of her, of a man wearing archaic clothing. He had a soulslayer mark on his face. *They did that?*

Generations ago, yes. "If you would rather speak privately, we can do so in my rooms."

Ulla nodded. *Let's.*

Fripp led the way upstairs to a suite a few doors down the hall from Ulla's. The Elder waved a hand toward the human-scaled sofa in a seating area exactly like the one in Ulla's front room.

Ulla sat. Napkins and an unopened pastry box sat on the table.

Fripp busied herself at the kitchen counter. "Would you like coffee, Child?"

"Yes, please." This room, much like Ulla's own, had no personal touches. Fripp did not live here, then.

Of course not. My home is at Castle Chisos. Fripp smiled like a human as she placed a mug of hot black coffee in front of Ulla. "I have found that food and drink help humans relax, especially when the conversation's subject matter is difficult." She set her mug on the table, opened the pastry box, and sat across from Ulla.

I wouldn't put it quite that way but, yes, you're right. Ulla reached for the biggest chocolate-filled pastry. "Thank you."

For at least a full minute, neither said a word. Was the Elder weighing her next words, now that they were face to face?

Ulla certainly was. She bit into her pastry, swallowed, and followed it with a sip of coffee. "I dreamed about you last night."

"You did." Fripp selected a crisp cake and took a bite.

Ulla wiped chocolate from her fingers. "From your reaction, I'm guessing you heard at least part of it."

Fripp chewed and swallowed. "Yes."

Ulla waited.

At long last, Fripp broke the silence. "We hoped you were too young to remember that night."

We? Mechanically, Ulla set down her mug. "We, who?"

"Your parents and I." *Losing your Gifts so suddenly had to have been beyond traumatic, especially at such a young age.*

That really happened, then. "You knew my parents?"

"Not well." Fripp set her half-eaten cake on a napkin. "That night was the only time your mother and I met."

"And Dad?"

"We met once before." Fripp took a bite of her pastry. *I had the opportunity to observe him in action during the Pendarian evacuation.*

"You were there?" The Yotne attack on Pendaria, during a week of high-level meetings there, shortly before most of Ulla's cadet class had been born, was standard reading at the Academy.

"Yens Govinderson and I were the Alliance delegates at that meeting." Fripp sipped her coffee. *Your father acquitted himself brilliantly."*

Mama never said. But then, Mama had never said anything about Dad. And Dad only ever brought up his combat history when he was chasing a new contract.

Ulla reached for her coffee and thought better of it. Her hands shook. "Are you saying I was born with the Gifts I have now?"

Yes, Child. "You have always had them," Fripp said. "The night your mother refused to let you come with me, I concealed them."

Tears ran from the corners of Ulla's eyes. *WHY?*

Because your mother was about to take you and your brother to live in a place where Gifts can get you killed.

"Did Andrew have psi talent too?"

"No, Child." Fripp picked up her mug. "Just you." *Your Gifts blossomed early; your nanny caught on and wanted your parents to tell the Guild.*

Ulla caught herself smiling. "She can't have minded looking after a baby who could retrieve her own pacifier."

"I'm told that mind-moving was your first visible Gift." Fripp reached for Ulla's hand. "Your parents had their reasons for not involving the Guild."

???

Fripp squeezed Ulla's hand gently. "You were—and are—a spinner of wyrd, destined to serve here in the star system you call Bailey-Duran."

"Now, wait just a minute!" Ulla yanked her hand out of Fripp's and jumped up to go—where? Heavily, she sank back onto the sofa. "The academics say spinners can change the fabric of time and space." *Why not just do it? Blot the Yotne the hell OUT!*

Child, do you think that has never occurred to anyone before? Fripp settled into her pile-of-rocks mode. *The chain of consequences for such an act is extraordinarily complex.*

It would be. Ulla slumped in her seat.

A faint smile creased Fripp's otherwise immobile face. *Sit still with me, Child, and breathe. Think of nothing for a while. Then you may revisit the logic of what you just said.*

Reluctantly, Ulla grabbed a sofa pillow and rolled it up underneath her as she sat cross-legged, eyes closed. Quieting her thoughts would take some time.

* * *

"Child?" Fripp's voice nudged the peaceful spot where Ulla's mind had finally settled.

Ulla opened her eyes and took a moment to get her bearings.

While Fripp still sat quietly, she no longer looked like a pile of rocks. "Someone taught you well. I am glad."

"Mr. Sanders, on Farwell. Mama hired him to teach Andrew and me to speak and write Standard." *He wound up being a family friend.*

"When your little family disappeared through MitSmith's Houston commercial Gate, I thought we had lost you forever." *I so regretted concealing your Gifts.* Fripp smiled. *It seems Fortune provided for your needs.*

Had Mama meant for them to disappear? Probably. Ulla pulled the sofa pillow out from under her, fluffed it up, and hugged it to her. "I had Gifts similar to, say, little Stelle Pietersdaughter. I went headblind at a young age, with no explanation and no support." She cradled the pillow in her lap. "Why did I not grow up to be a serial killer? Why did I not commit suicide?"

Your chosen profession, Starfighter, rules out neither choice.

That was bleak.

It is true. Fripp reached out her hand to Ulla.

This time, Ulla grasped it.

"You were surrounded by adults who, however flawed, loved you dearly. You were not without support."

In the deserts of far west Texas? Ulla found that hard to believe.

"Your grandmother found a teacher," Fripp said. "You may remember her as Tía Sara."

The woman with the vegetable garden! *She was nice.* "Tía was always after me to 'use my words.'"

She is an empath, that much I know for sure. If she has other Gifts—which is highly likely—she hides them well. "Her official job was to prepare your older brother for school. Comm in that place, even now, is intermittent; hololessons were not an option." *Your father paid, quietly, for her to care for both of you.*

He hadn't abandoned them then! "You kept tabs on us."

"In Texas, yes."

That had to have irritated Mama no end.

It did. When your mother had a chance to move to the other side of explored space from here, she took it.

Ulla took a sip of her coffee; it had grown cold. She reached for Fripp's mug. "Shall I warm yours too?"

"Yes, please." The Elder's face was animated once more. She stretched.

Ulla put both mugs in the warming oven and switched it on. "You were at Binder Station."

"Only in projection, after you were—hurt—but yes."

That was some weird shit that went down.

The Elder shrugged. *Your Spinner's Gift almost got you killed.*

The warmer beeped. Ulla carried their hot coffee back to the table. "How did you find me?"

Fripp picked up her half-eaten pastry. "At Binder Station? That was easy. Most of the adepts in known space heard your cry."

"What about—before?"

"When you came of age and chose to be a citizen of the Republic of Texas, your name was flagged for an administrative error. An—acquaintance—in the United Worlds and Nations bureaucracy knew I was looking for you. He let me know."

Ulla had thought her citizenship had been approved without incident.

By the way, Texas was a wise choice.

???

They almost never allow other nations to interfere in their citizens' affairs. Fripp set down her coffee. "When your application to the SpaceCom Academy encountered similar administrative issues, I resolved them."

Ulla sat down. "Resolved, how?"

Fripp gestured with the pastry in her hand. "The Spinner's Gift is best practiced in small doses. Divert the subject's attention from a critical event, or roll a pinecone under an attacker's ski. In your case, a clerk found reason to update one checkbox in a form."

Ulla gazed at the pastry box and decided against having a second. "Why?"

"You are a spinner," said Fripp. "This world needs you."

"You're a spinner; why don't you just...make it happen? You know SpaceCom wants me back in the sky as soon as possible."

Oh, Child. Fripp's shoulders sagged. *Much as I could manipulate SpaceCom's bureaucracy, power like yours cannot be forced.* "I hope one day, before it is too late, that you will reconsider." The Elder's voice grew stronger. "A trained spinner of wyrd in her prime is much more effective against the Yotne than any starfighter can hope to be."

"I can reconsider all you want, but I have orders for the *Resolute*." Ulla drank the last of her coffee. "With a war heating up, SpaceCom'll have me in the sky till it's over." *Or till I'm dead.*

Fripp's eyes widened just the slightest bit. "Do think about it, Child. Please."

Ulla carried her coffee mug and napkin to the counter. There was no fold-down platform for humans at this one, so she put the mug on the chin-high counter rather than risk dropping it in the sink. *Why?*

We have covered that, Child.

Not quite. "Spinners are local to here, aren't they? I'm not. Why am I, of all people, a spinner?" *And please don't quote me the Hidden Spinner Prophecy; it's cheesy.*

For a long moment, Fripp said nothing. Ulla opened the door to leave.

Fripp sat very still. *Ask your father.*

Chapter Twenty-Nine
Back to SpaceCom

Less than a week later, Ulla stood outside the Trade Ministry's back door. She picked lint off her black uniform trousers as she waited for Skuli, who was supposed to drive her to Headquarters. She would have been more than happy to walk across Landfall Square to Hotel Row and catch the headquarters shuttle there, but Skuli had insisted.

"You've seen the new order from the Council of Chieftains about ground travel for valuable assets," he'd said. "You're a spinner. Unless Padraic Willemson or the High King tell me otherwise, you will be accompanied by a soulslayer and a spotter who's also a bodyguard."

"I'm a soulslayer," she'd told him. "I can do my own spotting." *Do I need a bodyguard? Seriously?*

"You are on the injured list until the doc says you're well. If anything happens to you while you're on this world, Padraic Willemson will have my head"—*if Thom doesn't kill me first.*

To fill in the gaps in Ulla's backcountry wardrobe, Yasmin and Skuli had gone with her to the shops, where she'd been measured for new uniforms, shoes, and civilian clothes. Per Admiral Rosen's order, Ulla had a short, tapered haircut that managed to conform to SpaceCom's personal grooming regs and still be the height of On'oi ladies' fashion.

Skuli drove up in a Balanced Trade Enforcement sedan. Aden Fournier, Ulla's new Matthias Carroll

Memorial Society mentor, rode in the front passenger seat.

"Never in anger, Starfighter," Aden said. *Black and whites? The other starfighters at HQ wear flight suits.*

Ulla's starched white shirt stuck to her sweaty shoulders as she reached for the door handle. *Now you tell me.* "Never in anger." She slid into the back seat. "Soulslaying duty?"

Her mentor nodded. "Day shift." *At least the Society put me indoors this time.*

"What about the shop?" The Fournier "shoe shop" was more like a small factory.

He shrugged. "It'll be fine. I put Geoff Tully in charge while I'm out."

Then they drove off through Newcastle's narrow streets.

* * *

"Never in anger." Aden greeted the soulslayer at the entrance to the Headquarters building.

"Never in anger." The young On'oi woman gave a thumbs-up to the SpaceCom guard, who let him in, and Aden disappeared up the stairs.

"Ulla?" Skuli said, "Let me know when you're ready to leave this afternoon."

If Council insists. Ulla folded her cap flat and tucked it into her belt.

I'm serious. "See you this afternoon, Starfighter. I have a meeting in ten minutes."

The young soulslayer gave another thumbs-up. Skuli went in, turned left, and disappeared down the corridor.

The soulslayer added "Never in anger" to her next thumbs-up. She must have known who Ulla was.

"Never in anger," Ulla replied and pulled up her SpaceCom ID on its chain around her neck. She waved it in the general direction of the pickup and got a green light. She stepped forward and smacked into a force field.

"Sorry, ma'am." The guard really did sound sorry. "Let me check your biometrics."

Of course. With the heightened alert status, he would need both ID and biometrics. Ulla stepped aside and let a handful of people go in. "It's probably these; they're recent." She pointed to the little scar on her face and held her scarred right hand out for inspection. She fished her readpad out of her back pocket, tapped at it, and showed him the screen. "I have an appointment in Personnel to update my profile."

"Of course." He peered at her readpad. "That's four hours from now," he said. She sensed suspicion bloom in his mind. "You're way early."

Ulla tapped at her readpad again and showed it to him. "That's because I have an appointment with the flight surgeon right now." If they didn't sort this out quickly, she'd be late.

"Yes, ma'am." He tapped at the comm panel on his counter. "Says here you're cleared—but you'll need an escort to get you through checkpoints until Personnel fixes your profile."

The young woman on soulslayer guard duty rolled her eyes. *Seriously? When you have a valid ID, and I can verify you're Flint Clan's Hidden Spinner?*

Ulla shrugged. *There's the right way, the wrong way, and the SpaceCom—wait! I'm what?*

You're famous. The soulslayer verified two more spacers coming in. Her brown eyes sparkled as she smiled at Ulla. *Cara Giovannisdaughter. Honored to meet you.*

The guard's comm panel beeped again. "Medical is sending somebody for you."

* * *

Dr. Lym tapped at a comm panel in the drafty exam room while Ulla shivered in a flimsy medical gown.

Was she cleared to fly? Or not? She resisted the urge to read his mind.

He swapped her earlier images on the screen with the ones he had just taken. She couldn't help overhearing one stray thought: *Not possible.* He turned to face her. "Your lungs look good," he said out loud. "My compliments to the Elders."

Ulla drummed her fingers on the exam table and swung her bare feet. "Am I cleared to fly?"

Lym turned back to the comm panel and brought up another image. "Stand up."

Ulla slid off the table and stood barefoot on the floor. The gown parted in front; she grabbed it and held it shut.

"Stand on tiptoe."
She did.
"Stand on just your right foot."
She did that effortlessly.
"Go up on tiptoe."
She did.
"Now stand on just your left foot."
Ulla did.
"Up on tiptoe."
Nothing to it. She teetered a little, but only because she was too proud to lower her heel before he said to.
"Sit down." Dr. Lym smiled. "You've been doing your ankle exercises. Good."
Damn straight, she'd been doing them. There was the sky to get back to. Ulla didn't mention that Fripp had shown her how to repair the ligaments she'd reinjured at Summer Pasture.
"Congratulations, Lieutenant. Medically, you're cleared to fly." The flight doc tapped at his comm panel. "As soon as the Guild rep signs off on your psych clearance, you can fly wherever Ops wants to send you."

* * *

Once she was dressed, Ulla stopped by the clerk's desk in the flight doc's outer office. "Is there a checkpoint between here and the Guild rep's office?"
He thought for a minute and nodded. "She's on the same corridor as the rest of the command staff."
Damn. "I have an appointment with her in ten minutes," Ulla said. "I need an escort to get through checkpoints until Personnel fixes my biometrics profile."
Thanks be, a break! He smiled broadly. "I can get you there."
Ulla kept a straight face. "Thanks."
He shut down his comm panel and stood.
Ulla Thorsdaughter, Olwyn Dara Wittber-Argeles.
"Just a minute, sorry," Ulla said to the clerk. *Ulla here.*
So sorry, Ulla, but I have to receive an urgent message. Can we reschedule?
Ulla pulled her readpad out of her pocket. *Sure.*
The clerk stared. "Psi?"
"Guild rep needs to reschedule." Ulla opened her

readpad, quashed two "new document" alerts, found her calendar, and watched the small screen as Olwyn pushed their appointment to tomorrow.

Now that Ulla had an hour of unexpected free time, she could catch up on reading her messages. One of the "urgent" documents was from Admiral Rosen. That one needed her attention right now. The other had a "sensitive information" flag and couldn't be opened in this semi-public waiting room.

Mags worked in Ops; they might have an unoccupied desk with a comm panel she could borrow. "Where's Ops?" Ulla asked the clerk.

"At the top of the stairs by the main entrance." He pointed. "The command post is secured, but you should be able to get into their office area—it's right next to the command post."

Her readpad vibrated again. She silenced it and headed upstairs.

* * *

The door to the empty office suite labeled "Operations" stood open. Where was everybody?

Heya, Starfighter. Aden Fournier nodded to her from his seat in the corridor next to an armed guard outside the closed door to the command post.

Uncle Aden! "Never in anger."

"Never in anger." He turned and whispered to the armed guard. "This is Lieutenant Thorsdaughter."

"Honored to meet you, Lieutenant." The guard inclined his head toward the closed door. "Morning briefing just started. Colonel B. said let you in if you made it up here in time." He opened the door and motioned for her to go inside.

Who was Colonel B? Not that it mattered; her messages would have to wait. Ulla slipped inside. Her readpad went quiet; no doubt a comm blocker covered the room.

She found a place to stand behind two flight-suited men. If they stood still, she could look between their shoulders and see the main display, which took up a three-meter round space, floor to ceiling, in the middle of the room.

Bailey-Duran, the star, took center stage as a

luminous ball more or less to scale in the display. Planets, ridiculously larger than scale so they could be seen at all, winked in their orbits; the third one from the star was Bailey-Duran Three, the world under the floor of this building. Out from BD3 lay two sparkling asteroid belts, three more planets, a few comets visible only by their labels, and a lot of nothing.

Glowing labels and markers, bigger than any natural feature of the star system, floated about the display. There were the designated jump zones, the shipping lanes, BD3 Station, commercial satellites, SpaceCom vessels, and a few mineral-extraction operations among the asteroids and one on BD3's moon. A cloud of Yotne explosive mines, all but one marked "neutralized," blocked the regular shipping lane; a line of blinking labels for merchant ships must be a detour.

The last Yotne mine winked from bright red to muted pink. The flight-suited man on Ulla's right muttered, "Go, *Dauntless*!" Much of the tension in the room dissolved.

Valiant's sister ship, the *Dauntless*, was in-system? Ulla glanced at the listings on the far wall. Yes, the *Dauntless* had arrived a few weeks ago. As had an assortment of other ships; SpaceCom had a proper task force in-system now. Starfighters had been blowing up mines while Ulla cooled her convalescent heels at the Trade Ministry.

The briefer paused, listened to something in his earpiece, then said, "This just in from the Guild."

On the main display, a new cluster of red labels—a Yotne task force—moved from outside the farthest planetary orbit, on the Edge side of the system, to a spot that was still far away but definitely on course for BD3.

Shit. They could be here by Midsummer.

Chapter Thirty
New Orders

Ulla, being last in, was first out the door when the meeting broke up. She went back to the Operations office suite and got out of the way as people, most of whom she did not recognize, streamed in.

"Spider!" Mags Pappas looked delighted. "Come in." She led the way to a big room filled with desks and plunked down her readpad on a desk next to a holo of Nik.

Ulla looked around the shared office and spotted an unused desk with a comm panel on the other side of the room. Good; she wanted to use a full-sized screen to look at her damned messages. "May I use that comm panel?"

"It's all yours." Mags sat down at her desk and activated its comm panel. "Spider, I'm so glad you're back. You look great!"

"Thanks." Ulla logged in at the empty comm panel. Mind-seeing, unbidden, told her when she touched it that Skuli Branson had been the last person to power it on.

"Sorry to abandon you." Mags put on a set of headphones. "I'm on a deadline."

"No worries." Now that she was logged in, the comm panel beeped unmercifully. What was so urgent?

"Lieutenant Thorsdaughter." A broad-shouldered officer emerged from a private office behind Ulla's borrowed desk. "Good, you're early." The insignia on his ground utility uniform said *colonel*; his name tag said *Becenti*.

Early for what? Ulla stood up and poked the comm panel to quiet it.

Colonel Becenti held out his right hand. "Welcome."

"Thank you, sir." Ulla shook his hand. She could punch through his psi block but decided against it. She could always ask—or sneak a look at the comm panel.

Becenti glanced at Mags's screen. "Lieutenant Papas."

Mags took off her headphones. "Sir?"

"Your presentation to Admiral Rosen got pushed back two hours."

"Thanks be." Mags grabbed her water bottle and drank. "That'll give me time to incorporate the data *Dauntless* sent; it ought to be here in half an hour."

"Good. That's what she thought." Colonel Becenti glanced at the readpad in his hand. "Lieutenant Thorsdaughter, have you seen your comm in the last hour?"

"No, sir."

"Read it. Then go see Admiral Rosen. She'll be free in about ten minutes."

Ulla's new document alerts winked at her from the comm panel. Still standing, she pushed aside Olwyn's calendar change and a note from Medical and went straight to the document from Admiral Rosen marked Urgent.

The brief message contained a single attached document—a new set of orders. Ulla read the first line and sat down abruptly.

SpaceCom had assigned her a desk job.

* * *

Ulla stood outside Admiral Rosen's open office door. The admiral looked up from her desk. "Please, come in. Have a seat."

Ulla did as she was told. She tried to cover her anger by inspecting the decorations on the admiral's office walls. Printed, framed accolades and gaudy service plaques vied for space with fashionably flat family portraits and a few very good pieces of local artwork.

"Like it?" Rosen caught Ulla eyeing a small, elegant tapestry. "Cara Giovannisdaughter, the soulslayer, made it. You may have seen her on Dweller guard duty."

"I met her this morning, yes."

"We only have her for a few more days. She's from Esperanza, only in Newcastle till her ship leaves for Earth."

Rosen admired the tapestry. "Art school in Paris."

Neither of them spoke.

Finally, Admiral Rosen broke the silence. "You're a soulslayer too."

Ulla blinked. "Among other things."

"That's what Mr. Branson says. Guild Member Wittber concurs." Rosen glanced at a document on her comm panel. "Ms. Wittber approved your psych clearance for duty, by the way—though she still wants you to come and see her."

"Why did SpaceCom move me from a flying billet to Headquarters?" Ulla still felt as though the wind had been knocked out of her.

The admiral put her elbows on her desk and leaned forward. "We need local tactical perspective here in Ops. The Alliance liaison with General Zhou's staff has been helping us out, but he can't be in two places at once. You have a solid background in UW&N history and SpaceCom operations, and you've completed SpaceCom's leadership classes."

Ulla tried not to squirm. Was Admiral Rosen trying to sugarcoat a desk job?

"Your experience with local psi methods and tactics is limited, but I think you have the contacts to overcome that."

Ulla had skimmed over her new orders. What had she missed? "What are you asking?"

Rosen shook her head ever so slightly. "I'm not asking. Just explaining what I expect of you in your new position as LTLO."

Local Tactics Liaison Officer. "Isn't the LTLO supposed to be a ground pounder?" In Ulla's current mental state, tact was off the table.

"Bald Mountain looked like a ground action to me." Admiral Rosen's comm panel beeped; she silenced it. "Technically, at least, you are On'oi. You're a citizen of the Alliance, and also, you're a SpaceCom officer. You're trained in local psi protocols, you speak fluent Dialekt, and you can get by in City English. It's a good fit."

Ulla had noticed a "combat" flag on her new orders. Maybe, just maybe—"How does the combat piece work?"

Rosen laced her fingers together. "If and when the balloon goes up—and there is every reason to think it will—you leave here and go fight."

Ulla allowed herself to hope. "In a Goshawk?"

The newly promoted admiral whose call sign had once been Rosie looked at the oldest unit plaque on the wall, and the picture next to it of a group of starfighters in front of a cargo Gate. *Once a starfighter, always a starfighter* leaked past Rosie's psi blocker.

That was a side of leadership you didn't see very often.

Admiral Rosen cleared her throat. "No, Spider. Your new combat billet is with our allied force on this world's surface—unless their leadership chooses differently."

Ulla sat very still and concentrated on listening.

"You're to become fully qualified in your new operational specialty." The admiral looked up from the comm panel. "Specialties."

Oh. "To whom do I report, for..." Ulla's voice cracked. She swallowed. "...for combat duty?"

"The Elder, Fripp." Rosen glanced again at the document. "Or to her deputy, if she assigns one."

"On the ground." Ulla realized too late that she'd said it out loud. Once lapsed, her Goshawk qualification would be extremely difficult to restore. Words deserted her.

"Spider."

Ulla straightened.

"I am so very sorry." Admiral Rosen tapped at her comm panel; its screen went blank. "Your psi talents make you a very high-value asset. The Alliance has asked for your help, and they are willing to train you." She paused, sighed, and went on. "You—and your talents—will be much more useful and much safer with them. Knowing what I know now, I cannot in good conscience put you back in harm's way in a Goshawk."

Shit, shit, shit! Ulla barely kept her mouth shut.

Admiral Rosen was still talking. "...nor can I hold you back from your potential to completely eclipse the substantial contribution you have already made—and could make in the future—as a starfighter."

She had a point. Ulla had not yet come to terms with said point, but it was valid.

"The Guild rep says your psi talents include leaving your body to fly independently." The admiral's eyes wandered again to the starfighters in the picture on her wall. "I would love to know what that's like."

Spider's Wyrd

After that, Admiral Rosen was all business. "You'll live in the Pordenone Hotel with the other officers who work here. As LTLO, you report to the Director of Planetary Operations, BD3. That's Colonel Becenti; I think you've already met him. He will fill you in on the details. I believe you are already acquainted with Balanced Trade Enforcement Agent Skuli Branson."

"Yes, ma'am."

"Mr. Branson is the Alliance's liaison with the commander and his staff; I'm sure he can give you some pointers about your new job." The admiral sipped from an enameled coffee mug. "It'll be up to Colonel Becenti, of course. You'll likely work closely with Intelligence, probably most often with Lieutenant Commander Nkosi. She heads a workgroup that studies Dwellers."

They'd put Mary on the ground, too? Ulla had looked forward to working with her again. On the *Resolute*.

"You'll probably see a lot of Ensign Strom—he's Intel's Ground Forces Analyst for this planet."

The brand-new officer who had inventoried Ulla's things and assembled her ribbon rack?

"Which brings me to the next point." Admiral Rosen handed Ulla a paper document headed with the Alliance Trade Ministry's logo. "To SpaceCom, Lieutenant Thorsdaughter, you are an experienced starfighter with useful local expertise. To the Alliance, you are a VIP with highly valued psi talent. They would like to see a bodyguard and a soulslayer accompany you any time you go outside this installation, the Alliance Trade Ministry, or secured contract quarters like the Pordenone."

Was this Skuli's doing? He'd been on his way to a meeting in the Commander's wing this morning. No. The signature on the paper was Padraic Willemson's, dated yesterday and marked "for the Council of Chieftains."

"We got them to modify the terms." Rosen handed her another sheet of paper. "You're a SpaceCom officer; you can protect yourself. And your experience as a soulslayer speaks for itself."

Thanks be! Ulla's shoulders relaxed a little.

"You will carry a sidearm any time you are outside the presumed safe locations the Alliance stipulates." Rosen activated her comm panel, brought up a document on the screen, and scrolled until she found what she was looking for. "When you entered the Academy, you had a black belt in karate. Have you kept up your practice?"

"Yes, ma'am. At least I did, before..." Ulla's voice trailed off. Before the *Valiant* exploded.

"Understandable." The admiral silenced her comm panel again. "You'll be working with Mr. Strom, anyway; I think it would be a very good idea for you to ask him to help you get back up to speed on unarmed combat."

"*Ensign* Strom?"

Rosen laughed. "Spider, he was a Marine for ten standard years before he enrolled in the Academy and earned his commission."

When an admiral in one's chain of command gave voice to a "very good idea," one turned to and did it. Ulla looked forward to meeting the enigmatic Ensign Strom.

"There is an administrative hurdle you need to clear before the position is permanent." Rosen brought up another document. "Personnel has an administrative hold on your record; there's a request from the Matthias Carroll Memorial Society that you meet at least weekly with your mentor."

"A 'request'?"

"Personnel doesn't mess around with 'requests' from the soulslayers." Admiral Rosen scrolled through the document. "We've dealt with this before."

They had? Oh. Mary Nkosi.

Rosen scanned the document one more time. "I don't see anything here that keeps you from visiting BD3 Station or our ships in-system, but Personnel says 'restrict to BD3 surface.' Can you shed any light on that?"

"No, ma'am. Aden Fournier might. He's my mentor."

"Put me in contact with him, then."

At least Ulla had one easy thing to do today. "He's on Dweller guard duty in front of the command post." She inclined her head in that direction. "Shall I go cover for him for a few minutes and ask him to see you?"

"Perfect! Send him in."

* * *

The next morning, Ulla trudged along the gravel path beside the road leading from SpaceCom's headquarters to its warehouse complex down by the sea docks. She carried a duffel full of brand-new flight suits and the worn-out gear she'd had on when she landed. She had to trade it in for ground combat gear and utility uniforms.

Ulla had decided against taking the installation's circulating shuttle. She hadn't had nearly enough fresh air lately, not since leaving Flint Clan's summer pasture feet first on a stretcher. After one look at Ulla's face when she'd arrived this morning, Colonel Becenti had suggested she take some time outdoors.

Her new boss had seen her desolation. Not a good start to a working relationship. Ulla pressed on, her white shirt stuck to her sweaty back.

Heya, Starfighter! Skuli Branson pulled up beside her in one of the ubiquitous little open voiturettes people used to get around on the installation. "Want a ride?"

"Thanks, but I'd rather walk. It's a glorious morning," Ulla walked on, hoping her facial expression could be interpreted as a smile.

Nice try. Skuli nudged the voiturette forward and stopped next to Ulla. He patted the passenger seat. *Want to talk?*

Ulla hesitated, then tossed the duffel onto the voiturette's cargo shelf and climbed aboard.

"I'm going to the sea cargo pier." Skuli got them moving again. "You heading for Personal Equipment Issue?"

"Yep." Ulla stared straight ahead. *I have to turn in my flight gear.*

She heard his mind consider and reject several responses. Mercifully, he said nothing.

Ulla tightened her grip on the passenger handrail. *After everything that's happened, I'm still just SpaceCom's fucking pawn.*

Skuli kept his eyes on the road ahead. *You play chess, then.*

Not well. Ulla had taken SpaceCom's money and sworn SpaceCom's oath. She'd become a damned good starfighter. She had the medals and the bad dreams to prove it.

He eased the voiturette over a bump. *Then you know that with skill, effort, and luck, a pawn can become a queen.*

In chess, the queen can move as far as she wants to in any direction.

Exactly. Skuli pulled up by a door marked "Personal

Equipment Issue" in the middle of the street-facing wall of a huge warehouse.

"This is the other side of the chessboard," he said. "You might as well embrace it."

Chapter Thirty-One
Micky Bravo's

"Better, Lieutenant!"

Ulla rolled, grinding more grass stains into her physical training clothes, stood up, and faced Ensign Strom. She had yet to land a punch, but at least this time, she'd avoided getting fake-killed.

He was average height for a human man, all muscle and brains, and he was whipping her butt at unarmed combat drill.

His reach was longer than hers, but maybe, just maybe, if she watched for the right opportunity—

She sailed right past him, rolled, and got up again.

"Stop!"

Fine by her. Ulla took the opportunity to cough; she spat on the manicured grass of their practice area behind the headquarters building.

"Lieutenant, I'm bigger than you." Strom wiped the sweat off his forehead. "Why don't you use your feet?"

Ulla adjusted the athletic ankle brace the doc had given her. "Got out of the habit, I guess."

"Well, get back in the habit! Go!"

Ulla watched him move, watched where his eyes tracked. She dodged his attack, turned, and landed a kick.

"See, Lieutenant? You CAN make contact!" Then he sent her rolling again.

Discerning his next move was hard. Reading thoughts behind his buzzing psi blocker ate up mental bandwidth she needed to stay in the fight. When had she become so dependent on psi?

Since you discovered your 'Today, I am lucky' trick at Mining Station Beta Three.

Fripp?

Yes, Child. HEADS UP!

Purely on instinct, Ulla blocked Strom's attack and sent him rolling.

"Stop!" Strom stood up and grinned. "Good situational awareness, Lieutenant." His eyes tracked to a spot behind Ulla's shoulder. "Who's that?"

Ulla stood her ground. "You're not making me look over my shoulder so you can whup me again."

"No, really." He stood straight, arms relaxed at his sides.

Ulla turned. Fripp's projection watched them with great interest. "The Elder? Gaining commander for my combat billet. Also, my mentor for psi stuff."

His eyes widened just the tiniest bit when Fripp's projection winked out. "I'll bet you can incorporate psi into your fighting technique."

"Guess so." Ulla thought back to Flint Clan kids horsing around on trek. Strom had a psi block, so she was limited to ordinary headblind misdirection in that department—but mind-moving was another matter. "Do we have time for one more round?"

"Sure." He glanced toward Bailey-Duran. This far into Newcastle's northern summer, it was hours away from setting. "Ready?"

Ulla assumed her stance.

"Go!"

They circled around each other for the barest second before he closed in. Ulla ducked and changed direction. Strom countered. As soon as he lunged toward her, Ulla reached out with mind-moving. He was mid-lunge when his feet slid out from under him, and he fell, hard. Automatically, she rolled him over, held him down with her knee, and twisted his arms behind his back.

He pounded the ground with one foot. "Stop!" His voice was almost inaudible.

"You okay?" Had she hurt him? Ulla sat back, appalled.

He found his breath and sat up. "Excellent job, Lieutenant. You used your knee correctly; falling on my back is what knocked the breath out of me." He grinned.

"But you won't catch me like that again."

Good to know. "Let's call it a day," Ulla said. "I'm meeting the other *Valiant* starfighters for supper downtown at Mickey Bravo's. Want to come?"

He stood up. "The starfighter bar?"

She nodded.

"No, thanks." He fished a towel out of his duffel. "Enjoy."

"I plan to," she told him. "And I'll think up some more psi tricks for tomorrow."

Strom brushed grass clippings out of his hair. "I want to talk with Mr. Branson and see what he can teach me about psi and fighting."

What a good idea! "See if he can join us tomorrow afternoon," Ulla said. "Oh, and Ensign?"

He wiped grass clippings off his arms. "Ma'am?"

"You're a junior officer; I'm a junior officer. It's time we started using each other's names." Ulla unzipped her duffel and pulled out her towel from its place on top of the uniform she'd worn today. "Mine's Ulla. Call sign's Spider. What do you want to be called?"

"Mikko is fine."

"Thanks, Mikko. Good workout." She wiped mud off her face. "You must have been a drill sergeant in some past life."

"I was a drill sergeant in this life." He shook out his towel. "After a string of back-to-back deployments, I took a garrison job for a breather." He grinned. "Replacement Depot on Reynoso Tres—that's where I met my wife."

"She was a recruit?"

"Heavens, no!" He blushed. "Abby's father is a SpaceCom officer at the sector headquarters."

So, the quiet ensign had a life. "Do you have an image of her?"

He fished a small flat-picture case out of his pocket and opened it. From one side of the case, a pretty, young woman smiled. In the picture on the other side, she held a tiny baby.

"They're beautiful." Where had Ulla seen Mikko's wife before? "What's your child's name?"

"Jovvá." Mikko paused. "Well, Arthur Jovvá; his mother's father calls him Arthur."

Abby. Arthur. Sector headquarters in the Reynoso

system. Ulla studied the woman's image again. "Is your wife related to Admiral Shinn?"

Mikko nodded. "He's her father."

An enlisted man need not even think about marrying a flag officer's daughter. "I wondered why you switched, mid-career, and went for a commission," Ulla said.

Psi blocker or no, the look on Mikko's face told her his young family was worth all that and more.

* * *

In her hotel room an hour later, Ulla ran her fingers through her clean, wet hair. She opened the armoire and pulled out a dress Yasmin had helped her choose. The skirt was long enough to satisfy SpaceCom's requirement not to scandalize City-States people and short enough not to trip her up. She pulled it over her head and was pleased with the result. Thom was going to Mickey Bravo's with her, and she wanted to look good.

Ulla removed her Flint Clan earring, shined it up, and replaced it in her left earlobe. Glad as she was that she and Thom had managed to rise above their awkwardness at the Trade Ministry, she was out of practice at girly things.

There was a knock at her door. *Starfighter?*

Thom! Ulla used mind-moving to spin the lock and let him in.

"I think you're brilliant at girly things," he said.

She kissed him enthusiastically. *My, uh, girly things won't make it out the door if you keep talking like that.*

Another time?

Absolutely. Ulla disengaged from Thom and reached for her new jacket. Newcastle's hot, sticky days cooled down fast after Bailey-Duran set.

Thom glanced at her holstered weapon. "Unless you want to give the good people of Newcastle the vapors, you'd better wear your jacket."

It's still warm outside! But she let him help her into it anyway. Her sidearm disappeared under its generous folds. She reached onto the top shelf of the armoire for a stylish Newcastle cloche.

"You're wearing that?"

"Newcastle women cover their heads in public; SpaceCom requires we do the same when we wear civilian clothes here."

Thom shook his head. "That's the letter of the policy. The spirit, I'm sure, is that you not antagonize indigenous personnel."

???

"You're On'oi now." He took the hat from her and put it back in the armoire. "That makes you indigenous personnel."

Out of uniform, Ulla had no use for hats except as protection from dirtside elements. She was not a fan of hat hair either.

"There you are, then." He held out his arm to her. "Shall we join your shipmates?"

* * *

Ulla and Thom rounded a corner. A colorful sign with the letters *MB* swung from a standard that stuck out of the wall on the right side of the street.

Ulla stopped in the middle of the sidewalk. "Thom, you ought to have a heads-up."

"What?"

"One of my—exes—will be there."

"Fergus McCauley?"

Of course, he already knew. This was a reunion for the *Valiant*'s surviving starfighters, and Fergus's name was on the list Thom had procured for her weeks ago. The night he'd shown her his notebook full of drawings, Thom had heard Fergus's name again and Ulla's anguish.

Thom glanced sideways at her. "Do I need to fight him?"

"No." Ulla relaxed into Thom's easy companionship. *Spark's gone.*

Are you sure?

Ulla shrugged. *Doesn't matter. He's over me.* That orbit had decayed years ago. "We're still good friends—more like siblings, these days." Which made Fergus the only brother she had left. *I'll not change that.*

Booze and all?

You heard, then.

Ed Jeppeson said one of your friends is trying to drink away a Gift he won't own up to.

Ed had been on guard duty the day the starfighters

had visited her. The Trade Ministry was such a small town!
—and the starfighter community isn't?
Indeed. Ulla held out her hand to Thom. "Hey, Guardian. Wanna come play with the starfighters?"
He put an arm around her shoulders. "Let's."
They ducked through the door into Mickey Bravo's. As Ulla's eyes adjusted to the dim interior, she took in tables of well-dressed Newcastlers alternating with groups of Standard-speaking spacers.
Heya! Neal Erikson smiled and waved from where he sat between Mary Nkosi and Colonel Becenti. Admiral Rosen was with them, as was the captain who ran Intel, and a bevy of trim, middle-aged spacers Ulla hadn't met—command types from the *Resolute,* most likely.
Heya, cousin. Thom waved back at Neal. *We're in the cheap seats tonight.* He led the way to the starfighter bar at the back of the building.
Ulla waved to Neal and Mary and followed Thom down the aisle between tables. *A person might think you've been to the starfighter bar before.* Mind-talking worked so much better than speech in the crowded dining room!
Nope. Thom stood back to let her go first. *Everybody knows it's back there.* He grinned. *When you're all in the sky, we ordinary people go in and gawp at your squadron plaques on the walls and your signatures on the ceiling.*
A thought struck Ulla. *If you weren't with me, you'd fit in at that table full of brass.*
Yup. He caught up to her. *Spinner Ulla, you belong at a table with your commanding general and my da.*
Ulla so wasn't ready for that yet.
He gave her a quick squeeze. *I hear starfighters are more fun.* "After you."
"Spider!" Mags waved from a long table at the other end of the room. The backs of two empty chairs leaned down on the table's edge. She pointed to the chairs. Fergus and Nik waved. José, formal as ever, pulled out a chair for a young local woman Ulla had never seen before. Having seated his date, he smiled. Ulla and Thom sat down.
A server brought platters of grilled fish and fried potatoes. There were fresh carrots, radishes, and other vegetables cut to finger-food size. Nobody would go hungry while waiting for the main course. "Drinks?" he asked.
Ulla and Thom asked for beer; others at the table were

ready for a second round. Conversation flowed; Thom was his charming self, in fluent Standard. Ulla relaxed.

One well-placed grenade . . .

That was random. Ulla looked around. *Fergus?*

He parodied a salute from his seat on the other side of the table. *The* Resolute *has a down day tomorrow. That's no secret. A lot of her leadership and most of her starfighters are here; we're a fecking target.*

Ulla heard variations on *What the hell?* from Thom, Neal, Mary, Skuli, Olwyn, and one of Mickey Bravo's security staff. Wait! Skuli and Olwyn were here too?

Heya, Starfighter. That was Skuli. *We're outside in the beer garden.* There was a pause. *He's right, you know.*

"Fergus." Ulla said his name out loud.

"What?" His beer glass was empty. He picked up a tiny glass and downed its clear liquid contents in one go.

"Psi. You're projecting to everyone who can hear." His range might be short, but gods, he was loud.

"Oh." He blinked. "Sorry. It's just that—something awful is about to happen." As the server cleared away the empties and replenished everyone's drinks, Fergus picked up his fresh tiny glass, tossed back the contents, and settled in with his beer.

Ulla set her beer down. *Thom, do you mind if I...*

Thom was already well into a conversation with Mags and Nik. *Please. Do what you need to.*

Ulla stood up. "Fergie, let's dance." That would give them a chance to speak privately.

Chapter Thirty-Two
What Went Down

Ulla stuck to speaking aloud as Fergus whisked her around the dance floor. "I won't ask if you're okay."

"Good." Fergus raised his arm, guiding Ulla through a turn. "How do you do it?" he asked.

"Do what?"

"Keep yourself to yourself." The music changed, and he changed step with it. Drunk or sober, he was a great lead on the dance floor.

Ulla thought for a bit. "I learned; so can you." She sent him a telepathic impression of the hangover she'd shared with Flint Clan.

They danced through a few more figures. "I'm doing that, aren't I?" he said.

"Mm-hmm." Ulla twirled underneath his outstretched arm. "There're too many distractions here tonight for me to teach you, but it's not hard. The Guild rep can show you tomorrow."

"The newbie on the *Resolute* who replaced Ms. Wittber-Argeles?" *Not a chance.*

"Then come dirtside and see Ms. Wittber."

"Maybe." Fergus led her through another dance figure. "Can she teach me to shut out the infernal noise from other people too?"

In an instant, Ulla understood what was bothering Fergus. Her psi had blossomed among civilized, discreet adepts, who had trained her as soon as they saw the need. His had emerged here in Newcastle, among headblind City people and spacers. He'd had to deal with the constant mind-chatter Ulla had long since tuned out.

"How do you sleep?" she asked.

"My rack's not too bad if everybody in—earshot?—is asleep at the same time. Just so long as nobody has any nightmares. There's a couch in the wardroom where the only psi I hear is white noise—must be a psi shield node in the bulkhead behind it. When we're on different shifts, whiskey does the trick if I can't use the wardroom." He stepped and turned to the music. "Timing's an issue because I only fly sober."

It took a lot of whiskey to damp down unwanted psi. Ulla hoped Fergus never found out how well poppy juice worked.

He led her to the edge of the dance floor. "Wait a minute." He pulled his readpad from his pocket and tapped at it. "We've no signal here, but this'll remind me to make an appointment. Thanks for kicking my butt, Spider."

"Any time, Fergie." They danced back out onto the floor. Ulla relaxed and followed Fergus's polished lead.

Fergus led her through another turn. "Tell me about your Guardian friend."

"Thom Yensson?"

"I think you two are crazy about each other."

"I spent most of those weeks on the ground trying not to be. Crazy about him, that is." Ulla danced a few steps. "But we couldn't not bond."

"He seems like an okay guy."

Fergus McCauley was vetting her dates now? The nerve!

"I'm the only brother you have left, remember? Do you love him?"

Ulla nodded, starting to answer, then rephrased. "I think so. I'm not sure how love works."

"I know."

"I treated you like shit back in the day." Ulla sighed. "I'm sorry."

Fergus kept up his cheery outward facade. "Yeah, well, nobody died." He stopped them in the middle of the dance floor and looked into her eyes. "If you think this guy's the one, Spider, let him into your heart." *True love really can last more than five standard months. Just—don't force the poor man out to arm's length like you do the rest of us.*

That hurt. But Ulla supposed she'd earned it.

Just then, a beam of light flashed from Fergus to a spot in the air about a meter from his head.

Shit. Dwellers!

Time seemed to slow.

Neal raced outside and traded places with Olwyn, who joined Mary inside. Mary was already fielding Dwellers that were bouncing off the psi blockers of the senior officers at her table. Scanning the area, Ulla sensed at least twenty Dwellers in the street outside. She risked a quick projection into the air above the building to get a better look. Ordinary Newcastlers milled about; one sat, head drooping, on a public bench. Had he been the recent host of the Dweller Fergus must have just banished?

Ulla would digest that bit of information later. In the meantime, people were staring at her.

Ordinary headblind people might not be able to see Dweller-killing energy beams, but they'd just watched the offworlder Guardian split in two, waft about, and reunite herself.

A bouncer whispered to a pair of servers. "Dwellers outside! Give her room—she's a soulslayer."

"In here!" Ulla dragged Fergus by the hand and pushed him through the door into the starfighter bar. She slammed the door behind them as Thom killed two Dwellers in midair.

Another Dweller hovered over Mags, bounced off her psi blocker, changed course, and possessed a starfighter across the table from her. He stood.

Flash! Ulla destroyed the Dweller.

The starfighter sank back into his chair. "What the hell was that?"

"Dwellers!" Ulla felt waves of adrenaline surge among their fellow starfighters. "I just killed the one that almost got you."

He leaned on the table, spent. "Thank you."

"Dwellers?" Two starfighters from the *Resolute* jumped up, ready to fight.

"Sit down!" Ulla dispatched another Dweller, midair. The damned things were coming in straight through the walls. "If you want to be useful, don't let anybody in here that a soulslayer hasn't cleared."

"Soulslayers? Where?" The short starfighter from B

flight moved to cover the kitchen door.

"Thom." Ulla pointed. "Me. Commander Nkosi and her date."

Fergus nailed a Dweller.

Ulla took a deep, centering breath. "Fergie, too, may the gods have mercy."

Two more flashes from Thom.

"Thom was at Bald Mountain; he knows what he's doing. Do what he says." Ulla did a quick scan; Neal and Skuli had made it out into the street.

Watch and learn, Lieutenant McCauley. Thom did not look away from his task.

Good. Fergie managed to tell his brain to ignore his blood-alcohol content and mostly followed Thom's lead.

Pairs of starfighters divvied up, guarding the doors to the kitchen and dining room, the bar pass-through, and three windows overlooking the street. Physical security was a drill they understood.

Some part of Ulla's mind heard servers going table to table in the dining room and beer garden, asking customers to stay where they were.

"Sit down, shut up, and get out of the soulslayers' way!" Olwyn's voice carried through the closed door. *Mary! Two Dwellers! There!*

They needed crowd control, and fast. Ulla raised an arm over her head and cruised her prone projection holoshow-superhero-style over the customers in the main dining room, through the wall to the beer garden, and back again. That ought to convince them weird shit was going down. She left Olwyn to her Dweller-spotting.

Mary had the dining room, Thom had the bar, and Neal was making headway in the street outside. The kitchen! Ulla scanned the area. One Dweller. She sent her projection in for a better view. The Dweller possessed a cook, who reached for a pan of boiling water.

Flash! The cook crumpled to the floor, clear of the stove and empty-handed, thanks be.

She returned to her body in the starfighter bar in time to see Fergus pick off a Dweller in midair. *Good, Fergie, stick to killing the ones in midair. Leave the double-souls for soulslayers who know what they're doing.*

Fergie kept scanning for Dwellers. *Will do. I'm buzzed, not stupid.*

There might be hell to pay from the Matthias Carrol Memorial Society, but right now, Ulla didn't care. *Oh, shit!* What about SpaceCom's contract hotels, like the Pordenone? What about Whiskey Row, down by the port and chock-full of spacers?

Society's on it. And the City Guard's on the way. That was Skuli, outside. *Neal! Behind you!*

Ulla remembered to breathe.

Two more flashes from Thom.

Somebody needed to unify their Dweller-killing efforts here at Mickey Bravo's. Ulla could do that in projection, but she didn't want to repeat what had happened at Bald Mountain. If she could find a secure place to park her body while she projected very, very carefully...

"Ma'am, there's a basement." The bouncer who'd helped with crowd control stood right behind her.

"Show me."

He led the way through a door in the back of the kitchen, opened it for her, and locked it behind them. They had no sooner reached the foot of the stairs than electric power went out, and they were left with dim light from the slit windows at the top of the basement walls.

Had someone thought to shut off power in case a Gate lay hidden nearby? Or had the lights just gone out? The former, Ulla hoped. Skuli had said somebody called the Newcastle City Guard.

She grounded herself on the hard, cool floor and sent her projection up on the roof. She stuck a ghostly hand through a standpipe to remind her to keep her projection insubstantial.

Half a dozen men in City clothing lay inert on the cobblestone street outside Mickey's. The first former Dweller host she'd seen still slouched on his bench, staring straight ahead. A trail of unconscious and barely conscious people led to the end of the street, where Neal and Skuli worked what she hoped were the last remaining active Dweller hosts. She scanned again, found two Dwellers just outside Neal's range, and banished them. One host tumbled to the sidewalk and the other wobbled to a nearby bench and collapsed.

Holy shit! That came from the bouncer in the basement.

He'd seen the flash then. Ulla dissolved her projection and asked, *Do you have the Gift?*

He nodded, and they got back to work. From her seat on the basement floor, she scanned the area for Dwellers. None nearby. Where had they and their hosts come from? Seemingly out of nowhere. She tried mind-seeing and found a Gate in a boarded-up shop three streets over. *Hey, Olwyn.*

The Gate? Got it. Olwyn sounded tired. *Newcastle City Guard just arrived; I'll tell them.*

Ulla accepted the bouncer's offer of a hand up. "Thanks."

"Any time."

"Does the management know?"

"Know what?"

"That you can mind-talk." In the city-states there was a small but vocal minority who were afraid of people who had psi talent. Ulla thought back to the Newcastlers who had warned her and her offworlder friends not to trust the On'oi.

"My boss knows," he said, "and Mickey Bravo's seems okay with it, but..." The conversation tapered off.

"But what?"

"Not every employer is as accepting," he said as he led the way to the stairs. "I'd appreciate it if you don't mention it."

Ulla sighed. "If the Guard ask, I have to tell the truth."

"I suppose you do." He didn't look happy about that.

She followed him up the stairs. *I shouldn't think it would occur to them to ask. I certainly won't bring it up.*

Thank you. The bouncer opened the door for Ulla, and they walked back through the kitchen and out into the restaurant.

Chapter Thirty-Three
After

Ulla pushed her empty plate away, grateful the City Guard had allowed Mickey Bravo's to serve dinner to all the witnesses stuck here waiting for the investigators to interview them.

Fergus sat, looking chastened, at the center of a conversation at the other end of the room between Neal Erikson and a well-dressed spacer who, it turned out, was Lieutenant Commander Warner, Fergie's flight commander from the *Resolute*. Olwyn and Skuli were with them, as was Admiral Rosen.

The young cook who'd been Dweller-ridden perched on the edge of his seat across from Ulla, waiting for his ride home. He shivered, caught himself, and sat up straight. She read his memories, now entwined with a River Pack foot soldier's memories and the memories of the Dweller itself, which reached back to before human habitation of this part of the galaxy. The poor man was in for a lifetime of nightmares.

Ulla and Thom had already given their statements, but Admiral Rosen had asked Ulla to stick around. Thom waited with her. Mary Nkosi sat with them, waiting for Neal.

Ulla linked minds with Mary. *So, you and Neal are an item then?*

Outwardly, Mary shrugged. Her inward thoughts were more candid. *Yes. And we had plans for tonight.*

Commander Warner approached their table. "Spider,

may I have a word with you?" He motioned toward the only empty corner of the room.

"Yes, sir."

Once they were away from the others, he didn't leave her in suspense. "SpaceCom is putting a Goshawk squadron on BD3 Station. Mr. McCauley's a candidate. I need a character reference, and I need your perspective as Headquarters Ops LTLO."

Had the Society already restricted Fergie to the star system? *Neal?*

Never in anger, Starfighter. Neal Erikson waved from where he sat. *And yes, we have.*

Ulla chose her words carefully. "Fergus McCauley is a—close friend. I'm not unbiased."

"I know."

Right. Ulla had heard flight trainers use the story, with names removed, of her and Fergus's ill-fated Goshawk-school romance as a cautionary tale. They were part of starfighter lore. She sighed. "Ask away."

"How long has he been a soulslayer?"

"Just since the Dwellers hit Mickey Bravo's."

"Lieutenant…"

"I'm not being snarky, sir. He has always had, uh, remarkably accurate premonitions. His granny, back on Earth, gets them too. But full-on psi talent, no." Ulla caught herself fiddling with her Flint Clan earring. "He's developed short-range telepathy just since the *Valiant* blew—maybe during the week or so the survivors spent dirtside?"

"Go on."

"He's been trying to hide his psi talent—afraid it'd pull him out of starfighters and into a paranormal billet." As hers had. "But with no training, he can't filter what he hears telepathically. He told me this evening that other people's thoughts are background noise for him all the time. He hasn't had a decent night's sleep in weeks."

"What about the booze?"

Ulla took a deep breath. "He drinks, we all do. But until—here—I've never known Fergus McCauley to let drink be a problem."

"Why now?"

"Alcohol interferes with psi. He says it helps him get to sleep." Ulla met Commander Warner's stern gaze.

"The problem is that the stronger the psi talent, the more alcohol it takes to turn it off."

"And he's a soulslayer. That's a strong talent, right?"

"Yes, sir."

"Professor Erikson has offered a remedy." The crease between Warner's eyes deepened.

"Does it get Fergie back in the sky?" Ulla asked.

"Professor Erikson says yes if Mr. McCauley does the work. I'm told there's an oath involved. What can you tell me about that?"

"The one that begins and ends with 'Never in anger'?"

He nodded. "It's...draconian."

Yes. Yes, it was. "It's similar to our 'use of deadly force' agreement for small arms," Ulla said, "but soulslaying is a psi talent. There's no way to lock it safely away in an armory."

She took a deep breath. "Understand, sir, that if Fergie takes that oath and then demonstrates that he cannot live safely with his Dark Gift, the Matthias Carroll Memorial Society will send you his ashes in a box. They'll have followed their own due process, and there is no recourse."

Warner blinked. "He keeps drunking himself up, that'll happen."

"I don't think he has a drinking problem," Ulla said. "I think he has a psi problem."

"Are you sure?"

"He won't be the Society's first." Ulla thought about Granny Kate. "My first soulslayer mentor was a recovering alcoholic. She had to have been well into her seventies, standard calendar. I never knew her to touch a drop."

"You're speaking of her in the past tense."

"Katrin Ostapsdaughter died killing Dwellers on Bald Mountain," Ulla said. "But before that, she raised a strong, caring family. She loved them all, and they loved her back."

Fergie's flight commander cleared his throat. "Professor Erikson and Lieutenant Commander Nkosi say Mr. McCauley was a hero this evening. Though they're not happy about his using the Dark Gift while under the influence."

Fergie'd had deadly accurate aim and had killed at least half a dozen Dwellers when he was at least four drinks in. How powerful would he be with all his faculties intact?

"Professor Erikson has invited Mr. McCauley to stay with him for a week of psi training," Warner said. "If he does well, he takes the oath, joins the local Matthias Carroll Society, and returns to duty."

"And then?"

"If he keeps his nose clean, he joins our advance team on the station and flies Goshawks."

"I think he'll like that," Ulla said. "I recommend you take Neal Erikson up on his offer." *Fergie, you lucky shit! You get to fly!*

* * *

"That's all you brought, Fergus?" Cara Giovannisdaughter asked from the driver's seat of an aging van in the Pordenone Hotel's loading zone. Ulla and Thom stood on the pavement outside her window, keeping her company.

Fergus, with paper checkout receipt in hand, tossed a small overnight duffel into the back of the van and climbed into the passenger seat. "I only meant to spend one night dirtside." *Hotel's too loud.*

Neal, in the van's rear seat, winced. *Speak for yourself, buddy.* A couple of lights winked on in the hotel windows above them. Mary, sitting beside Neal, winced too.

No worries, Fergie. It gets better. With Thom's warm arm around her shoulders, Ulla watched them drive away. "How'd Cara get taxi duty?"

Thom yawned. "She's staying with the Rogerses. That van is theirs, and they live across the street from Neal. Over by the university."

So, Mary's going home with Neal anyway. That would be a full house, with Fergus there too.

Thom laughed. *Mary's going home to the guest house she rents from the Rogerses.*

Oh. Ulla knew Mary had rented a place downtown; she just hadn't known where. *Aubrey and Miles?*

Yep. They all kind of bonded in Landfall. "Let's get you home."

An odd word to use for a hotel room, but that's what it was. They went inside and took the stairs.

Ulla unlocked her door. *Would you like to come in?*

Yes, please.

No sooner had Ulla shut the door than her knees nearly buckled. She barely made it to the couch in time to sit, not fall.

Thom plopped down next to her. She reached out to him. They sat, hand in hand, and trembled.

Presently, Ulla gained a little control and stood up. She found a bottle and glasses and poured drinks. *Here's to, uh, tonight's victory.* They raised their glasses.

Thanks. Well done, Starfighter.

Starfighter? "Please don't call me that." She set down her empty glass. "You know I'm grounded."

"Jealous of Mr. McCauley?"

"A little," she admitted. Destiny was so kicking her butt down the spinner path.

Yes, it is.

You're eavesdropping.

Yup. Thom pulled her onto the couch and nibbled her ear.

That feels good. As they kissed, she hiked up her skirt, straddling one knee across his lap so she could face him. She undid his belt buckle and began work on his trouser buttons.

That's pretty definite. He reached for her underpants.

Yes, Guardian, it is. She undid the last of his buttons, pushed his pants down, and allowed him to help her wiggle out of her undies. He did physical, human things with his hands that felt better than any magic.

Once they linked minds, things happened fast.

* * *

A few hours later, Ulla woke. Her arm had gone to sleep; Thom was lying on it, snoring. Gently, she eased her arm out from under him. She stood up in the half-light of Newcastle's city night and walked over to the open window. The fresh air felt good on her skin. She leaned against the sill and watched Thom sleep.

The ground isn't such a bad place to be, she thought. *The company is good here.*

A lifetime ago, Kate Ostapsdaughter had told Ulla she'd want to take up with someone and had recommended Thom. Back then, Ulla had been so very focused on getting back to SpaceCom, back in the sky, back in a Goshawk.

Back to fighting the Yotne and their Dwellers, which she and Thom had just done, no Goshawks required.

A few bright stars remained visible in Newcastle's well-lit night sky. Were those constellations hers? Was this her world now? And what about the man asleep on her sofa?

She tiptoed through the half-dark to the desk, powered up her readpad, and quietly settled on the edge of the bed, flipping through backlit documents until she found a form she'd downloaded but hadn't filled out.

She took a deep breath and started filling in the information. She was as ready as she'd ever be.

Separation request? From SpaceCom? Thom was awake; he sat down beside her. *Are you sure?*

She tapped her readpad. *My current service obligation's up two weeks before local Midwinter.* It wasn't as though she'd be unemployed. Destiny, or Fripp, or both, were doing everything short of dragging her by the ankles to get her into Castle Chisos.

There. The form was complete. Ulla slid off the bed and stood barefooted on the cool floor. She set the readpad to search for a connection.

What are you doing?

I learned a long time ago never to tap Send in bed. Ulla's readpad pinged when it found the hotel's signal.

He laughed. *Good policy.*

Once she'd submitted the form, she felt oddly content.

"That's all it takes?" he asked.

"Oh, no. On Monday, I'll have to explain this, face-to-face, to Colonel Becenti and Admiral Rosen and ask for approval."

Your boss, and your boss's boss.

Yup. And maybe my boss's boss's boss. General Zhou. Ulla hoped not.

What about Fripp?

Fripp, too, no doubt. SpaceCom had listed Fripp as Ulla's gaining combat commander. *She'll be delighted.* Ulla yawned. "I'm going to bed. You're more than welcome to join me."

"I'd love to." *You might want to take off the rest of your clothes first.*

They undressed and nestled into the hotel's big bed. Ulla laid her head on Thom's shoulder. He put his arm around her. She relaxed completely, closed her eyes, and slept.

* * *

The next time she woke, Bailey-Duran's first tentative rays had only just upstaged Newcastle's city lights.
You're awake, then. He put one hand on her breast. Lower down, something twitched and firmed up. They linked minds and made love again.

Afterward, she lay next to Thom, thinking. She'd fancied men before, but this was different. The chemistry was certainly there—but this was more, much more. Was this undefinable "more" what Fergus had been talking about last night? Was this what opening one's heart felt like?

Hungry?

Why, yes, she was. They needed coffee. And a bath. And clothes and getting up to resume their lives. But was any of it worth getting out of a bed that had Thom in it?

Stay put. Thom rolled out of bed and found a printed cardboard menu on the desk by the comm panel. *I'm buying breakfast.*

He ordered breakfast entirely by tapping codes into the hotel's comm panel. Not once did he activate voice or video. *That's slick.* It also gave her—and SpaceCom—plausible deniability in case some outraged Newcastler complained about female spacers allowing men in their rooms. *You're such a gentleman.*

I try. He found his pants, pulled his wallet out of a pocket, filled an envelope with cash, and settled back into bed with her. *Where were we?*

Mmm. Ulla's mind flashed to the picture of their imaginary child Thom had drawn in his notebook.

That's encouraging. He nuzzled her shoulder. *I thought you couldn't.*

Not now. But as soon as my separation from SpaceCom's approved, I can see the doc about it. If all went well, Ulla might be fertile by Midwinter.

He sat up. "You're serious."

She nodded. *I've been doing some thinking.*

Apparently. His thought-stream rambled for a minute before he shielded it.

Ulla did not pry. She felt a little like she'd lost her mind. But if wanting this man's baby was madness, she was okay with that.

There was a knock at the door.

Thom got up and shoved the envelope under the door. They heard a muffled "Thank you!" Footsteps receded.

Thom cracked open the door and looked both ways. *Coast is clear.* Naked, he opened the door fully, brought the tray inside, and set it on the coffee table. He made sure to lock the door before pouring coffee. He tore off a piece of bannock and set it on a plate. Thoughts still shuttered, he walked toward her with the coffee cup and little plate. He stopped short.

What's up?

"If you're serious about having my child," he said, "I want to be right there with you."

Ulla wasn't sure what to say.

He gestured with the plate and cup, splashing a few drops of coffee onto the floor. "Tradition says coffee and bannock."

???

"They're the traditional betrothal gift." He stood there, naked and caught between cultures. *You pigheaded spacer, I'm trying to ask you to marry me.*

Oh! She got out of bed and reached for the plate and cup before he could spill any more. "If you want to marry a pigheaded spacer, I'm all yours." *Are we supposed to share the bannock and coffee?*

Blushing, he nodded. *It didn't occur to me you wouldn't know how this works.*

She set the plate down on the nightstand and tore the piece of bannock in two. Unsure what to do next, she fed him half. He picked up the other half and fed it to her.

"How do we do that with a single cup of coffee?" she asked.

He grinned. "We don't; it's too hot. Taking turns will suffice."

Chapter Thirty-Four
Family

Monday morning, Ulla sat at her desk and worked on a briefing script about Friday evening's Dweller fight. She tried not to fiddle with the new half-size betrothal earrings in her right ear. Thom's uncle Padraic had installed the one for Raven Clan at last night's private celebration in Renata and Padraic's quarters at the Trade Ministry. The High King himself had placed Ulla's Worldtree earring and his wife, Marta, had done the honors for Thom's Flint Clan earring. Auntie Renata had insisted on doing the piercings.

Marta had Gated in for the party with Ingeborg and Dannel; Yens Peacemaker was already in town. Ulla hadn't fully processed what she thought of her future father-in-law; the High King came off as larger than life, even in an intimate family gathering. Marta, on the other hand, was every bit as likable as people had said.

Ulla pushed back against a mild hangover and reflected that she was better off than Ingeborg, who had passed out early last night.

Early this morning, Thom had Gated off to the Planetary Restoration Project headquarters in north Terrandessay—something to do with the regular job they paid him for. She missed him already.

"Spider?" Colonel Becenti looked over Ulla's shoulder. "How's the briefing coming?"

"Ready, pretty much." Ulla changed another sentence. "Just wordsmithing." And trying not to panic. She hated public speaking. Especially public speaking scheduled right after a meeting this morning with Admiral Rosen about her separation request.

"It looks fine to me," he said. "Upload it to the morning briefing packet."

Ulla tapped at her comm panel. "Done." Even though the speaking part still loomed, the writing part was over. She relaxed a little.

"You'll do fine, Spider." He smiled. "Also, congratulations."

"Thank you, sir." She turned around in her chair to face him. "What's the word from the *Dauntless* task force?"

"They're regrouping now."

Everyone in Ops had been recalled yesterday morning for a few hours to help launch the *Dauntless* and her task force. If the task force didn't hold, the Yotne would be here in less than a fortnight.

Colonel Becenti placed a sheet of paper on her desk. "This is for you, from the Alliance. You'll want to read it before you see Admiral Rosen."

"Orders?" she asked.

He nodded.

That was fast. Yesterday, General Zhou's staff car had been parked behind the Trade Ministry when she and Thom arrived for their betrothal party. The general, Fripp, and the High King had pulled Ulla aside and briefed her, explaining how Ulla's wartime duties with the Hjralma-On'oi Alliance would start immediately. The Elder Spinner had farmed Ulla out to Neal Erikson's group, which was doing their best to pry the Landfall Ring from the vault wall where it had materialized.

"You've seen my orders, then."

Becenti nodded. "Admiral Rosen says she got the Alliance to let us keep you for a few hours a day. You'll still report here in the mornings. After the daily briefing you'll join Professor Erikson."

"That's what Mr. Branson did, wasn't it?"

"Yes, when he wasn't with the CO's staff, or the local harbor patrol, or the Newcastle Guard, or working some special Trade Ministry project." Becenti inclined his head toward the bare wall behind Ulla's desk. "You'll still have sole use of this desk and this comm panel. Why not print up your diplomas, unit plaques, and family pictures? You can display them right there."

"An 'I love me' wall?" Ulla wasn't sure about that.

He pulled out the chair beside her desk, turned it around, and sat. He folded his arms on the chair back. "It'll help you remember who you are."

So it would. "I need that."

"Someplace downtown did a great job with Admiral Rosen's 3D files. She can tell you where she had them done."

Hand-painted, digitally routed hardwood would not come cheap, but Ulla didn't mind. "It's not like I've been spending much money lately."

"That's more like it, Spider."

Ulla's mind drifted to how she might arrange the collection she'd never had printed up before.

Colonel Becenti's expression grew serious. "Thorsdaughter, you have a hell of a career change coming up. If you need to talk about it, come find me."

Ulla snuck a peek under her boss's psi blocker and found that he actually cared. She counted herself lucky. "Uh, sir?"

"Yes?"

"You know what a spinner of wyrd is, right?"

"I've read up on it; not sure I understand completely."

"Me either." Ulla sighed. "I am so not ready for this."

"I'd be more worried, Lieutenant, if you were raring to go. 'Spinner of wyrd' may only be a group of psi talents, but some cultures associate those talents with gods."

Ulla shivered. "I'm no god."

For a long moment, he didn't say anything. Finally, he said, "Glad to hear it, Spider." More silence, then a searching look. "How'd you get your call sign?"

What did that have to do with anything? Ulla felt her face get hot. "At initial flight school, they had these ginormous spiders that wander in out of the desert."

"Go on."

Ulla knew she was blushing. "I stepped on one, barefooted in the middle of the night, on my way back from the loo in the barracks. I, uh, made a lot of noise."

"That's it?"

Ulla thought it was plenty. "Why do you ask?"

"Something occurred to me." Colonel Becenti shook his head. "Never mind."

***

"This concludes the briefing." Admiral Rosen looked around at those assembled. "Are there any questions?"

Having survived her public speaking ordeal, Ulla prayed that nobody had any.

Nobody did. Everyone snapped to attention as General Zhou stood up and left. The rest of the audience streamed into the corridor behind him.

A man in a Berserker uniform shouldered his way forward against the tide of people. "Good job, Little Bear."

"Dad!"

He swept her up in a big hug. The facility's psi shield didn't block audible comments, so Ulla heard plenty.

"Isn't she engaged?"

"He's her father."

"What's he doing here?"

"Bjornson's Berserkers have the defense contract for MitSmith's Landfall Mainland properties."

"And?"

"He's Thor Bjornson."

"That explains a lot."

Ulla didn't care. She had new orders, and Admiral Rosen had approved her separation from SpaceCom. And she hadn't seen her father in over a year. She hugged back. "You're who they turned the psi shield on for."

Thor shook his head. "Not me."

Ulla probed. Her father's thoughts were hidden behind a personal psi blocker. His Berserkers did nothing by halves; he likely had a Guild member on his payroll.

Somebody turned the briefing room's psi shield off, and Ulla sighed with relief.

"You okay?" he asked.

"Much better now." Ulla dug a finger into the worst knot on the side of her neck. "Damn shield gives me headaches." She pocketed her readpad and the small paper notebook she now preferred.

"It is so good to see you." His readpad lit up with a string of messages; somebody must have powered down the room's comm blocker. He glanced at the readpad and stuffed it into his pocket. "I've heard stories."

"Have you seen your personal messages today?" Ulla asked.

He nodded. "Congratulations." He smiled, eyes on Thom's betrothal set in her right ear. "When do I get to meet the lucky man?"

"He's in Terrandessay for work; won't be back till Midsummer." Ulla rubbed her neck. "How long are you in town?"

"Until early tomorrow. Berit and I have a room at the Pordenone."

Ships passing in the night. "Another time, then." So Berit was in Newcastle too!

"I hear you have orders."

Ulla shrugged. "Wartime billet. After work today, I'm moving house from the Pordenone to the Alliance Trade Ministry."

"Would you like help moving?"

"Thanks, Dad, but I don't have much stuff." She was all packed; Skuli would drive her to the hotel after their sparring session with Mikko and help move her two duffels to her new rooms at the Trade Ministry.

"Do you have plans for dinner?" he asked.

"Not yet."

"Then you're dining with us. Berit will be wild to see you."

"I thought you two were in Landfall," Ulla temporized. Her father was obviously happy to see her, but her own feelings were so mixed. Tonight was not the night for family discord; could she even make it through dinner without asking him the questions that swirled in her mind?

"Landfall Mainland," he replied. "MitSmith wants us to protect two of their properties—the big resort near Kirkhilo and a pair of archaeological sites on property MitSmith owns."

"The Knobs?" she asked, hoping she'd guessed wrong.

"Great Knob and Lesser Knob. Pretty spot. You saw the map in the briefing; they're maybe eighty klicks down the coast from the hotel."

The Ring seat on Great Knob and its support facility in the newly restored villa on Lesser Knob. *Oh, shit.*

Thor glanced over his shoulder toward the door at the back of the room. "The area's already crawling with Home Guard, and they look damned lethal. But there's no way they, plus a ground unit our size, can secure a major Yotne objective."

He understands then. Ulla breathed a sigh of relief. "Word is the Alliance is on a war footing."

"Neither the Landfall Home Guard nor we are equipped to repel a spaceborne attack." He sighed and rubbed at a crease between his eyebrows. "Giving MitSmith's Landfall facilities director the benefit of the doubt. He's new to the Edge."

Ulla did one last check for any briefing materials she might have left behind.

"Well." Thor Bjornson grinned his deadly serious not-a-smile. "I'm here to see Jared about that. John Mitsui—he's in charge of MitSmith's affairs in the Bailey-Duran system—is with SpaceCom's local head of logistics right now. And Berit's talking to SpaceCom's chief of Medical Support."

"Isn't John one of THE Mitsuis?" Ulla asked.

"He is. John'll come through; he always does."

As for medical support, Ulla had seen her father's partner Berit in action. The Berserkers would have whatever SpaceCom had that she thought they needed. But—"Berit's on your payroll? I thought she'd retired."

"She did retire. This trip was supposed to be a low-key job combined with house-hunting." He paused to check his vibrating readpad and shove it back into his pocket. "But she's a damn fine administrator and her nursing credentials are still active."

If it came to that. Ulla poked at the loosening muscle in her neck one last time. "I don't think they'll need to push very hard. SpaceCom understands what's at stake."

"Mm-hmm."

"Who's Jared?" Ulla asked.

"Your CO, Jared Zhou. He and I have a meeting in a few minutes with Alliance and City-States leadership."

"You know General Zhou?" Ulla asked.

"We keep in touch." Her father waved at someone in the back of the room. "We were cadets together, back in the day."

Ulla saw the general in the doorway. "He's waiting for you?"

Thor Bjornson grinned a real grin. "Need to go." He paused. "Was that a yes or a no about dinner?"

"Yes." It would be small of Ulla to refuse; they might never see each other again. "I wouldn't miss it for the world."

He gave her one last quick hug. "See you tonight, Little Bear."

Chapter Thirty-Five
The Past Catches Up

That evening, Ulla knocked for the second time on what she was pretty sure was the correct door in the hotel corridor. She carried two bottles of wine Renata had insisted she give to her father and Berit.

"Ulla!" With a shopping bag in one hand and a basket in the other, Berit emerged from the elevator at the other end of the corridor and hurried toward her. "Sorry I'm late." Berit set her hoard on the carpet and hugged Ulla. "So good to see you."

"You too." Berit unlocked the door and invited Ulla inside. So this was what the suites on the top floor looked like! "Have you heard from Dad?"

"He's on his way back from SpaceCom Headquarters. Message pinged my readpad when I got signal here." She put the basket on a side table under a window. "This is what took so long. The seller in the produce stall insisted on wrapping each apple individually—she wanted me to pick which paper to use for each one."

"Fresh fruit is a big deal in Newcastle." Ulla liked the look of the brightly colored globes in the basket. "She probably upped her game because you're an offworlder." She held out the wine. "This is for you and Dad, from the On'oi, namely, Thom's Auntie Renata."

"Please tell her thank you!" Berit took the bottles and put them on the counter next to a grouping of good crystal barware. "She's their—Minister of Culture, right?"

Ulla was impressed. Berit and Dad had done their

homework.

"I have a breakfast date with her and your future stepmother-in-law tomorrow before Thor and I Gate back to Landfall." Berit selected three glasses, then poked in a drawer until she found a corkscrew. "They want to discuss wedding plans."

Wedding plans? Now? "Thom and I aren't getting married until local Midwinter."

Berit opened the wine. "It'll be a big wedding. He's the High King's son."

Oh, dear gods. That had not occurred to Ulla. She reached for the glass Berit offered her, raised it, and drank.

Berit recorked the wine and picked up her own glass. "Renata asked me to tell you that your friend Ingeborg's wedding is being downsized and moved up to this weekend. It'll be in Flint Clan's summer encampment."

Lucky Ingeborg and Dannel! Ulla knew they'd had mixed feelings about a huge Midsummer Gathering wedding. "I heard the Hoffnung On'oi were scaling back the Gathering."

Berit grabbed two napkins from the hotel's supply. "Renata Connersdaughter said all the Gatherings are scaling back this summer. They're leaving everything that's not to do with the Gathering's core political process at home."

That made sense with a Yotne fleet in-system. But... "Why are you three meeting tomorrow?" Ulla asked. "I'd think planning a Midwinter wedding would be the last of your priorities."

"Impending disaster is a terrible reason for putting life on pause." Berit's expression was unreadable. "We three will at least get to meet one another in person."

"Thom's aunt thinks like you do." Ulla followed Berit to a pair of overstuffed sofas in the corner. "When Renata found out that Thom and I weren't going to Summer Gathering, she wangled invitations for us to Newcastle's Midsummer Ball." She rolled her eyes. "She said it'd be good for us."

Berit kicked off her shoes. "So much better!"

"Long day?" Ulla's boots didn't come off as easily; she left them on and stretched out her legs in front of her.

"Yes." Berit tucked her feet under her and sat cross-legged. "But I think we have a fighting chance now." She raised her glass. "There will be no more talk of invasion tonight."

That was fine with Ulla. Mental hygiene aside, such talk was unwise in a hotel with thin walls and primitive comm. They sat in silence, enjoying each other's company.

Berit sipped her wine. "How'd you burn your face?"

"How'd I what?" Ulla was mystified. *Oh, that!* "Campfire mishap."

Berit's shoulders relaxed visibly. "Not a psi injury this time, then?" *Thanks be!*

"Not...entirely." While the flying cinders had been tangible enough, Ulla doubted she could keep much of anything from her might-as-well-be stepmother. *Did you just use psi?*

Berit nodded. *Still feels weird.* "I started getting headaches about a week after we arrived in Landfall," she said. "There didn't seem to be a medical cause, so I went to the Berserkers' Guild rep. He deactivated my psi blocker, and I felt better. He tested me for psi and found mid-range telepathy and a few other things I can't pronounce. Then he taught me how to keep my thoughts to myself and scheduled more lessons for when I'm back in Landfall." Berit took a sip of wine. "I never did like using a psi blocker, but it was necessary. Part of being with Berserker leadership."

"Knowing what I know now, I'm surprised you could tolerate a psi blocker at all." Ulla held up her glass and admired the way the light played off crystal and liquid. "You've always been an empath. You know that, right?"

"Not officially, but yes. And I was pretty sure I had what the On'oi call the Healing Gift."

Fripp, Ulla reflected, had said as much. "After—Binder Station, right?"

"Yes."

Ulla drank deeply and resisted the urge to polish off the last centimeter in her glass. "Fripp told me."

"Fripp?" Berit's eyes narrowed. *The ghost?*

Ulla gave in and finished her wine. "She's a BD3 Elder, as real as you are. She's my new boss." *She was at Binder in what the Guild calls astral projection.*

Not a ghost then. Berit drained her own glass, stood, and reached for Ulla's. "More wine?"

Ulla held out her glass, then reconsidered. "No,

thanks." Where this conversation was headed, alcohol wouldn't help.

You're right. Berit set her glass down next to the wine bottle and reached for a colorful paper-wrapped apple. "Want one?"

"Sure, thanks."

Berit unwrapped two apples. "This paper is so pretty." With a spacer's sense of economy, she flattened the two paper squares and left them on the table for future use. She handed Ulla an apple and settled back down on the couch. "You remember anything more?"

Ulla had just bitten into her apple. *About Binder? Some.* She chewed and swallowed. "I remember the first two missions. We were stepping for the third when somebody spotted Dwellers on the flight deck." She thought for a minute. "After that, not so much." Her Gallantry Star notwithstanding, the official report read like an overwrought holoshow script.

Oh, Child. Did I not unblock that memory? Fripp's tall projection appeared to sit on the floor across from Berit. *I apologize.*

Berit's eyes opened wide.

"Hello, Berit Gee." Well-being radiated from Fripp as her projection spoke. "I am glad to see that you are well."

Fripp and Berit clearly had a history, but what was it? Ulla thought back to the Battle of Binder Station and the days that followed. Memories that had so far eluded her suddenly filled in for the first time since all that had happened, like a dam being opened.

Mostly, it matched her nightmares. *Oh, dear gods.* "Bald Mountain wasn't my first shot at Dweller-killing, was it?"

Fripp's projection shook its head. "No, Child, it was not. As have many who are ignorant of their Dark Gift, you banished your first Dwellers in self-defense."

As Fergie had, two nights ago at Mickey Bravo's. Ulla took a deep breath. "There were—three Dwellers—on the flight deck?" She only remembered seeing two hosts, but she'd definitely banished three Dwellers before climbing into her Goshawk for that last sortie.

Fripp nodded. "The two on the flight deck intended to move from the maintenance technicians they possessed to you and your wingman. The third possessed a chief petty

officer in the flight maintenance control center."
There was another. Ulla hadn't been alone.
Commander Nkosi slew a Dweller in the station's main control center.

How long had Mary Nkosi been using her Dark Gift? Ulla would think about that later. "There were two more Dwellers, in flight," she said. "On Springs and Pigpen."

Berit's eyes widened. "Springs and Pigpen?"

Ulla explained, "Starfighter call signs for Carlos Pak and Alia Denys. They were supposed to be the other half of Torch's and my four-ship." Ulla caught herself squeezing the apple Berit had given her; she relaxed her grip. "They launched ahead of us." She'd picked off the two Dwellers in space, well beyond a soulslayer's expected range. Carlos and Alia would more than likely have blacked out, which would have made their Goshawks Gate automatically back to the flight deck. They'd survived—Alia was flying off of UW&NS *Wiwo'ole* in the Farwell Sector on the other side of the Edge and Carlos had a desk job on Reynoso Tres.

No wonder the Guild was unclear about what had happened.

There had been Yotne. Ulla and Torch—Gav Psarakis—had engaged them. The Yotne lost. Then there had been more Yotne. They'd lost too. Outnumbered, Ulla and Gav had flown and fought and flown and fought until they were out of ordnance, until SpaceCom replacement starfighters took their place, until the station had to Gate them back.

But one of Gav's jets had stuck open. His other jets compensated, so he didn't get spit out to kingdom come—but there was no way to get a Goshawk in that state back onto the flight deck without setting everything on fire.

"I reached out through space and turned Torch's manual shutoff," Ulla said, the final piece of the puzzle clicking into place. "I must have projected very substantially."

"Yes, Child. You cried out; we heard you here." Fripp reached for something in her physical space and a cup appeared in her hand. "Your Goshawk's emergency system Gated it back to the station when your vital signs dropped. After you'd shut off your colleague's emergency switch, you could not find your body."

Berit stared at Ulla. "When they brought you in, you were alive but unresponsive. I didn't see it happen, but there were stories of a Yotne-sized ghost dragging the ghost of a starfighter in full gear straight inside through the station's outer hull. But I was there when the big ghost sat by your bed and would not budge until your... psi-related episode was over." Berit looked to Fripp. "That was you, right?"

"Yes."

Berit set down her half-eaten apple and turned toward Ulla. "You had decompression sickness, which should not have been possible—your Goshawk never lost pressure." *The ghost—this Elder here—tried to tell us.* "You'd burned your hand inside your sealed gauntlet."

Ulla's nightmares matched all of that. "I still get queasy when I touch a Goshawk's manual shutoff switch." Now she knew why.

"You had the bends and a burned hand." Berit ran her fingers through her short hair. "Decompression sickness can present with neurological symptoms. At first, we thought that's what you had. But it turned out to be a psi issue. It cleared up—" She looked at Fripp. "Spontaneously?"

Fripp shook her head. "You and I, Berit Gee, helped her recover. Do you not remember me directing your Healing Gift?"

That was real, then. Berit leveled her gaze at the Elder. "I slept for a full day/night cycle after that little adventure." *Almost lost my job over that.* She squared her shoulders and faced Ulla. "Once you were conscious, the rest was treatable enough."

Ulla poked at her newly restored memories. "I tested negative for psi, right before I left Binder for Reynoso." *Was that you, Fripp?*

Fripp sipped her drink. *I concealed your Gifts that had manifested. You needed time to get here without making another dangerous blunder.*

As soon as Ulla had been cleared to fly, she'd received orders for UW&NS *Valiant,* which had deployed from Reynoso Tres to the Bailey-Duran system before Ulla had had a chance to find permanent quarters, let alone unpack. Had that been the Elder Spinner's work as well?

Only partly. Fripp's thoughts went shuttered. "You were due for a shipboard assignment, and the *Valiant* was happy to have a Gallantry Star recipient."

Ulla and Gav had each been awarded a Gallantry Star for protecting a shuttle full of the station's evacuees—mostly children—from the Yotne attack.

Gav's was awarded posthumously. Even though Ulla had shut off his jets, the inside of his Goshawk had caught fire.

Fripp glanced to her left. *I must go.* Her projection winked out.

Berit stared at the spot where Fripp had been. "Ulla," she said slowly, "I'm going to have another glass of wine. Want some?"

Oh, yes, please. Ulla leaned her head back against the cushion and closed her eyes.

* * *

Presently, a key turned in the door latch, and Thor Bjornson let himself into the room.

Berit met him with a hug. "Did SpaceCom and the Home Guard sign off on your request?"

"They did," he said. "How about garrison support?"

"Jared said 'Yes.'" They both relaxed.

Ulla did not ask; no doubt the two Berserkers were discussing something best kept for a limited audience. She stood up. "Hi, Dad."

"Little Bear!" Delighted to see her, he wrapped her in a big hug.

Ulla hugged back as best she could. *Ask your father*, Fripp had said, when Ulla had wanted to know why she was born a spinner. But aside from their quick greeting this morning, she hadn't seen Dad in over a year, not since the Berserkers left the Binder system. Now was not the time for pointed questions.

"You okay?" Thor asked.

"A very long day, is all." Ulla plastered a smile on her face. "The On'oi sent you some wine. Would you like a glass?"

"Yes, please." He took off his jacket, hung it up, and settled on the couch next to Berit, who rested her head on his shoulder.

Ulla had to open the second bottle to give him a decent pour. "Cheers."

He took the glass from her. "Looks like you two had a

head start."

Ulla sat down.

"The ghost we saw at Binder Station stopped by." Berit sipped her wine. "You just missed her."

Thor sat up straight. "Fripp, the Elder?"

"That's the one," Berit said. "She's Ulla's new boss."

He spilled wine in his lap. "Your wartime billet is with the Alliance."

Ulla waited for him to blot up the mess with a napkin before saying, "That's why I moved into quarters at the Trade Ministry."

He folded the napkin, making deep creases. "So that's how the eetee managed it..."

"Managed what?" Ulla tried to maintain outward composure.

"Fripp and I, uh, go way back." He went quiet again.

Don't ask! Don't ask! Don't ask! Ulla so needed to save her question for later.

Berit raised an eyebrow; Ulla remained silent.

"Little Bear," Thor said finally, "I am so very, very sorry."

She looked at his devastated face and the ground combat nightmare Fripp had called "the dream of another" clicked into context. Fripp had cooled a path through the Yotne firestorm for three soldiers and a handful of evacuees in exchange for—

She said it out loud. "You traded your firstborn daughter."

The look on his face told Ulla everything she needed to know.

The events in the firestorm dream had really happened, then. Ulla took a deep breath. "Dad," she asked, "who are Velasco, Cheylik, and Jones?"

Startled, he said, "Three of my troops, back when I was in SpaceCom. Why do you ask?"

"I used to dream about them. Regularly."

He put his face in his hands.

Ulla's morning headache returned with a vengeance. "Dad, I'm a telepath. I probably heard you dreaming when I was a baby." *Before Fripp came to visit. Before Mama left and took Andrew and me with her.*

She had never seen her father cry before. She waited. Finally, Thor looked up. "That was the Pendarian evacuation." His shoulders sagged. "Velasco died a year later. Jones left the service. And you met Cheylik at Binder Station. He died soon after of a virus. We all left SpaceCom around the same time; that's when Cheylik and I stood up the Berserkers."

That only left one question. "I'm supposed to ask you about spinners of wyrd." Ulla barely kept her voice from shaking.

"What about them?" he asked.

Ulla set her glass down. "Let's start with the one you made a deal with."

"She saved their lives." His voice was bleak.

Until that moment, Ulla had thought "seeing red" was just an expression. Now, the room had an ugly glow as the full realization of her father's actions hit her. "In exchange for my future as a normal human being!" The capillaries in her eyes must be bulging.

"I never imagined I'd live to have children. Hadn't met your mother yet." His voice cracked. "Little Bear, I am so, so sorry."

Chapter Thirty-Six
Talking Spider Down

"Don't call me Little Bear!" Ulla struggled to keep her voice even. Very carefully, she stood. If she lost control now, chaos would win. The Dark Gift was in her, coiled and ready to strike the man who had sold her into this position. Her father's lips moved, but she didn't hear what he was saying. With measured steps, she walked across the room, let herself into the hall, and shut the door quietly behind her.

The balcony door at the end of the hallway beckoned with light and a promise of fresh air. She bolted for it, flung open the door, and stood there, panting as she nearly collapsed against the railing. Below her, the people in Landfall Square went about their business.

Spider? Ulla turned and saw Fergus McCauley standing shirtless in the doorway. His wet hair stuck up at odd angles. She turned back to the railing, crossed her arms, and tried not to let him see her tremble.

"Spider, come away from there." He approached, but not so quickly as to startle her, as though he was afraid that she might—

Jump? Truly, that hadn't occurred to her. Though jumping had a certain appeal, she was appalled that Fergus thought she might actually do it. She took a step toward him. A tear rolled down her face, then another. He held out his arms, and she sank into them, her tears turning into long, racking sobs. She buried her face in his shoulder and bawled.

When she was through the worst of it, he guided her to an upholstered bench. They sat down. "Better?" he asked.

A little. Ulla wiped her face on her sleeve. *Thanks.*

"You need a hankie." Neither of them had one.

"I'll be back in a moment," he told her. "You're not to move, do you understand?"

I won't, I promise. Talking was hard.

It took him less than a minute to return with two clean handkerchiefs, a glass, and two bottles. He had combed his hair and put on a shirt, still unbuttoned. He set the bottles down. "Here." He held out a handkerchief.

"Thanks, Fergie." She took it and dried her face. "What are you doing here? I thought you were with Neal."

"He's still my boss." Fergus pulled his open shirt aside. A triangle in fresh blue ink was nestled among sparse, coppery hair on the pale skin below his collarbone. "Now that I've sworn the oath, the Society says I can sleep here. Plus, Neal's house was crowded. And tomorrow I'm Gating to an offshore Ring seat to meet my new mentor." Fergus broke the seal on the larger bottle, opened it, and poured a little amber liquid into the glass. "Here."

Ulla took the glass and sniffed. Whiskey. "Offshore Ring seat?"

"Neal put me to work." Fergus opened the other bottle and drank. "He found out what I did for a living before I joined SpaceCom."

"Diving? Like you did in the North Sea?" Ulla knew, vaguely, that some Ring seats would have to be on water. And that when young Fergus McCauley had left school, he'd gone straight to work for an Aberdeen company that kept Earth's petro-era well holes sealed up.

"The water is a LOT warmer where I'm going." He sat down beside her. "More than likely, I'll be linking with really powerful finders and mind-movers. They're bringing up artifacts from the seafloor."

Of course they are. Ulla stared at the whiskey in her glass. "Are you sure you want to drunk up the offworlder spinner?" Did she want to pour spirits on top of the Trade Ministry's wine?

"You've had a nasty shock." Fergus took another swig of the orange liquid. "You're safe enough; you rose above the temptation to strike your da."

He and every telepath in mindshot must have heard

that. Ulla drank. The whiskey was powerful and very smooth. She reached for the bottle and read the label—Three Mountains, distilled shortly before she and Fergie were born. It warmed her insides all the way down. *I thought you swore off booze.*

"I did." *Neal will kill me if I touch a drop.*

Not hyperbole. The Society did not screw around.

"I splurged on the Three Mountains the afternoon before..." His voice trailed off.

Mickey Bravo's?

He nodded. "I poured out the rest of my stash, but this was too good. I knew an occasion would come along."

A rough translation of the visible part of the label on the bottle he drank from said it contained "Bubbly Orange Delight"—mostly carbonated water, sugar, and caffeine. The "orange" part was made of artificial color and wishful thinking.

I was that close. Angry as she was, Thor Bjornson was still her father. Her shoulders trembled.

That close to what?

To killing him. Tears rolled down her cheeks.

"No. You were that close to blotting him out forever, soul and all."

The breeze picked up; it chilled her. She drew her knees up and hugged them.

The important part is that you didn't do it. Fergus wrapped his arm around her shoulders; she rested her head against him. It was warm there.

"That's what the Society is for, isn't it?" she asked. "To keep people from...doing that."

He took another swig of the awful-looking orange drink. "I suppose that makes this my first official moral support for another soulslayer."

"Discharging an obligation, are you?" Ulla tried to sound hurt, but Fergus did read minds.

We're friends. You know that. They had been through too much together to be anything less.

You're my conscience, McCauley. Thank you. She heard the delicate sound of liquid being poured; when had she finished her first glass? Warm as Thistle Clan's whiskey made her insides, she did not want to drink too much.

You won't. Fergus capped the bottle.

Won't what? Ulla was curious what he thought she

wouldn't do.

"You won't do anything," Fergus said. "As soon as you're ready, I'll see you back inside."

Ulla swirled the whiskey around the glass. She sniffed appreciatively but didn't drink. The sounds of Landfall Square floated up to where they sat. The Prophecy of the Hidden Spinner popped into her head.

Bred in fire,
Born in earth.
Tested in fire;
Found in water.
Confirmed in fire,
Protector in air;
Returned to fire.

Dad's story fit "bred in fire." Her life matched every line through "confirmed in fire." If the prophecy was real and if it was about her, then the last two lines were coming right up.

You might cut him some slack. He was barely out of the Academy. Younger than we are now.

Ulla's hand tightened around her glass. *He bartered my chance at a normal life for three of his troops.* Mama had left him over that and taken their children; Ulla suddenly realized her mother must have deserted from SpaceCom to do it. And taking the kids to Texas without Dad's consent was what attorneys called international parental kidnapping. Which, Ulla realized, was why Mama had taken them home to the isolated desert in Big Bend. The Republic of Texas almost never allowed its citizens to be extradited.

Fergus nodded. *The MitSmith mining settlement where you grew up? On Farwell? It's a Texas-registered corporation.*

And, Ulla remembered, they'd used a MitSmith company Gate to board a MitSmith company ship to get there.

She shivered as she worked out that, from the night Fripp came to collect on Thor Bjornson's promise, Mama had spent her life on the run.

Had Dad let her? Or had he tried, and failed, to get them back? Either would have been the end of his

SpaceCom career.

No wonder Fripp had needed to pull strings to allow Ulla to leave Farwell a generation later.

Fergus sipped his orange drink. "Ever stop to consider how things would have played out had you come here with the Elder? Grew up here?"

If Ulla's life had gone according to Fripp's original plan, she'd be a trained, fully functional spinner of wyrd—whatever that was—and BD3 would be her firmly established home. But—"I'd never have been a starfighter."

"You and I likely never would have met." Fergus put his arm around her. "And that would have been a shame."

You're right. Ulla leaned into his hug. "There's another thing."

"What's that?"

"Stelle Pietersdaughter." Ulla was not proud that after landing in the backcountry she'd avoided the first people she saw because one of them was an Elder. But if she had gone with them instead of heading into town, who would have pulled Stelle out of the river after the ferry accident?

Was the entire universe made of what-ifs?

Fergus chuckled. *Pretty much. But as it happens, we're here now.*

Why had fate been so persistent? *Why did Fripp choose Dad?*

Fergus made a noncommittal noise. "Think about it. You take after him. Maybe the Elder saw in him something Bailey-Duran needed." *Like go-to-hell compassion.*

Ulla drained her glass and held it out for more.

"No." Fergus grinned, took Ulla's glass, and set it just out of reach.

"You asshole!"

"I said I'd help you over a rough bit, not drunk you up." Fergus reached to scratch his new tattoo and thought better of it.

"How do you know so much about Dad?"

"Thought I was going to have to ask him for a job." Fergus blushed. "Back when I almost got thrown out of SpaceCom for—oh, never mind." He paused. "Let's just say I did my homework."

Ulla caught herself smiling. "You know the Berserkers are groundies. At best, you would have been a rotorcraft driver."

He chuckled and shook his head. "Underwater demolition—same skill set Neal's getting out of me."

Ulla stood up. "Thanks, Fergie. I better go."

Fergus tossed his empty Orange Delight bottle into the bin marked *glass*. "Take care, Spider." He held out the almost-full bottle of whiskey. "For you."

"Thanks," Ulla said as they hugged one more time.

"Are you still having dinner with your da and his partner?"

Ulla nodded. "If they'll have me, yes. And thanks for kicking my ass up between my shoulder blades about the open-your-heart thing." *You were right. Sorry I didn't learn it when you and I were—*

That's in the past. His thoughts went completely shuttered. Then he smiled. "Good luck, Ulla. All the best for you and Thom."

PART 3

The Rings Get Real

Chapter Thirty-Seven
Flint's Villa

A few days later, Ulla, dressed in her old trail clothes and carrying a small rucksack, emerged from the Gate uphill from Flint Clan's summer pasture.

Fripp had wasted no time putting her to work for Neal Erikson, who was still trying to unstick Flint Clan's erstwhile Ring so it could be installed in its historical seat on Landfall. But first, Ulla had to learn Ring song. Given how strong her Gifts were, she needed to make her beginner mistakes well out of earshot of any major Ring.

Summer Pasture worked.

"Heya, Starfighter." Ingeborg stood just outside the Gate, waiting for her. "You're looking good."

"Heya yourself." *We're going to be sisters.* They hugged.

Ingeborg grinned. *You sure you want to spend your life with my brother?*

Ulla walked downhill with her toward Flint's camp. *You sure you want to be stuck teaching me Ring song with your wedding coming up this weekend?*

Oh, most definitely, yes. "Ma's here. I need the distraction." Ingeborg pointed to a distant group of three women deep in conversation. *My ma, Dannel's ma, and Emli Clarksdaughter. They have Dannel and me up to our necks in wedding planning.*

With Midsummer Gathering stripped down to its political-process essentials, their Midsummer wedding had been moved forward and downsized. Ulla detected relief on Ingeborg's part.

From what Ulla had gleaned from Auntie Renata, the swiftly approaching "small, rustic" wedding was still a panic-worthy event spanning at least two days and two clans' summer pasture encampments.

Ingeborg sidestepped a rock in their path. *Da's the High King. This is as modest as it gets.*

Ulla refused to think about what that meant for her and Thom, come Midwinter.

If they were still alive, come Midwinter.

Ulla changed the subject. *Emli's here?*

"She arrived not long after you went to Newcastle," Ingeborg said. She's taking over Kamna's apprenticeship." *With Hanni dead, and me leaving with Dannel for Mountain Clan next week, we were short of healers.* "Nathan's staying on too."

Ulla wondered if Nathan's other employer approved. "What's Flint Clan doing for mind-talkers?" Dmytro was good, but Council needed a telepath who had longer range. Emli Clarksdaughter, maybe? She'd monitored Ulla's cognitive abilities all the way from Chisos after the debacle on Bald Mountain.

Nope. Emli's continental-range, like Dmytro. "Maribet's back," Ingeborg said as they passed Council House. *She's working this afternoon.*

???

Ingeborg kept her eyes on the path. "They called up the Home Guard last week." *Her Home Guard post is with Flint Council.*

"What about her partner in Newcastle?"

"The widow Schiller?" Ingeborg grinned. "She and Maribet are still quite the item; City society was starting to talk." *It's just as well Maribet got called up.*

Ulla looked around. The Alliance had not been idle. Two artillery pieces pointed skyward. *Anti-atmospheric-craft artillery?*

Mm-hmm. Ingeborg pointed. *There and there, from Thistle Clan.* She sighed. "We sent them snipers. Mountain's sending Thistle some people who are good at what SpaceCom calls 'asymmetrical warfare.'"

???

Chieftains cut a deal. Flint and Mountain never needed modern weaponry before.

Oh! The Electronics Unreliable zone would have kept

modern combat machines away. "Because the big Ring's gone?"

Neal Erikson's mind-voice popped into Ulla's head. *Better get it up and working again real quick, Spinner Ulla.*

Neal! Ulla had thought he was working away at the stuck Ring in Newcastle. She followed Ingeborg around an overland camion parked in front of the single ladies' tent. There he was, chatting with Dmytro Robson and a trim older woman.

Neal motioned for them to join the conversation. "Heya, Starfighter." *Out loud, please. Aubrey's headblind.*

"So, you're the spinner who fell out of the sky." The woman smiled and held out her hand to Ulla. "I'm Aubrey Rogers."

Was this grandmotherly person the archaeologist who'd evacuated New Vatersay Dweller survivors in a small boat on her "beer runs"? Ulla shook her hand. "Pleased to meet you."

Ingeborg opened the camion's passenger door. "Look what they brought." She gestured toward several cased utility Rings stacked behind the passenger seat.

They? Who was the archaeologist with?

"Greetings, Spinner Ulla." An Elder waved from the driver's seat. "I am Vani. We meet again."

Again?

He made a deep rumbling sound that Ulla had learned, with Fripp, to associate with laughter. "Do you recall seeing three people in the woods on the morning when your pod landed?"

Ulla nodded.

I am the 'troll' whose presence so frightened you. Vani's implied quotation marks were hard to miss. Ulla was relieved he hadn't said it out loud.

Ulla tried to find words. She couldn't. Instead, she took a deep breath and offered the Elder her hand.

He took it. *Fripp tells me you are making progress.* His wrinkled gray face broke into the Hjralma equivalent of a smile. "I am glad to have the opportunity to work with you, Ulla Thorsdaughter."

"What are we waiting for?" Ingeborg called from the camion's rear cargo bed. Once Dmytro, Neal, and Ulla joined her, Aubrey taking the passenger seat, Vani put the camion in gear and they drove down the track in the direction Flint Clan had come from weeks ago, away from Bald Mountain.

"Where are we going?" Ulla asked.

Ingeborg settled against the back of the tall cab, out of the wind. "Ancients' villa."

"The ruin?" Ulla remembered Miles Rogers's notes at the back of *Bailey-Duran Three: A World Remade*. "That dig is Aubrey's baby, isn't it?"

"Yep," Dmytro said. "She spent four summers working with a crew out there. Still comes back from time to time to check on one thing or another. That villa helped her make her name as an archaeologist—she's the galactic authority on the Ancients." *My first trek as an adult with Flint was the year Miles and the kids came too.*

Ulla was intrigued. "What's the family like?"

"Nice people. Very bright." Dmytro let Ulla sense his memories of the young family and went on, "They all spoke passable Dialekt when they got here. By the end of that summer, Thad and Eliza were indistinguishable from the On'oi kids."

"What a glorious way to grow up!" Ulla envied Thad and Eliza.

"I'm sure it was," Dmytro said. *Might as well use mind-talk for now. It's easier.*

He had a point, what with road noise and wind. It wasn't as though Aubrey was with them to be excluded.

Ulla rested her back against the camion's cab. *Why are we going to the ruin?* She'd thought they were going to work on Ring song.

Council's using their utility Ring today. Villa's well out of earshot, so your lessons there won't interfere. Neal spread his arms along the cargo bed's side railing. *And Aubrey wants to poke at the frescoes again.* It was clear, just looking at Neal, that after weeks of trying to unstick the Ring from its dark warehouse vault in Newcastle, he was happy to be outdoors.

* * *

The ruined villa was bigger than it had looked from a distance. Its original roof was long gone, and a modern roof on tall posts sheltered a rambling collection of once-grand rooms. Their broken hewn-stone walls were still covered in big swaths of painted plaster. The patterned tile floor looked remarkably well-preserved.

Vani pulled the camion up under the shelter, parked in front of a gap in the villa's outer wall, and he and Aubrey made a beeline for a section of wall in the middle of the site, deep under the protecting roof. Neal was not far behind.

Dmytro, Ingeborg, and Ulla climbed down from the cargo bed. Dmytro reached behind Aubrey's seat and pulled a utility Ring from the top of the stack. "This one is yours to keep, Starfighter. No need to borrow Council's anymore."

Her very own Ring! "Thank you." Ulla said, taking it from him in its brand-new case. "Where did these come from?"

"Kettlerest," said Ingeborg. "They found about fifty of them in three different sizes when they were hunting for Dwellers."

Ulla was mystified. "How did anyone have time to dig?"

"They didn't." Dmytro set aside four shallow Ring cases on the camion's passenger seat, moving the taller case from the bottom of the stack to the passenger footwell. "One of them tripped over what he thought was a rock." He put the four smaller cases back behind the seat. "The 'rock' turned out to be a Battle Ring—part of a cache the Ancients left behind."

What was a Battle Ring? No matter, Ulla decided; with the Yotne so close, of course the party would have brought back as much of the cache as they possibly could. But— "Don't archaeologists usually excavate super carefully and document everything?"

"Mm-hmm." Ingeborg nodded. "But in this case the Council of Chieftains sent in a team of expert mind-seers with shovels and pickaxes to make sure nothing important got left behind. Aubrey's still pissed off." *At least she understands.*

"Come on, Starfighter." Dmytro shut the camion's passenger door. "Let's find a shady place to sit and have your lesson."

* * *

Ulla's new utility Ring was a joy to work with—very

responsive, and its runes were clear and easy to see. Of course, learning to read what the runes said would take more than a single afternoon.

"You'll get there." Ingeborg pushed a wisp of hair off her sweaty face. "Sing it down."

Ulla and Dmytro had been working on a dual-voiced protocol. Dmytro sang the last part of the lower-octave exit song and stood up to stretch before Ulla even started the final singing-down.

The Ring's surface went opaque as Ulla sang her last few notes. She leaned over, grabbed the Ring case's lid, and buckled it shut. Rather than stand up, however, she lay back on the layer of pine needles that littered the ground. The terrace they'd chosen lay between the roofed archaeological site and the river. It was pleasantly shaded by old trees and decorated at regular intervals by even older pieces of sculpture. Most of the statues were nudes that left one in absolutely no doubt as to their subjects' species.

"I thought you said Ancients built this villa," she said idly.

"They did." Ingeborg leaned back on her hands. "Scholars are pretty sure the family who built the villa also moved the major Ring from Landfall to Bald Mountain."

The explicitly human statues dotting the landscape depicted people of all ages and sizes doing everything from making love to bargaining for goods in a market. They were a far cry from the generic humanoid illustrations in SpaceCom's Bailey-Duran system orientation guide. Here was a little boy—the sculptor had made it obvious he was a boy—rolling a hoop along a path, and over there, a saggy-bodied elderly couple, still very much in love, sat arm-in-arm on a stone bench.

Oh, that.

Ulla sat up and saw Neal walking toward them.

"Opinion is still divided among scholars across explored space." He laughed and waved his hand toward the circle of sculptures. "We locals think that if the Ancients were alive today, they could at least interbreed with modern humans. It's even possible that a few were still here when the First Settlers arrived, and they did just that."

"Did any of their genetic material survive?" Ulla asked out loud because Aubrey and Vani had come up behind

Neal.

"Among the artifacts on this world? No," Aubrey said. "Well, there's a little. Not enough to tell us much. We do know the Ancients were a space-faring people, and that there was a diaspora in the years leading up to the Yotne takeover. Between that and the likelihood that some humans on this world today are descended from them, they are unlikely to have vanished completely." She glanced at Vani. "Miles has recorded Hjralma stories about bands of what they call 'short people' who hid in the wilderness until the Yotne left."

All that, Ulla knew now, had been less than a thousand standard years ago. Was there no historical record?

"That was the Time of Abandonment, Spinner Ulla. My forebears had enough to do securing food and clean water while forming a strategy for restoring the atmosphere, land, and seas." Vani sighed. "They kept meticulous records for planetary restoration but had no time for more than that."

"But there are stories," Neal said. "The only reason Miles Rogers hasn't recorded them all is that there may be one or two people on this planet he hasn't met yet."

Dmytro laughed. "I was learning Ring song the summer Miles spent with us. He sat in, every chance he got."

Vani glanced at Neal and inclined his head toward Ulla. "Shall we ascertain if the spinner can activate the thick utility Ring?"

Neal nodded. "Yes, let's."

Ulla stood up. "Is the thick one a Battle Ring?"

Vani shook his head. In that much human body language, he was fluent. "No. Our theory is that the thick Rings are meant to be used with a major Ring. Some of the Ancients' legends refer to maintenance Rings. We hope that is what it is. Also, we hope you can activate it."

"Me?" Ulla inclined her head toward Dmytro and Ingeborg. "You have expert Ring workers right here."

"Dmytro and Ingeborg are masters at precise Ring work. But this Ring needs to sense a psi profile none of us have. You, as a spinner, may be able to activate it."

Ulla took a deep breath. "Why a spinner?" *You know I mustn't*—

She remembered Aubrey and continued out loud. "You know I'm forbidden to use the Spinner Gift."

Neal led the way back to the camion and extracted the

thick utility Ring from the footwell. "There's a lot you can do short of using the Gift itself. We're hoping all this Ring needs is your psi profile."

"But the Ancients made the Rings, right?" Ulla said. "Did they even have spinners?"

"We know the Ancients used psi." Aubrey had followed them. "Their records don't mention spinners as such, but some of the Ancients in the legends had comparable Gifts."

Hero legends? Maybe. Or they might be actual history. "Fripp already tried, right?" Ulla asked.

"It flickered a little for her but didn't activate," Neal said, "and her voice is pitched too low for Ring song."

Of course. And little Stelle, the only other living spinner, was still a child, with a child's psi profile and a child's voice.

That left Ulla, the offworlder, who was painfully aware of how little she knew about this place and everything in it.

Neal handed her the cased Ring. She took it to a shady spot, sat down on the soft pine needles, and opened the cover. "How many thick Rings are there?"

"Eighteen from Kettlerest," Neal said. "A dozen or so more, sunk with the major Rings offshore." He brightened. "Your buddy Fergus has been a big help with bringing them up, Starfighter."

Fergus was in his element, Ulla decided. "Have they let him dive yet?"

"Some—but only for old time's sake." Neal sat down next to her in the shade. "Mostly he's linking with our strongest finders and mind-movers. They got the last of the maritime major Rings up from the seafloor today. Should be in place by the end of this week."

Ulla touched the Ring lightly, mind-seeing.

"Look!" Neal stared. The Ring brightened under Ulla's touch. Shining glyphs floated to its surface. The unfamiliar symbols behaved just like the runes in the few utility Rings Ulla had handled.

Ingeborg plopped down across from them. *Oh. Dear. Gods.* "Can you read that?" she asked Neal.

Neal peered at the Ring. "Mostly. I'd need to look up a few." He reached into his pocket for a notebook and pencil, then transcribed furiously. The glyphs faded back into the Ring. "Touch it again, Starfighter."

The glyphs winked back on as her fingers made contact.

Neal finished copying the string of glyphs, then handed the notebook to Aubrey. "Does this look familiar?"

The archaeologist pulled a set of reading spectacles out of her pocket, planted them on the bridge of her nose, and pored over Neal's transcription, scribbling Elders' runes underneath Neal's tidy row of glyphs.

Elders' runes? Why not Standard or Dialekt? Or City English? Ulla had no idea what Dr. Aubrey Rogers had just written. And why did the thick Ring have hieroglyphics instead of runes?

You'll learn, Starfighter. Ingeborg read over Aubrey's shoulder, translating for them. "'Maintenance Ring for'"—she spat out a near-unpronounceable word that apparently contained no vowels—"'Ring, on standby mode.'" She looked up. "That's an island off the Esperanza coast, isn't it?"

"There's a Ring seat there," Neal said. *Dammit. I was sure this one went with the Great Knob Ring.*

The Ring from Bald Mountain, that was stuck in Newcastle. Ulla ran her hand over the maintenance Ring's smooth surface and set the glyphs flowing again. "Shall I sing it up anyway?"

"Sure." Neal sat down opposite Ulla.

Ulla used the activation song Hanni had taught her, her voice prompting a new set of glyphs, which settled into an orderly flow across the Ring's surface. Neal transcribed furiously in his notebook.

Out of habit, Ulla sang to activate the Ring's default privacy shield. Nothing changed; this Ring didn't seem to have one.

A few seconds later it vibrated under her touch. A bright glow bloomed from deep inside and spread until it obscured the marching glyphs.

Neal reached over and touched the Ring. "Ow!" He jumped back and stuck two fingers in his mouth. "Sing it down!"

Ulla did. *What the hell...* "What happened?" The thick Ring's surface faded to its expected dark luminosity. She laid a single, experimental finger on it; it was still plenty hot.

"It must have already come up in standby mode inside

its case," Ingeborg said.

How did that even work?

Neal and Aubrey huddled together, puzzling over the hieroglyphs he'd scribbled while the much taller Vani bent down to watch over Neal's shoulder.

Maribet's telepathic voice popped into Ulla's mind. *Ring keeper from*—there was the unpronounceable place name again—*Ring seat, for Neal Erikson and the, um, spinner.*

Maribet had replaced the Ring keeper's colorful adjective with "um," but Ulla had heard what he said. Neal and Aubrey were oblivious, still poring over the glyphs in his notebook.

Ulla called to him. "Professor Erikson!"

Neal took a moment to disengage from his notebook. "What?"

Ulla practically heard Maribet's patience fray. *You take the link, Starfighter. I've got another contact request.*

The minute Ulla linked the Ring keeper with Neal, he turned to a blank page in his notebook. "Vani too," he said.

Ulla included Vani in the link and settled back to relay.

The stranger opened with, *Neal Erikson, what in the hell are you doing?*

Chapter Thirty-Eight
Rings

With the pissed-off Esperanzan finally satisfied and gone from her link, Ulla stood up and shook out her limbs while Ingeborg and Dmytro gathered up their things and loaded the camion. Aubrey and Vani had wandered off to pick some more at the section of plaster they found so interesting.

"How did I manage to sing up a major Ring halfway around the planet?" she asked.

"You didn't." Neal went over his notes from the conversation and thought for a minute. "There was a prepared script recorded on the thick Ring you sang up. Your psi profile activated the script, and your Gift transmitted it there, is all."

Ulla sat back down and closed her eyes. *You'd think a Ring that can do that would have a privacy function.*

You'd think. Neal was quiet for a bit. "Hmm."

Ulla opened her eyes. "What?"

"Privacy function." He looked around. *Where's your utility Ring?*

Over there. Her new Ring and the thick Ring they'd almost exploded were the only things Ingeborg and Dmytro hadn't tidied away and packed. She walked over to her utility Ring, sat down, and opened the case.

Neal joined her. He sighed. *Of course.*

Ulla stared at the still surface of her inactivated utility Ring.

Neal absently scratched the sunburn on his ear. "We

have always used utility Rings mostly for privacy—even though we thought they were meant for practicing Ring song."

The singers have to get it right the first time with a major Ring, don't they? Ulla asked. Even with a utility Ring, bad things could happen if you messed up a song—which was really a command sequence for a sophisticated artifact. If adolescent Thom had scorched a table with a utility Ring, what might happen if a singer botched a song for a major Ring?

Neal stifled a laugh. *He told you about that?*

I...stumbled upon the evidence. Ulla rubbed at a tight spot in the back of her neck. *He told me you saved his butt.*

Thom must really love you if he said even that much. Neal smiled. "More to the point, even though we use major Rings mostly to redirect power, they have the same privacy functions as a standard utility Ring—and at full power, a major Ring can cover a lot of ground."

Ulla thought back to when Hanni had shown her how to use a utility Ring to make a force field about three meters across that didn't let ANYTHING in or out—not heat, not light, not sound, not psi, not weaponry, not air. And she had made Ulla create and then undo such a force field over and over again. Once Ulla was sufficiently impressed by the little Ring's lethal potential, they had worked on the other permutations of its privacy functions. Hanni had taught Ulla how to use it for full-on force fields, for mild barriers that could keep headblind neighbors' thoughts from intruding in their homes, and for all the gradations in between.

That was why a beginning Ring singer like Ulla could sing a Ring down even when awakened from a deep sleep.

"It takes two people, singing different octaves, Neal explained, "to do pretty much anything with a major Ring."

"If that's the case," Ulla asked, "what just happened?"

Wouldn't I like to know! Neal retrieved the thick utility Ring and set the case down about a meter from Ulla's Ring. "Think you can sing it up again?"

"Are you sure you want me to?" The gods knew what would happen when Ulla did. More than likely, it would involve the angry Esperanzan.

Not now. Vani's telepathic voice reached them from where he and Aubrey Rogers were carrying on an animated conversation about early Ancient hieroglyphics. *First we must learn more about how the new Rings work.* He droned on, citing what must have been academic references, and Ulla barely stifled a yawn. Neal pulled out his notebook and pencil and scribbled as fast as he could.

Suddenly there was a loud pop. Ulla jumped at the sound and turned to see Vani and Aubrey leap back. The field of hieroglyphics they'd been peering at had just split in two; the wall had cracked from top to bottom.

There was another loud pop, then all was quiet. Vani examined the base of the wall but jumped back. Even at a distance, Ulla could see fresh motes of dust and flakes of old plaster puff out from the wall into the dappled sunlight. Birds fluttered away from the commotion while a disgruntled squirrel chattered on the nearby ruined wall.

Neal and Ulla ran to see what had happened. Behind them, Dmytro and Ingeborg caught up fast.

"Stand back, Aubrey, let me use mind-moving." Vani and Aubrey had already stepped back a good two meters. "If the wall cracks again, it will likely collapse."

Aubrey took a deep breath and left the Elder to it. She set her readpad to record video and aimed it at the wall as Vani worked. Everyone else stood behind them, watching as chunks of broken plaster floated smoothly to one of the better-preserved sections of tile floor outside the wall's probable fall zone and arranged themselves as they had been on the wall. The second layer of plaster had writing on it, too, and the academics grew even more excited about that.

Neal propped his readpad to record from a nearby stone pedestal facing Vani's growing collection of plaster bits.

Once the Elder had cleared away the loose plaster, his activity centered on the most prominent cracks: a rectangle near the base of the wall.

"No." Aubrey spoke up just as Vani mind-moved the plaster front of the rectangle that had not yet come entirely loose. "From here, we excavate properly."

Neal and Vani glanced at each other; even Ulla could not hear the thoughts they must have exchanged.

"The Ancients hid something in there," Neal said. "The top layer of plaster is contemporary with the Kettlerest Ring cache; the layer it covers could be important."

Aubrey peered at the exposed glyphs on the second layer of plaster. "That's the same style as the glyphs inside the Bald Mountain Ring Seat."

Ulla had no idea what the archaeologist's usual technique would be for exposing the second layer. No doubt it would be excruciatingly slow and would only happen after they shored up the wall.

"Starfighter," Vani said, "how far along are you at mind-seeing?"

"I can puzzle out what the underlying layers look like," said Ulla, "without touching the wall, if that's what you're asking. But my drawing skills—"

"—stink," said Ingeborg. "Ulla, why don't you and Vani link minds? He knows what to look for. You do the mind-seeing; he can draw."

The Elder pulled a notebook and pencil from his pocket.

"Okay." Ulla began settling herself for the task.

Providence saved them the trouble; the wall cracked one last time and tumbled down.

Providence, Spinner? Neal shot Ulla a searching look.

Don't look at me; it just collapsed. Ulla was annoyed that Neal would think to ask.

The group waited for plaster dust to clear. The main section of stone and plaster wall had toppled away from them, leaving a boxy structure that had been its base. A corner of a bent metal door lay exposed. Was the box a reinforced cabinet?

Was the thing inside what Ulla thought she'd sensed? It would be so much easier to find out if she could touch what was left of the wall's base.

It wasn't as if there was anything left to fall on her. Crouching down, she touched the crumbled plaster and stone and immediately snatched her hand back, the hot masonry nearly burning her. She wrapped part of her shirttail around her hand and tried again. She lost some mind-seeing sensitivity through the cloth, but not enough to matter. "There's a utility Ring in there. A thick one. And a couple of lumps of—something. Feels like Rings, but they're not."

Aubrey checked to make sure her readpad was still recording. Ulla had the impression the usually meticulous archaeologist was as eager as the rest of them to unearth what the Ancients had hidden.

Neal thought for a moment. "Starfighter, there's a tool bag in the camion. Would you please mind-move it over here?"

"Sure." As she found the tool bag and flew it to him, Ulla heard a stray, poignant memory that Neal must have thought he'd shielded. His brother Piet had loved extending their collective reach in just this way.

When Ulla plunked the tool bag down in front of Neal, he opened it and pulled out a pair of heavy work gloves. He put them on and carefully pried out the rectangular chunk of plaster. He set it aside, opened the door, and pulled out two flat, more-or-less round things that could have been abstract sculptures or petrified cow droppings. The remaining item, thoroughly coated with dust and many layers of scorched insect webs, was a twin of the thick utility Ring Ulla had inadvertently overheated. "A little help here," he called over his shoulder.

Ulla glanced at Vani; the Elder's hands were too big to fit in the Ring's cabinet.

Aubrey rummaged in the tool bag, found a second pair of work gloves, and knelt beside Neal. They extracted the Ring from its hiding place and set it on the tile floor.

Vani set his readpad to record, aimed it at the filthy Ring, and got to work with his fine brush. The Elder had no trouble handling the Ring bare-handed as he cleaned off the webs and dust.

Ulla wondered if she had inadvertently sung it up while working with the Esperanzan Ring.

Vani nodded. *Yes Spinner Ulla, you did.* "It appears that this Ring was in standby mode when it was hidden. That is the simplest explanation for the layers of burned material surrounding it. There must have been other occasions when someone activated it inadvertently."

"That explains wall warmers!" Neal blurted.

Aubrey chortled but otherwise said nothing. Dmytro and Ingeborg looked at each other quizzically.

Ulla was at a loss. "What's a wall warmer?"

Dmytro finally spoke. "I always thought it was what spacers call an 'urban legend.'" He used the Standard term.

Aubrey shook her head. "I've seen it happen."

"Seen what happen?" Ulla wished they would get to

the point.

Neal gestured toward what was left of the Ring cabinet. "There's a tradition in Flint and Mountain clans that if headblind people get too close to this wall, it will get warm."

Dmytro snorted. "It's a myth."

"Not all headblind people have that effect," Aubrey said. "All four of my family tried, that summer Miles and the kids were here. The wall didn't warm up for any of us."

"See?" Dmytro said. "Myth."

Aubrey and Neal exchanged glances. Finally, Neal spoke. "Tell that to Thom's Newcastler friend Geoff Tully."

Ulla immediately thought of the scorched table in Thom's Trade Ministry attic hideaway. Thom had mentioned Geoff at the time.

"I got Aubrey to hire Geoff, Thom, and Skuli to help on the dig one summer," Neal said blandly. "Young Geoff set off that wall every time he got within three meters of it."

Vani cleared his throat. "Be that as it may, it would be prudent for Spinner Ulla to activate this Ring properly. Only then can it be sung down."

"Wait!" Neal looked around until he spotted Ulla's utility Ring. "Starfighter, may I use your Ring? I want to try something."

"The privacy function?" Ulla asked. "Sure."

He retrieved her utility Ring, set it down about a meter from the Ring they'd just found, and started to sing. Three notes in, Ulla heard no birds, no animals, no rustling leaves, no sound of water in the creek. Aside from the minds of those assembled around the Ring, there was none of the usual background psi chatter. A breeze wafted her cheek; at least Neal hadn't locked down their air. Or their light. Vani walked right through where the dome-shaped barrier surely must be.

"This is how we shielded the broken Ring in Newcastle—except there, we have four utility Rings working in concert." Neal glanced down to check the runes in her Ring. "Dmytro, I'd like you to contact Stef Nicson in Newcastle. He's in charge of today's guard on the Landfall Ring; I want somebody to monitor it while we work with this one."

Dmytro stepped outside the utility Ring's privacy circle, closed his eyes, and concentrated. "He's on it. I also gave Flint Council a heads-up."

Thanks. "Go ahead," Neal said. "Let's find out what we have here."

Ulla reached out and touched the Ring. Up popped one group of glyphs, then another, then another.

Neal grinned broadly. "This is it! That's the glyph for Great Knob, Landfall!"

"Do you still want me to sing it up?" Ulla asked.

"Sure. You heard Vani." Neal ran a hand over the top of his head, where he must once have had hair. "We have to deactivate it for transport; you can't do that properly till it's completely activated."

Ulla sang. More glyphs appeared. She finished the activation song and symbols flowed across the Ring's surface and through its depths.

Neal watched intently. "There! Sing it down!"

Ulla sang the next notes just as a series of glyphs lined up as they had in the maintenance Ring that had just tried to reset a Ring halfway across the planet. The glyphs faded, and the thick Ring assumed the blank sheen one expected of an inert utility Ring.

Dmytro opened his eyes. "Stef says nothing unusual happened to the Ring in the warehouse. Want me to link you with him?"

Neal shook his head. "Tell him 'Thanks.' We can talk about it when I get back." He sang down Ulla's utility Ring, then stared into space for a minute, lost in thought. He glanced at the camion. *Road's too dangerous, and it'll take too long.* "Ulla, do your SpaceCom liaison duties include getting us a rotorcraft?"

Ulla nodded. "To take this Ring to Newcastle?" She fished a SpaceCom conventional comm unit out of her rucksack.

"This one, yes, and the ones in the camion too." *No way am I sending Rings through a Gate.* "And two passengers. I'll be one." Neal thought for a moment. "They'll have a soulslayer and spotter on board, right?"

"That's required all over the Bailey-Duran system now," Ulla said. "The Society has a contract with the Guild."

"Which I helped write." Neal patted the pocket where he kept his notebook. "Dr. Aubrey Rogers will be the other passenger. In case we need to tend the Rings en route."

Ulla was puzzled. "But Dr. Rogers is—"

"—a headblind offworlder?" Neal asked. "Yes, and also a very accomplished Ring singer. She only needs somebody to read the markings for her; I've been doing that since I was her husband's grad student."

Ulla had always thought Neal Erikson's field was more scientific.

"I recreate what happened in the folktales Miles collects." Neal shrugged. "I guess you could call it 'applied anthropology' in Standard." *One culture's technology is another's magic.*

He cleared his throat. "I'd like you to send your utility Ring back with the rest, if you don't mind."

"Um, sure." Why the deferential air? The man was her boss. Ulla was accustomed to orders, not requests.

"I need you in Newcastle," he said. "You'll need the Ring for practice; we'll find you a new pair of teachers." *SpaceCom may have listed me as your reporting official, Ulla Thorsdaughter, but the fact remains that you are a spinner of wyrd.*

* * *

By the time Ulla had summoned a rotorcraft, Vani had requested anti-grav crates from Castle Chisos, Dmytro and Ingeborg had taken the stack of assorted utility Rings to Council House for safekeeping, Dmytro had gone off to help his brother Yanek with the capraglamas, and Ingeborg and Ulla had brought the camion back to the villa with Vani's first installment of empty crates, Ulla was starving.

"Mind if I eat my lunch?" Ulla asked as she sat with Ingeborg on the camion's tailgate, soulslayer and spotter guarding a hastily assembled crew packing up bits of newly important stone and plaster under Vani's and Aubrey's close supervision. The academics would reassemble the layers of plaster for study in the comfort—and security—of Castle Chisos.

"Go ahead." Ingeborg glanced up at Bailey-Duran's mid-afternoon position in the sky. "I thought you already ate."

Ulla opened her rucksack and fished out a SpaceCom box lunch she'd brought from the Headquarters dining hall that morning. "My body's running on Newcastle time—it's just past midday there." She wanted to keep things that way too. She unwrapped a sandwich and took a bite. *You didn't have to come back, you know. I don't need a spotter.* Her mouth was full; psi had its uses.

Ingeborg laughed. "If I were in camp, Ma'd have me planning menus, seating arrangements, dances, and who knows what else. The Council of Chieftains' directive calls for soulslayer AND spotter to guard overland journeys and high-value targets."

Ulla, having just taken another bite, raised an eyebrow. *We are in the middle of nowhere. How necessary is a guard?*

Plenty, Starfighter. You raised a ton of energy when the Ring almost blew. That was bound to've been noticed. Ingeborg swung her legs. *Besides, I'll be with Dannel and Mountain Clan next week. It won't hurt Flint to learn to get along without me.*

Ulla finished her sandwich and dug out a half-liter of berries she'd filched from the Trade Ministry kitchen. She held it out to Ingeborg. "Want some?"

"Sure, thanks." Ingeborg reached in and grabbed a handful. They sat there eating berries, scanning for threats, and enjoying the brilliant summer weather.

Ulla scanned again and, unsurprisingly, found no threats. She glanced at Ingeborg. *As long as we're sitting here on our butts, you may as well teach me something.*

Ingeborg popped a berry into her mouth. *What do you want to learn?*

How about Battle Rings? Ulla waved away a buzzing lace flier.

Ingeborg swallowed. "They, um, enhance the Gifts of whoever sings them up. The legends are full of Battle Rings, but nobody living ever saw a working one until Magnus Lemaire tripped over the top of the Kettlerest cache."

Which implied that non-working Battle Rings were a known thing.

"They're a single-use item; they melt once you've finished singing them." Ingeborg tucked a stray wisp of hair behind her ear. "Those lumps of Ring material you found with the maintenance Ring over there? They're melted Battle Rings."

Ulla thought back to a carefully polished round,

blobby—sculpture?—she'd seen displayed in a glass case in the Trade Ministry's reception hall alongside a slew of archaeological finds. *Oh.* She'd wondered if the Ancients venerated cow droppings. "How do you know the skinny Rings are Battle Rings?"

Ingeborg almost choked on a berry. *Cow droppings?* She coughed, then swallowed carefully. "Neal had Dmytro and me sing one up. Our Gifts got really strong. Then the Battle Ring melted." *Now that you mention it, it looks kind of like a cow pie.* "Dmytro says his mind-talk range went system-wide for a while there." She shivered.

"My range got longer too. But the best part was that I could finally see clearly—and repair—all kinds of things that are ordinarily way too tricky. Saw Dev had a budding heart-valve problem even Emli hadn't spotted, so I fixed it. Thom was out here tying up loose ends on the Bald Mountain investigation, so I checked him over more thoroughly than is usually possible—he's fine, by the way."

Why wouldn't he be fine? Ulla was curious.

"His ma died young of a heart problem that's genetic. That's not happening to anybody I care about while I'm around." *I was even able to examine Padraic in Newcastle, from here.*

Why Padraic?

He's Thom's ma's brother.

Oh. Ulla felt faintly stupid. *How's Padraic?*

Ingeborg went back to eating berries. *He's fine too.* She sat up straight and rolled her shoulders. "I cornered as many of Thom's close relatives as would sit still for me. Found a few issues, but nothing life threatening that they can't get taken care of where they are." She paused to grab more berries. "As long as I was poking around in Newcastle, I had a look at your ankle."

Ulla popped a berry into her mouth. *Nosy.*

Ingeborg was unrepentant. *The way you bounced around Summer Pasture before Bald Mountain, you set yourself up for a chronic sprain that'd never get better on its own.*

Hey! I was careful!

Ingeborg wagged her handful of berries in Ulla's face. *You hurt it again the day we arrived.*

Busted. *I landed wrong, getting off Snowball.*

And then you pretended it didn't happen. Ingeborg swallowed. "Did Fripp heal it, then?"

Ulla shook her head. "I did. Fripp provided adult supervision." Between the energy involved in tightening up a handful of wobbly ligaments and her body's need to finish healing in the usual way, Ulla had been flat on the couch for two days afterward.

Ingeborg grew sober. "You've seen the price of the Healing Gift, then."

"Coming down off of what you did had to have been a bitch," Ulla said.

"It was." Ingeborg blushed. "That's why I went face down in the dessert at your betrothal party."

So it had been exhaustion, not alcohol. Ulla had wondered.

Ingeborg nodded. *Exhaustion, yes.* She paused to scan for Dwellers. "We fired up the Battle Ring two days before your betrothal party. I went from buzzed to full stop right there at the table." *Just so you know, sleep is not part of the Battle Ring experience.* "So glad Dmytro and I are not a conjugal pair."

What? Ulla's mind formed the question before her mouth could ask out loud.

Ingeborg cleared her throat. "According to the Ancients, if it had been me and Dannel, or Dmytro and his wife, the effect would have been much stronger and lasted twice as long. It would have been stronger yet if we—and the Battle Ring—were surrounded by people who were directly affected by whatever we needed to step up our Gifts for." *Oh, and heads up: Neal has you and Thom in mind for such time as the Alliance needs to deploy a Battle Ring for real.*

A "conjugal pair" surrounded by people? For Ring work? Ulla was not particularly shy in that regard, and she was pretty sure Thom wasn't either, but—*eww!*

Ingeborg burst out laughing. "No worries, Starfighter. The Ring senses a couple's shared affinity. Just as it senses a person's psi profile."

"So all we have to do is Ring song?"

"Just Ring song." Ingeborg's eyes twinkled. *Though you could add a certain flair—*

Ulla sat up straight, eyes on the tree line. *Dwellers!*

Ingeborg jumped. *Where?*

In my imagination. It was Ulla's turn to laugh. "If you

could see your face," she said as she wiped her eyes.

Chapter Thirty-Nine
Unsticking a Ring

A few days later, Ulla was back in Newcastle, tucked into the corner of a warehouse behind a half-meter-high fragment of thick wall that had once been part of a high-value cargo vault. The other parts of the vault wall that the Ring from Bald Mountain hadn't exploded when it materialized had been knocked down and carted away, as had the vault's heavy ceiling. Not that Ulla could see much of the Ring; half the people she'd met telepathically in the lead-up to Bald Mountain, plus Miles Rogers, were crowded around it.

The warehouse roof loomed high overhead.

"Watch and learn," Neal had told her before transferring his attention entirely to the Ring, which sat on a hastily thrown-together frame of heavy wooden beams. A crust of broken concrete and rebar remained stuck tight in the Ring's erratic force field.

Emma Lemaire, who'd taken the day off from her MitSmith office job and Gated in from Kirkhilo, lay flat behind a remnant of vault wall next to her brother, Neal Erikson's grad student Sean Patel.

"Ready?" Neal asked.

Sean and Emma sang a few notes to establish a common pitch.

Neal and Miles joined Ulla in her corner.

Emma sang in a clear mezzo-soprano. Her brother sang the Ring song's baritone counterpoint.

Any luck? Skuli, who stood guard outside, had been

pestering Ulla for news for the last hour.

Nope. Ulla pressed her face into the floor as a fist-sized chunk of concrete popped off the Ring and flew past her.

More chunks popped off. Sean and Emma didn't miss a beat of Ring song. Ulla risked a peek as the undulating, dust-filled force field spat out concrete bits and sizzling-hot rebar.

"It's working!" Miles Rogers alternated between watching and ducking chunks of debris.

Sean and Emma sang until the space between the force field and the Ring's surface cleared. Chunks became bits. Bits turned to dust that flew until the Ring was clean. The Ring's glowing runes cycled to its surface and back in. They'd done it!

Then the dust settled in a smooth layer about five centimeters above the Ring's surface.

Damn. Neal stood up and went to the Ring. He brushed the dust aside and studied the swirling runes through the Ring's now-clear force field. *So close.*

Emma sat up and wiped the sweat off her face. "At least you can read them now."

What happened? Skuli, again.

Ulla filled him in.

Neal walked up to Ulla and Miles. "You okay?"

"Yeah." Ulla sat up. So did Miles.

Neal peered at the Ring's swirling runes. "Why the hell didn't that turn off the force field?"

Miles brushed cement dust out of his hair. "Good question."

This from the planet's foremost human authorities on Rings. Ulla tried not to think too hard about that.

I heard you. Neal sounded nothing like his usual professorial self.

Ulla wiped her hands on the seat of her pants. *Sorry. None of us has seen anything like this before.*

"What happens next?" Ulla asked.

Neal thought for a moment. "Add in Song 201?"

The older man consulted his notes. "Maybe the Landfall variant—201.6."

Neal looked at the singers. "You up for another?"

"Only if it's quick," Sean answered. "Test of concept, maybe." His voice was starting to get hoarse.

"What do you want to try?" Emma asked.

"201.6. But with capraglama support."

"You're joking, right?" Sean started to roll his eyes at his advisor and must have thought better of it. *Nearest capraglamas are at least a hundred klicks away.*

Range, kid. Range. Neal turned to Ulla. "Starfighter, Piet said you're pretty good with capraglamas."

He had? Ulla was flattered.

"Ask Yanek if he and maybe two of Flint's capraglamas can spare us half an hour. Just for a quick test."

"Um, sure." Ulla sat up straight, relaxed, and hailed Flint Clan's new head keeper, Dmytro Robson's brother, Yanek.

Heya, Starfighter! Wait one minute. Ulla waited while Yanek tightened the last bolt on a sturdy new keeper's perch with four seats. She felt Neal link with them, felt his stomach lurch right before he broke his link, and his relief that nobody else would risk getting trampled to death like his brother Piet had.

Should she send her projection to Summer Pasture? *Wouldn't want to spook the capraglamas.*

Yanek's attention pivoted from his task to their mind-talk link. *It's okay. They know you.*

Ulla grounded herself and sent a faint projection into the bushes a few meters outside the fence while Yanek put away his tools in a new wooden shed. At least half a dozen fence rails were new. They'd sunk a new gate post and hammered the gate's hinges back into shape.

"Heya!" Ryan called out loud; he must have been working nearby. The animal healer and his shadow, young Wat, rounded up a pair of capraglamas and nudged them toward the pen.

A third capraglama ambled toward Ulla's projection.

"Starfighter!" Young Wat, standing between the two capraglamas in the pen, shouted and waved. "It's all right; they're happy to see you."

Ulla moved her projection and settled it on the top fence rail. She murmured sweet nothings to the capraglamas while they poked their noses through her shadowy feet and legs.

Yanek, Wat, and Ryan climbed up on the keeper's perch. *Ready?*

Ulla faded her projection from Flint Clan's summer pasture and settled herself in the ruined vault. "They're ready when you are." She linked Yanek, Sean, and Emma. Neal, Ryan, and young Wat tagged along.

The singers got up and stretched, then took their places. Inside the Ring, swirling runes sped up and changed color as they sang. The layer of dust on the force field's boundary sagged a little. Ulla and Yanek channeled capraglama energy through Sean and Emma, who doubled down on Ring song. The force field shrank but did not dissolve.

They kept singing for a few long minutes.

When the song ended, Emma rolled over and lay on her back, exhausted.

Sean sat up. "Capraglamas helped." *But not enough.*

Neal brushed dust off the force field again and peered at the runes. "That was the right song, but it needs more power."

"You mean brute force." Sean wiped sweat off his face. "I felt us getting there, but we just couldn't."

Miles considered. "Let's revisit this another day. Maybe with two pairs of singers who can work in shifts."

Emma sat up. "What about the maintenance Ring you found? There's at least one legend about singing into one of those and replaying the song over and over."

Neal shook his head. "Not enough time."

"Why not?" Emma ran her fingers through her hair and pulled a pair of hairpins from her pocket.

"It's been in the ground on Kettlerest since before the Hjralma arrived on this world," said Neal. "Its major Ring has been in continuous use; unlikely they're still matched."

Which, they'd found, was why the maintenance Ring Ulla had sung up at the Ancients' villa had almost fried its companion major Ring on the other side of the planet.

"It'll take weeks of troubleshooting to get the maintenance Ring up, running, and matched," Neal said. "If the *Dauntless* task force doesn't hold—"

"—the Yotne will be here on the ground any day now." Emma sighed and twisted her hair, pinning it back into the neat bun she'd worn earlier in the day.

"If brute psi strength is what we need," Sean mused, "what about a Battle Ring?"

Ulla thought about what Ingeborg had said.

"Starfighter," Neal asked, "want to sing up a Battle

Ring?" *I've already talked with Thom.*

Who would not only have said "yes" but "hell, yes." "Um, sure," Ulla said. "When?"

Neal thought for a minute. "Legends say the turning points of the year are the most effective times to sing up Battle Rings—that might just be Ancients' superstition, though."

Miles spoke up. "An awful lot of what we thought was superstition is turning out to be accurate."

"Midsummer is next week, and you and Thom will need time to practice." Sean stood up and brushed dust from his clothes. "Can the task force hold off the Yotne that long?"

Ulla hoped so. But she had her doubts. There was another matter to deal with too. "Thom and I are supposed to be at Newcastle City's Midsummer Ball." Maybe having to sing up a Battle Ring would get them out of what had to be the most stultifyingly formal social event of the season!

"Perfect!" Neal looked ecstatic.

"You're joking." *I was hoping to get out of going to the damn ball.*

"Ancients maintained that Battle Rings work best when surrounded by people who need the strength, the magic." Neal warmed to the topic. "All the cities send representatives to each other's important social functions. Padraic and Renata will be there to represent the On'oi. SpaceCom will have been invited; Ulla, you make sure they send somebody in addition to you."

"General Zhou's going." The protocol officer had ordered Ulla to wear the SpaceCom semiformal uniform in solidarity with the general. She had been looking forward to at least getting to wear a pretty ball gown of Renata's impeccable choosing. But no, she would wear SpaceCom black, encrusted in gold braid and clanking with medals. Hers—the version with a long skirt—had just arrived from the tailor. She'd confuse the misogynistic Newcastle leadership just by walking through the door in that getup.

"But how do Thom and I get up in front of all of those people and sing up a Battle Ring?" she asked.

"I'll ask Renata Connersdaughter. She'll think of something." Neal paused. "We need at least one Elder from Castle Chisos there too."

That made things interesting. The City-States people

preferred to think of the Elders as historical figures, occasionally sighted in the hinterlands. Newcastlers never failed to affect surprise when faced with a living, breathing Elder.

"Aubrey and I have been invited," said Miles. "If Renata can't wangle an invitation for the Elders, we'll find a way."

Neal closed his notebook. "That's it for today. Flint and Mountain clans have a wedding to go to."

As did Raven, Worldtree, and several hundred friends, for the first night of Ingeborg and Dannel's wedding.

Ulla brushed grit off her pant legs. Thom would be at the Trade Ministry by now; she needed to get cleaned up and Gate out to Bald Mountain with him in less than an hour.

Chapter Forty
Preparation

Midsummer afternoon was upon them. Bailey-Duran was still high in Newcastle's evening sky as Ulla met the Berserkers' second-in-command, Jan Martin, by the Trade Ministry's back entrance. Colonel Becenti and Mags's boss, Captain Nault, slid out of the SpaceCom van after him and surveyed the area as an Atmospheric Forces officer Ulla hadn't met got out. Mikko Strom parked the van next to the nondescript sedan Neal had just arrived in with an equally nondescript-looking Newcastler.

"Detective Matti Brown, Newcastle City Guard." The Newcastler extended his hand. "Never in anger, Lieutenant." *Honored to meet you.*

Ulla shook hands with him. "Never in anger," she repeated automatically. *I had no idea the Guard had—*

—soulslayers? Not officially. The inspector's eyes sparkled with intelligence. *But being who I am is—useful.*

Ulla could imagine. Never mind the Dark Gift; this man would be a whiz at interrogations even with short-range psi. *Why aren't there more like you?*

City prejudice. He stood aside to let the SpaceCom officers through the door. *For now, let us speak out loud.*

They trooped down the hall to the conference room where Fripp and Ed Jeppeson, the BTE agent who worked at the Trade Ministry, waited with a representative from Landfall's Home Guard.

Neal opened his notebook and checked the roster. "Where's Thom?"

"On his way. There was a line at the Gate in Terrandessay." Ulla took a seat at the table.

Neal frowned. "Why'd he go back?" Thom had been in Newcastle, practicing Ring song with Ulla since the Coalition had decided to go forward with Neal's plan.

Ulla shrugged. "Said he needed to settle some things at work." *Thom?*

Almost there. I'm through the Gate; just got a taxi.

She relayed the information to the group as they found places at the big conference table. "Isn't the Guild sending somebody?" She poured herself a glass of water from the pitcher on the table. Where was Skuli Branson? He was supposed to be here too.

Skuli and Olwyn walked in and sat down next to each other. They weren't late; everyone else was early.

Ed took the utility Ring out of its locked cabinet, set it on the table, and sang it up for privacy while the offworlders watched, fascinated.

The sound of running footsteps in the hall belonged to Thom, who entered quietly and found a seat next to Ulla. He gave her hand a quick squeeze under the table just as the anachronistic clock in the Trade Ministry's entry hall chimed. *Right on time.*

Everyone's here; good. Neal scribbled the finishing touches of a meeting agenda on a writing board on the wall. "We haven't much time. Here's the updated outline of the plan; please have a final look. This is the last chance for questions, answers, and last-minute deconfliction."

Ulla and Thom had practiced their part until even the Ring song was sheer muscle memory. She reviewed what Neal had written.

Same basic plan, thanks be. Under the guise of showing off On'oi Ring song during a break in the Midsummer Ball's official entertainment, Ulla and Thom would sing up the Battle Ring among people from all over the planet. Mayors of all the city-states in Hoffnung, or their representatives, would be in attendance. Dignitaries from Esperanza and Landfall would be there, as well as a couple of higher-ups from the Planetary Restoration Project's Terrandessay main office. General Zhou would represent SpaceCom.

Wait a minute! There were three senior SpaceCom officers at the table. Captain Nault was here about the spaceborne piece. If their plan to use the Rings to block the Yotne worked, SpaceCom's fleet would be cut off from the planet's surface just as effectively. The Atmospheric Forces officer had committed a cargo flittercraft and crew to carry the Ring and those attending it to Landfall, and atmospheric fighters would provide cover along the way. Colonel Becenti was here for the land piece—a ground war could easily break out, especially in Landfall. Colonel Martin was here because the bulk of offworld ground fighters on Landfall Mainland were Berserkers. Why was Mikko at the table?

Skuli glanced at Ulla. *Lieutenant Strom is General Zhou's newest aide.*

Lieutenant Strom?

Skuli grinned. *He got a promotion too.*

The embroidered pips that meant "Lieutenant, Junior Grade" on Mikko's dark utility uniform were so muted they were almost invisible. "Congratulations, Lieutenant," Ulla said. "Glad to see you here." *Skuli, why didn't you say something?*

Skuli shrugged. *I just did. You've been busy.*

"As for security for Pioneer Hall," Neal said, "the Matthias Carroll Memorial Society will send two soulslayers; they'll arrange for their own spotters. Ulla and Thom, with you on-premises; that makes four soulslayers. Ed will spot for Thom if it comes to that—and, Ulla, you don't need a spotter."

True, but—"If I have to work in projection, I'd like help with physical security for my body," she reminded them.

"Like the bouncer did at Mickey Bravo's?" Mikko asked. "I'll do it."

"What if the general needs you?" Skuli asked.

"He won't." Mikko took a sip of water. "His driver will be there too; I'm to work with you."

Neal pointed to the next item on the agenda. "At the orchestra's break, Ed will set up the Battle Ring."

Ulla stopped doodling in her notebook. "How will he get in?"

Ed grinned. "I'm the Trade Minister's armed assistant."

Thom snorted. "When did Padraic Willemson start needing a bodyguard?"

"Since he and Renata Connersdaughter received an invitation to Midsummer Ball. Everybody there who can afford one is bringing an 'assistant.'" Ed waved his fingers to make air quotes.

Oh.

Detective Brown spoke up. "I have an update about the organized crime packs."

Neal tapped his pencil on his notebook. "Go on."

"Hard as the Society has worked to get rid of Dwellers, they keep popping up. We're seeing a lot of them in River Pack—probably getting in through River's smuggling operation." Matti glanced at his notes. "We confirmed this morning that River Pack is actively colluding with the Yotne. Some of the other pack families may be too."

"Any idea how many?" Skuli asked.

"Not yet," Matti said. "Some families are against the idea; the packs are on the verge of warring among themselves. But the takeaway right now is that not all your threats will be Dweller-ridden. You'll need conventional deadly force—not just soulslaying."

Ulla took a deep breath and hoped for a peaceful, though busy, Midsummer's night—with backup.

Starfighter.

What?

Skuli Branson's eyes met hers. *All those headblind armed assistants. Beginning with Lieutenant Strom. We need to talk.*

Let's talk, then, right after this meeting. Ulla looked straight at Mikko and silently moved her lips; he got the message.

"Let's hope it doesn't come to that." Neal ticked off another item on the writing board, then continued to rapidly move through the rest of the prep. "After Ulla and Thom sing up the Battle Ring, Skuli will drive them to the warehouse."

Where, with luck and Battle Ring power through Ulla and Thom, Emma and Sean would be able to free the Landfall Ring, Neal's party would pack it up, and they'd drive it five kilometers to SpaceCom's airstrip.

"Your cargo flittercraft is standing by, Dr. Erikson," the Atmospheric Forces officer said. "Your party's personal bags are already aboard."

They'd likely spend several days in Landfall—not to mention Ulla and Thom would need to change out of their formal attire as soon as they could.

Neal continued. "The Ring seat at Great Knob is

ready, and the Landfall Home Guard is on alert. The nearest capraglamas and their keepers, assembled at their respective pens, will add power if needed; all the rest are on call. And the Guild representative will Gate to BD3 Station immediately after this meeting, along with all spaceborne forces not assigned to ships."

Ulla sensed Skuli squeeze Olwyn's hand under the table. So, they were an item.

Elder Spinner Fripp stood ready to keep inexperienced Spinner Ulla from turning into, as Olwyn had put it, a loose cannon. Nobody said that out loud because everybody at the table already knew.

"Anything else?" Neal looked around the room.

Silence.

He erased the board. "Let's do it."

* * *

After a quick huddle with Skuli, Mikko, Detective Brown, and Ed, Ulla and Thom walked down the corridor with Fripp and Landfall's Home Guard representative.

When they reached the elevator doors, Fripp gave Ulla and Thom each a quick hug. "I will see you later, in projection." *Now you must get some rest.*

"She's right," said Thom. *But when?*

Right now. The elevator doors opened, and Ulla followed Thom inside. "When do we have to be at Pioneer Hall?" she asked.

"Officially?" Thom asked.

Ulla pressed the button for her floor. "Realistically." She did not select the floor where Thom was staying with his aunt and uncle. Instead, she held her hand in front of the button array and smiled. *My place.*

Thom did not argue. "Program says introductions begin at 20:00, which, with that crowd, ought to put the mayor's entrance at about 21:00 or so. As long as we get there before he does, we'll be fine. The middle of the pack will get there about 20:30." *Our Battle song is about an hour before the solstice.*

That would be about a quarter after 22:00; this year's northern summer solstice would be at 23:17 Newcastle time. They stopped in front of Ulla's door. She yawned. "Plenty of time for a nap."

How can you even think about sleep? Ulla could hear thoughts racing inside Thom's brain.

"Amateur!" she chided gently. *I'll show you.*

She led him inside. They got most of their clothes off on the way across the sitting room and through the hallway before they fell onto the bed together.

* * *

Wake up! The telepathic jolt came from the guard downstairs. *Your hairdresser is here.*

Mmmph. Waking from a deep sleep, Ulla slid out from under Thom's arm. *Five minutes?*

I'll tell her. The guard broke the link.

I heard that. A bit of cloth snapped against her behind. Thom, already wearing pants, grinned as he put on his shirt.

You asshole! She leaped out of bed. They kissed, then Thom grabbed the rest of his clothes and went to change in his own room.

After a quick wash-up, Ulla put on her good lingerie. She was pulling the semiformal uniform's stretchy under-top over her head when there was a knock at the door. *Heya. It's unlocked.*

Sonya, the hairstylist who had given Ulla such a good haircut a few weeks ago, opened the door. *Let's get to work. We haven't much time.*

Ulla sat on the plain chair at her desk, which doubled as a dressing table.

Sonya opened a small bag, laid out scissors and combs, and set a curling iron to heat. "Do you have to wear a hat tonight?"

Ulla shook her head. "Hat's not worn with this uniform." The protocol officer must have overlooked that detail. *Newcastle can deal with my uncovered female head.*

They'll get over it. Sonya chuckled. "I'll cut your hair the same as before and give it some curl to fancy it up a bit. You'll make a gorgeous barbarian."

Ulla was happy to experiment with feminine things, but her experience was limited. "What do you have in mind?"

"No worries. Give me a free hand, and I'll fix you right up." Sonya wrapped a towel around Ulla's shoulders, then ran her fingers through Ulla's hair and got to work.

It wasn't long before she handed Ulla a mirror. A woman with a symmetrical mass of brown curls stared back. *Is that me?*

Sonya took the mirror back from Ulla. "Looks good, Starfighter."

* * *

After Sonya left, Ulla put on her skirt. She was delighted that the updated semiformal uniform skirt was divided and lined with satin so a person could move. She could ride a camdeer in this thing or hide a small artillery piece in its folds. The designer deserved a commendation. Or maybe the local tailor had improved on SpaceCom's specifications.

The latter, Ulla decided, as she strapped on a holster for the small pistol Ed had issued her last week before the uniform's final fitting at the tailor's. It fit nicely inside the skirt's waistband at the small of her back and nothing sagged when she holstered the loaded weapon.

Her new semiformal jacket looked like the one she'd left in storage, except that it fit perfectly and did not bulge over the pistol. Even with its high collar and many buttons, the jacket was not at all restrictive; she put that down to skilled tailoring, slippery lining, and a few hidden and quite nonregulation gussets, gores, and slits. The black wool fabric was encrusted with shiny gold-colored braid, especially on the collar and sleeves. She pinned on her medals and her starfighter hedgehog; for once, she felt unabashed about showing off her Gallantry Star. The shiny bits filled the space between her left breast and shoulder and made the uniform even gaudier.

Ed had given her enough ammunition to survive a siege. She distributed as much as she could about her person but stopped before her pockets sagged. After all, a woman needed room to carry some money and a hankie.

Dressing for this ball felt remarkably like suiting up to fly.

Heya!

Ulla opened her door for Thom. He wore black trousers, a long, flawlessly tailored cutaway jacket over a pressed white linen shirt, and the ugliest cravat she had ever seen.

He carried a length of pale, soft cloth.

Never mind the formal Newcastle tie; this'll cover it up. He shook out the cloth; it was a hip-length cape woven of natural capraglama fiber. The threads were lumpy, the weaving skillful enough but not great. A tailor having more skill than the spinner or the weaver had attached a blue silk brocade lining and made it into—what?

Don't tell me you haven't seen a sorcerer's cloak.

She was mystified. Then she remembered seeing a soft, elegant cloak tumble out of Ingeborg's bag once when Ingeborg was hunting for something. Ulla hadn't asked, but she had wondered why Ingeborg had brought such a nice item of clothing on trek. And then she'd noticed Maribet had one too.

"Oh, we're rarely without them." Thom held it out for her to touch. "My sister is a more enthusiastic weaver than I, and much, much more Gifted."

Ulla ran her hand across the soft fabric. "You made this?"

"Sure. Everybody spins and weaves their own during training at Castle Chisos." He made careful folds in the fabric and fastened some hidden snaps. Then, checking his progress in the tall mirror on the wall next to Ulla's bedroom door, he fastened the cape's collar over the dreadful Newcastle tie. Blue silk and capraglama wool flowed in sleek folds over his shoulders and back, leaving his arms free. Looking more closely, Ulla noticed little triangles woven into the blue brocade lining.

"You look like a cleaned-up barbarian." Ulla grinned, taking in the view.

"That's the idea." Thom made some tiny adjustments to the folds.

"Do the triangles mean what I think they mean?" Ingeborg's cloak had been lined with plain green silk.

"Soulslayer? Yes." *Listen to the City folk tonight; they'll whisper among themselves until somebody figures it out.*

"Do they get real quiet all of a sudden?"

Yep. "We need to go. Do you have everything?"

"I think so."

Oh! He reached into his pocket and handed Ulla a conventional comm transmitter.

"Thanks." Ulla put it in her ear and did a quick test; Mikko answered immediately.

Thom opened the door for Ulla. "Let's go."

Chapter Forty-One
Midsummer Ball

Chattering people filled Pioneer Hall's front gallery. They rushed to greet friends, compare notes, and show off their fancy clothes. To look at them, one would think Newcastle City was oblivious to the Yotne advance in space above their heads.

One would be mistaken. Almost every rich and powerful man in attendance wore a discreet comm transmitter in his ear. Many were armed; Ulla could tell by mind-seeing, though she spotted more than one weapon print underneath their expensive formal jackets. At least two dozen of the "personal assistants" Ed had mentioned stood about the grounds, pretending idle chitchat. To a man—and they were all men—they wore transmitters that kept them in touch with their employers. She spotted Mikko conversing with a small group by the entrance. His black SpaceCom dress uniform and the aiguillette on his shoulder blended right in with the polished livery of his City-States counterparts.

"Lieutenant, Mr. Yensson." He saluted her as she and Thom reached the outer edge of the portico.

She returned his salute. "Good evening."

"Hope so, ma'am." Underneath his psi blocker and his pleasant though formal mien, he was in full hunting mode.

Once inside, Thom led the way to the back of the crowd where the Hjralma-On'oi trade minister and his wife, the culture minister, waited.

The older couple were resplendent in their finery. Padraic wore his chain of office over a black cutaway coat and knee-length sorcerer's cloak. "Glad you could make it," he said.

Thom blushed.

Renata wore a simple evening gown of dark green silk. Where a cloak would have been, lined folds of the same fabric, heavily embroidered in sparkly thread, cascaded down her back from two shipsmetal clasps at her shoulders. Her carefully styled hair was uncovered and pinned up with matching shipsmetal combs; City-bred ladies with even the latest headgear would be envious. To complete the ensemble, a transmitter was nestled in her left ear.

Renata surveyed the queue at the top of the wide staircase leading down to the ballroom. "You should get in line. You're next."

Thom held out his arm to Ulla and they slid to the front of the line waiting for their names to be announced as they entered the ballroom. A jolt of recognition alerted Ulla to Maribet's presence two couples behind them, with Susana Schiller.

Can they do that? In Newcastle?

Of course they can, Thom answered. *But that they ARE doing it has got to be a first.*

If we're all going to die anyway, let's do it right! That was Maribet. Ulla glanced over her shoulder and saw the two women give each other a great big socially incorrect hug.

"Thom Yensson, Hjralma-On'oi Alliance Planetary Restoration Project, and Ulla Thorsdaughter, United Worlds and Nations Space Command, attached to Hjralma-On'oi Alliance, Space-Time Continuum Management Branch." The announcer made a total hash of the Hjralma words.

Really?

Bureaucratese for spinner of wyrd. Thom smiled and waved, so Ulla waved too as they stepped into the ballroom.

With Newcastle's upper crust busy digesting that mouthful, a Guardian with a starfighter on his arm would be less memorable. That was genius on Renata's part.

They stood to one side and watched the next few couples walk down the stairs.

"Susana Marie Johnstone Schiller, of Schiller

Enterprises and Newcastle Mercantile Guild, and Maribet of Flint Clan."

There's the bitch who won't give up her late husband's Guild seat and *Look! That's the Elliot girl who ran off with the herders!* were the mildest thoughts Ulla heard running through people's minds.

Maribet did not react. Instead, she smiled and waved. Hand in hand, she and Susana made their way down the steps into the ballroom. Ulla spotted a middle-aged couple on the other side of the room staring at the two women; they discreetly looked away when they saw she'd noticed. By their musings, they would be Maribet's parents, the Elliots, whose name had pointedly not been used.

Ulla decided that coming of age in a company mining settlement on the Edge had not been so bad after all.

Across the room, lines of gentlemen moved toward a side table with three elegant glass water dispensers as fast as the servers could fill glasses and hand them out. Thom joined the line, leaving Ulla to mingle with the other ladies. They smiled politely; she smiled back, trying not to eavesdrop on what they didn't say. Their curiosity outweighed contempt, but Ulla still felt like a crow among tropical birds.

Thom emerged from the line and handed her a crystal goblet of water.

"Thank you."

Water is a popular choice tonight.

Ulla glanced at the almost-unattended bar. While Newcastle's upper classes might be stubborn, hidebound, and ethnocentric, they were not stupid.

"Would you like a bite to eat?" a server asked, holding out a tray piled with fruit and cheese. *Victor sent Henri Brown and me. Henri's in the kitchen, covering the back of the house.*

Spotters? Thom asked.

Assistant dishwasher's spotting for Henri. The server inclined her head toward another uniformed waitstaff member circulating with a cleanup tray. *Mine's over there.* Ulla recognized the Gifted bouncer from Mickey Bravo's.

Including Thom and Ulla, there were four soulslayers present. They'd had four at Mickey Bravo's, five if you counted Fergie's debut. But Mickey Bravo's was a middle-sized restaurant and bar. This place was huge. Ulla looked around, sizing things up. *This is the damnedest party I've ever been to.*

Indeed. Thom guided her to a place where they could stand with their backs to the wall. *Let's hope it is the dullest.* They watched the showy parade of dignitaries still walking down the steps into the ballroom. Judging by their heavy, gaudy chains of office, the current crop were the mayors of other city-states and their wives. Then came a pair representing MitSmith Corporation.

Padraic and Renata were next, representing the Hjralma-On'oi Alliance.

There was a lull.

"Where are the Rogerses?" Ulla whispered. She hadn't seen any Elders in the ballroom either.

Thom spotted them at the top of the stairs. *Over there.* Aubrey Rogers and Vani, dressed to the nines, stood in animated conversation with General Zhou.

Vani offered his hand to Dr. Rogers, and they descended the stairs together as their names were announced.

"Dr. Aubrey Tilston Rogers, Newcastle University and United Worlds and Nations Society of Xenoarchaeology, and Elder Vani, Hjralma-On'oi Alliance Castle Chisos Research Facility and United Worlds and Nations Society of Xenoarchaeology."

Vani coughed discreetly. *Dr. Miles Rogers sends his regrets.*

Thom's mouth was full. With almost superhuman effort, he swallowed before he could spray water everywhere. *Should have known they'd pull something like that. Aubrey loves these shindigs; Miles hates 'em.*

General Zhou waited at the top of the stairs until the room quieted. As the guest who had traveled the farthest to be there, he immediately preceded a well-preserved man in late middle age who could only be the mayor of Newcastle, with his equally well-dressed and well-preserved wife. They reached the foot of the stairs just as the background music ended.

The musicians queued up paper sheet music on their stands. As their director raised his baton, the hall filled with dance music. The mayor held out his hand to his lady, sweeping her onto the dance floor, and the party really began.

***

When Ulla and Thom left the dance floor, General Zhou was waiting.

"Good evening," he said, glass in hand, appearing for all the world to be watching people and enjoying life. "May I have this dance?" He set down his glass and held out his hand to Ulla, who barely managed a graceful nod and "Yes, thank you" instead of "Yes, sir." She took his arm and followed, grateful that the music was neither too slow nor too fast. She didn't dance with generals every day.

Things improved once they were out on the floor. The general was a good dancer; Ulla had only to follow his lead. "I'm proud to make your acquaintance," he said as he guided her expertly through a turn.

"And I, yours." Was it the spinner business or something else? They danced the next few steps in silence.

"'From those to whom much has been given,'" he quoted, "'much will be required.' I know it isn't easy."

Did he read minds? No, Ulla decided, he didn't. But he was a very competent reader of people. Nor had he brought up what she had been given, because they both knew.

"Your father and I were classmates back in the day," he said, "and I met your mother once, before..." He stopped talking and seemed relieved that the dance took an intricate series of turns. He led flawlessly. "That was a lifetime ago."

Ulla concentrated on the dance. Step, step, turn. Step, step, turn.

"You are Thor Bjornson's child," he told her. "That and your service record tell me you will do well at whatever you take on."

Ulla almost tripped. "Thank you," she said as he steadied her.

"I should thank you," said the general. Then, in an almost fatherly tone, he added, "You'll do fine."

The dance was over. As the general turned and walked away, Ulla did her best to avoid standing there with her mouth open.

***

When the band took a break, Padraic Willemson

stepped up to the podium. A pair of uniformed waitstaff set the conductor's music stand aside and replaced it with a small sandbox. Ed stood behind Padraic, holding the Battle Ring.

"Thank you so much." Padraic nodded toward the departing band members. Then he faced the crowd. "For your entertainment during the band's intermission, piper Mik Fowler of Thistle Clan will play us a tune. Then Thom Yensson and Ulla Thorsdaughter will treat us to a rare exhibition of On'oi Ring song."

It's rare, all right. Thom squeezed Ulla's hand. *First time ever, in front of City folk.*

Mik struck in the drones on his pipes, Padraic stepped back, and Ed set the Battle Ring case on the floor. He opened the case, lifted the Ring out, and set it in the center of the sandbox.

People who had drifted toward the doors stopped, standing as though riveted in place while the piper played.

Ulla did too. *That stuff's compelling.* The pipes were loud, but she didn't care.

Thom grinned. *That's why he's here. We need these people's attention.*

Ulla and Thom faced each other across the Battle Ring, knelt, and placed their hands on it. When the piper's tune ended, they began to sing.

Several notes in, the atmosphere changed. A fountain of light rose up from the Battle Ring, curled around the ornate chandeliers, and spiraled back down, enveloping everyone in the room. People stared at the ceiling, awash in light. As the Battle Ring melted into the sand, the mass of light contracted and flowed into Ulla and Thom. Energy filled her entire being with more strength than she'd thought possible, both physical and mental. Because their minds were linked, she felt the same happen to Thom.

* * *

After an awe-inspiring show, Ulla and Thom stepped outside and waited for the dance music to begin again.

Men and women in evening dress mingled about the lawn, drinks in hand, chatting and enjoying the evening's mild weather. The Midsummer sun had finally set. The sky was clear, and a handful of faint stars glimmered.

Flowering shrubs on the grounds of Pioneer Hall and nearby Landfall Square scented the night air.

Skuli Branson drove an unmarked BTE van right past them. *I'm going around the block; pick you up when there are fewer onlookers.*

Ulla and Thom drifted toward a stand of shrubbery in Pioneer Hall's side yard, near the service entrance. To the rest of the partygoers, they looked like a couple hunting for privacy.

Which they were. Buzzed from singing up the Battle Ring, Ulla needed time to get control of her enhanced Gifts. She sensed Thom doing the same.

"Some evening we're having." Ed, almost unnoticed, had joined them.

"Indeed," said Thom.

Ulla felt it too; something wasn't right.

Mikko Strom detached himself from a group on the portico and wandered casually toward Pioneer Hall's service entrance.

The transmitter in Ulla's ear crackled to life. "Lieutenant! Over here! There's better cover." Mikko's shadowed silhouette stood by a cement window well in front of a row of darkened basement windows.

Ulla sensed half a dozen folk nearby who hadn't been there before. *Gate?* She squeezed Thom's hand and walked casually away toward Mikko.

Skuli's telepathic voice cried out. *Dwellers behind Pioneer Hall! Need a soulslayer NOW!*

Chapter Forty-Two
Fight

Ulla jumped feet first into the window well. She felt Thom reach out and kill a Dweller at five times his usual range.

Where was the Gate? Ulla combed through the neighborhood with mind-seeing. There! Inside an apartment over the shops across the street. She reached out to the Gate operator: *Today, I am luck—*

No, Child.

Shit! That was Fripp.

You will not use your Spinner's Gift tonight.

Seconds ticked by. Two more Dweller-ridden humans stepped out of the Gate. Ulla killed both Dwellers; their hosts fell conveniently unconscious on the narrow stairs leading out of the apartment.

Child—

What? Couldn't Fripp see they were up to their asses?

Use the Gifts you have practiced.

Feeling slightly stupid, Ulla investigated further. Thanks be, this Gate was a commercial personnel Gate without the hardened kernel she'd seen on the military Gate on Bald Mountain. She found its power supply and concentrated. Mind-moving did nothing. She concentrated harder and melted the power supply's innermost workings.

Fire and Ice for the win.

As Ulla did the same for the Gate's control system, she heard Fripp sigh with relief.

Slightly disappointed that nothing had exploded, Ulla

mused that at least the property owner would still have a building when this was over.

Attention back on her immediate surroundings, Ulla was pleased to note that all the Dwellers were gone.

Mikko pushed her onto the floor of the window well just as an incoming bullet smashed the glass where her head had been.

"Where's Thom?" Ulla whispered. There was silence where Thom's thoughts ought to be.

Mikko nodded toward the van in the street. Thom crouched beside it while Ed exchanged fire with a small group in the street.

Never in anger, Starfighter. A man wearing a white chef's jacket and carrying a meat cleaver ducked behind a packing crate. *We're on your side.* His aproned companion—undoubtedly his spotter—shot methodically at the figures in the street.

Skuli was nowhere to be seen. Oh! There he was, slumped inside the van, barely conscious. *No worries, Starfighter. Thom got the Dweller that got me. Just give me a minute; I'll be—*

Skuli's telepathic voice went quiet.

More shots in the street. What the hell had happened to Thom and Skuli?

Ed peered around a corner of the van and returned fire.

Please, please, please, let him be all right.

What did I tell you about using your Spinner's Gift? Fripp, again.

Was Ulla not allowed to hope?

Of course, Child, but not in that tone. Then Fripp was gone.

Three shadowy figures headed for the loading dock. "Where's the spinner?"

Ulla got up and raised her pistol.

Mikko pushed her down. "Don't!" he whispered. "They want you to show your position!"

Ulla so wished she hadn't taken the oath about the Dark Gift.

Me too. But I never took an oath about this. The young chef stood up and sent his meat cleaver flying.

Thunk! One assailant fell. But not before releasing a shot at the steady-handed chef, whose body jerked and fell to the ground.

The two remaining men advanced; the soulslayer's spotter must have run out of ammunition.

Mikko and Ulla both took aim and fired, dropping them. Ulla fired several times and gave thanks for Mikko's expertise.

The fight was over.

Ulla?

Thom! Thanks be! Ulla scanned the area for hostiles and found none. "Coast is clear," she told Mikko. Together, they sprinted to the van.

They reached it just as Thom staggered to his feet. The right side of his sorcerer's cloak had come undone; it was red and sticky.

"I shot you." Skuli, appalled and visibly exhausted, stared out through the van's open door.

"No." Thom poked at his arm under the red stain with his good hand. "The Dweller that possessed you shot me. It's a flesh wound; would've been way worse if you hadn't fought back."

Ulla helped Thom remove his cloak and cravat. He grunted when she helped him take off his jacket. Rather than repeat that with his shirt, Ulla ripped the damaged cloth.

The bleeding had stopped. The bullet's entrance hole smoothed and healed as in a fast-motion holo. Experimentally, Thom moved his arm so they could see the exit hole. It, too, was healing itself along with, presumably, the path the bullet had taken through the muscles in his upper arm.

Skuli stared at Thom's closing wound. "Battle Ring power?"

"Has to be." Thom looked at Ulla. "Unless you're using your Healing Gift."

"Nope." Ulla shook her head. "It was pulling itself together before I ever touched you." Emergency vehicle sirens wailed and grew closer.

Mikko broke in. "Lieutenant."

Ulla forced her attention away from Thom's arm. "Yes?"

"If you have a psi talent for healing, the kid who threw the meat cleaver needs your assistance."

"He's alive, then?" Ulla scanned; the young soulslayer

had regained consciousness. *Oh, Mikko.* "I have the Gift but not the training," she said. But she left Thom and sprinted toward the fallen soulslayer anyway.

Correct choice.

Where had that come from? *Fripp?*

Yes, Child. Fripp's towering projection popped into view. The spotter, who had been trying to stop the soulslayer's bleeding, lost concentration. Blood flowed freely.

Ulla approached the spotter. "Please allow us." As they changed places, Ulla linked her mind with Fripp's and slowed the man's bleeding while Fripp examined his torn-up insides.

* * *

Endless minutes passed. Ulla pressed her hands on the soulslayer's wound and watched with her mind's eye as Fripp worked. She was vaguely aware of emergency vehicles arriving and of at least one soulslayer who hadn't been there earlier. But her focus was on the wounded young man on the ground bleeding out in front of her.

Somebody placed a hand on Ulla's shoulder. "Lieutenant."

She jumped, startled, and saw a City of Newcastle medic.

He nodded to her. "We'll take it from here."

Ulla was unsure. *Fripp?*

Yes, Child. The Elder's imposing projection kept up an unbroken conversation in perfect City English with an older medic. *They are quite competent. Also, he is no longer in mortal danger.*

The medic handed Ulla a clean, damp rag. "You'll want this."

She cleaned up as best she could, then joined Thom and Skuli by the van.

Out in the street, Newcastle City Guards pulled dazed former Dweller hosts to their feet. She heard the words "River Pack" more than once. Dead assailants outnumbered the living, but all told, there were no more than a dozen, including those inside the apartment across the street.

Another Newcastle Guard cruiser pulled up to the

curb. Two men got out.

One, who wore On'oi clan earrings with City business attire, waved to Ulla. *Never in anger, Ulla Thorsdaughter. I'm Victor Jamesson. Pleased to meet you.*

So, this was the president of the Matthias Carroll Memorial Society. He was at least twenty meters away, surprisingly long-range psi for a soulslayer.

Never in anger. Underneath his polished demeanor, Ulla detected anguish. Her mind blurted, *What's the matter?* before she thought to filter.

I must see to Skuli Branson and ensure he comes to no harm after being Dweller-ridden. He nodded toward the scene in the street. *And there are Dweller hosts the Guard apprehended.*

Ulla could tell that, while a valid concern, the condition of recent Dweller hosts was not what weighed on the man's heart.

The medics by the loading dock slammed the ambulance's big rear door. The head soulslayer watched it depart. *I assigned Henri Brown to this job.*

Ulla thought all working soulslayers had been volunteers.

Well, yes. Victor waited for the ambulance to pass between them. *He did volunteer. But I never meant for anyone to—*

The ambulance, having gotten past the clot of people, sped away with sirens blaring.

Die? Ulla asked.

He nodded again.

Um, sir—

Ought she to call him "sir?" Ulla had no idea.

All she heard from him was desolation.

Sir, ambulances only go that fast and loud for the living.

* * *

Fripp's projection turned from the conversation she'd been having with the other new arrival, who turned out to be an inspector from the Newcastle City Guard. She found Ulla and Thom. "You must go. Quickly."

"You are free to go," the inspector said, "but check in with the City Guard at your earliest convenience." It was so obvious he was aching to hear their side of the story that Ulla wondered if he had latent psi talent.

Ed intervened. "Once these two get the Ring out of the warehouse, we expect to be in flight for several hours," he said. "I can take their statements once we're aboard and forward them to you through the BTE."

"That works."

Ed took Skuli's place in the driver's seat, and Mikko climbed into the passenger seat next to him. Ulla and Thom slid onto the seats behind them. Despite everything that had happened, the shot-up van started and ran normally.

Skuli and Victor paused their conversation. *Godspeed.*

Chapter Forty-Three
Moving a Ring

They reached the warehouse with no further incident. Ulla and Thom stepped inside the chilly, ruined vault to find Neal Erikson wiping sweat off his forehead.

A crease between Neal's eyes relaxed and disappeared. "You two look like hell. Go get cleaned up, and we'll get started."

Ulla and Thom spent a few minutes in the washroom in an adjacent warehouse bay. While Ulla had already wiped her hands clean, her jacket and skirt front were soaked in blood. She took off her jacket; her under-blouse was relatively clean. She kept the divided skirt on because the vault felt cold after all their activity in the steamy Midsummer night—well, that, and the fact that she had no desire to work in only her underwear, shoes, and a pistol.

Thom took off what was left of his shirt and dropped it in the trash can. His jacket was long gone, but he'd hung on to his sorcerer's cloak. He dabbed briefly at the cloak's quickly-setting bloodstains, gave up, and put it on.

Let's get to work.

Neal wasted no time as Thom and Ulla took their places behind Sean and Emma. "Let's hope you have enough Battle Ring power left over to do some good."

Ulla linked her mind with his, briefly.

His eyes widened. *I'll take that as a yes.*

"No worries, Professor." Sean had already linked with Thom. *They're wired.*

Ulla linked her mind with Emma's.

"Flint's capraglamas are ready." Neal brushed his hand across the Ring's force field. "Starfighter, call on them."

Yanek Robson, Ulla Thorsdaughter. Ulla hoped they'd make quick work of what came next; all her senses were working overtime, and the vault floor was hard and cold.

Thom, sitting beside her, reached over and wrapped his sorcerer's cloak around the two of them.

Yanek Robson here. Flint Clan capraglamas are ready. The animals' busy minds join with Ulla's. *The other clans' capraglamas are on standby; Dmytro Robson will coordinate through the Trade Ministry.*

Ulla listened more closely. The capraglamas were using words! Not words she knew, but words. She wanted to know more. But first, they had to get this Ring up and running in its proper Seat.

Then the Flint Clan capraglama called Marigold said, in Dialekt clear as day, *Heya, Starfighter. We know. Work now; talk later.*

Ulla and Thom joined hands. Ulla put her free hand on Emma's shoulder; Thom put his on Sean's.

Sean and Emma began to sing.

The Ring's force field softened and disappeared. Runes swirled to its surface, quivered, stabilized, and flowed smoothly. Neal watched their progression like a hawk over prey. *Begin repair sequence.*

Not a command one would say out loud. It would interfere with Ring song.

The singers made eye contact and modulated into another key and tempo. If Ring song could even be said to have key or tempo. Ulla brushed off that distraction and settled down to concentrate on the singers in front of her.

The next bit was monotonous, bordering on hypnotic. Every aspect of the Ring had to be evaluated. Occasionally, Emma and Sean paused and varied their song to make a repair. Fortunately, the Battle Ring had given Ulla and Thom not only greater power but greater ability to focus.

The floor was still hard and cold.

Humans! Marigold the capraglama was amused.

Ulla checked all their psi links and leaned everybody into the job at hand.

*　*　*

Done! Power it down! Neal's tone was jubilant as Sean and Emma did just that. Ulla had to wait to close their link until Marigold finished a string of capraglama words that sounded both congratulatory and snarky. *Later, you. We'll talk.*

You bet we will, human! Then even Marigold was gone.

The five of them picked up the heavy Ring, put it in its case, closed the cover, and sealed it. In silence, punctuated by the sound of the rattling wheels of the transport case on the concrete floor, they maneuvered it out of the vault, down the hallway, and out the door, where a SpaceCom Ground Forces armored utility vehicle waited. Mikko drove, and Ed rode shotgun in Skuli's place. Two City Guard cruisers—their escort—waited.

Nobody spoke as they loaded the Ring into the cargo bed and set off for the airstrip.

*　*　*

Ulla closed her eyes and rested her head on the seat back as they bumped over cobblestones. There would be no sleep in her near future, but maybe she would not be overwhelmed if she closed her eyes and was quiet.

Me too. Thom reached for her hand and held it.

She let her mind explore the nearby cityscape. Three blocks away, a fight was taking place. A City Guard cruiser raced past them, going the other way. Ahead, to the right of their course, the Guard was chivying people out of some kind of social establishment. The actions seemed related to each other but not to the Ring or the people transporting it. Was the Guard running a sting on the packs?

Ed glanced back at her. *Yes, they are, Starfighter.*

Ulla was curious. *Why didn't the Newcastle detective mention it in the briefing?*

Ed turned his attention back to their surroundings. *You didn't need to know. Bonus is, it's keeping the packs out of our business tonight.*

Except for the small matter of them trying to kill us behind Pioneer Hall. Ulla shifted her position against Thom and stretched. She was still wired but yawned anyway.

That was Yotne-driven, Ed told her as Mikko pulled

them to a stop at the airstrip's security gate. *Different thing.*

The gate guard waved them through. Ulla rested her head on Thom's shoulder. The sting must have taken months to plan. What were the chances of it happening tonight, of all nights?

The chances were excellent.

Ulla sat up. *Fripp?* Had the Elder used her Spinner's Gift to enhance those chances?

Enhance the chances and have to deal with consequences? Ulla could almost see Fripp shaking her head. *No, Child. I asked them to time it so.*

Coordination and planning, then. But—how had Fripp known when such a diversion would be needed?

I am a spinner, Child. Watch and learn.

As they neared the airstrip, atmospheric fighter escorts bobbed up into the air and scooted off into the sky where they would fly in sedate circles until the transport joined them.

They rolled to a stop behind a winged transport. Mikko stayed in the driver's seat while the Ring party manhandled the cased Ring out of their vehicle and up a ramp onto the flittercraft's central cargo floor. Mikko drove off while the six of them boarded the transport and took their seats on the wide benches along the bulkheads facing the Ring.

The big door closed. The transport rolled down the airstrip and climbed into the sky toward Landfall.

* * *

Once the transport had reached cruising altitude and was flying straight and level, Emma yawned, took off her jacket, rolled it into a pillow, and lay down on the wide bench, asleep in moments with the practiced efficiency of a parent of young children.

A uniformed loadmaster emerged from the flight deck and walked aft to join them. He pointed to a row of bags. "Your stuff is over there," he whispered.

Gratefully, Thom and Ulla found their bags and changed out of what was left of their ruined formalwear into cleaner, warmer clothes.

While they were doing that, the loadmaster pointed to a bin full of blankets and another of pillows. "Those are for you."

Sean took two of each, gently replaced his sister's jacket with a pillow, and tucked a blanket around her before lying down and falling fast asleep.

Thom had already settled in to sketch. "Maybe later, thanks. Not sleepy."

"Starfighter?" Ed had just spread out a bed for himself, but he let it be and pulled a readpad from his pocket. "The Newcastle Guard wanted your statement hours ago. Let's get to it."

Neal Erikson's gentle snores punctuated Ulla's recorded deposition. By the time Thom finished his deposition and Ed had a chance to lie down, all the sleepers were quiet.

Ulla got to her feet and stretched. She walked forward; the door to the flight deck was open. She peered past the pilot and crew into the darkness ahead.

"Can you drive one of these?" the pilot asked conversationally, not turning to look around at her.

"No. Not really." Her initial training had included familiarization with rotorcraft and winged flittercraft, but once selected for starfighters, she hadn't gone near the controls of anything atmospheric again.

She peeked through a clear port in the bulkhead immediately behind the flight deck. The weather was clear and the stars shone brilliantly. The barest hint of dawn lightened the sky on the horizon behind them. In other circumstances, this would be a beautiful night.

It still is a beautiful night. Thom had gotten up, too, and was standing behind her. *Just more, um, interesting than we would've liked.* He put one hand on her shoulder.

His touch ignited a streak of desire all the way to her toes. Apparently, their enhanced sensory response covered sex too.

Yeah. He took his hand off her shoulder. *But we'd wake them.* Thom nodded toward Sean, Emma, and Neal. *Best let the Ring installers get their beauty sleep.*

You're right. Ulla sighed. *Dammit.* Saving the world did take priority.

Chapter Forty-Four
Ring Seat

Ulla Thorsdaughter, Ring Group: Olwyn Dara Wittber-Argeles, Bailey-Duran Three Station.

That was formal. What did Olwyn want? Ulla fished her notebook and pencil from her pocket. *Ulla here.*

Olwyn. Yotne are attacking Lesser Knob, Landfall.

That got Ulla's attention. Lesser Knob was where they were supposed to land with the Ring. Ulla scribbled in her notebook. *Ulla. Copy.*

Olwyn. SpaceCom recommends your flight divert to Landfall Resort Airstrip near Kirkhilo. Transport to Great Knob is being arranged. Advise your captain and aircrew.

Ulla. Will do. Ulla headed for the flight deck. Why didn't they just use comm?

Olwyn. We aim to let the Yotne think for as long as possible that you don't know.

Oh. Ulla paused before entering the flight deck. *Ulla. With whom do we coordinate?*

Olwyn. One moment. Another telepathic voice joined their link. Its owner introduced himself. *Levi Dirkson, Bailey-Duran Coalition Headquarters, Newcastle.* Less formally, *Heya, Spider. We meet again.*

Again? Ulla racked her brain to remember anyone named Levi Dirkson.

Levi. Your emergency beeper isn't squawking in the background this time.

Ulla's face warmed. She was glad she hadn't yet entered the flight deck; nobody back here except Thom was awake to see her blush.

Levi sent her a nonverbal affirmation. Then he said, *You've come a long way, Ulla Thorsdaughter. I'm honored to work with you.*

Ulla knocked on the flight deck's open doorframe. "Captain, there's a new development."

* * *

Hours later, the flittercraft's engines changed pitch. They angled down through clear morning light toward steep mountains and jagged, dormant stretches of black lava rock that met the ocean at a tiny scrap of beach and green lawn. As they got closer, the airstrip near MitSmith's Landfall Resort hotel came into view.

Levi Dirkson, Ulla Thorsdaughter. Status in Landfall Mainland?

Levi. MitSmith Resort area quiet. Great Knob secured with minimal damage. Fighting at Lesser Knob is centered on the airstrip.

They landed. No sooner had the pilot stopped their engines than a mid-sized camion with a crew cab raced up behind the flittercraft. The loadmaster tossed their personal bags out on the ground, where a crew with a van bearing the resort logo grabbed the bags and carried them away. Ulla, Thom, Ed, Neal, Emma, and Sean rolled the cased Ring down the ramp, loaded it into the camion's cargo bed, and piled in.

After a drive of maybe half a kilometer, they stopped in front of a bright yellow rotorcraft.

Ulla was dismayed. At least the rotorcraft was big and sturdy; it likely belonged to the contractor who'd refurbished the Ring seat. But where were the military rotorcraft SpaceCom had sent to Landfall?

'Yours' is on fire at Lesser Knob. The others are busy.

Who said that? Ulla saw a man peering at something inside the rotorcraft's open maintenance panel. He stood up, waved to her, and went back to work. She hopped out of the camion and sauntered over to meet him.

Damn! A small bolt slipped from the mechanic's wrench and fell deep into the rotorcraft's insides. She watched as the bolt danced gently back up into the palm of his hand. On his second try, a cable moved out of the way so he could get at whatever he was working on. "Heya, Spinner! I'm Sumeet," he said, and returned to his task. Four earrings glinted in the sunlight.

"What are you doing?"

"I'm beefing up the force field that keeps people and tools from falling out."

He must be the flight engineer. *Does it work both ways?* Ulla asked.

It won't stop a bullet, if that's what you're asking. And I just made sure that it won't interfere with flight operations. He shut the access panel, secured it, and shrugged. *It's better than nothing.*

Ulla helped heave the Ring onto a forklift, whose operator placed it gently and expertly into the rotorcraft.

Fortunately, the contractor's rotorcraft was rated for a much heavier cargo than this jam-packed compliment of living beings crowded inside it around the cased Ring. They lifted off easily and sped toward the Knobs.

They hit a patch of bumpy air. Looking through the open door at the ground, Ulla gulped and hoped Sumeet's adjustments worked.

A spent artillery round bounced off the rotorcraft's force field.

Starfighter. That was Ed. *We need better. Is there anything you can do?*

Maybe. She'd caught a bullet on Bald Mountain; might that apply to their current predicament?

No, Child. Fripp's projection hung disconcertingly half-in, half-out of the rotorcraft. *Not that way. You can, however, use mind-moving to redirect the energy.*

Another round connected with the shield, slid sideways, and spun away to who knew where.

Like that?

Yes, Child, like that. Fripp was breathing hard. *You will need much strength if this keeps up for any length of time.* The Elder's projection disappeared.

Ulla focused on the shield as Fripp had. Another round obligingly rose up for her to bat away. *Got it.* This was HARD! *Some help here?*

Thom linked his mind with hers. Together, they had enough Battle Ring strength to deflect three more rounds. Sumeet linked up just in time to help deflect a fourth.

The Ring seat might be fortified, but first, they had to

get there. Ulla felt capraglamas join them, group by group, and the task became doable.

Starfighter. That was Sumeet. *The guns.*

Ulla was breathing hard. *What about them?*

I don't have your strength, of course, but now that the capraglamas are linked, Thom Yensson and I can handle this long enough for you to melt the guns.

Ulla deflected another round and grunted with the effort.

I heard you melted a Gate in Newcastle. The man wasn't going to take no for an answer.

Ulla wasn't sure she had enough left in her to do that. But they had to try. Far below, something exploded, and the artillery went quiet. *The Berserkers got it.*

The rotorcraft pilot put the craft down inside the fortified Ring seat. Ulla closed her eyes, leaned her head on Thom's shoulder, and fell fast asleep.

* * *

Someone shook her by the shoulder. "Time to go."

The light was softer now, and it came from low on the other side of the sky. It was late afternoon. Except for the birds, it was quiet.

"It worked then." Ulla had to speak out loud because she had no energy left for Gifts.

Ed handed her an energy bar. "Planetary shields went up just like in the legends. Nobody's gotten in from space since they set the Ring this morning."

The rotorcraft pilot broke in. "There are still Yotne on the surface. We need to get out of here."

Ulla yawned. Why couldn't they just stay here inside the Ring's barrier? All they needed was food and water.

But he was right; they couldn't stay at the Ring seat indefinitely. Ulla and Thom sagged against the seat back. There would be soft, warm beds inside the resort hotel turned troop garrison.

Neal reached into his pocket. "You two need food."

"Thanks, I've got some." Ulla held up the energy bar Ed had given her. Sumeet pulled a napkin-wrapped bundle from his jacket pocket and tucked into a soft flatbread wrapped around something that looked delicious. A workman's lunch, possibly packed this morning by the wife whose clan earrings he wore.

While Ulla envied Sumeet his homemade lunch, her energy bar tasted just fine, especially after Neal gave her a bottle of water to wash it down with.

Then she and Thom went back to sleep.

* * *

Sometime later, Ulla woke up just enough to sit up, stretch, and snuggle back on Thom's shoulder. She linked her mind with his; he seemed far away. Maybe that was to do with the Battle Ring. *Love you,* he said. *Take care of our family.*

His big ornery extended family who had made her one of them? Of course, she would. *Love you, Thom.* She went back to sleep.

* * *

"Wake up! We're at the hotel!" Neal sounded entirely too chipper.

Ulla didn't feel like moving. She buried her face in Thom's shoulder. Something wasn't right. She woke up fast. "Thom?"

He didn't move.

"THOM!" She rested her head on his chest, listened for a heartbeat, and heard none. He wasn't breathing. She tried linking her mind with his and couldn't.

Neal turned to the rotorcraft pilot. "Get an ambulance out here, now! And an On'oi traditional healer if they have one. Or at least a Guild rep."

While a part of Ulla's mind registered exactly what was going on, she could not will her body to do anything to help. She was still screaming his name when the Battle Ring's aftereffects dragged her back to sleep.

Chapter Forty-Five

Tears and Sweat

Ulla rolled over in bed. She opened her eyes; a night light revealed the inside of an upscale hotel room.

Thom was dead. Of that, Ulla was certain. Enough ragged bits of her psi talent had come back that she knew she would have found him, if that were possible. Which it wasn't...

Even though she felt completely drained, she couldn't sleep anymore. She closed her eyes again. Maybe if she closed them hard enough, she'd see Thom. She felt like her soul had been ripped open.

She could just barely hear Maribet saying something like, *Berit, she's awake.*

What was Maribet doing here?

Ulla rolled over and rested her head on her arm. Something hard poked her in the face. Why was there a hospital-style diagnostic cuff on her wrist? She peered at the cuff's time-and-date display. It was three days ahead. That wasn't right; Midsummer was last night. Wasn't it?

Can't go now; I'm assisting in surgery. Berit's voice. *Thor's at the Knobs. Get Neal.*

Maribet's voice came back. *Heya, Ulla. We're here for you. Except I'm at Summer Pasture.*

Heya, Maribet. Ulla wrapped her arms tight around a pillow and curled herself into a ball.

The solid core in her middle, who she really was, was still there. That was something. She closed her eyes, lay still, and tried hard to think of nothing at all.

* * *

Bright sunshine. Right in her face.

Oh. Morning. Landfall. Ulla rolled over and burrowed away from the window into damp pillows that tasted like salt.

Presently, she sat up. There would be no more sleep today.

Heya, Cousin.

Neal?

Right outside your door, if you need me.

Thanks. She forced her brain to work. *Give me a minute. I'm not dressed.*

She forced herself out of bed. Someone had left an automatic kettle full of water next to the room's generous coffee carafe that was already set up to brew.

Ulla ought not keep Neal waiting. She turned on the kettle, padded into the bathroom, and splashed water on her face. If she remembered correctly, that Berit had marched her through the shower last night, why was her face so sticky?

She licked her upper lip. Salt. Well, tears, of course. But where was the scent of unwashed human coming from? Ulla woke up a little more and studied the time-and-date display on her hospital cuff again. Maybe three days had passed after all.

She took a quick shower. The bathroom was spotless except for a dozen or so energy bar wrappers on the floor. Automatically, she picked up the wrappers and put them in the wastebasket.

Two unopened energy bars sat next to an empty glass by the sink.

Ulla filled the glass with water and drank the whole thing down. She was so thirsty! She filled it again, drank about half, and set it on the counter.

Now that she was not as dehydrated, her stomach growled. She ate an energy bar and tossed the wrapper into the trash. The action felt somehow familiar.

Oh! Neal was still waiting! She'd better get dressed.

She found her toiletries kit on the counter on top of a stack of neatly folded clothing. A paper note in Berit's handwriting said, "Wear these." There was a flowing shirt of muted green silk, a pair of well-made trousers, and a generously cut light woolen jacket, all in her sizes. And socks and underwear. Ulla's boots stood on the floor next to her travel bag.

Fine by her. The decision was already made: no SpaceCom uniform today.

The key to her rooms at the Trade Ministry, a wooden toothpick, and a small pile of Newcastle euros lay on the counter next to the new clothes; they would have been in her pockets.

There was no sign of her pistol, its holster, or the extra cartridges she had stuffed in her pockets a lifetime ago. Where had they gone? She would ask.

She dressed and cleaned her teeth. Her hand went to her throat; her SpaceCom ID and little turquoise bear were where they belonged on the thin chain.

The kettle boiled and turned itself off, so she went back to the bedroom and poured water over coffee grounds. Tears threatened; she took a deep breath and sat down on the couch to wait for the coffee to brew. Unable to trust herself to walk across the room, Ulla used mind-moving to unlock the door for Neal.

He came in, took one look at her, and swept her into a big hug. *I'm so sorry.*

Tears came this time for both of them, and they sat, cousins, together.

* * *

Neal coaxed Ulla downstairs to breakfast, which consisted of a row of heated pans on a table at one end of the resort's smallest dining room. This late in the morning, the selections were picked over, but she managed to fill the next-to-last plate with beans, the last of the scrambled eggs, some berries, and a roll.

The room was near empty; any seat would do. She set her plate on the closest small dining table and sat down.

"Here's coffee." Neal set down a cup for her and a cup for him.

They ate in silence. Or rather, Ulla ate. Neal had grabbed the last misshapen sticky roll from the corner of the pan to eat with his coffee.

I had breakfast hours ago. He broke the sticky roll in half. *But these are too good to pass up.*

That, Ulla thought, explained the first impression one got of Neal—though she knew now that what looked like pudge on him was mostly muscle.

He sighed. *I heard that.* He put the roll back on his plate, uneaten.

Oh, gods. She hadn't meant—

I know, Cousin. No worries. He looked at her. "Stress-eating. Especially sweets; they're my go-to."

She put down her fork. "You miss him too."

Of course I do. "When I first went to university, I spent almost every weekend with Renata and Padraic. Thom lived with them; he was a kid, same age as my baby brother Piet."

Who had also died recently.

Neal, done with words, applied himself to the sticky bun. When he had eaten the torn-off half, he said, "Renata put me in touch with the Rogerses—I studied under Miles." He sipped his coffee. "They introduced Thom and me to the Tullys and the Fourniers." Neal made a face and added more sugar to his coffee. "That's bitter."

Ulla hadn't noticed.

"Through them, we met all kinds of City people who have Gifts and know how to use them—it's a whole subculture. I think you've met some of them."

Aden Fournier is my Society mentor, Ulla reminded him.

Oh, that's right. "Anyway, I felt a lot less lonely, and Thom made friends with kids his age." He tore his remaining piece of sticky bun in half.

What Neal said clicked with what Ulla knew from linking minds with Thom. "He thought of you as an older brother."

"Yeah, I guess." Neal laughed. "For a few years there, he was my little shadow—until he and Geoff Tully were old enough to get into trouble on their own. Then Thom started going on trek with Raven Clan and became friends with Skuli Branson." Neal raised the pastry to his mouth, paused, and set it down without eating. "When Skuli was in town, the three of them were inseparable." He pushed his plate away. *I should never have proposed we stand up the Rings like the Ancients did.*

Did Neal think he was responsible for Thom's and Piet's deaths? For Hanni's? Ulla gave him time while she finished her beans. Fork empty, she pointed with it. "How many Yotne have landed since we stood up the Rings?"

"None," he answered. "But SpaceCom, BTE, and the merchant ships can't land either. And here, on the surface, we're cut off from satellite navigation. We still have line-of-sight conventional comm, and we can bounce some conventional comm off the inside of the Ring barrier and reach a little farther—but for true long-distance and off-planet, mind-talk is all we have."

Ulla picked up a berry and ate it. "We all knew that ahead of time."

But...the cost. His shoulders sagged.

Yeah, I know. All that and the *Dauntless* task force pretty much obliterated while buying time for Bailey-Duran. That'd be one for the annals of history but bringing up *Dauntless* in this conversation would serve nobody. "I don't remember you forcing any of us to work with the Rings," she said. *Maybe me, a little, but that was SpaceCom and Fripp.*

"Thom volunteered the two of you," Neal confessed, "for the Battle Ring."

Thom would have. Ulla almost smiled. "I didn't know Piet well," she said slowly, "but I got the impression he was born to work with stock." *Especially capraglamas and camdeer.*

Neal ate the piece of sticky bun he'd pushed away. "Even as a little kid on trek with Mountain Clan, Piet followed the keepers everywhere they'd let him. After he hit puberty and went on trek with Flint, our old head keeper took him on as an apprentice." *Piet was so thrilled.*

Ulla decided to be blunt. "A Dweller killed Hanni. Last I heard, Dr. Neal Erikson of Newcastle University is not in charge of Dwellers."

He reached for his coffee cup but did not drink. "True."

She made eye contact with him. "So, stop it."

"Stop what?"

"Blaming yourself."

What the hell am I supposed to do?

You're asking me? Ulla poured milk into her bitter coffee. *You're my boss.*

He tapped his Flint Clan earring. "Until Berit and Thor can get here, I'm the closest thing you've got on-site to next of kin." His shoulders sagged. "But I'm doing a terrible job of it."

"No worries." She choked back a tear. She would have hugged him if the table hadn't been in the way.

"I feel like I have to do something."

"Me too," Ulla said. *Not sure what, though.*

How about we just do the next thing—whatever that is.

Ulla thought for a moment. "Berit ought to be free soon. I'll track her down and get this hospital cuff taken off. Do you know what happened to my sidearm last night?"

"Last night?" Neal asked. "Midsummer was three days ago."

"Oh," Ulla said. "So it was."

Neal's thoughts went shuttered. "You need to ask Berit about your sidearm."

Well, then, Ulla would do that. "What's your 'next thing'?"

"We're already looking at fine-tuning the Rings to allow select traffic on and off the surface," he said. "But it's slow going because the research team is spread out."

Spread out, how?

"There's Miles and the rest of them at Newcastle University," Neal told her. "Two researchers in the sky, collecting data at BD3 Station"—he downed the last of his coffee—"and Vani's team at Castle Chisos. Then there're the Ring seats." He set his empty cup on his plate. "With so much else going on, we're strapped for long-distance mind-talkers." *Especially mind-talkers who can coordinate multiple parties.* "I'd meant to wait a few days before asking you."

Thanks. Ulla wasn't sure she could do a damned thing today. Other than find Berit, find her sidearm, and find out why she was wearing a diagnostic cuff. *How about tomorrow?*

"If you feel up to it," he said. "Meet me at breakfast, and I'll show you where. My grad students Sean, Thad, and I are using a conference room on the ground floor."—*When we're not running around the Knobs helping MitSmith with their damage report.*

"Thad Rogers?" she asked as she stacked her cup and flatware on her plate.

"Miles and Aubrey's son. He helped restore the Ring seat at Great Knob." *He's living here for now.*

For now?

Neal sighed. "Yotne rocket hit the kitchen in his apartment at Lesser Knob. Blew hell out of the building." *Good thing nobody was there when it happened.* "Anyway, Thad may be headblind, but he's an expert at Ring song, and his perspective keeps us honest."

Ulla felt a headache coming on; she rubbed her temples. *So, so much to process.*

Neal stood up and came around to her side of the table. "See you tomorrow morning?"

"Sure." As long as everybody involved understood that she might lose her shit at a moment's notice.

That's part of the deal, Cousin. He gave her a quick hug. "Just keep doing the next thing."

Chapter Forty-Six
The Next Thing

As soon as she hugged Neal goodbye, Ulla walked through the hotel's sumptuous lobby and through the etched glass doors of its unused spa, where she found the office Berit had commandeered for Berserker logistics. Inside, a Berserker with one arm in a sling sat at the reception desk where Ulla and her friends had booked massages less than a local year ago.

"Berit Gee? She's not back yet." He pushed a pad of paper and a pen across the desk. "Would you like to leave her a message?"

No, Ulla wouldn't.

She wandered out onto the hotel's wrap-around veranda and gazed past the wide lawn toward the mountains. Ruts marred the resort's pristine lawn along with a SpaceCom Ground Forces transportable field hospital, which sat smack-dab in the middle of what would have been an unimpeded view of the ocean.

She used psi to scan in every direction. All was quiet at the Knobs and around New Vatersay. The far-flung island group west of New Vatersay—what did they call it? Oh, yes, the Littles—was a different story; people there were still fighting Dwellers and a few remaining Yotne.

Yotne mines dotted the waters pretty much everywhere in Landfall. *Eesh!*

Ulla thought she spotted her father's psi blocker with a dozen other psi blockers in what had to be an airborne command post. No, that wasn't Dad; he'd be out on the ground, or in a boat, with his Berserkers. Besides, Berit had told Maribet he was at the Knobs. She scanned again. Yes! There he was, at Lesser Knob. Alive.

Of course. The Berserkers' contract was to protect the MitSmith properties on Landfall Mainland. She'd heard Dad wasn't known for allowing mission creep. She let out a breath she didn't know she'd been holding.

The here and now offered only the usual potential for stupid mistakes. The sky was blue, with puffy clouds for variety. The air was warm but not too warm, tempered as it was by the ocean breeze.

Here and there, on the rest of the hotel's grounds, a handful of people weeded garden beds, set out flower seedlings, and mowed grass.

Hadn't most of the resort staff been evacuated?

Yes, except for a few key personnel. The voice was unfamiliar.

Curious, Ulla went down the steps and walked across the lawn toward the voice.

A SpaceCom Ground Forces major in a utility uniform knelt, pressing dirt around flowers he had just set in the ground. "I apologize for eavesdropping." He stood up to greet her. "I'm still learning about telepathy."

He must have been among the newly Gifted who got sent dirtside for training and were stuck here now.

Ulla straightened and took her hands out of her pockets. "It gets easier, sir."

I certainly hope so! He brushed dirt from his hands. "You must be Thor Bjornson's daughter."

"Yes, sir." They shook hands.

"Chaplain Taleb." He set one last plant in the bed and patted dirt around its base. *Irrigation will flow here soon; we're good.* He gathered his tools and headed for a barn behind the main building.

Ulla walked with him. "Who are those people working over there?"

"Convalescents, mostly. Dweller survivors who need time to recover, and wounded fighters from the Littles. A few from Lesser Knob are starting to show up for light duty," he said, hanging his tools up on hooks in the barn that doubled as a garden shed. "Neither the Berserker leadership nor the Home Guard believe in idle hands, and the few remaining resort staff can use the help." The chaplain tossed his empty seedling containers onto a pile of similar ones. *Some of us just need a quick break to remind ourselves why we do what we do.*

* * *

Ulla went looking for Berit again and found her at her desk, deep in discussion with the infantryman-turned-clerk about the day's requirements. Ulla stood to one side and waited. Finally, the man walked away down the hall, list in hand.

"Ulla!" Berit came around from behind her desk, arms open wide. Her sweaty hair lay plastered to her head. The mask marks on her face accentuated the dark circles under her eyes. *So glad to see you!* They hugged. "Would you like coffee?"

"Sure, thanks." Ulla sat down in the chair; it was still warm.

Berit stepped out and around the reception desk to a small table in the front hall, turned two mugs upright, and drew coffee from the spigot of a seven-liter urn. Her hands shook as she offered a mug to Ulla. *I won't ask how you are feeling.*

Thank you. Ulla wrapped her hands around the hot mug, winced, and set it down on a stack of papers to cool.

They sat in silence. The comm unit on the desk beeped, and Berit swatted at its Ignore switch. She glanced at the text on the screen, deleted it, and tapped some more.

"You can take off your diagnostic cuff now," she told Ulla. "They paused the feed when you left your room; the alerts were too distracting. I just saved your data and reset the cuff."

Ulla unfastened the cuff and set it on Berit's desk. "Why was I wearing it?"

Berit tossed the cuff into a basket on the credenza behind her desk. "We didn't want to lose you, too." She didn't look at Ulla.

Maribet, and maybe others, had monitored Ulla while she slept. If they were so worried, why hadn't they put her in the hospital out back?

It's full. Berit tapped again at her comm panel. "You weren't ailing—just exhausted. Once you started getting up to drink water, relieve yourself, and look for food, we moved you out to make room."

Ulla fished unsuccessfully for memories of doing any of that. But the energy bar wrappers had landed on the floor somehow. "Has it really been three days?"

"You were as soundly asleep as it is possible to be," Berit told her. *Only asleep, thanks be.* "Now that you are up and about, I'll have a tech remove the diagnostic comm repeater from your room. You don't mind them going in there, do you?"

Ulla shook her head.

"Oh," said Berit. "You're to clean your own room. Fresh linens and cleaning supplies are at the end of each hall."

That made sense, with most of the hotel staff gone. The resort was a troop garrison now—which led to the next thing on Ulla's list. "About my sidearm…"

Berit rubbed at a red mark on her forehead. "It is clean and stored safely."

"I'd like to have it back."

"Why?" Berit sipped her coffee. *Hot!* Her eyes opened wide, and she set the mug down with a *thump*. Coffee sloshed onto the desk.

Because I feel naked without a weapon?

"Unless things change, you are unlikely to need your pistol here in garrison." Berit reached for a towel, mopped up the spill, then draped the towel over the edge of the wastebasket. "Ulla, I'd like you to wait a bit. Please."

"Please," from Berit Gee, in this context, might as well be an edict from the gods. *What about the psi talents you know I have? How is that safer than me carrying a weapon?*

It isn't. But the rest of us breathe more easily knowing you don't have a gun on you.

Ulla was shocked. *I would never—*

"Of course you wouldn't," Berit said, "not on purpose. But right now is not the time."

Ulla covered her unease by picking up her coffee and taking a sip. It burned her mouth; she drank it anyway.

"From what I can tell, you're having trouble lining up two thoughts in a row."

True, but—*For fuck's sake, I just woke up.* There had been too much time to think on that long flittercraft ride, incredibly strong psi Ulla hadn't known existed, too many deaths. Ulla had awakened from a deep sleep with her arms around Thom's dead body. Now that she was halfway coherent, the simple act of closing her eyes put her right back in that moment.

My point, exactly. Berit rubbed at a spot next to her left temple and tried again to drink coffee.

Had she worked straight through last night? Ulla thought so.

Berit stood up, wobbling a little on her feet. "I'm going upstairs to get some sleep. Want to walk with me?"

"Thanks, but I need fresh air." A comfy chair on the veranda would be about Ulla's speed. She hugged Berit, picked up her cup of too-hot coffee, and headed outside.

She found a chaise longue on the veranda. If she pushed it half a meter to one side and turned it just a bit, she could see the ocean past a corner of the field hospital. That put the chaise longue in the shade; the part of her that had grown up in the deserts of west Texas and Farwell approved.

She settled into the chaise, set her coffee cup on the deck, pulled her jacket tightly around her, and stared at the ocean.

Eventually, she reached down and picked up her coffee. It was stone cold, but she drank it anyway—she was probably still dehydrated. She ought to get herself a glass of water.

Ulla Thorsdaughter, Syver Marcson linking for—

The voice was not familiar. Who wanted to talk with her? Especially now?

—Yens Govinderson and family.

Ulla had no words.

Oh, beloved of my son. She felt raw emotion the High King rarely let anyone suspect. *Words are for another day.*

Heya, Starfighter. That was Ingeborg. Ulla felt Dannel's quiet presence in the background.

Dear, I so wish we could be together. Marta Charlesdaughter. It was clear that the woman, whom Ulla had only met a few times, was sincere.

Ulla brushed back a tear. *Uh, we kind of are.*

Padraic for Renata. We're here. Ulla felt him squeeze Auntie's hand.

Padraic. What she said. That got a faint cheerful impulse among those assembled.

They stayed linked but silent for a long time.

While Ulla did not feel particularly better, she did feel

loved in a way she hadn't anticipated, and more competent than she had felt all morning. *Uh, Syver Marcson, Ulla Thorsdaughter. I can handle the link from here.* Thom had, after all, asked her to take care of their family.

Syver. ???

Yens. Concur. Thank you.

Syver out.

Ulla kept their family linked until the time was right for everyone to go their separate ways.

Chapter Forty-Seven
Back at It

By the end of their first week in Landfall, the Ring workgroup had developed a routine. They spent between two to four hours linked with their counterparts in Newcastle, Castle Chisos, and BD3 Station every morning. Afterward, Ulla was free to do what she wished unless they needed to contact a Ring seat in another time zone. On one such evening she had tried linking them from her favorite chaise on the veranda but had to admit that remote meetings worked best when she could see the figures on the board with her own eyes.

Ulla, Sean.

Ulla here. She climbed up the few steps cut into the hill behind the resort and turned to finish watching Bailey-Duran rise over the water. *What's going on?*

Sean was already in their conference room. *Vani's at the Ancients' villa by Flint Clan's summer pasture. He wants to talk with the BD3 Station folks and with Miles Rogers.* Through Sean's eyes, she saw new scribbles on the writing board. If it was going to be a scribbles-on-the-board kind of day she definitely needed to be in the room.

Ulla headed back down the trail. *On my way.* On her way back to the hotel she passed Ed, who was admiring the view from a bench set back a few meters from the path. She waved; he waved back.

You have time, Sean told her. *Miles's relay mind-talker is about ten minutes out from his place.* Still, she could tell he was excited about something.

*　*　*

An hour later, Neal drew yet another diagram on the board while Thad cleared away the remains of the breakfast the four of them had ordered in and eaten during the meeting.

Ulla trusted that Neal knew what he was doing, but the diagram looked like a bowl of noodles to her.

Watch and learn, Child. Watch and learn.

Dammit! Vani was calling Ulla "Child" now, just like Fripp did.

Compared to us, you are one. Via psi, the Elder's laugh sounded almost human. *Please direct your attention to the upper-right corner of the board; I want to see those figures again.*

She did what he asked.

—and please keep your unschooled opinions to yourself. It is distracting.

Ah, life with unfiltered Elders. Ulla was glad the station rep had already signed off.

Then, with almost no warning, *Thank you. Vani out.*

Ulla blinked. "Any progress?" she asked.

"Maybe." Neal drew a line connecting two groups of runes on the board. "Have to test it first."

*　*　*

Later that morning, Sean and Thad left to take a break. Neal finished writing a string of Elder runes on the board and set down his marker. "Do you have a minute?" he asked Ulla.

"Sure." Ulla sat back down. "I've got an appointment with Berit this afternoon, is all."

???

"She's the person to ask about helping the resort staff keep this place up." Ulla wanted a spot among the amateur groundskeepers she'd seen on her first day here. *I need something to do.*

You have that with us. "You're doing a great job, by the way," he said.

"I'm glad my Gift is useful, but it hardly fills my day." She could only read and walk on the beach for so long. "I need to do physical work."

Neal sighed. *Thinking gets hard?*

Ulla would prefer not to think at all, but how could she tell her boss that?

He gave her "the look." He clearly heard that last bit.

Ulla returned his gaze. *Busted.* "So, what's up?"

He opened his readpad. "Do you have your readpad with you?"

"Yes." It pinged as she pulled it out of her pocket.

"That's the autopsy report for Thom."

Ulla glanced at the alert and put her readpad back in her pocket. *I can't.* She took a deep breath. "Have you read it?" She could probably handle a verbal summary.

"His brain just stopped working," Neal said. "The examiner can't find a definite cause."

Of all the things. *Was it the Battle Ring?*

"Maybe, maybe not." Neal sounded miserable. *There's so much that we just don't know.*

Chapter Forty-Eight
Still Here

Laundry. Ulla pushed a cart of clean towels from the dryer to the automatic folding machine. *Why'd it have to be laundry?*

Because the resort's executive housekeeper, Mrs. Echon, had released the previous laundry helper back to his regular duties on the day Ulla had asked Berit for something to do. So, Ulla had spent her afternoons these last few weeks becoming an expert at folding the hotel's linens.

The Berserkers and the SpaceCom troops might clean their own rooms, but they dried themselves with towels and slept on sheets, at least when they were in garrison.

For the combat troops lately, that wasn't often. Logistics and maintenance troops, plus the hospital staff, plus the handful of hotel employees who had stayed on, ensured that laundry never quite stopped falling out of the chutes.

Ulla's other job was to wheel big carts of clean laundry daily to the field hospital and collect their soiled laundry. Ship's Serviceman Amanda Potts processed that; she had the professional credentials the hospital required.

Fair enough, Ulla thought to herself as she ran the zillionth towel through the folding machine. *Potts is a good kid.* Their paths didn't cross often. It might have felt odd to be working for a person so junior to her in the SpaceCom hierarchy, but the reality was that both Ulla and Ship's Serviceman Potts currently worked for Mrs. Echon.

* * *

The next day, Ulla added lunch with Neal, Thad, and Sean to her new mental hygiene regime. There would be no more grabbing takeaway to eat alone on the veranda. She set her tray next to Thad's and sat down.

Even with Emma joining them—MitSmith was giving her Thursdays off from her regular job to help with the Rings—their morning meeting had been singularly unproductive.

Some days are like that. Neal passed the saltshaker Ulla was about to ask for.

Ulla tucked into her lunch. Cabbage salad again! It was delicious.

They ate in silence. Thad set down his fork, grabbed a fresh napkin, and drew a diagram on it. He passed the drawing to Neal.

Neal studied it carefully for a moment. "If all the Ring singers make the same adjustment within seconds of each other, that might work." He added one line to the drawing and set it in the middle of the table for all to see. "Include this."

"Good catch," Thad said. "Sean?"

"Yeah, that should work."

Vani's projection popped into view, half-submerged in the floor at the end of their table.

Thad pointed to a group of converging lines on the diagram and sang a snippet of Ring song in a clear baritone.

"Seriously?" asked Sean.

Thad, Neal, Vani, and Emma nodded in unison.

"Heya, guys." Ship's Serviceman Potts, unfazed by Ring song and half an Elder projection, set her tray down next to Ulla's. "Good to see you, Lieutenant. This is a pleasant surprise."

"Please, call me Spider. What would you like me to call you?"

Potts smiled. "My name's Amanda."

Neal redrew the diagram on another napkin, adding some lines and squiggles. He handed it to Sean.

Sean sang some upper octave Ring songs in a squeaky falsetto while his sister Emma rolled her eyes.

"Don't mind them, ma'am, uh, Spider." Amanda cut up her entrée. "They do this all the time."

Neal looked up from the scribbled napkin. "I'd like to do a test of concept using practice Rings this afternoon, while Emma's here. Ulla, are you up for coordinating forty Ring singers plus our little group?"

Forty, maybe fifty human beings? Ulla had coordinated that many capraglamas—while under the influence of the Battle Ring. Without the Battle Ring, she could and had linked groups of people with one another. But that many?

She took a deep breath. Somebody had to do it, and she had yet to find the limits of her Gifts. "Sure."

He gave her a searching look. "Are you certain?" *Bravado has no place here, Starfighter.*

The nerve! Ulla set down her coffee cup. "I can do it."

"You remember Ansel Flett."

"The mind-talker who linked you with Flint's soulslayers when you got back from Kettlerest," Ulla said. *Right before Bald Mountain.*

"Ansel's on-site today, helping plan a private organization's remote meeting," Neal said. "He told me he can spare an hour for us this afternoon—and he lives in Kirkhilo, so we can hire him again as needed." Neal pushed his tray back from the edge of the table. "We'd need to scale back the test; his limit is thirty people."

They could scale back a test, but to adjust the major Rings they'd need Ulla's Gifts. "Let me try." She drank the last of her coffee. "If there's a problem, you can bring in Mr. Flett next time."

They trooped back to the conference room. Neal lined the song sequence out on the writing board while Ulla contacted Ring singers at all the Seats across Bailey-Duran Three.

She had to rouse about a third of them out of bed. *No, you don't have to haul tail out to your Ring seat,* she repeated over and over. *It's only a test; just grab a utility, uh, practice Ring.* Everybody still stumbled a little over the fact that now there were three kinds of utility Rings, not just one.

Contact built upon contact until at least sixty people had joined Ulla's web of cooperative consciousness. Yawning bedmates wanted to watch, and Ulla had no trouble including them.

Sean and Emma took their places on either side of the practice Ring in the center of the conference room table and began to sing as soon as they linked their minds with Ulla's.

Thirty-eight other singers heard the Landfall singers through Ulla's ears, saw the board through her eyes, and matched pitch and tempo as they sang their Rings up, making adjustments in unison as the network of practice Rings hummed in concert.

It worked! Everyone sang down their Rings. Ulla sighed with relief.

Neal cleared his throat. *Folks, please stick around.*

Ulla remembered just in time to relay out loud for Thad.

I'm on it. Sean sat down next to Thad and whispered in his ear. *You handle the link.*

Ulla sat there, gratified at how easily everyone's questions, answers, and suggestions flowed. Her mind was no more and no less than a clearinghouse for all these people's psi. So this was what using her psi talents could look like. She'd take it.

In the middle of their animated discussion, the link dropped abruptly. Neal ask out loud, "Starfighter, are you all right?"

Later, she wasn't sure what had happened. She may have been tired. Maybe it was that Raven Clan's male singer had a telepathic voice that could have been Thom's. Or maybe it was just bad timing. But at that moment, Ulla found herself doubled over in a wave of grief that washed in from out of nowhere.

* * *

Alone in the laundry an hour later, Ulla dumped a load of towels out of the dryer into a cart. She rolled the cart to the folding machine and started feeding towels into it. One by one, they dropped from the other end into a tidy stack of Esperanza cotton rectangles. She loaded the stack of folded towels onto a cart bound for the SpaceCom maintenance crews' floor and went back to the head of the machine to feed more towels in.

She brushed away tears. What had she been thinking, telling Neal she'd jump in and do, untutored, a psi thing she hadn't done before?

And that being the case, why wasn't Fripp here to

jump her ass?

Once she'd finished folding the towels, she moved on to a basket of sheets that needed to be folded by hand because the sheet-folding machine was broken. Even the careful ministrations of Mrs. Echon and Ship's Serviceman Potts could not bring it back into service.

No matter, Ulla decided. Folding sheets was about her speed.

BOOM!

Ulla dove for the floor and instinctively reached out with psi to find out what the hell had just happened.

Home Guard mind-seers and mind-movers, along with SpaceCom explosives experts, were clearing Yotne mines from Kirkhilo Harbor. Tardily, Ulla remembered yesterday's message from SpaceCom to that effect. Feeling sheepish, she got up, brushed herself off, and placed the basket of sheets next to the big folding table.

As she picked up the first sheet and shook it out, she heard a flittercraft take off from the resort's airstrip.

She'd worked halfway through the basket when a pair of rotorcraft took off. Was another battle getting ready to happen? Already happening?

She turned the current sheet and made another fold. As she did, she used her Gifts to see what was going on in these islands. Yup, the Home Guard were engaged with the Yotne way out in the Littles, same as they'd been for days. The craft she'd heard take off were part of SpaceCom's support.

Why the hell was she standing here folding sheets?

Because, Ulla decided, she wasn't fit for the psi billet Fripp had forced her into.

When she turned the sheet to make another fold, her hand slipped, and she dropped the sheet on the floor.

Shit! This backwater world's all-seeing, all-powerful Hidden Spinner couldn't even fold laundry effectively.

Child, you did beautifully today. Fripp sat her projection on the other end of the folding table.

Ulla left the sheet right there on the floor. *Don't patronize me. I screwed the link up completely.*

Did you, Child?

Ulla let that remark hang unanswered between them.

Child—

What? Ulla was in no mood to play games with Fripp.

You are human. Yet, you kept human weakness at bay until the critical part of this afternoon's mind-talk transaction was complete.

Human weakness, eh? Ulla picked up the sheet and wadded it into a tight ball. So, human weakness was at fault; what would Fripp have her be?

I would have you be yourself. Fripp's projection winked out from its perch on the folding table.

Myself? Who the hell even was she anymore? Thom was dead. They'd have no life together; their plans were dashed. SpaceCom was cutting Ulla loose next Midwinter because she'd effectively committed herself to becoming the Bailey-Duran system's great hope.

Just how, exactly, was she supposed to deal with that?

She threw the wadded-up sheet at the wall, stood still for a long moment, then sank to the floor. Trembling with all the grief she hadn't been ready to feel, she closed her eyes and howled.

* * *

After a great while, she breathed deeply, consciously. Ship's Serviceman Potts would be here any minute, and Ulla would not, could not allow Potts to see her falling apart like this.

* * *

When her shift was done, Ulla skipped supper, went back to her room, and cried until she couldn't cry anymore.

That night, she slept straight through until sunup. When she woke, there was a message from Neal on her room's comm panel:

Be ready for a full day of work with the Rings.

Chapter Forty-Nine
Pulling Together

Up and dressed early, Ulla peeked inside the dining room. A few SpaceCom types lingered over their coffee, but most had already eaten breakfast and gone. She didn't see Neal, Thad, or Sean; they'd likely be down in half an hour. Ed was somewhere around; she sensed his psi profile but didn't see him.

She'd get in a walk before breakfast. She crossed the veranda and went down the steps toward the water.

A man—not Ed—sat on a bench near the temporary barricade MitSmith had flung up to keep people off the beach. He stood up when she approached. *Heya, Lieutenant.*

She'd met him before, but where? *Uh, heya.*

He held out his right hand. *I'm Ansel Flett.*

Of course. The mind-talker from Kirkhilo. Ulla shook his hand.

"I love coming out here," he said. "MitSmith has good taste in ocean views."

So MitSmith did. Ulla watched the last of Kirkhilo's city lights wink out in the morning. In the other direction, she'd be able to see the Knobs, just barely, once the morning mist cleared. The ocean itself stretched in front of them as far as the human eye could discern.

The wind was brisk; Ulla was glad she'd worn her uniform jacket. *Neal Erikson hired you, didn't he?*

He did.

Fair enough. Ulla sighed; it was time to be an adult

about what happened yesterday. *Thanks for coming. We can use your help.*

The mind-talker from Kirkhilo watched a flock of sea birds dive for fish. *I hear you had a zinger in front of the whole Ring community.*

Ulla squirmed. *There's a word for that?*

"It's my word," he said. "I'm sure there's a professional term with lots more syllables."

So, it wasn't just her.

You're human. It's normal. He turned toward Ulla. "My first wife drowned in a boating accident." *I won't tell you I've been where you are, but I know the territory.*

Ulla noticed then that despite his lack of patronym, Ansel Flett wore two clan earrings in his right ear and four in his left. There was not a scrap of blue enamel among them.

You've remarried.

It took a while. He brushed at something dry and flaky on his shoulder. "Dammit. I forgot there was spit-up on this jacket too."

He had a child.

Two. Flett scraped the spot with his fingernail, gave up, and smiled. "A son and a baby daughter." *They're brilliant.*

"Neal and the rest of them will be at breakfast soon. Want to join us?"

"That's why I'm early. MitSmith does breakfast well."

Ulla made a face. *You must not have heard.*

Heard what?

"SpaceCom cooks are running the kitchen," she said. "You're about to see what they can do with MitSmith's pantry."

* * *

The meeting after breakfast was mercifully short.

"Castle Chisos has the simulation up and running," said Neal. "So far, things are looking good; we should know for sure in a couple of days—maybe even tomorrow."

Simulation? Ulla remembered to speak out loud. "What simulation?"

"They have a big sphere there, made of practice Rings," said Neal. "They're testing the sequence we came up with yesterday; they just got started because they had to set up the no-fly zone first."

Ulla wondered if that Ring array had caused the static that kept her from hailing Rescue those first days on the ground.

Sean glanced at Ulla. *That was us. Sorry it messed with your comm.* He rested his elbows on the table. *Fripp said go ahead and run the tests anyway, that you'd be fine.*

Ulla resisted putting her face in her hands. She forced her attention back to Neal, who was still talking.

"The setup blocks physical intrusion; they'll try conventional comm next, then Gate impulses." Neal paused. "Assuming that works, they'll try adjusting individual Rings."

So, Ulla interpreted him to mean, the Rings' barrier around this planet could be opened and closed selectively.

Neal scribbled some names and locations on the board. "Sean, Thad, and I will stand by for questions and discussion. Ansel is here to help with long-distance mind-talking."

Oh. Ulla inspected her fingernails and dug out a sliver of grime she'd missed earlier. Given what happened yesterday, she braced herself for awkwardness.

Done with the board, Neal sat down at the table. "Ulla, you have a training opportunity right here on-site."

Ulla swallowed. In SpaceCom, "training opportunity" was often a euphemism for a spectacularly awful task reserved for someone who had screwed up badly. Did Neal know that?

The professor? The corners of Mr. Flett's mouth twitched. *I don't think he does, Lieutenant.* "I've been asked to facilitate a remote meeting for a regional choral group who usually have their annual music festival and business meeting here at the resort this time every year."

"They're meeting anyway? Now?" Ulla decided these people must be uncommonly dedicated to their hobby.

"Music is what gets most of 'em through." Ansel shrugged. "But even if the Gates were working and there were no mines in the water, the chorus still couldn't have a normal conference here because their venue has been turned into a troop garrison."

Merciful gods. Ulla hoped MitSmith had refunded the

singers' room fees.

Ansel was still talking. "...but then a lot of singers are in the Home Guard and can't be here anyway."

In short, Ansel's sister, who was on the board of the Archipelago Chorus, had wangled meeting rooms and conventional comm from MitSmith and roped Ansel into linking as many people as he could because they were going to sing together come hell or high water. Of which they had both, Ulla reflected.

"I can link thirty people effectively," Ansel said. "Their plans keep growing. I know it'd be new for you, Ulla, but I don't have the capacity to do what they have in mind. If you link for the chorus, I'll gladly take your place with these guys for Ring Q and A."

"It would be good practice for you, Ulla," Neal said. "They're a large, dispersed group who have to match pitch and tempo."

Exactly the skill set she needed to coordinate Ring song. "I'll give it a go," she said, "but they need to know I'm new at this."

"You'll be fine." Ansel grinned. "Nobody's ever done what they're asking; they'll be happy with whatever you can give them."

"The music festival is two-and-a-half days long." Neal scribbled something in his notebook. "By the time it's over, I want you to be able to handle that kind of link in your sleep."

* * *

Ulla and Ansel wasted no time; the choral group's business meeting was this afternoon, followed by—they hoped—an informal long-distance singalong, dinner, and concert.

Ulla fired off questions as she followed Ansel down the hall. *Is it just singers?* She thought back to the one semester of choir she'd had in school. *What about accompanists?*

He opened the door to the hotel's ballroom. *Oh, yes. You'll need to work out a way to hear and project their instruments to musicians and singers at other sites.* "They haven't been able to rehearse together since the Gates stopped working, though my sister Lori says a few smaller groups have gotten together."

Spider's Wyrd

When they weren't fighting Yotne or trying to put their island communities back together. Ulla declined to verbalize that. "Why not use conventional comm?" she asked.

"There's a lag, even at short-range." Ansel stepped out of the way of a woman who hurried past them carrying an instrument case. "They can't sing or play together."

"Can they all mind-talk?" Ulla asked.

Ansel switched back to psi; a group of musicians were tuning their instruments. *A little over a hundred of them mind-talk well. About another, oh, three dozen or so can't, but every local ensemble has at least a few solid mind-talkers.*

How many local ensembles?

Twenty-seven. Kirkhilo's the biggest; most are tiny. Family groups and individuals who get together on remote islands. He thought for a minute. *My numbers may be off because a lot of them are in the Home Guard.*

Any groups in the Littles?

Fifteen, maybe more.

???

Groups in the Littles are smaller and spread out, he explained. *They're unlikely to sing, but you'll want to scan periodically in case somebody out there wants to check in.*

His subtext was that the people in the Littles were busy not getting wiped out by the last of the Yotne.

She wrenched her brain back to the here and now. Even with, say, a third of the individual singers gone, the number of groups would likely compare evenly enough to the number of Ring seats she'd linked up yesterday— but with more people in a much more eclectic mix. Good practice, indeed.

Around them half a dozen people unfolded and set up a bank of risers they'd pulled from a deep closet, as though they knew exactly where everything was. They'd already placed a semicircle of folding chairs around a conventional comm pickup with a big holo display. *They seem awfully familiar with this space.*

Ansel laughed. *This is where the Kirkhilo branch rehearses.*

Ulla took in all the activity. *It's the middle of a weekday. Don't these people work for a living?*

Ansel waved to a woman who had left her station with

the riser setup crew and was heading their way. *Most of them have had this on their calendars since last year.*

Didn't these people know there was a war on?

Yes, Starfighter. The woman had reached them. *Yes, we do.* She held out her hand to Ulla. "Hello," she said brightly. "I'm Lori Gooding, Ansel's sister. So glad you could come and help us out."

Ulla shook Lori's hand and felt deep melancholy under the woman's pleasant veneer of excitement.

"Remembrances start in an hour," Lori said, "followed by our business meeting—but we'll use conventional comm." She glanced over her shoulder at the room, which appeared to be completely set up. "We'll use conventional comm for the evening concert too. But I'd like you to link us for the afternoon meet-and-greet and the informal singalong—it'll be a good way for all of us to get used to linking with each other. Can you be ready two hours from now?"

"Sure." Ulla was relieved that Ms. Gooding understood she'd need time to settle into any kind of link with this many people. "I'll need help finding all the groups to hail them the first time."

"Of course." Lori Gooding looked almost ready to hug Ulla. "Ansel knows everybody; he can help you get started." *He says you have Gift enough to link everybody.*

Ulla probably had—but this job was shaping up to be a master exercise in cat-herding.

Lori got a "mind-talking with somebody else" look on her face and went silent.

Ansel grinned. *Far better you than me, Starfighter.*

Gee, thanks.

Lori was back with them. "Sheltertown lifeboats just got an alert. Two basses, two tenors, and an alto are on the crew." *Please let them be safe and back with us soon.* She pulled a readpad from her pocket and tapped at it. "Here's the schedule."

Ulla's readpad buzzed. "In Memory" was the document's first subtitle, at the top of a list of names that went on for three pages.

* * *

At lunchtime the next day, Ulla set her tray on the

dining room table, sat down, and closed her eyes. The singers from Kirkhilo had invited her to share their catered lunch in the ballroom, but she just couldn't. *So. Many. People.*

An hour from now, they were going to do it all again.

In the meantime, Ed's psi profile was here in the same room. Ulla opened her eyes and watched him fill his tray. She waved. *Heya, Ed. You might as well sit down right here.*

Heya. "How's the community choir treating you?" he asked as he set his tray down across from her.

Don't call them that to their faces; they'll hurt you. Ulla shook out her napkin. "They're pretty good." They'd sounded even better once she'd figured out, under Ansel's instruction, how to link the section leaders with each other, listen through their ears, relay what she heard back to all the leaders simultaneously, wait for the sections to even things out, and only then link the rest of the ensemble. She was still mulling over how best to link the household of three percussionists and one soprano with the rest of the mix.

"They are good." He picked at the cabbage roll on his plate. "I listened in."

Ulla cut up her cabbage roll and began to eat. *Haven't seen you much lately. What've you been up to?*

I've been around. "I'm attached for the moment to the BTE office at the Port of Kirkhilo." He gave up on the cabbage roll and reached instead for butter to slather on his bread. "Just till we can get home." *Mostly same old, same old.*

Ulla swallowed her food. "Protecting the spinner?"

Me and your da. Ed nodded. *A Berserker almost killed me for following you before Neal made it clear to her that that's my job.* He bit off a chunk of buttered bread. *We're sharing now; your da's people have the evening and night shifts.* He swallowed. "Until Stelle Pietersdaughter grows up, you're the only adept in this system who can coordinate all the major Rings—maybe the only adept anywhere. The Guild says it's outside their skill sets." *And as of yesterday evening, it's public knowledge that you are still alive.*

Well. Ulla applied herself to eating her lunch. *Um, thanks.*

Don't thank me...yet. Ed pushed his uneaten cabbage

roll to the edge of his plate. "It would make all our lives easier if you stopped taking your solitary walks."

Even here on MitSmith property?

Yep. Especially down by the water.

Hey! I always check for mines. But Ulla had to admit he was right. She sighed and gave him a parody of a salute. "Will do." *But if you're supposed to shadow me, you'd better develop a taste for long walks.*

Starfighter, I've been tailing you since we got here.

Seriously? Ulla must really have been in a funk.

It happens. You're getting better. "Also, Berit wants you to come and see her—something about getting your sidearm out of her safe."

???

You'll need it when you go to the Ring seat; Neal says the tests are going well. Ed stood up. "I'm going to find something else to eat. Want me to bring you anything while I'm up?"

Oh, yes, please! Ulla finished the last of her cabbage roll. "See what they have for dessert."

* * *

Three days later, Landfall's morning dawned sunny and cloudless. The only Yotne left on BD3 were pinned down on the far side of the Littles. You couldn't have picked a better day for a rotorcraft ride.

A yellow rotorcraft landed in a loud swirl of leaves and dirt on the resort's pad. Ulla and Ed, Emma and Sean, Neal, and Thad climbed aboard and set out for Great Knob.

"Heya, Starfighter!" Sumeet waved.

Same rotorcraft, same crew. Different day, thanks be. They flew through the morning and landed on the big, cantilevered platform.

Neal and Ed—soulslayer and spotter—took positions near the edge of the platform. The rotorcraft's crew stayed aboard while the rest of the group trooped into the Ring's seat, a mood of anticipation about them. Ulla imagined the Ring was waiting impatiently for them to begin.

No, Child; the Ring is but an artifact. You feel what we all are feeling, nothing more. Fripp's projection drew a wrap over her shoulders; the air at Castle Chisos must be brisk.

After Ulla's stint with the chorus, linking forty Ring

singers, half a dozen professional mind-talkers, and two Guild reps was simple in comparison.

Ulla sat on the ground where she had a good view of Sean and Emma by the Ring. She got comfortable and started roll call. *Thistle, Chisos, Mountain, Trinacria, Falcon, Lobo, Gaulois, Worldtree, Dolphin, Waterbasket, Raven...*

Everybody was ready. *Levi Dirkson, Bailey-Duran Coalition Headquarters; Ulla Thorsdaughter, Great Knob Ring.*

Levi Dirkson here. Olwyn, at BD3 Station, chimed in as an observer.

Sean and Emma sang the master pitch. Through Ulla's link, the other singers matched it and began the song sequence that would make the Rings allow communication and selected Gate traffic on and off the surface of Bailey-Duran Three. Forty people, at twenty Rings scattered over the surface of the planet, sang together in call-and-response through the sequence the team had worked out and rigorously tested.

If this worked, Bailey-Duran Three would not have to choose between commerce and being secure under the Rings' shield. Communication between surface and space would no longer be limited to the handful of adepts who had extremely long mind-talk range. This world would no longer be cut off from the rest of the universe.

On a personal level, everyone here on the ground could see for sure if the Yotne were gone.

Ulla. Levi, check Headquarters' status boards. Ulla, and by extension everyone in the link, watched the command post's big status boards through Levi's eyes. One by one, automated labels in colored lettering replaced the larger, irregular lettering of manual entries for status of friendly forces, Yotne forces, Dweller incidents, equipment status, personnel numbers, whatever information a commander might need to formulate the next move.

An adept spoke up from—Raven? *What are we looking at?*

Levi turned to face the BD3 surface situation display. Through his eyes, they took in the enormous world map, with a few bright clusters of lettering, almost all green, and a smidge of red in west Landfall. Levi moved closer so they could read the names of the surface combat units spread across the islands there. Green Contract, SpaceCom, Home Guard, and BTE tracks outnumbered the red tracks indicating the last Yotne enclaves.

One small, worrying cluster of red labels remained.

An update rippled through the automated display. The numbers on a green Home Guard/SpaceCom track dropped slightly, and the adjacent red Yotne track faded to a dull pink and winked out. Two other red tracks faded with it.

Levi backed up again for a view of the entire map. Nothing but green.

Ulla. Levi, please show us the space situation display. Levi turned and focused on the three-dimensional display in the middle of the command post. While plenty of labels had dimmed, the bright ones were all green. Task Force Bailey-Duran had been busy.

Through Levi's ears, they heard excited murmurs; voice and video comm units crackled to life. In the background, someone on the command post floor yelled, "They did it!"

Levi panned to the list of commercial and military Gates throughout this world and around the system. One by one, red listings switched to bright green, the list of surface navigation satellites next to it gradually following suit.

At the Great Knob Ring Seat, Fripp's projection sent a wave of joy to Ulla. *Well done, Child.*

All assembled, Great Knob Ring. Mission successful. It was all Ulla could do to maintain the link.

The group sat together in stunned silence. Could this really be it?

Does anyone have anything more to say?

Nobody did.

Great Knob Ring Out. Ulla jumped up and threw her arms around the two people nearest her, who happened to be Neal and Emma, while her mind hummed with the collective energy of all the people at the other Ring seats doing the same. *They're gone! Hooray! We won!*

This time.

Chapter Fifty
Ashes

The silence in their conference room back in the resort that afternoon was remarkable. As the world's comm systems reconnected, routing messages and sending them where they belonged, Ulla, Neal, Sean, and Thad sat with their noses in their readpads, catching up with—and mostly deleting—old correspondence. Emma had gone back to Kirkhilo to hug her husband and children. She'd said she'd start hacking at the backlog of work in her office tomorrow.

Neal broke the silence. "I have us a ride back to Newcastle." He tapped at his readpad; three other readpads pinged in unison. A rotorcraft sped overhead and landed next to the hospital. Ulla recognized her father's psi blocker aboard. *Oh gods.* She bent the rules and used her spinner strength to peek through the blocker. Dad was an escort, not a casualty. She gave thanks and resisted the urge to pry further.

Sean opened Neal's message. "That's not till next week," he said, oblivious to the mini-drama that had just occurred inside Ulla's head.

"Medevac goes first," said Neal. "The commercial Gate operators want to do more testing before they resume service, so flittercraft and surface ships are all there is."

"What about the SpaceCom and BTE Gates?" Ulla asked.

"Same issues." Neal's readpad pinged. *Dammit.* "We may have to adjust the Rings again before all the Gates work like they should."

BOOM! The minesweepers were working down by the Knobs today. Ulla didn't even jump.

Thad snapped his readpad shut. "Do you need anything else today, Neal?"

Neal shook his head. "Nope."

Thad drank the last of his coffee. "I'd like to go to Lesser Knob. MitSmith says my apartment is ready to move back in."

Neal closed his readpad. "Go."

Sean paused in mid-message. "I want to go see my folks in Kirkhilo."

Neal stood up and stretched. "Let's call it a day."

That was fine by Ulla, who was already yawning. Dad and Berit had invited her to dinner with the Berserker leadership. If this evening was going to be a big one, she needed a nap first.

* * *

Ulla went outside to soak up some late afternoon sunshine before heading for her room. Idly, she watched a van wind its way up the road toward the resort. As it drew closer, she recognized the chaplain and the injured Berserker who seemed to have become Berit's more-or-less permanent admin assistant. They parked in front of a pair of unassuming double doors several meters short of where Ulla stood. They both got out and met at the back of the van.

The two men stood quietly for a moment before the chaplain opened the liftgate. Then he tossed a set of keys to the Berserker, who unlocked the doors to the building, propped them open, and disappeared inside.

The chaplain reached inside the back of the van and hauled out a big square crate that moved as though it had an antigrav slider/lift attached. It looked heavy. Antigrav or no, mass was mass.

Ulla walked down the path to meet him. *Would you like some help?*

He didn't accept right away. *You know what's in the crates, right?*

She nodded. *Ashes. The remains of the fallen.* The men would not have rendered honors to crates of anything else.

In that case, yes, please. "Turning corners is the hardest part."

She grabbed a handle on the front of the crate to keep it from bashing holes in the walls. The chaplain pushed from behind as they threaded their way through plain service corridors to a pair of hand-carved wooden doors in a lavishly carpeted hallway. The two of them wrestled the crate to a standstill; the Berserker had to try several keys before he found the one that unlocked the doors.

They maneuvered the crate inside. The chaplain let the antigrav set it down on the carpet by some shelves on the back wall of a showy room with an entire wall of windows meant for an ocean view. For now, it overlooked the field hospital. One of the hospital's side doors opened, and a tall man in a Berserker uniform stepped onto the lawn.

"Thanks, Lieutenant," said Chaplain Taleb.

"Oh!" Ulla, startled, brought her attention back to him. "No problem, sir."

"We can get it from here." Taleb and the Berserker clerk headed out the door. Ulla followed them back to the van and watched the chaplain slide a smaller but still substantial box partway out of the cargo area. This box was made of finished wood and had attractive metal handles.

The clerk no longer wore a sling, but Ulla didn't need psi to see that his arm still bothered him. She stepped forward to help.

Let him. He has one good arm. The chaplain grabbed the handle on one side of the box. *You can close up the van and shut these doors.*

The Berserker grabbed the other handle, and the two men carried the box inside. Ulla closed the liftgate and went back to release the catches that held the hotel's service doors open.

Lieutenant? The chaplain must have thought of something else.

Ulla peered down the hallway but didn't see him. *Sir?*

The Berserkers' Sergeant Major Tolliver is running late. Do you have time to wait by the door and let him in?

Sure. Want me to close up after he gets here? She heard, through the chaplain's ears, the thump of the box being set on a table.

Yes, please.

* * *

"Good afternoon, Lieutenant." The tall man she'd seen exit the field hospital held a local-style cardboard folder for paper documents in his left hand.

"Sergeant Major." Ulla returned his salute. Given Tolliver's extraordinarily commanding presence, she felt a little like she ought to salute him instead. "Were you in the rotorcraft with Dad?"

He nodded. "Colonel Bjornson is fine. Colonel Martin is injured."

Dad's second-in-command and oldest friend.

A brief worried look flashed in the sergeant major's eyes before he quashed it. "Not life-threatening."

Ulla got the impression that this steady rock of a man said that as much to reassure himself as to reassure her.

"He's in good hands," Tolliver said. "Ms. Gee and a local adept just started work with that psi thing the locals call the Healing Gift." He shook his head. "I've never seen anything like it."

It never, ever ends, does it? Ulla remembered, belatedly, to repeat that out loud.

"No," he said, "it doesn't. But it often slows down enough that one can still find joy." He caught himself and resumed his outwardly invincible demeanor. "Your father asked me to tell you that tonight's dinner gathering is canceled."

Ulla thought that was a no-brainer, with Dad's second-in-command in the hospital and Berit sound asleep once she'd done what she could for him. "Thank you."

"That said, I'm sure your father would like to see you." It was obvious the sergeant major would not discuss the subject further.

"Are you looking for the SpaceCom chaplain?" she asked.

"Yes. I had intended to join him earlier."

Ulla inclined her head toward the end of the hall. "Turn left at the end of this corridor. It'll be the second door on your right."

"Thanks." He set off.

Ulla closed and locked the double doors and followed

him to the big, bright room where the SpaceCom chaplain and the Berserker clerk already had the big crate open.

Tolliver set down his cardboard folder. "Thank you, Corporal. I'll take it from here."

The clerk, visibly relieved, left the room. Ulla watched the two older men empty the crate, box by compact box, onto shelves at the back of the room.

The remains of the fallen.

The chaplain must have seen Ulla's expression. *Are you all right, Lieutenant?*

Nothing I haven't seen before, sir. Ulla swallowed. *Thanks.* But her knees failed her, and she sat down.

"Lieutenant Thorsdaughter?" Tolliver's face showed concern.

"I'll be all right." Ulla concentrated on breathing evenly.

The men developed a system as they worked: Chaplain Taleb reading a name off the label on a box, Sergeant Major Tolliver shuffling through the folder for the corresponding sheet of paper and folding it gently, the chaplain opening the box, tucking in the folded paper, and placing the box on a different shelf. Groups of boxes formed, sorted by destination. The people whose remains these were had come from all over known space. Mostly combatants from offworld, comprised of SpaceCom and Berserkers.

So many people. So many families. In this way, Ulla and Thom were far from unique.

Chaplain Taleb finished double-checking a completed shelf. "The Kirkhilo mortuary staff packed all the remains that need to be shipped off-planet in one crate."

Knowing, no doubt, that the Berserkers and SpaceCom would take care of their people no matter what. "What about the other box?" Ulla asked.

"Alliance members from Hoffnung; that box is ready to go." The sergeant major handed a folded paper to the chaplain. "They'll travel with your workgroup next week."

Alliance members from Hoffnung. *Oh.* Ulla had no idea what to say.

Chaplain Taleb walked over to the wooden box. He took off the lid, set it to one side, then removed two larger-than-usual individual boxes and put them on the table.

Elders?

Yes. He set aside three boxes from the next layer, found the one he was looking for underneath, and slid it

out from its place among the others.
Ulla sat down.
The chaplain handed her the box.
Thom's ashes. Tears came as she cradled the box in her lap.

* * *

By the time Ulla was in a position to notice, the two men had almost finished matching documents to boxes.
Words from the collection of verses Mama had insisted she and Andrew memorize as soon as they could read came to her then. She recited them out loud:

"All living beings die.
That day will come for every one of us.
But as creation fades and is reborn,
a good name will forever honor
the one who earned it."

The chaplain looked up from the shipping cover he had just opened. "Thom Yensson earned a good name."
Ulla agreed. She could not trust herself to speak.
Thom's father had asked her to formally join their family. A custom among the On'oi, she'd learned, to maintain family and clan bonds, especially when children were involved.
Only she and Thom would have no children.
One warm tear escaped from her eye and flowed down her cheek.

Chapter Fifty-One
Going Home

Outwardly, the flittercraft they boarded a week later for the flight to Newcastle looked exactly like the transport they'd used to carry the Ring. Inside was a different story: a command-and-communications module filled most of the cargo bay, save just enough space for the polished wooden box of ashes that was already tied down to grommets in the deck outside the module's personnel hatch.

Neal and Ulla paused to honor the dead. Ulla let her hand linger on the smooth wood before she followed Neal through the hatch into the module. Inside, they found seats in front of powered-down comm units. Sean and Thad were already buckled in, their seats locked in forward position for takeoff.

"Heya, Sean." Neal strapped himself into a seat. "What'd they give us for lunches?"

"SpaceCom Surprise." Sean pointed to a closed compartment overhead. "Box lunches are up there when you want 'em."

"Heya, Thad," Ulla said as she found her seat. "I thought you were staying in Landfall."

Thad shook his head. "My dissertation defense is next week." He glared at Neal. "Did you have anything to do with that?"

"Hey, I had them push it back for you twice." Neal smiled blandly. "These past few weeks, you've been… otherwise engaged."

Sean elucidated. "What the professor said was, 'My

student, who was scheduled to defend on the second Wednesday after Midsummer, was presented a unique opportunity to empirically test the theories put forward in said dissertation. His theories were proved reliable in praxis, thus saving the planet Bailey-Duran Three from the Yotne Dominion.'"

How's yours coming? Ulla realized just in time that Neal's question was intended only for Sean.

She couldn't help overhearing Sean's answer. *My dissertation? It's on hiatus. That whole saving-the-world thing.*

Ed was the last to duck inside. He closed the hatch behind him, sat down, and buckled in. The crew powered up and shut the big cargo door. Then they were off.

* * *

Once the flittercraft reached altitude, they unbuckled and got out their box lunches.

Neal ran his fingernail underneath the seal on his and opened it. *Not again.* He looked up. "It's pickled cabbage."

Ulla opened her box lunch and dug out a recyclable fork and a little tub of pickled cabbage from underneath two beef pasties and a pear. In about five bites, she polished off her shredded cabbage and peppers in a delectable vinegary sauce with just a touch of sweet. Then she unwrapped a pasty.

"If you like that swill, you can have mine." Neal held out his pickled cabbage for her.

"Trade you my pear for it." Ulla didn't really like pears.

"No, thanks; please keep the cabbage." Neal munched on his pasty.

Ulla finished her pasty, then ate all of Neal's pickled cabbage. She unwrapped her second pasty.

"Mine too." Thad handed her his tub. "I don't ever want to see cabbage again."

"They say the resort overbought on cabbages the week before the Yotne attacked," said Sean. "SpaceCom cooks were trying to use them up before they went bad."

The food had been pretty good, Ulla reflected. Cabbage salad, stir fry, cabbage rolls, New Shrewsbury boiled dinner, cabbage soup . . .

Starfighter, that's disgusting. Stop it. Ed set his pickled cabbage in front of her growing collection.

Me? You're the one who's eavesdropping. Ulla scraped out the last bit of juice. She licked the spoon.

Sean laughed and gave her his too.

Even after eating everyone's cabbage, she was still hungry, so she ate the pear after all. It was delicious.

Ulla boxed up the remains of her lunch and tossed it into the garbage. "If this workspace module is what I think it is," she said, stretching, "there'll be racks in the forward compartment."

"Racks?" Sean asked.

"Beds." Ulla yawned. "I could use a nap."

* * *

Wake up! The telepathic voice was Neal's, in boss mode.

Mmm? Ulla rolled over and caught herself just in time to avoid falling out of the flittercraft's narrow bunk as the engines changed pitch.

We're almost there!

Oh! I'll be right out. Quietly, so as not to disturb the sleeping crew member in the bottom rack, Ulla slid out and onto the deck.

She was putting on her boots when a bright light filled the sleeping compartment. The man woke quickly, put on his boots, and disappeared through the forward hatch.

Ulla belted herself into a seat just in time. The flittercraft descended, landing with a mild bump. The pilot drove around for a while on the ground before stopping and powering down.

The forward hatch opened and the flittercraft captain poked his head inside. "It'll be a few minutes. There's a party coming to greet you."

The flittercraft's big rear ramp unfolded on the ground with a thunk. The rear hatch opened, and a SpaceCom petty officer hurried in, carrying a hanging clothes bag and a pile of capraglama wool.

"Welcome back!" He set the pile of wool on a work surface and gave the hanging bag to Ulla. "This is yours, ma'am."

He shook out a sorcerer's cloak lined in blue. "Dr. Erikson?" Neal stepped forward, checked the snaps, straightened the folds, and put it on.

Ulla ducked into the sleeping compartment to change out of her utility uniform and into her SpaceCom service dress uniform. The black pants were tight and her white shirt gapped in front. She immediately regretted calling Neal out for stress-eating. The jacket, thanks be, was cut full enough to cover her transgressions. Glad that she'd set up all her insignia on the jacket when it first came from the Newcastle tailor's, she forgave SpaceCom for the jacket's high, tight collar and slipped her readpad into its inside breast pocket.

She opened her duffel and removed a paper-wrapped package from a Kirkhilo garment cleaner. She rolled up the empty hanging bag and stuffed it and her utility uniform into the space the package had vacated. Then she closed the duffel and handed it through the door for Thad to place on the group's small pile of luggage.

Ready? Neal's voice again.

Ulla took a deep breath and unwrapped the paper from Thom's sorcerer's cloak. She draped the folded cloak over her left arm and emerged into the main cabin, joining the rest of the group. "Let's get on with it."

Ed and Neal ducked through the hatch and picked up the crate with the ashes in it. Sean and Thad waited just inside. Ulla stood there, at a loss. Outside, the flight crew stood at attention at the foot of the ramp.

Over here, Starfighter! Neal gestured with his free hand to the spot directly behind the crate, in front of Sean and Thad. She ducked past them and took her place. Then they started down the ramp toward the gauntlet of honors rendered and images taken.

Padraic Willemson and Renata Connersdaughter, decked out in their best diplomatic daytime attire, stood with Yens Peacemaker, Marta, and two Elders at the foot of the ramp. Skuli, Olwyn, Mary Nkosi, Geoff and Yasmin Tully, and the Rogerses were with them, as were Dannel and Ingeborg. Behind them were over a hundred other people who, from the stew of emotions spilling over Ulla where she stood, had to be family members of the deceased.

Mik Fowler, with bagpipes ready, stood off to one side of the crowd. He struck in his pipes and played a lament.

It might have been the bagpipes that got her. Ulla was

never sure, afterward, how they all got down the ramp and into the waiting limousine, but they managed.

Chapter Fifty-Two
SpaceCom's Spinner

The next morning, Ulla stood at the Trade Ministry's breakfast buffet, her readpad in one hand and a piece of crisp flatbread in the other. She eyed the coffee urn, but she just couldn't face coffee yet.

"Good morning." Renata started filling her plate. "Is that all you're eating?"

Ulla shook her head. "No worries. I'll get breakfast at the SpaceCom dining hall."

She watched Renata's gaze stray from the piece of flatbread to her waist. Great. A tight-fitting sports bra had taken care of the shirt-gapping problem but she could not hide how snug her black pants were. Her readpad wouldn't even fit in its accustomed pocket. She would stop by the tailor's this afternoon and have some alterations made—maybe even order a new pair of pants to tide her over until she lost the weight.

She stood aside for Skuli, who had just arrived and wanted coffee.

Thanks. "I'm your ride today; ready when you are." He poured himself a fresh cup, then did a double-take and spoke out loud. "That was fast."

Ulla poked at her right ear; she was still getting used to the full-sized earrings she'd been given less than ten hours earlier.

He set down his coffee and gave her a big hug. "Welcome to Raven Clan."

"Padraic and Yens did the honors yesterday while

Yens and Marta were still here." While Thom's family had not wanted to waste any time including her, the ceremony had, of necessity, been intimate and low-key.

Skuli stood back and picked up his coffee cup. "Is Thom's memorial service still set for Saturday at Raven Clan's summer pasture?"

Renata set down her plate. "Yes, it is."

"Olwyn and I will be there." Skuli tipped back his cup and drank. "We both have the day off."

"The Gates should be working in west Hoffnung by then." Renata picked up flatware rolled in a napkin. "If they aren't, you're welcome to ride with us."

"Thanks." Skuli walked over to the dirty dishes tub and placed his cup on the pile. "You ready, Starfighter?"

Ulla finished her flatbread, hugged Renata goodbye, and followed Skuli out the service-yard door. *Looking forward to seeing Olwyn, are you?*

Skuli tipped back his head and laughed out loud. *You've been out of the loop, Starfighter; I just had breakfast with her.*

* * *

Olwyn Wittber's office door was closed, so Ulla looked for a place to sit and wait. Skuli disappeared down the hall.

Starfighter! You're early! Maribet bolted out of a tiny office across from Olwyn's and swept her up in a big hug.

Maribet! "So glad to see you."

Maribet led the way into her office and offered Ulla a chair. "Before you ask, I've moved out of Susana's house. I've got a spot at the Guild school. I'm working for Olwyn temporarily and staying in the new quarters here on post until the passenger liners start running again."

Did you and Susana, uh—

Break up? Not as such. We drifted apart once we got to know each other better. Maribet sighed. "Susana will always have a special place in my heart. We got each other through that awkward adolescent time when she and I were the only two girls at our school who had the guts to be who we really were."

Ulla had wondered. Susana's personality seemed so much more strident than Maribet's.

Maribet laughed. "You mean Midsummer Ball?"

"You two made quite the stir. Newcastle society will never be the same."

"Good thing too. I'm glad."

They sat there, savoring the memory. "How's Stelle Pietersdaughter doing?" Ulla asked.

"Pretty well." Maribet laughed. "I hear she's a handful; her grandparents have their work cut out for them." *I think they'll be relieved when our wee spinner takes up studies at Castle Chisos.*

Olwyn's door opened. Footsteps crossed the hall.

"Lieutenant?" That was General Zhou's voice.

Ulla sprang to her feet, turned around to face him, and stood at attention while Maribet watched in amazement.

"Please, stand easy. Guild Member Wittber told me you'd be in here."

Ulla tried to keep her facial expression neutral. *Please, no condolences. Not again.*

"Thank you and your—associates—for what you've done with those Rings. Everyone in the Bailey-Duran system owes you."

Ulla braced herself for what she knew was coming.

"I'm so sorry to hear that your fiancé died. How are you doing?"

"I've been better, sir. I'll be all right." There, that was done.

Apparently, General Zhou concurred. "I had lunch with Jan Martin yesterday. He says the Berserkers are standing down once their contract here is done."

Dad had planned to announce his decision at the dinner party they never had, the day the Rings finally got sorted and Colonel Martin got hurt. A leftover motion-sensing bomblet had rolled out from behind a rock and targeted him, Dad, and Sergeant Major Tolliver. He'd picked it up—never mind the nerve-disrupter coating everyone knew the Yotne used—and threw it as far away as he could. He'd saved their lives and almost lost his hand.

"Man has a good arm," General Zhou remarked.

"Did you serve with him," Ulla asked, "when he was with SpaceCom?"

"Jan was a year behind Thor and me at the Academy. We played several different sports together." The general paused—remembering? "He told me about Berit's Healing Gift; that's amazing."

"You know Berit Gee?"

Zhou nodded. "She's a force of nature and a natural-born logistician. While Thor was negotiating SpaceCom communications support and overhead cover for the Landfall piece, she backed me into a corner and insisted we deploy support personnel and a field hospital."

That would be classic Berit. Ulla could just see her getting ever-so-politely in the general's face.

"How are she and your dad?" the general asked.

"They're doing well, sir," Ulla said. "Right now, they're in Landfall, tying up loose ends."

"And then?"

"They're going to retire."

"Thor's been saying that for years. What's different this time?"

"Dad accepted the Landfall Home Guard's bid for the Berserkers' on-planet equipment in exchange for cash and a nice piece of land in the hills above Kirkhilo."

* * *

Ulla found the Guild rep tending houseplants on a shelf by her office window.

Spider! So good to see you! Olwyn set down a small watering can and rushed over to give Ulla a hug.

Once they'd hugged, Ulla stood back and examined Olwyn's right ear. *Raven and Worldtree?* "Skuli, right?"

The Guild rep nodded, smiled, and raised a hand to her set of full-sized earrings, so new that Ulla spotted traces of disinfectant around the piercings.

"You're married." Ulla hugged her again. "Congratulations." *That rat-bastard! All he said was that you'd moved in together.*

"We'd already planned for me to move in with him when I came back from the station," said Olwyn. *He had bannock and coffee waiting just inside our door.* "We skipped the formal engagement and got married quietly last week; Padraic Willemson did the honors." *We are neither of us spring chickens; there's no time to waste if...* Olwyn's telepathic voice trailed off. She blushed.

"If you want to have kids," Ulla said gently.

"That didn't seem like the most tactful thing to say," said Olwyn. *Under the circumstances.* She led Ulla to the comfortable chair beside her desk. "But this is your check-in appointment, not mine." *How are you holding up?*

"All right, I suppose," Ulla said. *Some days are better than others.*

Olwyn leaned back in her chair. "Berit Gee says you're bouncing back pretty well."

"Seriously?" Ulla wasn't sure she agreed.

The Guild rep nodded. "It's not just Thom's death, you know."

Ulla knew. The life she'd built as a starfighter was gone. Most of her shipmates from the *Valiant* were dead. Unexpected paranormal talents had brought wrenching career change. New love had led to abrupt loss.

Ulla did not trust herself to speak.

"You won't hear any platitudes from me," Olwyn said. "When you do want to talk, get yourself in here." *I wish I could just fix the universe, but I can't.*

"Fixing the universe is, actually, one of my psi talents." *They say the price for doing it is too damned high.*

Indeed. Olwyn squared her shoulders and took a deep breath. She tapped out a message on her comm panel. "I'm sending you contact information for a Guild member who specializes in grief counseling. She's not in-system, but with your telepathic range, that won't be an issue." *Please, Spider, don't be too proud to use her services.*

They sat quietly for a long minute until Olwyn spoke. "Congratulations on joining Thom's family."

Ulla's full-sized earrings felt heavy. "I'm still not sure how family relationships work around here, but there's a good chance you and I are cousins now." *Maybe in-laws?*

I have no idea. Olwyn paused. "Is there anything else you want to talk about?"

"Not really." *I probably ought to ask the doc; I don't think it's psi-related.*

"Try me," said Olwyn.

"I get really tired in the middle of the day lately, and that's not me." *Depression, maybe? Changing time zones?*

"Could be either." Olwyn thought for a moment. "I'm told you like cabbage."

"I do. It's tasty." *Where was the Guild rep going with this?*

"Lieutenant, when did you last have your period?"

"Before Bald Mountain, Ulla said. "It would have been a few days before we reached Summer Pasture." How long ago was that? She could think in the standard calendar or the local calendar. Converting between the two made her brain hurt. In any event, Olwyn's question was irrelevant because combat—or even intense training—almost always put Ulla's cycle on pause. *Why do you want to know?*

Two words: Mags Pappas. Plus a few others. Olwyn tapped on her comm panel. "Spider, before you leave today, I'd like you to stop by the medical lab. They have an order on file for you."

"All right." The Guild rep could order her to pee in a cup, but that wouldn't make the impossible happen. "Anything else?"

Olwyn smiled. "You tell me."

Ulla shook her head. "Not right now." *I'm sure I'll be back.* She stood up to leave.

Olwyn stood too; they walked together to the door. "By the way, you did a masterful job of telepathic linking last week. Are you sure you don't want to join the Guild?"

Ulla managed a smile, and they hugged goodbye.

* * *

At lunchtime, Ulla stood in the doorway of the dining hall and looked for Mags. There she was, already in line next to a red-headed man in a flight suit. Fergus? What was he doing dirtside?

Ulla picked up a tray and automatically tried to put her readpad in her pocket. Since her pocket had grown no roomier in the past five minutes, she put it on her tray and hoped she wouldn't forget it again.

Lunch looked good: roast beef, carrots, beans, potatoes, braised cabbage. Bins of fruit and bread sat on a side table, and slices of cake were lined up on little plates for dessert. All the food was local to this planet; everything except the coffee had probably been grown right here in Hoffnung.

And the oranges, Starfighter. They come from North Esperanza. Maribet had joined the line a few places behind Ulla. She smiled and waved.

I'm eating with them. Ulla inclined her head toward

Mags and Fergus. *Want to join us?*

Sure. Thanks!

Ulla loaded her tray with a little bit of everything except for potatoes and cake. There would be no cake until her pants fit. She carried her tray to the table for four that Mags and Fergus had staked out.

Skuli and Olwyn occupied a table for two in the corner, where Skuli had a good view of the main entrance—and of their table for four.

"Heya, Spider!" Fergus pulled out a chair for her.

"Heya, yourself! Fergus, what brings you dirtside?"

"Teaching." Fergus, seated now, unrolled his napkin. "You just missed most of *Resolute*'s B Flight; they were here doing classroom training all morning."

She tried to mask her disappointment by setting her food on the table and arranging flatware. She shook out her napkin.

He cut up his roast beef. "No worries; they'll all be at Mickey Bravo's tonight if you want to see them."

Ulla brightened. "You're still at the station then. Are you flying yet?"

"Yup." He speared a chunk of potato with his fork. "We got our Goshawks up and operational just in time."

Jealous, Ulla filled her mouth with beans so she wouldn't say anything snarky.

Fergus grinned at her. *Nice try, Spider.*

Damn, his psi talents had grown!

Still getting used to that. "Will you be working half-days here, like you did before—"

Before my entire life changed? Ulla managed to swallow her mouthful of beans before it got her into trouble.

Dammit. Sorry.

Ulla took a drink of water before risking audible speech. "I'm still the LTLO for Ops. The plan is for me to fly a desk here in the mornings, like before." She set down her glass. "I'm to spend afternoons, uh, training in my new career field." She suspected that meant she'd stay in Newcastle and bounce between the Rogerses and Neal Erikson's Ring study team until Midwinter, when her obligation to SpaceCom would be finished and she could begin studying with Fripp at Castle Chisos. "We're still working out the details."

"The Ops office will be busy," Fergie said. He switched

to a conspiratorial stage whisper. "I'm told one of your fellow officers will take extended leave any day now."

Mags rolled her eyes. She looked very, very pregnant. Maribet, tray in hand, walked up to them.

"Heya, Maribet!" Ulla pulled out a chair for her. "Guys, here's someone I'd like you to meet."

Mags smiled and held out a hand to Maribet. "Mags Pappas." The others followed suit.

"You're Ulla's friend from last spring's trek?" Mags asked.

"Yes." Maribet moved her lunch from tray to table. "I just joined the Guild; I leave for training as soon as the commercial ships start running." She went to stack her empty tray on top of the others and found a readpad sitting on the top tray. She held it up and asked, "Is anybody missing their readpad?"

"It's mine," Ulla said. She felt herself blushing. It was definitely new pants time.

Since Fergus was closest, Maribet handed him the readpad to pass to Ulla. As he grasped it, the screen winked on.

Spider? Fergie's thoughts were heavily shielded, just for the two of them. *Were you expecting a high-priority message?*

Ulla looked up at him and shook her head. *No.*

You need to see this. He handed her the readpad. *Is this happy news? Or not?*

The words on the screen blurred as soon as she read them. *Happy.* She blinked back tears.

May I tell them?

Yes, please. I—can't talk right now. There was a catch in Ulla's throat.

Fergus set down Ulla's readpad. "Spider's pregnant."

- - -

AUTHOR'S NOTE

Spider's Wyrd is set in our far future on BD3, which stands for Bailey-Duran Three, the third planet of the star Bailey-Duran. BD3 has thriving ocean life, three inhabited continents, a slew of islands, and one moon. Its atmosphere, gravity, and length of day are similar to Earth's. Its biology is startlingly earthlike because the settlers who left Earth in the mid-2100s and settled here had to start almost from scratch with what they brought from home. Bailey-Duran is located on the Edge, a swath of space that the extraterrestrial Yotne Dominion and the humancentric United Worlds and Nations (UW&N) both think is theirs.

Humans from Earth "rediscovered" the "lost settlement" in the Bailey-Duran system a few generations ago. The humans and Hjralma who were already there are not lost and have mixed feelings about having been "rediscovered." That said, they have embraced interstellar commerce and joined the United Worlds and Nations. Bailey-Duran relies on the UW&N's SpaceCom to keep smugglers and pirates at bay.

The neighbors include:

Humans: Enough said. Human nature is what it is. On BD3, humans have subdivided themselves into the commercial City-States and the paranormally gifted On'oi who form an alliance with the Hjralma. Both factions think they own the planet. More recent arrivals include Second-Wave settlers and offworlders.

Hjralma (Elders): Tall, gray-skinned humanoid aliens who were on BD3 before the first humans arrived. Most have paranormal skills. When they are very still, they look like piles of rocks, reminiscent of the trolls in northern European mythology. "Troll" has become a derogatory term for them that civilized people do not use.

Ancients: A vanished people of unknown origin who lived on BD3 long ago. It's thought they developed Bailey-Duran's energy-concentrating Rings.

Yotne: Aliens who are exploring the same space in the Edge that humans are interested in.

Dwellers: Disembodied spirits that must possess sentient beings to survive. Most Dwellers are allies of the Yotne.

A Word About Italics

Many characters in this book converse telepathically as well as audibly and often mix the two. Telepathic dialogue and distinct, articulated thoughts are italicized.

GLOSSARY

Ancients: A vanished people of unknown origin who lived on Bailey-Duran Three long ago.

Bailey-Duran Three: The third planet of the star Bailey-Duran. Those who grew up there call it "the world."

BD3: Commonly used abbreviation for the world Bailey-Duran Three.

cabrio: small roadster-type vehicle.

camdeer: Very large draft animal indigenous to BD3.

camion: truck.

capraglama: Showy, llama-sized animal developed to assist with paranormal activity.

Dwellers: Disembodied spirits that must possess sentient beings to survive.

finding: Part of mind-seeing; includes water witching and the like.

fire and ice: A rare mind-moving Gift that includes fire starting, fire quenching, and ice making. Very rare subset of mind-moving that works on the molecular level, perhaps smaller.

First Settlers: First historically recorded human settlers on Bailey-Duran Three.

Gift: Paranormal talent.

ground pounder (groundie): Very informal term for a soldier who fights on the ground on a planet that can sustain human life.

the Guild: The United Telepathic and Paranormal

Practitioners' Guild, which fosters and regulates paranormal activity in the rest of explored space.

headblind: On'oi term describing a person who has no paranormal talents—what the humans in the city-states and the rest of the known universe would consider "normal."

herders: Derogatory term for the On'oi, who usually bring herds of capraglamas, camdeer, and more prosaic livestock along on trek.

Hjralma (Elders): Very tall, gray-skinned humanoids who were already on BD3 when the first humans arrived. Most have paranormal skills.

Hjralma-On'oi Alliance (the Alliance): Bailey-Duran system-wide governmental entity originally developed by the Hjralma and the On'oi to regulate terraforming on BD3 and enforce balanced off-planet trade. The Alliance effectively controls the system's natural resources and is a member of the UW&N.

keeper: A person who works with capraglamas or other Gifted stock.

lace fliers: Bug-like creatures native to Bailey-Duran Three, with the same size range as butterflies and moths. They often have gossamer wings with lace-like veining.

League of City-States: Bailey-Duran system-wide organization of independent cities, mostly ports or hubs of industry. The League of City-States effectively controls the system's commerce and is a member of the UW&N.

Matthias Carroll Memorial Society (MCMS; the Society): Protective/regulatory organization for soulslayers.

mind-moving: Telekinesis.

mind-seeing: Remote viewing; includes finding and water witching.

mind-talking: Telepathy.

mindborne healing; healer's Gift: Ability to use paranormal talent to diagnose and treat ailments and injuries. A very special blend that includes mind-seeing and mind-moving.

Mr. and Ms.: In the larger community, these words are used in the usual way. In SpaceCom, officers might refer to officers who are junior to them as Mr. or Ms. instead of articulating what rank. This is not done in the other direction.

On'oi (also called Guardians): 1) Human First Settlers who found they had developed paranormal skills, then created a social structure to help them manage that. They became the primary allies of the Hjralma to finish terraforming Bailey-Duran Three. 2) The Hjralma word for "World Guardian."

planetary restoration: Terraforming.

projection: Very rare Gift of appearing to others in a place where one's physical body isn't (apparitional experience).

psi: Paranormal talent.

Rings: Artifacts left behind by the Ancients that concentrate energy to be used for various purposes, most often for customized force fields. Legend says the major Rings, each just under a meter across and quite heavy, were once used to protect the planet. Smaller, dinner-plate-sized Rings are used for many different applications.

Second Wave: People who have immigrated to Bailey-Duran Three in the hundred standard years or so since its "rediscovery."

sing up: Power up a Ring by singing the appropriate string of syllables.

sing down: Power down a Ring.

soulslayer: Human with the rare paranormal ability to extinguish a soul.

SpaceCom: Short for United Worlds and Nations Space Command. The military branch of the UW&N.

spinner of wyrd: Person whose Gifts include the ability to alter the space-time continuum. Similar to the three Fates in Greek and Roman mythology or the Norns in Norse mythology.

trek: Annual journey, usually in summer, by On'oi clans to inspect/maintain/enforce terraforming rules on the lands the clan is responsible for.

troll: Derogatory term for Hjralma.

United Worlds and Nations (UW&N): The overarching galactic coalition that provides structure (and teeth) for what is basically human hegemony.

voiturette: small open vehicle for getting around big, flat places.

wyrd: Destiny; fate.

Yotne Dominion: Alien empire that aims to take over the swath of space that includes the Bailey-Duran system.

ACKNOWLEDGEMENTS

Dreaming up stories is a solitary activity, at least for me, but it takes a community to create a book. Many thanks to beta readers Harry, Jennifer, Kelli, Maria, and Shelly. Your willingness to read an unfinished manuscript and be candid about what it needed made *Spider's Wyrd* a better book.

Editor Erika Steeves helped get the manuscript ready to submit. Her expertise, enthusiasm for speculative fiction, and tactful corrections make my writing a better version of itself.

At Brick Cave Media, Bob Nelson took a chance on a new author and signed a book contract. Sharon Skinner's edits pulled the story and all its parts into focus. Ben Manning caught the mistakes the rest of us didn't.

A special shout-out to the Arizona State Library's Writers in Residence program, which makes it possible for published authors to teach classes and provide one-on-one guidance for new writers at Arizona public libraries. Words cannot express how much I learned while working with authors in residence Betty Webb, Kelli Donley, and Sharon Skinner. For more information, see https://azlibrary.gov/libdev/arizona-center-book.

Last, but very much not least, many thanks to my family. I could not have done this without you.

ABOUT THE AUTHOR

Adrienne Bengtson, who writes science fantasy as Adrienne Miles, picked back up her lifelong interest in writing after retiring from the U.S. Air Force and a 25-year career as a librarian.

During her time in the Air Force she served as an intelligence support officer, working with pilots and command staff at an F-15 fighter unit in Germany and later served for many years with an Air Force Reserve F-16 wing that deployed multiple times in support of operations in Iraq and the Balkans. She retired as a lieutenant colonel, having juggled family responsibilities, a civilian career move to a big suburban public library, and her Reserve commitment. She has always wanted to write, and collected her first rejection slip as a teenager. Spider's Wyrd is her first published novel.

In addition to reading and writing, she enjoys travel, hiking, fiber arts, and doting on her daughters, sons-in-law, and grandchildren. She plays Celtic traditional music on the penny whistle and keyless flute, and has been known to play the great Highland bagpipes in public. She lives in Mesa, Arizona, with her husband and their cats.

www.ingramcontent.com/pod-product-compliance
Lightning Source LLC
LaVergne TN
LVHW021210090325
805348LV00006B/15